IN SEARCH OF US

Maria Duffy is the author of numerous bestselling Irish novels, including *Any Dream Will Do*, *The Letter* and *One Wish*.

In Search of Us is her seventh book.

She lives in Dublin with her husband, Paddy, and their four children.

Follow her on Twitter at @mduffywriter or visit her website at www.mariaduffy.ie

ALSO BY MARIA DUFFY

Any Dream Will Do

The Terrace

The Letter

A Love Like This

One Wish

Falling Softly

In
Search
of Us

MARIA
DUFFY

HACHETTE
BOOKS
IRELAND

First published in Ireland in 2018 by HACHETTE BOOKS IRELAND
First published in paperback in 2018

1

Cataloguing in Publication Data is available from the British Library

ISBN 9781473673137

Typeset in Adobe Garamond Pro by Bookends Publishing Services
Printed and bound in Great Britain by Clays Ltd, Elcograf S.p.A.

Hachette Books Ireland policy is to use papers that are natural, renewable and
recyclable products and made from wood grown in sustainable forests. The logging
and manufacturing processes are expected to conform to the environmental
regulations of the country of origin.

Hachette Books Ireland
8 Castlecourt Centre, Castleknock
Dublin 15, Ireland

A division of Hachette UK Ltd
Carmelite House, 50 Victoria Embankment, EC4Y 0DZ

www.hachettebooksireland.ie

For Paddy –

thank you for always being my rainbow after the storm

Chapter 1

'My beautiful girls. Let me start by saying how much I love you. I love you both so completely that sometimes I feel I might burst.' Belinda Cunningham had been a powerful businesswoman and it was devastatingly sad to see her lying in a hospital bed ravaged by cancer, a mere shadow of her former self. She adjusted the pillow supporting her neck before clearing her throat and addressing her two daughters.

A smile suddenly lit up her face. 'You exploded into this world thirty years ago with angry red faces, screaming your frustration at being disturbed. And that's when my life changed forever.'

Ronnie swallowed a lump in her throat and glanced across at her twin sister, Elizabeth, who was sitting just a few feet away. There wasn't a hair out of place in her slicked-back bob and her expensive suit hung perfectly on her tiny frame. Others envied her figure and her style but not Ronnie. Elizabeth's face was stony and her lack of emotion irritated Ronnie. But she wasn't going to show it. Not today.

Their mother continued. 'I know I haven't been the perfect mother. I worked long hours and should have spent more time at home. I was probably too strict at times and other times not enough. I've always found it difficult to find the balance between work and home life but I did my best. Bringing you up alone was both hard and rewarding but I hope you know by now that everything I did was out of love and a desire for you both to become the beautiful, wonderful women you are.'

Ronnie's eyes were drawn to Elizabeth again and she was pleased to see a chink in the armour. A little bit of the old, softer Elizabeth. She was twisting a tissue in her hands and blinking quickly, as though to stop the tears. Ronnie wiped her own wet cheeks and sat forward to continue listening to their mother.

'Elizabeth. My beautiful, intelligent, wonderful girl. You make me so proud every day.'

A sob echoed in the room and Elizabeth looked as though it had taken her by surprise. She held the tissue against her mouth in an effort to stop another from escaping.

'From the time you were a little girl, you knew what you wanted to do. When other children were playing with dolls and board games, you were setting up stalls outside the house to sell yours. You were always going to be a businesswoman. There was no doubt about that. And you've become the best – better than I've ever been. You've been my saviour at work these last couple of years and I couldn't have kept the business going without you. I know you'll look after it well and continue to grow it like I have for the last twenty-five years. The future of Cunningham Recruitment is safe in your hands.'

Ronnie felt a slight sense of relief. For one awful moment, she'd thought her mother was going to beg her yet again to join the company. She'd spent years saying no to her but Belinda wasn't the sort of woman to give up when she wanted something. But thankfully she seemed happy to have Elizabeth run things alone.

'And Veronica.'

Ronnie jumped and shifted in her chair at the mention of her full birth name. She hated it, but somehow today it felt right.

'You, my darling, are the loveliest, kindest, purest heart I've ever known and I'm honoured to call you my daughter. I know I've been less than encouraging to you over the years. I was selfish. I desperately wanted both of my daughters working with me. I've mocked your lifestyle at times and made you feel I was disappointed in you but nothing could be further from the truth. You put me to shame. Your generosity of spirit and caring nature make you a far better human being than I'll ever be. I'm so proud of you for being independent and following your own path. You are an inspiration to us all.'

Ronnie's tears were flowing freely now and she didn't care. They were the most beautiful words her mother had ever said to her but they felt bittersweet. Her head was in a spin with emotion and her heart felt like it might burst out of her chest.

Their mother's face turned very serious then and she took a sip of water before continuing. 'I need to tell you something now. Something I should have told you a long time ago.'

Ronnie felt nervous and she could see at a glance that Elizabeth was feeling the same.

'It's about your father. I haven't been entirely honest with you both.'

She paused then to let that sink in. The sisters looked at each other and they didn't need words to say they hadn't been expecting *that*. As far as they were concerned, they didn't have a father. Their mother had told them from an early age that he was someone she'd met briefly and had disappeared just as quickly without a trace.

They'd asked her about him a few times but she'd always maintained that he was a one-night stand – an American businessman who was just passing through, and finding him would have been impossible.

'Your father was actually somebody I knew quite well. He was a good man but circumstances prevented him from being involved in your lives. Please believe me when I say that I lied to protect you, but not only that. There were other people involved. People whose lives would be devastated if the truth came out. I still stand by what I did and hopefully you'll understand in due course and can forgive me.'

'Understand?' said Elizabeth, pushing back her chair suddenly and standing up. 'Understand what? We need more than that.'

'Shhh, Elizabeth. Sit down.' But Ronnie felt upset too. Their mother had lied to them throughout their whole lives and it stung.

But Belinda began to look uncomfortable. In pain. And it was difficult to feel anything except compassion for the woman who'd brought them up single-handedly.

'I know this has probably come as a shock and you'll need time to digest it so I've written down a few things which might help you find him. Because that's what I'd like you to do – to find your father. When all this has sunk in, I hope you'll both agree that it's the right thing to do.'

Belinda Cunningham's smile faded and her face clouded over. Her spiky grey hair seemed to flop on the top of her head and her eyes filled with tears.

'I'm going to say goodbye now, my darling girls. I love you both more than you'll ever know. Keep being the wonderful women that you are and be happy.'

She blew a kiss and, just like that, she was gone. The room fell silent until Frank stood up and switched off the screen. Frank Logan was a dear friend of Belinda's and she'd given him power of attorney before she died. He looked at the two girls, his face as grey as his groomed beard. He looked older suddenly. Sadder.

'Is that it?' Elizabeth directed her fury at Frank but Ronnie could see that she was hurt. 'She drops a bombshell like that and then says goodbye?'

Frank looked uncomfortable. 'I know you must be feeling hurt and confused. But I have letters for you both too. Hopefully they'll explain a little bit more and help you understand.'

'So you knew about this and kept it from us all this time?' said Elizabeth, little red blotches appearing on her pale face. 'You knew about our father? About the lies she told us?'

He nodded and looked at his feet. 'Just in the last few years. She knew she didn't have much time left. She talked and I listened. It wasn't my place to tell you but she got me to help her make this video and made me promise to show you when things settled down after … you know …'

The words caught in his throat and Ronnie felt sorry for him. He'd been a great friend to all of them during the four difficult years that their mother had been ill, and they'd grown to love him. She went to him and hugged him.

'You must miss her too.'

'I do. So much.' His eyes filled with tears. 'It's been three months now but it feels like a lifetime. Sixty is far too young to die. She should have had so many more years.'

Suddenly Ronnie felt like she couldn't breathe as trickles of sweat dripped down the back of her neck. She needed to get out of that room. It was all so overwhelming. There was so much to take in.

To think about. And she needed to be alone to do that. She could tell Elizabeth felt the same so they said their goodbyes to Frank and left. As the two girls walked outside, Ronnie felt a spark of the old connection she used to have with her sister. Despite the fact they'd drifted apart, that twin bond would always be there. They hugged awkwardly and promised to speak again soon.

Ronnie walked to the bus stop in a daze. It was like her mum had just died all over again. Seeing her on that screen in front of them had been very strange. Trust her mother to do something like that. She'd always loved to shock people. She was probably looking down on them right now, amused by the whole situation. But hearing her beautiful words had given Ronnie a comfort she'd been craving. Her mother was proud of her. It had meant so much to hear her say it. Even now, after she was gone. She clung to the precious letter in her pocket and was both excited and nervous to see what it said. She just hoped that something good would come of it all but a little flutter in her stomach warned her that there might be some turbulence ahead.

Chapter 2

Ronnie ran her fingers along a thick-linked gold chain that had come into the shop as part of a collection. It never ceased to amaze her how people could part with such beautiful items. Especially if they'd belonged to somebody special in their lives. She held the chain up to her neck and glanced in the mirror that was kept on the counter for customers. Stunning. She was more of a silver girl usually but the red tint in the gold seemed to enhance her burgundy red hair. Ronnie's hair was her pride and joy. Long and wavy, she liked to emulate the styles of her favourite actresses from the 1950s like Maureen O'Hara and Audrey Hepburn by enhancing the natural curl and smoothing it back with a flower or a clip. She'd often joke to her friends that her hair was her saving grace because her body left a lot to be desired. But despite poking fun at herself, she was confident in her size 16 figure. She knew how to dress her curves and took inspiration from old movies, when they had proper, curvy women. According to some, even Marilyn Monroe was a size 16. She stared at her reflection for a moment before putting the chain back in its black velvet box. Beautiful as it was, with her birthday fast approaching she was hoping for something a lot more special than a piece of jewellery.

The bell on the door jingled as a young woman walked in and Ronnie nodded and smiled at her. Ronnie preferred to allow customers to browse and come to her if they needed help. She wasn't fond of the exuberance she saw in some shops where the customers were almost frightened off by staff overly keen to make a sale.

Ronnie loved working in Glisten, an antique jewellery shop huddled in one of Dublin's most exclusive side streets. Her walk down the cobblestones of Grafton Street each morning was a joy, as flower-sellers set up their stalls and the smell of freshly baked pastries from the many artisan cafés filled the air. The burgundy and gold façade of the shop was faded but still elegant and sophisticated and attracted many tourists throughout the day.

In Glisten, each piece they had for sale was special. Each piece told a story – or at least Ronnie liked to imagine the stories behind them. It was the same for her clothes. She loved rummaging through the rails in second-hand shops and finding something wonderful – something that had been worn and loved previously. She never understood the attraction of brand-new things direct from a factory floor. No matter how big or how shiny, there wasn't a modern diamond ring that could outshine an antique Victorian-inspired diamond cluster, or a modern synthetic skirt that could hold a candle to a 1970s chic tweed Chanel one. Ronnie was a vintage girl through and through.

She busied herself fixing the display of watches in the glass cabinet beneath the counter and was pleasantly surprised to see it was almost lunchtime. She was finished for the day at one and was looking forward to spending some time with her partner, Al, who was taking a rare day off. Al's tattoo shop was going from strength to strength. After studying in Central Saint Martins in London, he'd come back to Ireland to start his own business. It hadn't been long before word of mouth had seen his customer base soar and he was now even beginning to build an international reputation. The lead singer from Psychedelic Funk had travelled from Germany specifically for Al to ink a lion on his back and the tattoo had become legendary. So when Ronnie had decided to have a tattoo herself, there was no one else she would have trusted. She'd been nervous and unsure about what she'd wanted, but Al's suggestion of a small infinity sign had been perfect. The fact she'd fainted as soon as he'd produced the needle had sealed their fate. She'd been mortified but Al had been kind and patient and she'd left the shop half an hour later with a new tattoo and a date with the man who'd done it. Ronnie smiled at the memory and couldn't believe it was four years ago.

'How much is this one?'

Ronnie was startled out of her reverie by the woman, who was standing in front of her pointing to a rose gold bracelet.

'Beautiful, isn't it?' said Ronnie, taking it out of the display and placing it lovingly on a cloth on the counter. 'This one is a hundred and fifteen euros. Is it a present for somebody?'

The woman nodded. 'It's for my niece's christening. But that's a little too expensive for me. I was looking for something for around sixty or seventy euros.'

Ronnie nodded and replaced the bracelet onto the velvet display. 'That one is for an older child. How old is she?'

'Two weeks old tomorrow.'

Ronnie felt a stab in her heart but smiled at the woman. 'I think I have the very thing.'

She reached into the bottom shelf and pulled out a silver bracelet, thinner and more delicate than the previous one. 'This one is for a newborn and it's just fifty-five euros.'

The woman beamed. 'It's perfect. I'll take it.'

Ronnie felt a lump in her throat as she placed the item into a tiny box, carefully securing the exquisite chain with pins. Maybe someday she'd be opening presents just like this one for her own baby. She finally wrapped the box in pretty silver paper topped with a glittery bow and the woman left the shop delighted with her purchase.

Jean, who was working the afternoon shift, arrived minutes later and Ronnie was happy to be heading home. The delicate baby bracelet was still on her mind as she thought about the ovulation test she'd taken that morning. It had shown she was at the peak of her fertility and she felt excited. She and Al had the rest of the day to themselves and she was going to make the most of it.

She could see her breath in the cold air as she walked the short distance home. She'd never bothered to learn how to drive. Her mother had tried to persuade her on many occasions but with Dublin traffic becoming more and more chaotic, she was happier not to have the stress. Twenty minutes later she was turning the key in the door of their apartment, which was part of a complex nestled on the banks of the canal. They were surrounded by the hustle and bustle of traffic and shoppers and yet swans glided gracefully past their door each day. Ronnie loved the colour and the contrast of life in the city.

She felt exhausted but excited at the prospect of making a baby. Last year she'd thought that she'd be pregnant by her birthday. She'd been sure that it would happen quickly as they were both young and healthy. But it hadn't happened and then month after month they'd had disappointment after disappointment and she'd begun to lose hope. So here she was again with another birthday approaching and still no joy. But now that she had the science of the wonderful ovulation stick on her side, she was feeling more positive. This was going to be the month. She felt sure.

The football was blaring on the TV and Al didn't hear her come in. She stood at the living room door for a moment and watched him, his long, tattooed legs stretched beyond the arm of the sofa. His face was about the only part of his body that didn't have a tattoo and she loved that about him, despite her family's disapproval. She dropped her bag on the floor and he looked around in alarm.

'Ronnie! I didn't hear you come in. How was your morning?' He took his legs down from the sofa so that she could sit beside him.

'It flew. But I'm glad to be off for the rest of the day.' She kissed him gently on the lips before scrunching up her nose.

'What?' said Al. 'Do I smell or something?'

'No, but I think you need to get some conditioner for that beard. You'll have my face scratched to bits.'

He pretended to be annoyed. 'Is that any way to talk to the man who's just made you your favourite lunch?'

'You've made lunch?'

'Yes. I picked up a few bits in that Italian deli you like so there's a lasagne ready to go into the oven.'

Ronnie's eyes lit up. 'Oooh, I could kiss you. I'm starving.'

'But what about the scratchy beard?' His blue eyes twinkled.

'Forget the beard. And actually, let's forget the lasagne for now. We have something much more important to attend to.'

'And that is?'

Ronnie went to her handbag and produced the ovulation stick. 'This!'

'What the hell is that?'

'Remember I told you? Amber told me about these. She was doing a woman's hair and the woman was telling her about trying to get pregnant and nothing was happening and—'

'Okay, okay. Enough of Amber's stories.' Al began to tickle her. 'So what you're telling me is that we have to do the business when that yoke says so.'

Ronnie laughed. 'Well, yes. And it's telling us we'd better get going now.'

She didn't need to ask Al twice. He took her hand and led her into the tiny bedroom. Ronnie was into auras, and the purple-painted walls always made her feel relaxed and happy. She lit some lavender candles before joining Al under the crisp white duvet. He was already naked and he gently removed her clothes while planting kisses all over her face. He was a considerate lover and Ronnie knew that he'd pay attention to her needs before his own. But although she loved how he pleased her sexually, her focus was on just one thing. She closed her eyes and prayed that Al would give her the ultimate gift of a baby.

After a wonderful afternoon of love-making, and a dinner in front of the TV thanks to Al's lasagne, they were back in bed. But Ronnie couldn't sleep. She stared at a crack in the ceiling as Al snored contentedly beside her. She was awash with conflicting emotions and her head felt like it was about to explode. She was happy – really, really happy – but she felt guilty about it because her mother was barely cold in her grave. The excitement she'd felt earlier had ebbed with the knowledge that, even if she did become pregnant, her baby would never know his or her grandmother. And there was no doubt that her mother would have loved a grandchild. She'd always joked with them, saying she was far too young to be a granny, but Ronnie knew that secretly she would have relished the role.

The moon cast a shadowed light into the room and Ronnie's eyes fell upon the picture of her mother on her bedside locker. Tears sprang to her eyes. Belinda was laughing in the picture, her head thrown back, mouth open showing an expensive set of pearly white teeth. That's how Ronnie liked to remember her – relaxed and happy. Not how she'd seen her in that video. It was two weeks since she and Elizabeth had sat in Frank's office and watched their mother on a screen. Seeing her face and hearing her speak, yet knowing she wasn't really there, was the most confusing and sad thing that she'd ever experienced. And then there was the bombshell she dropped. Ronnie wished more than anything that she could talk to her sister. Properly talk to her. They'd spoken on the phone a couple of times since but, as usual, the conversations had been stilted and of no real substance. Elizabeth was the only one in the world who could really understand how Ronnie felt and it was sad that they were no longer close like they used to be.

When they were little, they'd been inseparable. They'd been best friends and had supported each other throughout their childhood, and especially through those awkward teenage years. Elizabeth had always been the popular one. She'd sailed confidently through her school years and had never had a shortage of friends or boyfriends. Ronnie's experience, on the other hand, had been very different. She'd been bullied because of her weight, because of how she liked to dress and sometimes for no reason at all. But Elizabeth had always had her back and had stood up to the bullies.

A loud grunt from Al startled Ronnie, and she envied his blissful state. But with a head full of thoughts whirring around, she didn't expect sleep to come anytime soon. When she and Elizabeth were in their early twenties they'd begun to drift apart. But it was only because of circumstance. Their lives had begun to change. Following a successful business degree, Elizabeth had begun to work in their mother's business. Both girls still lived at home but Elizabeth spent a lot of time on the road and would be gone for chunks of the week. Ronnie had flirted with a number of different jobs and found it hard to settle on anything in particular. Her love for travel made it difficult to take up a permanent position, as each time she'd work and save some money, she'd go off on another adventure. When the girls were twenty-four, Ronnie headed to Peru for a few months and it was only when she came home from that particular trip that she landed her dream job in the antique jewellery shop. She was beginning to tire of the travel at that stage and was happy to settle down to a steadier life in Ireland.

Following her return from Peru, Ronnie continued living at home with her mother and sister, but something had changed. Elizabeth was different. She was moody with her – distant. Sometimes she'd make snide comments but when Ronnie tried to talk to her about it, she'd plead ignorance. But it was on their twenty-fifth birthday that things came to a head. During a tea party their mother had thrown for them, Elizabeth let loose at Ronnie. She told her to back off – to stop stifling her. She said that they weren't little kids any more and she needed her space. She said a number of nasty things that shocked Ronnie to the core. Her outburst had come from nowhere and their relationship was never the same again. Soon afterwards, Ronnie moved out to a little apartment closer to her job in the city centre and away from the toxic atmosphere at home. A couple of years after that, she met Al and she finally felt settled and happy. Her life had moved on and Elizabeth wasn't her first priority any more.

She was wide awake now and knew she'd have to do something to kick her insomnia into touch. A hot chocolate usually did the trick so she carefully peeled back the duvet and swung her legs out of the bed. Grabbing her robe from the back of the door, she tiptoed out to the living room and through to the little kitchenette. She poured some milk into a pot and set it on the hob to heat. Al never understood why she didn't use the microwave but the only way to get the milk frothy was to boil it in a pot. Five minutes later she was sitting on the little two-seater red velvet sofa in the living room, her hot chocolate in one hand and her mother's letter in the other. She'd read it so often over the last couple of weeks, the page was crumpled and the writing a little more difficult to read. She made a mental note to photocopy it, for fear it would get so worn that she wouldn't be able to read the words at all.

The letter was mostly a repeat of what her mother had said in the video. Those heartfelt words that had filled Ronnie with love were now in print for her to have forever. And then there was the information about their father.

His name was Oliver Angelo. A free spirit, her mother had called him. A busker who wrote songs about love and peace and existed on the pittance that people dropped into his guitar case when he performed around the streets of Dublin. He hadn't been driven by money. He'd rejected conventional values and cared about the world. He wasn't the sort of man Belinda Cunningham usually went for but she'd been fascinated by him when they'd met and they'd become very good friends. Until that line had been blurred.

So her father was a hippy. The irony of the situation wasn't lost on Ronnie. All these years, her mother had tried to make her conform. To be more ambitious. But it seemed she'd inherited some of her father's values and, in a weird way, it gave her a little bit of comfort to know there was a reason for her oddness.

'Ronnie?'

The voice made her jump and a splash of her hot chocolate landed on the letter.

'For God's sake, Al. Look what I've done now.' She grabbed the edge of her robe and began frantically wiping at the stain.

'Sorry about that. I thought you'd have heard me coming down the stairs. Here, give me that.' He prized the letter from her hands and looked at it. 'It's barely marked at all. Only the corner. See?'

Ronnie put her head into her hands and began to cry softly.

'God, what is it, Ronnie?'

She wiped her tears with the sleeve of her robe. 'It's everything. Mum, the video, Elizabeth, us not being able to have a baby …'

He sat down beside her and wrapped his arms around her. 'Come on now. You've had a lot to deal with lately. It's going to take time for things to settle down.'

She nodded. 'I was coping. Or at least I thought I was. But this thing about my father has thrown me. I feel I should do something about finding him. To honour Mum's wishes.'

'But?'

'If I'm honest, I'm not sure if I want to. Not at the moment. I want to focus on *us*. On the baby. Does that make me selfish?'

'You, Ronnie Cunningham, are the least selfish person I know. You need to do what feels right for you. Whether it's now or sometime in the future, I imagine curiosity will get the better of you and you'll want to find him. But if not, that's okay too. I'll support you, whatever you decide.'

She smiled at him then. 'I don't know what I'd do without you.'

'Come on, let's go and get some sleep. We can talk about this more in the morning if you like.' He held out his hand and she took it gladly.

Ronnie was exhausted by the time she was back in bed and fell immediately into a fitful sleep where she dreamed she was part of a band of hippies dancing through the streets. Her mother was leading them and Ronnie was playing the bongos, feeding off the happy vibe surrounding her. Elizabeth was standing on the footpath, shaking her head in disapproval. She was holding a baby boy up in the air. Ronnie was confused for a moment but then realised the baby was hers. She went to take him from her sister but Elizabeth disappeared into the crowd. Ronnie could hear the baby crying but couldn't find him or her sister anywhere. She began to panic. Everything began to spin around and around and she didn't know what was happening …

She woke with a jolt and was shocked to realise she'd only been asleep for minutes. She pulled the duvet up to her chin and turned onto her side. She really needed to rid herself of all those negative thoughts. It wasn't doing her any good and it certainly wouldn't be good for the baby, if she was lucky enough to fall pregnant. Tomorrow was a new day and she was going to start by ringing her sister and arranging to meet. It was about time they put their differences aside. She missed her. She'd missed her for years but even more so now that their mother was gone. They should be pulling together and not tearing each other apart. It was with those happier thoughts that Ronnie finally fell into a contented sleep.

Chapter 3

Elizabeth sat at her desk and looked out the window. Her office was in a prime location overlooking St Stephen's Green, one of Dublin's oldest Victorian parks. It was the perfect oasis in the centre of a bustling city and Elizabeth loved to take a walk through the park when she needed to de-stress. But Stephen's Green was also where Grafton Street began and today it was thronged with people. One of the most expensive streets in the world, Grafton Street attracted shoppers from far and wide, and although Christmas was over, the January sales were still in full swing. It had been a difficult Christmas – the first one without their mother. Everywhere she'd turned there'd been carollers singing 'Jingle Bells' and Santas 'Ho-ho-ho-ing' through the day. She imagined her mother saying, 'If I hear "Silent Night" sung one more time, I won't be responsible for my actions.' The thought of her mother brought tears to her eyes and she swivelled around on her high-back leather chair to grab a tissue from the box on her desk.

When she and Ronnie were little, their mother used to take them out of school for a few days each December and head off to New York for some Christmas shopping. It had been the highlight of their year and the memory made Elizabeth smile. Sometimes she wished she could recapture that wonderful, innocent excitement of her childhood. The days when everything was simple and her biggest worry had been what to ask Santa for. The sound of a car horn from outside startled her and she gave herself a mental shake. The past was better left behind for all sorts of reasons. Thankfully Nathan wasn't a fan of Christmas, and with both of them so busy in their jobs, they'd managed to avoid as much Christmas cheer as possible.

Cunningham Recruitment was the brainchild of Belinda Cunningham and it had grown massively since its conception in the early nineties. At the age of thirty-five she'd become fed up working for other people and had taken the huge risk of starting up her own business. By then she was bringing up six-year-old twins alone and knew she wanted to create a better life for them. But thanks to her intuition and great foresight, she'd predicted that Ireland would come out of the awful recession it was in and she was going to be there to reap the rewards. Jobs would be plentiful again, she'd predicted, so a recruitment agency where she'd bring employers and potential employees together seemed like the perfect choice. She'd never looked back. She'd even managed to weather the recent recession, thanks to the solid business she'd built. The offices now occupied the top two floors of the building and they employed thirty staff.

There had never been any doubt in Elizabeth's mind that she'd come and work for her mother. She'd excelled at her business studies in Trinity College and had a ready-made job as soon as she left. But fearful of accusations of nepotism, she'd worked hard and earned her place in the company. She'd also gained the respect of her fellow workers by being a no-nonsense but fair boss. A tap on the door startled her and Amanda, her assistant, peeped her head into the room.

'John Lafferty is here for his three o'clock appointment. He's a bit early. Will I make him a coffee and ask him to wait?'

'Yes, please, Amanda. I have a few calls to make first.'

She sighed and pulled her chair in closer to her desk. It was only Monday and she'd need to get focused if she was to get through the week. But ever since she'd seen that video of her mother a couple of weeks before, she'd been finding it difficult to concentrate. It had really shaken her and made her wonder what else her mother had lied about over the years. Elizabeth had always prided herself on the close relationship she had with her mother. They'd told each other everything – or so she'd thought. Even when Elizabeth had married Nathan a few years previously, she'd insisted on buying a house just streets away from Belinda so they could be close. She couldn't understand why she hadn't just told her and Ronnie the truth from the beginning. She felt very hurt and betrayed.

And then there was the whole situation with Ronnie. They'd sat in Frank's office like two strangers and it had made Elizabeth sad. Sometimes she missed her sister. She missed the closeness they'd shared. The feeling that no matter what happened, they were always there for each other. But it was too late for them. It was six years since they'd fallen out and they'd been growing apart even before that, so Elizabeth didn't see any way back. If anything was going to fix their relationship it would have been their mother's illness but even that hadn't brought them back together. She had Nathan now, and he was her life.

She'd met him at a conference four years ago when she was at a particularly low ebb. More than a year had passed since her big bust-up with Ronnie and it had still been weighing heavily on her mind. And on top of that, their mum had just been diagnosed with cancer. Meeting somebody was the last thing she'd expected, but when Nathan had approached her at one of their tea breaks, she couldn't help falling for his charm. She smiled to herself at the memory.

'You look just as bored as I feel,' he'd said, his eyes twinkling.

She'd laughed, not entirely sure how to respond.

He moved closer to her so he could whisper. 'They're not telling me anything I didn't learn in secondary school. How about we play truant and go and get something to eat?'

'I … I don't know,' she said, torn between her strong work ethic and wanting to spend more time with this gorgeous stranger.

'Come on,' he said. 'Live dangerously. It's already half past three so we won't be missing much.' He held out his hand. 'Nathan Steele.'

She was completely under his spell. 'Elizabeth Cunningham. And yes, let's get out of here.'

He brought her to a little French restaurant close by and after checking she wasn't vegetarian, he ordered the boeuf bourguignon for both of them. She was content to let him take the lead. He was handsome and sophisticated and it was a novelty to have somebody make decisions for her for a change.

The following months went by in a haze of romance as Nathan swept her off her feet. Before she knew it, they were engaged to be married and Nathan was organising everything. Sometimes she felt as though she was looking in on her life from the outside as the wedding date drew closer, but in a strange sort of way, she liked it. Six months after meeting, they were married and Elizabeth felt blessed to have a man like Nathan by her side – somebody who loved and wanted her. Somebody she could rely on.

The sound of her mobile buzzing brought her back to the present and she rummaged in her bag to find it. 'Hello?'

'Hi, Elizabeth.'

She was surprised to hear Ronnie's voice, although she shouldn't have been. On the rare occasions her sister rang, it was always when Elizabeth was thinking about her. Twintuition, they used to call it. They used to laugh about it. Back in the day when they were friends.

'Elizabeth?'

'Sorry, Ronnie. I'm just up to my eyes here. Is it important?'

'I did try you a few times yesterday but it kept going to voicemail.'

'Sorry. I was on the phone for a lot of the day. So what can I do for you?'

'I won't keep you but do you fancy meeting for lunch?'

'Lunch?'

'Yes, Elizabeth. You know that meal that comes after breakfast and before dinner?'

'Smartass! Why do you want to have lunch?'

'I just thought we could talk. You know … about what Mum said.'

Elizabeth sighed. She wasn't keen on trying to find their father and she didn't need Ronnie putting pressure on her. 'I don't know, Ronnie. I'm not sure it will do any good.'

'Humour me,' said Ronnie, and Elizabeth knew she wasn't going to take no for an answer.

'Okay. When were you thinking?'

'Tomorrow at one o'clock in Carluccio's. It's close to both of us so no problem if you're a bit delayed.'

Elizabeth reluctantly agreed, and ended the call. A couple of hours later she was stepping into her silver soft-top BMW, glad to be heading home for the evening. She was lucky to have a space in the car park beneath the building, as parking in the city centre would be a nightmare otherwise. It was only six o'clock so Nathan probably wouldn't be home for an hour or so. A nice glass of chilled sauvignon blanc in front of the TV would be bliss. Nathan wasn't a fan of most things on TV, aside from sport. So Elizabeth recorded all her favourite programmes so she could watch when he wasn't there.

It only took half an hour to get to where she lived in Castleknock, a suburb on the west side of Dublin. She loved turning in to the opulent estate where each house was completely individual in style and screamed wealth and success. But her heart fell a little when she spotted Nathan's Mercedes already in the driveway. Catching up on *The Apprentice* she'd recorded would have to wait for another day.

'Hi, darling,' he said, greeting her at the door and planting a kiss on her cheek. 'You must have smelled the wine – I've just opened a bottle of white.'

'Great.' She kicked off her shoes and followed him into the kitchen. 'Will we just get takeout? I heard that new Thai restaurant in the village does a great curry.'

He swung around to look at her. 'You've forgotten, haven't you?'

'Forgotten what?'

'Dinner with Stephen and Gloria. Remember?'

'Oh, God, is that tonight? Do we have to go?' She sat on one of the kitchen stools and leaned on the counter. 'Can't we just make an excuse?'

'No. We. Can. Not.'

She didn't want to push him too hard but she really didn't want to go. 'I know he's your boss but he'd understand if you said I was sick or something. It's just the thought of having to talk to Gloria all night. You know what she's like.'

'I'll tell you what she's like, Elizabeth. She's the woman behind the man who owns me. Stephen says jump and I say how high. And he wants the four of us to go out, so we're going to do just that.'

Elizabeth sighed. She was fighting a losing battle. Nathan worked in the international finance centre of a German bank, having aced all his exams in college and subsequently been headhunted by several companies. He was fiercely ambitious and had been hoping for a promotion for the last two years. He'd do whatever he had to do to get on, and schmoozing with the boss was part of his plan to rise up through the ranks in the quickest possible time.

'So go on then,' said Nathan, staring at her. 'Get yourself ready. The taxi will be here soon.'

'I could probably save time if I went like this.' Elizabeth stood up to let him see her navy tailored suit, hoping he'd agree that she looked fine.

Nathan barely looked up from his phone. 'Wear the Louise Kennedy black dress. And not-too-high shoes.'

'But I'd be quicker just staying as I am. I have a lovely silver scarf that would—'

'Elizabeth, darling. Just do as I ask, will you? Now come on. We have to be out of here in half an hour.'

Elizabeth sighed and did as she was told and five minutes later she was stepping out of the shower. She'd managed not to get her face or hair wet, as she was planning on just touching up her make-up and leaving her hair as it was. It was her pathetic little protest at being told what to do. Elizabeth was a powerful woman in the workplace. She could stand her ground, argue her point and was very much respected by her staff. But at home she was different. She had a weak side, a submissive side. A side that Nathan Steele tapped into and for some reason she allowed it to happen.

She thought about going against Nathan's wishes and wearing her red Calvin Klein dress, but the last time she'd worn it, he'd said it showed too much cleavage. So she stepped into the Louise Kennedy one and stood back to check herself in the mirror. As usual, Nathan was right. It hugged her figure beautifully and was perfect for the occasion.

'Beautiful,' he said, rewarding her with a smile as she walked down the stairs. 'See? I know what suits you best.'

She noted that he hadn't bothered to change and was still wearing the grey suit and tie he'd worn to work that morning. But she had to admit he looked handsome. With silver streaks in his dark grey hair and his designer stubble, he had the look of George Clooney and she enjoyed seeing women swoon when he walked into a room.

'I'm just realising,' she said when they were in the taxi. 'I don't even know where we're going.'

Nathan put his hand on her knee. 'You'll see. I think it might just put a smile on your face.'

It wasn't long before they were in the city centre, and as soon as the car turned at St Stephen's Green, Elizabeth's heart lifted. 'Fire Restaurant,' she said, squeezing Nathan's hand. 'I love this place.'

'I know. Why do you think I suggested we go here?'

She suddenly realised she was starving and her stomach rumbled in anticipation as the car pulled up outside. The Mansion House was

the official residence of Dublin's Lord Mayor, and Fire Restaurant
was situated inside. It always made Elizabeth feel important to
walk up those steps. There was a great buzz about the place as they
entered and they were immediately shown to their table, where
Stephen and Gloria were already seated.

'Hello, Nathan,' said Stephen, standing up and shaking his
hand. 'And lovely to see you again, Elizabeth.' He kissed her on
both cheeks, allowing his lips to linger a little longer than they
should.

Elizabeth shuddered inwardly and turned to greet his wife.
'Hello, Gloria. You look lovely.'

'As do you, dear. That dress is divine.'

Formalities over, they settled into their seats and ordered some
wine before looking at the menu. The wonderful aromas were
making Elizabeth's mouth water and, despite the fact she wasn't
thrilled with the company, she couldn't wait for the food. She
quickly made her decision and was grateful for the speedy service
that had a waiter at their table in minutes.

'Gosh, there's so much choice. I don't know what to pick.'
Gloria's voice was high-pitched and annoying, reminding Elizabeth
of why she found her company challenging.

'Here, let me,' said Nathan, picking up the menu again. 'Do you
like seafood?'

Gloria nodded.

'She'll have the salmon for a starter and the baked Irish hake
fillet. Is that okay?' He flashed her a smile and Elizabeth noted the
flush in her cheeks.

'Perfect. Thank you, Nathan.'

'It's no problem. Elizabeth, are you ready to order?'

'Yes. I'll have the French onion soup and the roast monkfish, please.'

'Not the French onion soup. You won't like that.'

The waiter looked from Elizabeth to Nathan, unsure who to listen to.

'Oh, I love it. I had it here before when I came with Amber.'

'She'll have the wild mushroom salad,' Nathan said, addressing the waiter. He then spoke to her discreetly while Stephen was ordering. 'Garlic breath, Elizabeth.'

She was tempted to object but it wouldn't be worth it. Nathan wasn't the sort of man who took kindly to being challenged. And certainly not in front of his boss. So she just bit her tongue, even when she realised he'd ordered the wood-fired jumbo prawns for himself, which were cooked in garlic butter.

Thankfully the evening improved after that, mainly due to the delicious food. And although Gloria's giggling was annoying, Elizabeth had to admit she was quite funny after a few glasses of wine. She seemed to think Nathan was God's gift and kept reminding Elizabeth how lucky she was to have him. Stephen, on the other hand, didn't improve with wine. He touched Elizabeth's hand every chance he got and she caught him leering at her more than once.

She was relieved to see it wasn't yet midnight when they arrived home. She had an early start the next day and hated being out late during the week. The bed creaked as she brushed her teeth and she envied how easy everything seemed to be for men. She still had her make-up to remove and her night creams to apply before she could go to bed, and although she was tempted not to bother, she knew her skin would suffer for it. She eventually fell into bed exhausted and was surprised to see Nathan was still awake.

'You smell lovely,' he said, running his hand lightly over her face. 'Move in closer.'

She turned around so he could spoon her. 'I'm meeting Ronnie tomorrow. She wants to talk about what Mum said.'

'About your father?'

'Yes. What do you think I should do?'

'It's up to you, Elizabeth.' He wrapped his arms tighter around her and cupped her right breast with his hand.

'But what do *you* think?'

'I think we should make love.'

She gently pushed his arms away so that she could turn to face him. 'Nathan, seriously. I think Ronnie wants to look for our father. It feels strange to think she could be out there looking for him without me.'

He sniffed loudly, obviously not impressed by her rebuke. 'I thought you said you didn't want to look for him.'

'I know. But it's such a huge thing. And if I'm honest, I suppose I'm a little curious. Maybe I should give it some thought.'

'Seriously, Ronnie. It's late. Can we talk about this another time?'

'Okay.' She knew he wouldn't ask her about it again.

After her mother died, Nathan had been the perfect husband. He'd helped plan the mass, organised the death notice in the paper and even booked the venue for lunch after the burial. He'd had a supportive arm draped constantly over her shoulder and everyone had commented on how wonderful he was. The perfect husband. But behind closed doors he'd been entirely different. Elizabeth had been desperate for his compassion. She'd wanted him to understand she was grieving but he'd refused to acknowledge it. 'You need to buck yourself up,' he'd told her right after the funeral. 'You're not a child so there's no excuse for all that crying.' His words had really hurt but she hadn't shown it because she was fully aware that he just didn't do emotion.

She suddenly felt his hand creep around to her breast again and knew that they would make love. Because Nathan had said they would. There was no point in resisting. He would never force himself on her if she said no but the fallout wouldn't be worth it. He'd be in a bad mood until she'd eventually apologise for her rebuff. So she turned onto her back and he duly found his position on top of her. He kissed her around her face and she began to relax. If making love was the only way they could be truly close, then she'd take it.

But as he moved rhythmically up and down, she felt suddenly lonely. She was surrounded by so many people in her life but had nobody to talk to. She had no real friends. Nathan wasn't a good listener and Ronnie was like a stranger these days. Her mother had been the one she'd turned to when she needed somebody and now she was gone. Tears sprang to her eyes and as Nathan rolled off her and turned on his side to go to sleep, she let them fall freely. She thought about meeting her sister the next day and realised that maybe it would be nice to talk to her. They may not be close like they used to be, but they were still sisters, twin sisters, and they shared the common bond of the wonderful woman who'd meant so much to both of them.

Chapter 4

Ronnie had butterflies in her stomach. It was ridiculous to feel nervous about meeting her sister, but Elizabeth always had that effect on her. After a busy morning at Glisten, it was now lunchtime as she headed into the bathroom for a quick touch-up. She'd teamed a black pencil skirt with a black and white cardigan and as she glanced in the mirror, she knew she looked smart. She applied another layer of her deep-red Mac lipstick, one of the few luxuries she afforded herself, and ran a brush through her long, wavy hair. A last-minute addition of a white rosette clip in the side of her hair, and she was ready to go.

She crossed the road at Dame Street and headed towards Carluccio's, where they'd arranged to meet. Ronnie had picked that place purposely because she remembered Elizabeth raving about the smoked salmon they served there. Not that Ronnie would ever consider ordering anything fishy. She couldn't stand seafood, whereas Elizabeth practically lived on it. Not so when she was younger, though. Ronnie remembered a time when Elizabeth would hold her nose to stop herself from retching as she tried to down the fish their mother had put in front of them. Ronnie had just plain refused to eat it but Elizabeth, being the good girl she was, had suffered on. Funny how her tastes had changed along with so many other things.

Ronnie spotted her as soon as she walked in. Even though Elizabeth was small and slight, she exuded power. Her fitted smoky-grey trouser suit and crisp white shirt screamed *don't mess with me* and her slicked-back black hair gave her an air of confidence. She stood up as Ronnie approached the table and greeted her with an air-kiss on both cheeks. Ronnie hated that showbiz kissing. It was so false. Cold, even. Not that she'd expect warmth from her sister these days.

'I have to be back for a meeting at two,' said Elizabeth, shoving a menu across the table. 'I've gone ahead and ordered the smoked salmon on brown bread. I'm guessing you won't be having the same?'

Ronnie smiled. At least she remembered. 'You're right there. I can't stand the stuff. I'll have the steak and chips. You can't go far wrong with that.'

The waitress came and took the order, placing a jug of water and two glasses on the table in front of them. Ronnie was a little suspicious of the mint leaves and cucumber in the jug, but after a tentative sip, she had to admit it was delicious. They spent a few minutes making small talk about cucumber versus lemon in water until there wasn't much more they could say about it.

'So.' Ronnie looked at her sister and wished she felt more at ease around her. 'How do you feel about everything? I mean, about what Mum said. Now that you've had time to think about it.'

Elizabeth stiffened. 'Listen, Ronnie. You might think that this is all some great adventure. Some exciting project to embark on. But you have to understand that I don't feel the same. I've never felt the need to have a father. My life has been just fine without one, and at thirty years old, I don't feel the need to have one now.'

'Elizabeth, I think—'

'No, let me finish. I can't stop you if you want to go looking for him but you can't guilt trip me into it. It wouldn't be fair. And if you want my advice, you should seriously think of the consequences. I mean, what if you found him and he didn't want to know? What if he was horrible? What if—'

'I don't want to find him.'

'Sorry? What?'

Ronnie sat back in her chair, amused. 'Elizabeth, at the moment, I don't want to go looking for him either. And to be honest, I don't know why you assumed I did.'

'Oh!' Elizabeth looked sheepish. 'I'm sorry. I just assumed that was why you wanted to see me.'

'I asked you to meet me for lunch because you're the only person in the world who knows how it feels.' She tapped her hand over her heart. 'How painful it is to live our lives without her. But also to know that she'd kept something very important from us for our whole lives. Whether we like it or not, you and I are in this together.'

Their order arrived and it gave them a few moments to take a breath and gather their thoughts.

Ronnie continued. 'Now can we start again? I'll pretend you didn't go off on a rant and we can have a proper conversation.'

Elizabeth sniffed but nodded her agreement as she began to pick at her food.

'Was it an easy decision for you?' Ronnie asked, before shoving a mouthful of the succulent steak into her mouth. 'I mean, did you even consider searching for him?'

'To be honest, I didn't really give it much thought. As I said earlier, I've come this far without a father and I'm doing just fine.'

'But aren't you curious? I decided that now isn't a good time for me to go looking for him, but I don't mind telling you I'm dying to know more.'

Elizabeth looked unsure, before nodding. 'I know what you mean. It's only natural, I suppose.'

They both fell silent for a moment until Elizabeth spoke again. 'Do you think Mum would be mad at us?'

'What do you mean?'

'For not looking for him. She wanted us to find him. It was the last thing she asked of us. Her final request, and we've decided to ignore it.'

'We haven't ignored her request,' said Ronnie, happy to see Elizabeth's vulnerable side. 'We've just decided the time isn't right. That's not to say we won't look for him at a later date.'

'I suppose.'

Ronnie continued, 'I think Mum gave us that information because she felt it was the right thing to do. She wanted us to be armed with the truth and it's up to us if or when we decide to do something about it.'

Elizabeth nodded. 'And to think I came here ready to defend my position to you when all the time we'd come to the same conclusion.'

'Maybe our twintuition is alive and well. What did Nathan have to say about it all?'

The mention of Nathan seemed to startle Elizabeth. 'Nathan's been very busy in work these last few weeks. It's a really pressurised job. So we haven't had much of a chance to discuss things.'

'God, Al and I have talked about nothing else. He must be sick listening to me go on about it.'

'So what made *you* decide you didn't want to look for him?' Elizabeth's tone was sharp.

Ronnie thought for a moment. She wasn't sure how much of her personal life she wanted to share with her sister. She decided on caution for now. 'I'm not saying I'll never look for him but at the moment, I have other things going on in my life and I don't want to get distracted.'

'Other things?' Elizabeth held her fork in mid-air and looked at Ronnie questioningly.

'Just stuff.' Ronnie could almost feel the colour rise from her neck to her face.

'Oh, well, I'm sorry for asking. I forgot we don't share secrets any more.'

'There's no need to be like that, Elizabeth. There's no big secret. It's just … it's just …' She didn't want to tell her about trying for a baby but she felt she had to say something. 'Al and I have been together four years and we're just starting to talk about the future.'

'You're getting married?'

The suggestion startled Ronnie but she decided to go with it. 'Well, yes, maybe. Probably. We haven't decided on a date or anything but it's definitely something we're thinking about.'

Elizabeth shook her head. 'I can't believe you're going to marry *him*.'

'What do you mean by that?'

'Well, let's face it, Ronnie. Al is hardly the catch of the day. You could do so much better.'

'The cheek of you!' Ronnie's face flushed with anger. 'What

gives you the right to talk about him like that? You don't even know him.'

'I know enough. A tattoo artist is hardly going to set the world on fire. And have you thought about those tattoos he has? The Virgin Mary might be sitting pretty on his toned chest now, but imagine what it will be like when he's sixty and it's sagging down to his crotch.'

'Jesus, Elizabeth. You're a cruel bitch. I knew there was a reason I didn't like you any more. Do you think that working in banking makes Nathan a better person than Al? Is money what it's all about?'

'It certainly helps. But it's not just money. It's ambition and drive. In ten years' time, Nathan will be a senior manager at the bank and I'll be running an empire. What will you and Al be doing? He'll still be drawing tattoos and you, if you're lucky, might be selling some new jewellery instead of that second-hand rubbish.'

'Right, I've heard enough.' Ronnie stood up and glared at her sister. 'What happened to you, Elizabeth? What's happened to us? You've become so cold – so nasty to me. I honestly thought that by meeting up today and talking about Mum we might have connected again. How wrong was I about that!'

'The truth hurts, doesn't it? Well, now that Mum is gone and we're not going on some wild-goose chase to find our father, there's no need for us to see each other again.'

'Fine by me,' said Ronnie, resisting the urge to punch her sister right in the centre of her smug face. 'Goodbye, Elizabeth.'

She stormed out and walked at speed until she felt her lungs might burst. Stopping to lean against a wall, she realised that her face was wet from tears. How could her sister be so cruel? How could she say such horrible things? Ronnie always knew that

Elizabeth was driven by money and power but to put Al down like that was unforgiveable. She was glad now that she hadn't told her about them trying for a baby. No doubt she would have had something to say about that too and Ronnie wouldn't have been able to contain herself.

It was ten minutes to two so she began to walk quickly again to get back to work on time. Wait until Al heard what she said. He wasn't Elizabeth's biggest fan anyway but, after this, she wouldn't blame him if he hated her. At least she had Al to talk to. By the sound of things, Elizabeth and Nathan had such hectic schedules that they rarely spoke to each other at all. Ronnie would prefer her life to Elizabeth's any day. Her sister may have more money, but she and Al were rich with love.

She just barely made it back to work at two and didn't even have time to fix her make-up before returning to serve customers. It wasn't as busy as earlier but she was kept going and didn't have much time to dwell on what had just happened. However, one thought kept whirring around in her mind. Since Elizabeth barely knew Al and had only met him a few times, how the hell did she know he had a tattoo of the Virgin Mary on his chest?

Chapter 5

Elizabeth sat in her living room swirling white wine around in her glass. She wasn't really in the mood for alcohol but she needed something to take the edge off her mood. It was only three thirty but she'd decided to cancel her meetings and come home after that disastrous lunch with Ronnie. Every now and then she'd think that maybe she could forgive her sister – to go back to how things used to be. But when she'd come face to face with her, she'd always remember the events of seven years ago and she'd hate her all over again. She hadn't been able to face the afternoon in work so she'd rung Amanda to say she had a migraine and to cancel her appointments for the rest of the day. She was very diligent and rarely missed any time in work but she felt too emotional to face anyone now.

Nathan had texted her to say he was meeting a client after work so wouldn't be home until late and she felt relieved. She needed time to think and didn't need him telling her to pull herself together. She took another sip of the wine but it wasn't mixing well with the ball of anxiety in her stomach, so she took it into the kitchen and poured it down the sink. She filled the kettle with water and spooned some coffee into a mug.

She leaned against the white granite counter as she waited for the water to boil. It was a beautiful kitchen and had cost them over a hundred thousand euros. They'd ripped out the old pine units that were there when they'd bought the house and replaced them with ultra-modern high-sheen white ones. They'd picked lime green units for under the island in the centre of the kitchen and they contrasted the white beautifully. It was like a showroom kitchen and it remained impeccable because it got very little use.

She made her coffee and sat on a high stool at the counter. Her exchange with Ronnie earlier was still playing on her mind and she knew she'd gone too far. She just couldn't help herself. Ronnie had been so smug, going on about how Al was a great listener and how she spoke to him about everything. And planning a wedding so soon after their mother's death was just wrong. She hated how Ronnie seemed to be able to move on so easily when she felt her life would never be the same again.

Tears sprang to her eyes and she felt a desperate need to talk to somebody. But who was there for her? Nathan didn't do emotion – Steele by name and steel by nature. She had several acquaintances but no real friends. Amber had been her best friend once – hers and Ronnie's. But she'd chosen sides after the big birthday bust-up, and these days Elizabeth had barely any contact with her at all. She leaned her elbows on the counter and buried her head in her hands. She wished her mother was there. She was her one true friend. Someone she could rely on. Someone who'd listen and not judge.

A chill ran down Elizabeth's spine and her distress turned to anger. How could her mother have done it? How could she have lied to her and Ronnie for all those years? Watching that video had really shaken Elizabeth and made her question what had been real about her relationship with her mother.

Suddenly a thought struck her. If she wanted someone to talk to, she knew exactly who to call. She hopped down from the stool and went to find her brown Prada bag she'd discarded in the hall when she came home. A few seconds later she dialled a number and crossed her fingers it would be answered.

'It's me. Any chance you could come over …?'

Frank Logan stepped into the hallway and Elizabeth threw her arms around him.

'Hey, hey, Elizabeth. What's up? I came as soon as I could.'

Elizabeth was mortified and backed away. 'I'm sorry, Frank. I don't know what's come over me. Come on in.'

She led the way into the living room and sat down on the cream leather sofa, indicating for him to do the same. 'I'm sorry you rushed over, Frank. There's no emergency. I feel stupid now. I was a bit upset and I just needed to talk to somebody.'

'You can call on me anytime, Elizabeth. I've told you that repeatedly.'

She nodded gratefully. 'I've been meaning to ring you since you showed us that video but I just didn't know what to say. I still don't, to be honest.'

He sat back on the sofa and rubbed his bearded chin with his forefinger and thumb. 'I'm sorry if the video was a shock for you. That wasn't your mother's intention.'

'How can you say that, Frank?' Elizabeth raised her voice. 'How can you say it wasn't her intention to shock us? Of course we were going to be shocked. We're thirty years old and she's only telling us now the truth about our father. And she's not even here for us to ask her questions.'

Frank looked as though she'd slapped him in the face with the truth and she immediately felt bad for it. 'I'm sorry. None of this is your fault.'

'You're understandably angry,' he said, his tone gentle. 'I wouldn't expect anything less. But what I was trying to say was that your mother didn't do any of this out of spite. She only ever wanted to protect you and Ronnie.'

'But how was denying us a father protecting us? Unless …'

'Unless what?' He looked worried.

'Unless our father was some sort of monster. Maybe he was somebody we needed protecting from.'

'No way. I can assure you, that wasn't the case at all.'

Elizabeth glared at him. 'So did you know him? Did you know our father?'

'Our paths crossed once or twice. But I really can't tell you any more than what your mother has already shared with you.'

'I don't believe you. Please don't lie to me, Frank.'

'Why would I lie to you? I want you to find your father. And so did your mum.'

'You knew her back then, though, didn't you? Mum said she met you in college when she was twenty, so that would have been ten years before we were born.'

Frank sighed and ran his hand through his thinning silver hair. He was a good-looking man with fresh skin and beautiful teeth that wouldn't be out of place on a man half his age.

Elizabeth was still waiting for an answer. 'Tell me what you know about our father. Please, Frank.'

'I thought you didn't want to know.'

'Stop playing games with me,' said Elizabeth. 'I said I don't want to *find* him. That doesn't mean I can't ask questions.'

'Well, maybe it would be better to wait until you and Ronnie are together to tell you what I know. That's what your mum wanted.'

'Has she rung you?'

'What?'

'Ronnie. Has she rung you?'

'Well, no, but—'

'Has she looked for more information or told you she wants to find out more?'

'No.' He sank down further into the sofa and looked defeated.

'Well, I can tell you that I met her for lunch earlier and she's adamant that she doesn't want to look for him.'

He perked up at that nugget of information. 'You two went out for lunch? Together? Well, that's the best piece of news I've heard in ages. Are you working things out at last?'

'Sorry to disappoint you,' said Elizabeth, shaking her head. 'But it wasn't the sisterly hug-fest that you were hoping for. We met up to talk about what Mum said. We chatted. We argued. We went our separate ways.'

'You two are so frustrating,' he said, shaking his head. 'I wish I could knock both your heads together.'

'Huh! I doubt it would do much good. I know you and Mum were always conspiring to get us together but just face it, Frank. We've nothing in common any more. You can't force us on each other.' She really didn't want to talk about Ronnie. 'Well, if you won't tell me what you know about Oliver Angelo, tell me about

when you met Mum. What was she like? And how come you lost
touch for so many years?'

He smiled and his face lit up. 'We had a funny friendship, your
mum and I. We wouldn't speak for ages and then we'd meet and
wouldn't be able to stop.'

'So you were really good friends?'

'Not exactly. We were both studying in Trinity. She was doing
business and me law. We had some friends in common so we often
ended up at the same parties. I can't say I remember the first time
we spoke or met but she was always just there.'

'And that was it?'

'What do you mean?'

'I mean was it just friendship? There was no romance or
anything?'

'You already know this, Elizabeth.' His tone was sharp. 'We were
just friends. And besides, I had a girlfriend. She and I were in love.'

'Was this Shirley?'

'The very one.'

'And then you left Ireland. Where did you go again? Amsterdam,
was it?'

'Amongst other places. We moved around a bit. Things were
looking bleak in this country by the time we left college in the
early eighties, so, in 1982, Shirley and myself headed off to see if
we could make a living for ourselves in another country. We really
only intended to be away for a year or two but we ended up staying
away for all those years.'

'So is that when you and Mum lost touch?'

'Not quite. We stayed in contact for a couple of years, as I did
with all my friends in Ireland. But life has a funny way of getting in

the way. The letters and calls became less frequent and our visits back home likewise. We'd carved out a life for ourselves over there and your mum was working on becoming a successful businesswoman.'

Elizabeth was enjoying getting a rare insight into her mother's early life. 'Mum told me you and Shirley split up. Is that why you came back to Ireland?'

'Well, it wasn't exactly as simple as that. Shirley and I were together for years. And we were happy for the most part. Until one day she announced that she was heading off to do some charity work in Africa.'

'Oh my God. Seriously? And you had no idea that she'd been thinking about it?'

'I had an inkling. She'd trained as a nurse and had often spoken about working abroad with a charity.'

'So she left you just like that. Did you get a divorce?'

'Funnily enough, we were never married in the first place. We never saw the need. In hindsight, maybe it was just as well.'

'So did you come back to Ireland straight away?'

'What is this?' He laughed. 'Twenty questions?'

'I'm just curious. I often wondered what drew you back here when you'd made such a good life for yourself abroad.'

He looked at his hands and picked a piece of imaginary fluff from his suit trousers. 'I had a few bad years after she left. I'm ashamed to say I turned into a bit of an alcoholic and almost lost everything.'

'Ah. So that's why you don't drink any more?'

He nodded. 'I came home to Ireland for my father's funeral a few years ago and that's when I bumped into your mother again.'

'And you rekindled your friendship?'

'I believe things happen for a reason and your mother was

definitely my saviour. We got talking, and when I left again we stayed in touch. She made me see what a mess I was making of my life and persuaded me to come back to Ireland and start afresh.'

'Wow! I didn't know all that. But I do know that Mum loved you dearly. It's such a pity you only had those few years of friendship before she … before she …' Elizabeth choked on the words and Frank reached out and touched her hand gently.

'She was such a wonderful woman and I regret not having her in my life for longer. I think friendship is a very precious thing and we should cherish it.' He raised his eyebrows.

'What?'

'You and Ronnie.'

'That's emotional blackmail,' she said, pretending to look shocked.

'I'm just speaking the truth. Don't have any regrets, Elizabeth.'

She looked away when she saw the tears in his eyes.

'And on that note, I'll leave you,' he said, suddenly standing up and straightening himself to his full six-foot height. As usual, Elizabeth felt tiny beside him.

She walked him to the door and he folded his arms around her. 'We'll chat again soon, Elizabeth. We have so much more to talk about. And please do think about what your mother said. I know you feel hurt and angry now but maybe sometime soon you'll change your mind and want to find your father.'

'Maybe,' she relented.

He smiled at her before stepping into his Lexus. She waved until he disappeared around the corner and she felt better than she had in weeks. She made a mental note to keep in touch with Frank more often. It's what her mother would have wanted.

Flicking on the TV in the living room, she was shocked to see it was still only five o'clock. On a normal day, she'd have at least another hour of work to do before she'd even consider heading home. She lay down on the sofa, glad to know she'd have the house to herself for at least another few hours, and scrolled down to find her recorded episodes of *Revenge*.

The plot was beginning to confuse her and, as she watched, her mind wandered back to Ronnie. Maybe Frank was right. Maybe they should do something about their friendship before it was too late. But Elizabeth wasn't sure if she wanted to. It was difficult to forget that Ronnie had always taken everything Elizabeth ever wanted. Forgiveness didn't come easy to her. Besides, Ronnie was probably too busy with her marriage plans to even consider her relationship with her sister.

She felt her dark mood returning and cursed Ronnie. How could her sister still have such an effect on her? Elizabeth had spent years being angry with her and Ronnie seemed completely unaware of the reasons why. She glided through life with that tattoo-ridden guy on her arm like love's young dream, oblivious to the hurt she'd left in her wake. But Elizabeth didn't forget easily.

She couldn't be bothered trying to concentrate so she flicked the telly off and shut her eyes to think properly. She wished she could get rid of the ball of anger that seemed to inhabit her head all the time. Sometimes she didn't even know what she was angry about but talking to Frank had made her realise something. She was angry with Nathan for his lack of support and she was certainly angry with Ronnie for a lot of things. But most of her anger was directed at the one person she loved more than anyone else in the world. She was angry at her mother for dying.

Chapter 6

Ronnie was in a bad mood. She'd been hopeful that this month would be 'the one' but the arrival of her period that morning had smashed her hopes and left her feeling devastated yet again. She almost wished it wasn't Sunday. On Sundays, she had too much time to think. At least if she was in work, she wouldn't have time to wallow.

'Here you go, love.' Al arrived into the bedroom with a tray of tea and toast and she propped herself up in the bed to balance it on her lap. 'How are you feeling now?'

'Shitty, to be honest.'

'Physically or mentally?'

'Both. It's a double whammy, isn't it? Not only do I have the disappointment of not being pregnant, but I have to put up with roaring pains in my stomach too. It's bloody hard being a woman.'

Al lay down on the bed beside her and gently took her hand. 'I'm so sorry, Ronnie. I wish I could do something to make it better. I suppose we've just got to keep being positive.'

She glared at him. 'Positive? What is there to be positive about? Month after month I get my hopes up and it's the same thing every time. I'm really sick of it. I can't live my life like this – hoping, waiting.'

'But it's only been a year. And we're still both young. Some people try for years and years to have a baby.'

'Oh, that's a cheery thought.'

He looked sheepish. 'I'm not doing a very good job of cheering you up, am I?'

'You're doing your best.'

'It *will* happen for us, Ronnie. I know it will. I think you just have to relax about it and not get so worked up.'

Ronnie gave him a half smile but her heart felt heavy. Everyone kept telling her the same thing. '*Relax and it will happen.*' Her friend, Amber, was a hairdresser and, much to Al's annoyance, would give Ronnie tips she'd picked up from gossipy clients about getting pregnant. '*Exercise and diet – get that right and you'll be pregnant in no time.*' '*Put your legs up in the air for half an hour after sex.*' '*Don't shower straight afterwards because you'll wash the sperm away.*'

'… or go and see a movie?'

'What? Ronnie had begun to drift off into a lovely sleep when she realised Al was still talking.

'I was asking if you'd like to do something today to take your mind off things. It's pretty cold but the sun is shining so we could wrap up and go for a walk in the Botanic Gardens? Or if you'd rather not do anything energetic, we could go and see a movie?'

'Definitely nothing energetic,' she said, pushing the tray across onto his lap and snuggling down further into the bed. 'I vote for staying here all day. You could be my personal slave and we could just sleep and chat.'

'In your dreams!'

'Frank rang me yesterday,' she said, changing the subject.

'Frank Logan? What did he want?' Al placed the tray on the bedside locker and slipped under the covers. 'Go on.'

'He wanted to know if I had any further thoughts on finding my father. I told him I didn't want to do anything about it for now, but guess what?'

'What?'

'He said that Elizabeth rang him last week, saying she needed to see him. He said she was upset and angry and was asking lots of questions about Mum.'

'Understandable, I suppose. You've been the same a lot of the time.'

'Yes, but apparently this happened on the day I met her. She must have gone home and rung him straight away. I guess our meeting had more of an effect on her than I thought.'

Al nodded. 'Well, it sounded like a pretty horrible encounter. You were mad as hell when you came home too.'

'True. But there's more. Apparently now Elizabeth is thinking of looking for our father. She was adamant that she didn't want to find him when we spoke so I don't know if she's really changed her mind or if Frank is just trying his best to persuade us both.'

'And it's making you rethink things too?'

'Maybe. Frank thinks Elizabeth would do it if I would, but I can't imagine us joining forces. I'm still reeling from how she spoke to me last week. And the terrible things she said about you.'

'Don't worry about me,' said Al, kicking the duvet from his body. 'I have a thick skin.'

Ronnie sat up. 'It's sad really, isn't it? I had thought that Elizabeth and I might have become closer when Mum got sick but she's become so hard-nosed. So angry. It's impossible to break through her steely exterior. She never used to be like that.'

'You know I'm not Elizabeth's biggest fan but I can't help thinking that all that bravado is a front. I bet there's a softer, nicer girl in there just crying to come out.'

'You're such a softie, do you know that?' Ronnie looked at Al lovingly. 'So do you reckon we could find that nicer girl if we looked?'

'I reckon *you* could, Ronnie. I still don't know what happened between you two but I'm sure you could become close again if you tried. I'd do anything to have a brother or sister.'

Ronnie was about to disagree about becoming close to Elizabeth again but changed her mind when Al mentioned how he'd love to have a sibling. He was an only child and both his parents had died within a few years of each other when he was in his early twenties. He didn't speak about them much but Ronnie knew that he often felt lonely and sad that he didn't have any close family left in the world.

'I think Frank is playing it very clever,' said Al, breaking into Ronnie's thoughts.

'What do you mean?'

'He's manipulating the two of you so that you'll do as your mother asked.'

Ronnie thought for a moment before nodding. 'Maybe he's right. I think one of the reasons I've been so stressed lately is because if I don't try to find my father, I'm going against my mother's wishes.'

Al sat up and fixed the pillows behind his back. 'In fairness, your mother isn't here any more. You two are the ones who are living through this and, as I said before, you have to do what feels right for you. Don't feel guilty about following your heart.'

'I know what you're saying is true but I'm not sure what feels right any more. Maybe it wouldn't do any harm to follow up on a few leads. There are some details in the letter I can check out but Frank said he has some more information if we want to follow up on it.'

Al swung his legs out of the bed and stood up. 'I'll help you if that's what you want to do. But if having a baby is still a priority for you, you need to decide if this search is going to bring you too much stress.'

'What do you mean *if*? Of *course* a baby is my priority. And maybe a distraction would be a good thing. If I'm not thinking about getting pregnant every minute of every day, there might be a better chance of it happening. And also ...'

'Go on.'

Ronnie shook her head. 'No, it doesn't matter.'

'What were you going to say?' said Al, looking at her quizzically.

'It's just that if we have a baby ...'

'*When*, Ronnie. *When* we have a baby.'

'Okay then. *When* we have a baby, he or she will have no grandparents.'

Al nodded and smiled. 'Unless you find your father.'

'Exactly. I'm still not sure what I'm going to do but I can't think of any better motivation.'

'Right, come on.'

'What? Where to? I thought we were staying here for the day.'

Al grabbed her hand and tried to pull her out of the bed. 'Take your own advice, Ronnie. You'll have too much time to think if you stay here. It's not very often the sun shines in February so we're going out to make the most of it. The fresh air will clear your head and might even help you make a decision about what you want to do.'

Ronnie sighed but she knew he was right. 'Okay, give me half an hour to make myself presentable and I'll be ready to go. But I'm only going if you buy me lunch. I couldn't face cooking today.'

'Okay, deal. Now hurry up while the sun is still out.'

She was in the shower minutes later and as she let the water sluice over her body, her hand found its way to her stomach. Although she was a big girl, she carried most of her weight around her bum and thighs. Pear shaped, they called it. She wondered what it would be like to feel a bump. A proper baby bump and not just a fold of flabby fat. To feel her stomach expand every day and know there was a life growing inside. Instead of feeling sad or defeated, she suddenly felt excited. One day, she was going to be pregnant and she'd be the happiest girl in the world. And although her mother wasn't there any more, there was a slight chance that her baby could have a grandfather.

'Hi, Frank, it's Ronnie.'

'Ronnie. What can I do for you?'

'Sorry for ringing on a Sunday, but I was thinking about things again and I've changed my mind.'

'About finding your father? That's wonderful. You and Elizabeth should come in to the office during the week and I can pass on the rest of the information.'

'Well, actually it's just me. I'm going to see what I can find out myself, and Al is going to help me.'

There was no response and Ronnie looked at her mobile to see if she'd lost the signal. 'Frank?'

'I'm afraid I can't do that, Ronnie.'

'Do what? What do you mean?'

'I can't give you the information unless Elizabeth is willing to be a part of the search.'

'Don't be ridiculous. We're not one person, Frank. We can decide separately what we want to do. Elizabeth has told me herself she has no interest so I'll be doing this alone.'

'I'm sorry, but it was your mother's wish that you'd both do this together.'

Ronnie didn't know what to say.

'Talk to Elizabeth. I've told her this too. Tell her you want to find him and I'm sure she'll agree to help.'

'But what if I don't want her to? We don't exactly get along, you know.'

'I know that, Ronnie, but maybe this will bring you closer together.'

'Stop trying to push us together, Frank. It's not going to work.'

'Okay, okay. Forget about getting close to her but I'm still bound by your mother's wishes and she stated that no information, other than that in the letter, was to be given to either of you unless you both wanted to find your father. Together.'

'Bullshit. You're just saying that.'

'I have it in writing.' His voice was quiet. 'I'll check my diary in the morning when I'm in the office and I'll text you both with a time. You can let me know if you can make it in.'

'Okay.' She sighed. 'I don't suppose I have much of a choice. I'll talk to you tomorrow.'

She threw her mobile on the bed and felt like screaming. Why was her life so complicated?

'Ronnie, are you ready yet? I'm starving.'

'Coming.' She stood up to check her reflection in the full-length mirror on the back of the bedroom door. Her black and red swing dress was a bit over the top for a Sunday stroll but dressing up always lifted her mood. She took her brown faux-fur coat from the wardrobe to complete the look and she knew she looked good. It was going to be an interesting week ahead and she actually felt a little flutter of excitement thinking about it. As she stepped outside into the sunshine, hand in hand with Al, she thought about how wonderful her life was and how she could cope with anything if she had Al by her side.

Chapter 7

Elizabeth sat at the window of a little coffee shop on College Green watching the world go by. It always fascinated her to see people going about their business, oblivious to the turmoil that was going on in her head. There were foreign students gabbling in their native tongue, laughing and joking, people in suits rushing to appointments, shoppers running for the bus. Sometimes it felt like the world should stop and ask her if she was okay. Notice that she looked miserable. But it was a stupid thought.

She idly stirred her cappuccino and licked the froth off the spoon. It was already past five thirty and Nathan was half an hour late. The building where he worked was just around the corner but Nathan didn't like her to call to his workplace. He said it didn't look professional. She'd argued with him once about it, pointing out that she was a professional herself and wouldn't look out of place, but he'd been adamant so she hadn't pushed it.

'Can I take that chair?' A spotty-faced teen pointed to the empty seat in front of her and she nodded. Even if Nathan arrived now, there'd be no time to sit and chat. They were due in Frank's office five minutes ago and she hated being late for anything. No doubt Ronnie would already be there, sitting smugly with Al, looking at her watch and tut-tutting at the tardiness of her inconsiderate sister.

Elizabeth still hadn't made a decision about finding her father, but she was certainly more interested than she'd been initially. This was partly because Frank had been pestering her, telling her Ronnie wanted to do it, and partly because she was fed up with her life and needed a distraction. She'd agreed to meet with Frank today so she'd be armed with as much information as possible should she decide to go ahead with the search. She'd also read through her mother's letter again and again, and, each time, she'd become more curious.

Oliver Angelo. He sounded both exotic and intriguing. She'd repeated his name over and over in her mind these last few days and, the more she'd said it, the more she'd become interested in tracking him down. She didn't feel emotional about it. She wouldn't be falling into his arms, declaring her undying love for him and calling him Daddy. It was more a curiosity thing. And besides, it was something her mother wanted them to do and now that her anger was abating, she felt maybe she should respect her wishes. Nathan, of course, had been no help when she'd asked his opinion. She'd have preferred him to roll his eyes or tell her off for her indecision. Any sort of reaction would have been better than none at all.

Her phone buzzed in her bag and she pulled it out to see a missed call from Frank. They were now fifteen minutes late for the appointment and Elizabeth was raging with her husband. She dialled Nathan's number and was startled when a phone rang loudly beside her.

'Sorry I'm late, Elizabeth.' He bent over and kissed her on the cheek, his twelve-hour-old stubble scratching her face. 'Stephen called an emergency meeting and I couldn't get out of it.'

There was always something. She stood up. 'Come on, we're ridiculously late. I don't want them to start without us.'

'Do you really need me to be there?' he said, following her out of the shop. 'I honestly think you'd be better off doing this without me.'

She glared at him as she hurried down the road towards Frank's office on Dame Street. 'Yes, Nathan, I need you there. You're my husband and that's what married couples do – support each other.'

'But you know I'm not good at this … this emotional stuff. How about I head on home and start dinner? Wouldn't you like to come home and have a meal served up to you?'

'I couldn't care less about dinner. I need you by my side. Ronnie is bringing Al and I don't want to be on my own.'

'And there we have it,' he said, his long strides keeping up with her small, hurried ones. 'The very lovely Mr Alan Farrell.'

She stopped suddenly and stared at him. 'What are you talking about?'

'Come on, Elizabeth. You talk more about him than you do about your sister. What is it about him? Is it the muscles? The tattoos?'

'What exactly are you trying to say?' She couldn't believe what she was hearing.

'I think you protest too much about him. I reckon you're secretly attracted to the man.'

'Don't be ridiculous,' she said, marching forward at pace again. 'I can't stand him. You know that. I don't know why you're saying all this now.'

'I see how you look at him.'

'Nathan! Seriously. What are you on about? Why would I even look twice at him when I have you?'

'I often wonder that myself.'

'You're just being stupid. Really stupid.'

He grabbed her arm roughly and swung her around to face him. 'Don't. Call. Me. Stupid.'

'Nathan. Let go. You're hurting me.'

'Just remember who you're speaking to, Elizabeth.' He released his grip. 'Have a little bit of respect.'

She felt unsettled as they arrived at the door of Frank's office. He must have seen them coming because he buzzed them in before they rang the bell. They were over half an hour late and Elizabeth was mortified. And on top of that, she was reeling from her exchange with Nathan.

'I'm so sorry we're late.' She addressed Frank, who was sitting in a high-back leather chair at a round table. 'Nathan got delayed in work.'

'Don't worry. It happens.' He held out his hand to shake Nathan's and hugged Elizabeth.

Ronnie and Al were sitting at the table too and Elizabeth gave them a nod and a tight smile. She felt a little sheepish after her outburst over lunch with Ronnie and she guessed Ronnie would have told Al what she'd said about him. It felt awkward and she just wanted to get whatever information Frank had and leave. They both sat down and waited for Frank to speak.

'Okay, let's get started.' Frank leaned his elbows on the table and looked at them all. 'I'm really happy you've both decided to do this. It was what Belinda – your mother – wanted.'

Elizabeth was about to interrupt to say she hadn't made her mind up yet but she was afraid that Frank wouldn't give them the information he had if she said anything.

'And I'm delighted to see you two men here to support the girls,' he continued, nodding towards Al and Nathan. 'It's going to be an emotional journey – both finding your father and beyond.'

'Where else would we be?' said Nathan, putting his arm around Elizabeth and pulling her closer to him. 'That's what partners are for.'

Elizabeth forced a smile. Yet again he'd turned into the perfect husband while he had an audience.

Frank continued. 'So I have some information about your father which I'm going to share with you today. You can take notes if you wish, but I've typed out all the details so you'll have them for reference.'

'Thanks, Frank,' said Ronnie. 'But Al and I were just wondering something.'

Al and I, thought Elizabeth. Didn't she have a mind of her own?

'Why didn't Mum search for our father herself? I know she said there were good reasons initially, but it's been thirty-one years.'

'It will all become clear when I tell you what happened back then. She made a decision not to tell him she was pregnant and stood by her decision during the subsequent years.'

'So he doesn't know we exist?' Elizabeth couldn't believe it. She'd thought that he'd *chosen* not to be a part of their lives.

'As I said, she didn't tell him, but she had good reasons.'

It was Al's turn to join in. 'So when did she talk to you about it? When did she make the decision that she wanted the girls to find their father?'

'Actually,' said Elizabeth, 'can we stop referring to him as our father? It's making me feel uncomfortable. Can we just call him Oliver?'

Frank nodded. 'You can call him whatever feels right, Elizabeth. And in answer to your question, Al, it was really only when she got sick that she thought about you finding him.'

'But it still doesn't answer the question as to why she didn't do it herself,' insisted Ronnie. 'It would have made sense for *her* to find him. It would have been easier for her to trace him than it will be for us.'

Elizabeth almost spat the words out. 'Maybe it was a little matter of *the cancer* that distracted her. Maybe finding Oliver wasn't her top priority while her body was being ravaged by chemotherapy.'

Ronnie blushed and Elizabeth tried to hide her smile of satisfaction.

'Look, we're getting off the point here.' Frank tried to bring the conversation back to the search. 'The fact remains that your mother has left details to help you find your fa— Oliver. I'll tell you what I know and you can take it from there.'

'Go ahead,' said Elizabeth, looking pointedly at Ronnie. 'There won't be any more interruptions.'

Frank cleared his throat and sat back in his chair. 'You already know your father's name and a little about what he did. As your mother already said in the letter, he was a hippy, of sorts. He wrote songs with his girlfriend and …'

'His girlfriend?' Ronnie looked surprised.

'Shush,' Elizabeth warned.

'Yes, I don't think your mother mentioned that in the letter but Skye was his girlfriend. They lived in a shared rented house just off Baggot Street and made their money from busking around the city. Your mum met them at a college party and she was fascinated by them. They were different to the people she normally mixed with so it was a surprise to her when they became friends. But there was a special connection between her and Oliver. She didn't know what it was but they were drawn to each other. I think Skye sensed it and felt threatened by it so one day they announced that they were moving to Spain and planned to busk around Europe.'

'Poor Mum,' said Elizabeth. 'It seems like all her friends were moving away. Oliver, Skye, you …'

'It was the eighties, Elizabeth. College graduates along with other young people were leaving Ireland in their droves. Anywhere was better than here because jobs were few and far between and most saw their future as bleak if they were to stay.'

'So what happened then?' Al was on the edge of his seat and Elizabeth couldn't help wishing Nathan would join in too. Instead he was checking something on his phone, completely uninterested in the story that was unfolding.

Frank continued. 'According to Belinda, they kept in touch but she didn't see him again until the summer of 1986, when he came back to Ireland. Alone. Apparently, he and Skye had split up and he was devastated.'

'The summer of 1986,' said Ronnie, her voice barely a whisper. 'That must have been when it happened.'

Elizabeth felt her heart beating out of her chest but she held her breath, waiting for Frank to continue.

'Yes,' he said. 'He was confused and upset and she was a great support to him. It happened. Just the once.'

'And they regretted it?' Elizabeth was close to tears. She didn't want to think of their creation as a mistake.'

'No, no, not at all. In fact, your mother said nothing had ever felt so right. He felt the same way too but it wasn't meant to be.

Skye came over looking for him and he ended up going back to Spain with her.'

Ronnie sat forward in her chair. 'But how could he? If it felt right with Mum, how could he just leave like that?'

'It was complicated.'

'Complicated how?'

'Skye told him she was pregnant. They were going to have a baby.'

There was a gasp before the room fell silent.

'But before you ask, there was no baby. Skye miscarried a few weeks later but, by then, they were back in Spain and had decided to settle down.'

'But Mum was pregnant by then too,' Elizabeth cried. 'Why didn't she tell him? He probably would have come back to her.'

'Maybe,' said Frank, nodding slowly. 'But Belinda would never have put that pressure on him. He'd been pulled back to Spain because his partner was pregnant and then for her to pull him back to Ireland because *she* was pregnant just didn't feel right to her. And besides, you know what your mum was like. She was a strong, independent woman and she wanted to do it all on her own.'

'But did she love him?' Ronnie looked almost childlike as she begged for the story to have a fairy-tale side to it. 'Do you think they would have ended up together if he'd stayed in Ireland?'

Frank leaned his elbows on the table and ran his hands through his silver hair. 'Who knows, Ronnie? It would be nice to think they would have had a relationship but the truth is we'll never know.'

'So are we almost done here?' said Nathan, speaking for the first time. 'Because we have that *thing* tonight, Elizabeth. We should make a move.'

Elizabeth felt like disappearing as all eyes stared at her husband.

'We only have half the story.' Al looked like he was settling in to hear the rest and Elizabeth cursed her sister once again for having a man who was interested. 'I mean, what happened after that? Did they lose contact altogether?'

'Belinda kept track of him for a while through a friend of his. She wasn't sure initially whether or not she'd tell him about the pregnancy and then later about you girls when you were born. But as time moved on and she was settled and happy with her little family, it became less important.'

'So did they come back to Ireland?' Elizabeth asked.

Frank shook his head and shifted some papers awkwardly around his desk.

'Frank?' Ronnie looked as worried as Elizabeth felt.

'Skye was a New Yorker. She'd come to Ireland to study in her late teens before dropping out of college to pursue a more liberal lifestyle. But after the miscarriage, she became depressed and she missed her family.'

'You're not going to tell us they're in New York, are you?' said Ronnie, her face ashen. 'I thought this was going to be a search within Ireland – not halfway across the world.'

'I'm afraid that's exactly what I'm going to tell you, Ronnie. Through your mother's contact she heard that they went over to New York and settled there so that Skye could be around her family.'

Elizabeth's heart sank. 'New York is a big place. I hope you have an address at least?'

'I have an address that your mother was given when they first moved. She was still uncertain about contacting him at the time so she held on to it just in case.'

'And did she get in touch with him over there?'

Frank shook his head. 'No. There was no further contact so they could be anywhere now. But at least the address will give you a start.'

Ronnie looked as though she was about to cry. 'Is that all you have for us? If he's not at that address, then we have no chance of finding him.'

'As I said, Ronnie, I have everything written out for you. I have the New York address. I also have the address for Oliver's friend, Albert Dunne, although your mother lost contact with him a long time ago. And I have a picture which I've copied and—'

'A picture!' Elizabeth almost jumped off her chair. 'You mean you have a picture and you're only telling us about it now? Where is it? I want to see it.'

He opened the folder in front of him and took out a colourful picture and slid it across the table. Elizabeth pounced on it first. It was a bit blurred but she could see Oliver Angelo lying on the grass looking relaxed and happy, a huge smile on his face. He was on his side, leaning his head on his left elbow. His jeans were loose, held up by a wide brown belt, and he was barefoot. He had nothing but a tan suede waistcoat on his top half and wore a similar-colour bandana around his long hippie hair. Tears fell unbidden from Elizabeth's eyes and she was forced to use the sleeve of her navy linen jacket to wipe them. She felt an arm around her shoulder and suddenly felt glad that Nathan was there with her.

'Let me see,' said Ronnie, holding out her hand for the picture.

Elizabeth took a last look before carefully handing it to her sister. She watched as Ronnie's face showed the same emotions that Elizabeth had felt. Nobody said a word. Ronnie handed it to Al then, who passed it on to Nathan. It was an important and emotional moment for the girls and everyone seemed to respect that. Al was first to break the silence.

'He's not the sort of guy I would have expected your mum to go for.'

'What exactly does that mean?' said Elizabeth, glaring at Al.

'He's right,' said Frank, taking the picture back and replacing it in his folder. 'Oliver Angelo was very different to Belinda. And not somebody she would typically have gone for. She couldn't explain it herself. She said it was an initial fascination and then, I don't know, something more, I suppose.'

Ronnie nodded. 'Well, they say opposites attract, don't they? So where do we go from here?'

'It's in your hands now, ladies.' Frank handed them both an envelope. 'Take the information away, sleep on it, and let me know if you'd like to take the next step.'

'The next step?' Elizabeth was almost afraid to hear any more.

'Well,' said Frank, standing up and walking around to the front of his desk. 'You girls might want to clear your diaries for a bit.'

'You're not suggesting …?' Ronnie looked startled.

'Your mother has already booked flexi-date return flights to New York for you both. The hotel, transfers and everything else is sorted. You just have to tell me when and I'll have everything finalised.'

Elizabeth gasped. 'Go to New York? Together?'

'That's the idea,' said Frank, not meeting her eye. 'That's what your mother wanted. For you girls to find your father … together.'

'It's a bit of a shock, Frank,' said Ronnie, glancing at Elizabeth. 'I think we'll both need some time to digest everything.'

'Take all the time you need. I'll check in with you both in a few days.'

Nathan was already at the door, anxious to get out of there, so Elizabeth gave Frank a hug and said her goodbyes to the others. She really hadn't been expecting *that*. It was all getting very complicated. But as they walked down the street, her stomach was full of butterflies and she could hear her own heart pounding. It was funny, only last week she didn't want to know anything about her father. She'd got by this far without him and she didn't need him in her life now. And yet thoughts of him filled her head constantly. He was the last thing she thought of before going to sleep and the first thing that sprang to her mind when she woke.

'Well, that's that,' said Nathan, taking her hand as they walked across the road.

Elizabeth tried to read his face. 'What do you mean?'

'Think about it, Elizabeth. It seems like the only way you'll find out more about Oliver is by going to New York. And that's never going to happen.'

'Why not?' said Elizabeth, her head spinning. She hadn't even had a chance to digest the information and here was Nathan telling her it was all over.

'Of course you're not going to New York. You have commitments here. Maybe now you can put this whole silly fiasco behind you and move on.'

Elizabeth didn't respond but as she looked at her husband, something fired up inside her. Did he not realise how much this was affecting her? Did he not notice how upset and torn she'd been? It seemed like he didn't care about her at all. New York seemed like a crazy idea but one thing was for sure – it would be impossible to just forget about her father now, after all they'd learnt. As Frank had said, it would be difficult, but she knew now that she wouldn't rest easy until she found Oliver Angelo.

Chapter 8

'Right, let's take a look,' said Amber, balancing a glass of red wine as she opened her laptop. 'Oliver Angelo.'

She typed the name into Google and waited for the response. Within seconds a few matches popped up on the screen. There were also images, which almost caused Ronnie to spill her wine in her excitement to check them out.

'Oh my God! Look at those pictures.' She moved in closer to Amber on the sofa and held her breath as they scrolled through the images.

It seemed the name 'Oliver Angelo' confused Google because it brought up a myriad of different people. There were children, elderly people, women and men, people of every ethnicity imaginable, none of which were the person they were looking for. There was even a priest amongst them, which caused Ronnie to give a second look, but he definitely didn't fit the bill.

Ronnie sighed. 'This is hopeless, Amber. We're never going to find him this way.'

'Keep the faith, Ronnie. I'll have a look on social media now and see what that throws up.' Amber was always upbeat and Ronnie was grateful to have her in her corner. After the meeting with Frank the previous evening, Ronnie had sought her friend's advice. She really didn't want to go to New York with her sister unless there was no other way and thankfully Amber had come up with a few ideas. She was a bit of a social network addict, spending way too many hours on Twitter and Facebook, so she'd suggested trying to trace him that way. Ronnie was just the opposite and hated modern technology, so she'd been grateful for Amber's help.

But Facebook proved fruitless as they only found one Oliver Angelo who lived in Bangkok and wasn't even active online. Twitter proved much the same, producing an African-American woman called Oliver Angelo and a number of Angelo Olivers. Amber checked on a few more popular sites but it soon became clear that they weren't going to find what they were looking for.

She closed the laptop and put it on the coffee table. 'I'm sorry, Ronnie. I guess not everyone is online these days. I really thought we had a chance of finding him that way.'

'Don't worry,' said Ronnie, taking a huge slug of her wine. 'It was a long shot really. We'll just have to look at the other information we have and follow up on some things.'

'But shouldn't you really be doing this with Elizabeth? Even without going to New York, you could put your heads together and see if you come up with anything. You said that's what your mother wanted.'

Ronnie sighed. 'That's what Mum wanted alright, but Elizabeth has her head stuck so far up her arse that—'

'Vonnie said arse, Mummy. Arse, arse, arse.'

'Daniel!' Amber held out her arms and her little boy ran to her and hopped up on her lap. 'What are you doing up? You were fast asleep when I checked you a few minutes ago.'

'Hi, Daniel.' Ronnie felt sheepish. 'How's my favourite boy?'

'Why did you say arse, Vonnie? Is arse a good word now? Can I say arse?'

'That's enough, Daniel. Ronnie didn't mean to say it and she's very sorry, aren't you, Ronnie?'

'Yes, yes, I am. It's not a good word and I shouldn't have said it.'

''Kay. Guess what, Vonnie? Terence won't stop licking his bum and Daddy said it's 'gusting.'

Ronnie looked and Amber and raised an eyebrow. 'Terence?'

Amber laughed. 'Terence the shih-tzu.'

'I thought you called him Buddy?'

'Well, this little guy,' said Amber, nodding towards Daniel, 'decided he wanted to call him after one of the *Thomas the Tank Engine* characters. And actually it's quite funny having a dog with such a human name.'

'Hilarious,' said Ronnie, giggling. 'I can just see you in the park, shouting for Terence to come back.'

'Why are you drinking wine?' said Daniel, changing the subject.

'Because we're having some Mummy time,' said Amber, tickling him on the tummy. 'And you, my little munchkin, need to go back to bed.'

'Have you got a baby in your tummy, Ronnie?'

Ronnie was completely thrown by the question and instinctively sat up straighter to flatten out her rolls of fat. Amber reddened and shushed him, standing up with him in her arms.

'But I want to give Vonnie a hug,' he protested, holding his arms out for Ronnie to take him. 'Can Vonnie put me to bed and read me a story?'

Ronnie stood up. 'Of course I can, Daniel.'

'You don't have to, Ronnie. You didn't come over here for childminding duties.'

'It's no problem.' She held out her arms and Daniel hopped across to her. 'I love spending time with him. Come on, Mister Man. Let's get you back to bed.'

'You smell like Nanny's house,' he said, as they headed up the stairs. She hoped Mrs Webb had a Jo Malone French Lime Blossom candle, or else she'd have to rethink her personal hygiene. He picked a book off his shelf and hopped into bed.

'Is your hair supposed to be purple?'

'It's auburn, actually.'

'Well, is it supposed to be burned?'

'*Auburn*. It's a colour. Now, are we going to read this book?'

''Kay, Vonnie.'

She read him the story and was rewarded with a beaming smile and a hug when she was finished.

'Will you be here when I wake up?'

'I'm afraid not, Daniel. I'll be home in my own house. But I'll come and see you again very soon.'

''Kay.'

She kissed his white blond curls on the top of his head and tucked him in, before heading for the door.

'Vonnie?'

'Yes, Daniel?'

'Don't tell Mummy but I love your hugs better than hers.'

She flushed with pleasure. 'It will be our secret.'

'Because you're fat and your hugs are sooo squishy.'

She turned off the light and smiled to herself. There was nothing as refreshing as the honesty of a two-year-old. Amber was so lucky to have Daniel. He was a gorgeous, funny little child and Ronnie prayed that it wouldn't be long before she had a little Daniel of her own.

'I was just coming up to rescue you,' said Amber, meeting her at the end of the stairs. 'Come on, there's another bottle of red with our names on it. Roger won't be home until after eleven and he said he'd drop you home then.'

Ronnie sat back on the sofa in the sitting room as Amber went to open another bottle of wine. Amber lived in Cabra, just five minutes in a taxi or a twenty-minute walk from Ronnie's apartment, and Ronnie was grateful to have such a good friend so close. Roger, her husband, was a painter and decorator turned interior designer, so their little two-bed terraced house was like a palace. They were the perfect couple, with the perfect life, and although Ronnie was happy with Al, she envied both their home and their family situation. Amber often spoke about wanting a little sister for Daniel. She wasn't in a hurry but felt she'd like another baby in a couple of years. And Ronnie reckoned that her wish would come true. She was one of those people who had never suffered hardship and tended to get what she wanted in life. Both her parents were still alive and healthy, and helped out with Daniel's childcare, and her three brothers were very close to her and adored their baby sister. But despite her fortunate life, she was grounded and always grateful for what she had. She was a great friend and Ronnie cherished that friendship deeply.

'Here we go.' Amber arrived into the sitting room with an open bottle of red wine and a bowl of cheesy puffs. 'They're Marks & Spencer's ones. I know they're your favourite.'

'Yum! I've just had my dinner but I can't resist these.' Ronnie took a fistful of the snacks out of the bowl and shoved them in her mouth. 'Although I probably should ease up on the eating if it's making me look pregnant!'

'Oh God, I'm so sorry, Ronnie. He's always saying things like that.'

Ronnie laughed. 'It's okay. It would take more than that to offend me.'

'He'll get me into trouble one of these days. I hope he didn't blackmail you into reading too many stories.'

'He's adorable,' said Ronnie, licking her fingers. 'Do you know how lucky you are?'

'I do. Sometimes I feel like pulling my hair out, especially when he ends up in our bed and I spend the night with feet in my back. Or when he throws a tantrum in the middle of the supermarket. But then I look at those big blue eyes and wispy, golden curls and my heart melts.'

Ronnie bit down on her bottom lip in an effort to stop the tears that were threatening to fall. She didn't dare speak for fear her words would come out as a sob. Her desire to have a child was growing by the day and sometimes it felt like an actual physical pain. Amber noticed her discomfort and was quick to reassure her.

'It *will* happen for you, Ronnie. I know it will.'

'How?'

'Sorry?'

'How do you know it will happen for me? It's what everyone keeps saying but how do they know?'

'I'm just trying to be encouraging. To give you some positive vibes.'

'I know you're only trying to help and I appreciate it. Al is always saying things like that to me. But it's hard to be upbeat about it all the time.'

'Nobody expects you to be. It must be difficult.'

Ronnie nodded. 'It's hard to explain. It's the same thing month after month. It's like I'm walking up a mountain and just when I get to the top, I fall down and have to start all over again.'

Amber took her hand. 'Well, I can keep you company during that climb anytime you want. And if you want to borrow your godson, that could also be arranged. Even for a sleepover. Actually, *especially* for a sleepover.'

'It's a deal,' laughed Ronnie. 'Now come on, I didn't come over here to talk babies. Let's get back to the reason I'm here. What am I going to do, Amber? Now that I've started looking, I really want to find him. I just don't know what to do next.'

'Well, let's have a look at that picture again. Maybe it will give us some inspiration.'

Ronnie reached down to the side of the sofa and pulled her retro floral bag onto her lap. It was a mishmash of colours and Ronnie loved it because it went with everything. She rooted for a moment before producing the picture and handing it over to Amber.

'He was quite handsome, wasn't he?' Amber examined the picture carefully. 'And his hair is exquisite. Look at those natural waves. And the length of it!'

'But between that and his facial hair, it's hard to get a proper look at him. I can't even tell what colour his eyes are.'

'Well, you and Elizabeth both have brown eyes and your mum had blue, so I'm guessing his are brown. But did you see this?' Elizabeth pointed at Oliver's chest in the picture and Ronnie took it to have a closer look.

'I don't know what you're pointing to.'

'Look at his chest, right there at the edge of the waistcoat. It looks like a necklace but I think it's a tattoo.'

'Oh my God, you're right,' said Ronnie, triumphantly. 'It is a tattoo. How did we not see this before?'

'Maybe you weren't expecting it? Sometimes our eyes don't see what they're not looking for.'

'Oh you're full of philosophy tonight, aren't you? But you're right. I wouldn't have expected it. But I like the fact that he has one.' She strained her eyes to try and make out the detail. 'I think it's a peace symbol,' she announced, triumphantly.'

'That's what it looks like, alright. With a feather attached. You should get Al to have a closer look. He might be able to tell us more.'

'Good idea. I'm surprised he didn't notice it himself.'

'Do you think Elizabeth is doing this too?' said Amber, changing the subject. 'Trying to find him herself. Or do you think she's interested in going to New York?'

'You can be sure Elizabeth is doing some searching of her own. But as for New York, I doubt it. If you heard the way she spoke to me a couple of weeks ago, you'd realise how much she hates me.'

'Don't say that.'

'But it's true, Amber. She doesn't talk to me, she spits the words out and splashes them all over my face. Honestly, she can't even say hello without giving me a look of disdain.'

'And to think I used to be so jealous of you two in school.'

'Jealous of what?'

'Of your friendship, your closeness. I love my brothers but I would love to have had a sister. I used to imagine how cool it would be to have a twin. It makes me sad to see how you've grown apart from her.'

'Well, don't be sad, Amber. It's just the way it is.' Ronnie took a large sip of her wine and winced as the liquid burned her throat.

'I sometimes feel guilty, you know,' said Amber.

Ronnie looked at her quizzically. 'About what?'

'It's just … I don't know. It's just that you and I are such good friends. I sometimes feel like I've taken you away from her.'

'Don't be silly, Amber. Elizabeth has done this to herself.'

Amber nodded slowly and then her eyes lit up. 'Why don't all three of us arrange to meet up during the week and we can discuss ideas? We used to have some fun times, didn't we, all three of us? And we might get further with this if we all put our heads together.'

Ronnie wasn't sure but Amber wasn't letting it go.

'Come on, Ronnie. It might be fun.'

'I don't know about fun, but it might not be such a bad idea. I'm telling you one thing, though. I'll sit in a room with her and swap ideas. I'll even try my best to be nice. But one thing is for sure, if the Irish search doesn't yield anything, there's no way on earth I'm going to New York with her to find our father.'

Chapter 9

'There is absolutely NO WAY I'm going to New York with that woman.' Elizabeth was pacing up and down her office floor and Amanda, her assistant, was standing at the door. 'I mean, could you imagine it? We'd kill each other before we even got there.'

'Tell me again,' said Amanda, looking confused. 'You haven't been able to find him through the internet so you think you'll have to go over to his last known address? In New York?'

'Yes. And I've no problem going over there. In fact I'd quite like to. But just not with *her*. I know Mum wanted us to do this together, but seriously. The last time we went on a holiday together we were just naïve teenagers and hadn't even entered the real world yet.'

'Elizabeth, if you don't mind me saying so, you're getting ten steps ahead of yourself. From what you told me, there are other avenues to explore before you have to think about going all the way out there. And besides, even if you did go, it would hardly be a holiday.'

Elizabeth sat down at her desk and sighed. 'I know you're right but I don't have a good feeling about this. The leads we have here in Ireland are vague, to say the least. The only concrete thing we have is his address in New York.'

'And what does Nathan think about all of this?'

'Oh, he fully supports my decision to look for Oliver but he's worried about me too.' It was a lie. Nathan hadn't spoken a word about it since their meeting with Frank, except to accuse Elizabeth of giving Al the eye. It was ridiculous. He knew full well that she hated her sister's boyfriend, so accusing her of fancying him just didn't make sense. But then again, he was like that with every man that crossed Elizabeth's path. She was sometimes afraid to even glance at another man in case Nathan thought she was eyeing him up.

'So he'd go with you, then?'

'Sorry, what?'

'Nathan. He'd go with you to New York if you wanted to take that trip?'

'I don't know, Amanda. He's always so busy in work and finds it hard to get time off. But I'm quite happy to do it on my own, if I decide to go.'

Amanda looked at her understandingly and nodded. She knew. It was written all over her face. She'd been Elizabeth's assistant for the last ten years and had seen some exchanges between her and Nathan during that time. Nathan was always careful to appear polite and considerate in front of people but Amanda was very astute and would see through that sort of behaviour. Elizabeth suddenly felt embarrassed to be exposing her personal life at her workplace so she pulled her chair in closer to her desk and flicked the 'on' switch on her computer.

'Right, I can't sit around here all day moaning about family stuff. I have a heap of work to do. Can you dig out those files for the Delaney job, Amanda, please?'

'Of course. Will after lunch be okay? It's just that I've arranged to meet Adam at the gates to Stephen's Green at one fifteen.' Her face lit up when she mentioned her fiancé and she blushed slightly. 'It's five years today since we met and he's organising a picnic for us. Imagine … a picnic in this weather. But he said he's bringing blankets to fend off the cold.'

'How lovely.' Elizabeth wondered if Nathan would even know the date they met. She would have laughed at the idea of a picnic in the past, but seeing Amanda's face lit up with excitement and love, it seemed like the best date she could imagine. She was used to being wined and dined at the most expensive and exclusive places in the city but it didn't seem enough any more. She still liked the finer things in life and wanted to be successful but she also wanted more from Nathan, more from their relationship. She wanted to be truly loved and cherished.

'Elizabeth?' Amanda was still hovering at the door, waiting for confirmation that she could leave.

'Sorry, yes, you head off to lunch. And actually, I don't need those files today. You can take the rest of the day off.'

'What? Really?'

'Yes. Now go before I change my mind.'

'Thanks, Elizabeth. I really appreciate you doing—'

'Go! And, Amanda …'

'Yes?'

'Enjoy yourself. And appreciate the fact that he loves and cherishes you so much.'

She nodded, and disappeared out the door in a flash. Elizabeth smiled to herself. She wouldn't normally do something like that but Amanda deserved it. She was loyal and hard-working and sometimes Elizabeth felt that she was her only friend. They didn't spend any time outside work together but they did chat a lot during working hours. Elizabeth had told her about her mother's video from the start and Amanda had been asking for regular updates. Elizabeth was glad to be able to talk to someone because Nathan certainly didn't want to hear about it.

Her computer screen went into standby mode and she sat back in her chair to think. She needed some inspiration. She had the envelope with all the information about Oliver in her handbag so she reached down and pulled it out. She smiled to herself as she looked at the picture. Her mother looked really happy, as did Oliver. It was so sad to think that circumstances had pulled them apart when they should have been together. There really wasn't much to go on, but suddenly she knew what she wanted to do next. Her diary was clear for the afternoon so nobody would miss her if she did like Amanda and took the rest of the day off.

Albert Dunne was a friend of Oliver's. Belinda had kept in touch with him when Oliver first moved away and Frank had passed his details on to the girls. He had an address in Walkinstown and, if he still lived there, he could be the key to finding her father. She felt a flutter of excitement and grabbed her iPhone to type the address into Google Maps. She switched off her computer, grabbed her bag and was driving out of the car park within minutes.

It didn't take her long to get to the street and she parked outside number seventy-four. There were two women gossiping at the front of a house two doors down and they strained their neck to see who was in the strange car. Elizabeth felt uncomfortable so she picked up her mobile and pretended to be on a call. This gave her time to gather her thoughts and decide what she was going to say when she called to the door.

It was a typical Dublin end-of-terrace house with grey pebble dash at the front and silver railings surrounding the little garden. The door was varnished to a shining mahogany colour and the windows boasted gleaming white net curtains. Everything looked freshly painted and the garden was neat and tidy with colourful blooms around the edges of the lawn. There was a green area facing the house but, despite the sunshine, there were no children playing on it. It felt like a settled area – a place where people had lived for a long time. So maybe Albert Dunne still lived here after all. There was only one way to find out.

She stepped out of the car and smoothed her white blouse down over her Betty Jackson black trousers. She'd left her jacket in work in her haste to leave and was now regretting it as she felt a little exposed. Her blouse was perfectly respectable, but there was just something about how a jacket made her feel when she put it on. She felt powerful, in charge. She gave herself a mental shake. She should be showing her vulnerability rather than her power so maybe leaving the jacket behind was a good thing on this occasion.

The curtains twitched as she approached the door, making her feel both nervous and excited, but she rang the bell without hesitation. A woman's face appeared at the window and she felt her heart sink a little. Although, according to Frank, Albert Dunne was married back then and had three children. So this could be his wife. But what if Albert was dead and she upset his wife by asking for him. Suddenly this didn't seem like such a good idea after all and Elizabeth was tempted to run to her car and speed away.

'Can I help you?'

The voice came from her right-hand side and she almost jumped out of her skin when she saw a man standing beside her.

'Sorry, I didn't mean to scare you. I was just painting the side gate when I heard someone come up the driveway. Who are you looking for?'

He looked around seventy, so it wasn't looking good. 'I'm trying to trace someone who used to live here about twenty-five years ago. Albert Dunne. Do you know him?'

'I should think so.' He smiled, showing a mouthful of yellowing teeth. 'That's me. What can I do for you?'

'You? The Albert Dunne who lived here in the early nineties?'

'The very one. I've been here thirty-five years.'

'It's just that the man I was looking for is only around sixty.' She had the words out of her mouth before she realised, and wanted to disappear into a hole when he nodded sadly.

'It's the wife, you see. Puts years onto me. She's had dementia for the last five years and it's not easy to see her like that.'

'I'm so sorry,' said Elizabeth, and she meant it. He looked like a lovely man. And he'd been her mother's friend back in the day. She continued, 'You won't know me but I think you knew my mother. Belinda Cunningham?'

'Belinda Cunningham. Now that's a name I haven't heard of in a while. And now that I look at you, you're the spitting image of her.'

Elizabeth was relieved. He remembered her.

'And where are my manners? Come on inside and have a cup of tea and you can tell me what's brought you here.'

'Thanks. That would be great.' She followed him inside and he led the way into the little kitchen at the back of the house.

'Sophie is taking a nap. She always does in the afternoon and that's when I get some work done outside.'

Elizabeth was doubtful. 'I saw a face at the window. Was that not her?'

'Her bed is in the front room. She likes it there. Looks out that window for hours sometimes, she does. She sleeps lightly so must have heard you at the door.'

'Oh, I'm sorry. I didn't realise.'

'Of course you didn't. I'll check on her in a minute. Now come on, sit yourself down.'

Elizabeth sat down on one of the four oak chairs set around a small round table. 'I have to tell you your house looks beautiful outside. You obviously look after it really well. It's by far the nicest one on the street.'

'Well, aren't you lovely to say that.' Albert busied himself filling the kettle and pulling mugs from a cupboard. 'Sophie always took great pride in how our house looked and, even though she doesn't really care about stuff like that any more, I still want it to look good. For her.'

Elizabeth was anxious to explain the reason for her visit. 'You said you remember my mum?'

'Of course I do. A right little firecracker she was. I didn't know her that well but a mate of mine was very friendly with her.'

'A ... a mate?' She barely dared breathe.

'Yes. A guy called Oliver. Oliver Angelo. A hippie, he was. Into peace and love and all that mumbo jumbo.'

Elizabeth could hardly contain her excitement. 'Actually, that's why I'm here. I'm trying to trace Oliver Angelo.'

'Oh, really?' He placed two steaming mugs on the table, along with a jug of milk and a bowl of sugar. 'It's taken her a hell of a long time.'

'Excuse me?'

'Belinda. It's taken her a long time to go after him.' His eyes twinkled. 'I always knew she held a torch for him.'

'Did you? Did she? How do you know?'

'She used to ring me all the time.' He heaped three spoonfuls of sugar into his tea and stirred. 'Used to say she wanted a chat. But it was really to find out about Oliver. She thought she was being subtle but I could tell she liked him.'

Elizabeth was on the edge of her seat. It was more information than she could have hoped for.

'So how come she's looking for him now?' Albert continued. 'Wouldn't it be gas if the two of them got together after all this time?'

'Actually, she's not looking for him. *I* am. My mum passed away a few months ago.' She'd never get used to saying those words. Tears sprang to her eyes and she blinked quickly to stop them falling.

'Oh, love, I'm so sorry. What happened? I can't believe it. She was only the same age as myself.'

'Cancer.' She whispered the word.

He let out a long sigh. 'It must have been awful for you. Is it just you or did she have more children?'

'Just me and my sister. We're twins.'

'Of course. I remember her telling me she had twins. At least you have each other for support.'

Elizabeth nodded. She wasn't about to share her family problems with him and, besides, all she really wanted at this stage was news of her father.

'So,' she said, taking a sip of her tea. 'Do you have contact details for Oliver? Are you still in touch with him?'

He shook his head and she felt her heart sink. 'Not any more. We did keep in touch for a while. He used to write to me every few weeks in the beginning. Then he became more settled and the letters became fewer.'

'How long since you've heard from him?' She was desperate for even a little nugget of information.

'Gosh, let me see. I can't remember when we were in contact last. It's been too many years. I have an address for him somewhere, though. Maybe he's still there. Hang on.'

He disappeared out of the room and Elizabeth noted how he walked with a stoop. It was hard to believe he was the same age as her mother. Her mother had been fit and active with barely a wrinkle on her face. She'd always kept her hair on trend and made sure her clothes were in fashion. Albert, in his navy overalls with his wispy grey hair around his bald patch, looked like he could be her grandfather.

'Here we go,' he said, coming back into the room and placing a worn-looking address book on the table in front of her. 'That's where he was when we last spoke.'

It was the same address that Frank had given her. Her heart sank. She'd really got her hopes up that this man could be the key to finding her father but it wasn't to be.

'Copy it down,' he continued, tearing a strip of paper from the notebook and handing her a pen. 'Hopefully you'll still find him there.'

She didn't have the heart to tell him she already had that address so she took the pen and wrote it on the piece of paper he gave her. But she wasn't ready to let go yet. 'A phone number! Do you have a number for him?'

Albert shook his head. 'We never bothered with calls. Too expensive to ring international. It was just letters, I'm afraid.'

'Not to worry,' she said, trying to sound upbeat. 'And thanks. You've been very helpful.'

'It's no bother. It was lovely to see you.'

Elizabeth stood up and headed for the door. 'It was lovely to see you too, Albert. It's always nice to speak to people who knew my mum. It keeps her memory alive, if you know what I mean.'

'I sure do.' He opened the front door. 'Tell me to mind my own business if you like, but I'm curious. What do you want with Oliver Angelo?'

She hesitated for a moment. She wasn't sure if she wanted to tell him the real reason.

'Don't mind me,' he said. 'I'm just a nosy old man.'

She was quick to reassure him. 'Not at all. It's just difficult, you know. Mum spoke about Oliver before she died. We're just trying to learn some more about her earlier years.'

He shook his head. 'Very sad. Very, very sad.'

'Thanks again, Albert,' said Elizabeth, unlocking her car as she walked down the path. 'Maybe I'll see you again sometime.'

Amazingly, the two women were still outside talking as she left, and Elizabeth smiled to herself. She was disappointed that she hadn't found out any more from Albert but she meant what she'd said to him. It had been nice talking to him about her mother and especially hearing him describe her as a firecracker. She glanced at the display on the dashboard and saw it was only four o'clock. She briefly toyed with the idea of going back to work but quickly changed her mind. She had a few hours before Nathan would be home so she was going to have a look at the old photos she'd taken from among her mother's things. Maybe something there would reveal further clues about her father. Now that she'd started the search, there was no going back. She was determined to find Oliver Angelo, even if it meant putting her differences with her sister aside to do it.

Chapter 10

'She's not coming, is she?' said Ronnie, sipping at her orange juice. She'd decided to give alcohol a miss for a while to see if it would increase her chances of getting pregnant.

Amber glanced over at the door of Dolan's pub and her face fell. 'I'm sorry, Ronnie. I probably shouldn't have pushed you both, but …'

'Stop, Amber. Don't you dare apologise. You've done nothing except be a good friend to me. And even to Elizabeth, although she doesn't deserve it. If anyone should be saying sorry, it's her.'

'She seemed enthusiastic when I rang the other day,' said Amber, nursing her vodka and tonic. 'And she actually appeared to be happy to hear from me.'

Ronnie shook her head. 'You of all people should know what she's like. All smiles and promises on the outside but sometimes what's on the inside can be very ugly.'

Amber nodded sagely. 'What do they say – "All fur coat and no knickers".'

Ronnie almost choked on her drink. 'I think the phrase you're looking for is: "A wolf in sheep's clothing".'

'Oh yeah,' said Amber, giggling. 'That's the one.'

'So is this a private joke or can anyone join in?'

Both girls almost jumped out of their skin when Elizabeth appeared beside them. She hovered over them as though waiting for a formal invitation to sit and Ronnie couldn't help noticing how out of place she looked. With her pale grey slacks with matching jacket and white buttoned-up blouse, she looked more like she was heading to a business meeting than a casual drink in the pub.

'You came!' was all Ronnie could manage.

'Of course I did, Ronnie. I said I'd be here, didn't I?'

Amber moved closer to Ronnie to make room for Elizabeth. 'Come on, sit down. What are you having to drink? It's good to see you.'

Elizabeth slid into the little corner booth beside the girls, her mouth fixed in a grimace. 'So what's the big joke then?'

'Oh, it was nothing much really,' said Amber, glancing at Ronnie. 'I was just telling Ronnie about some of Daniel's antics. He's a real little …'

'Well, maybe we should move on to the reason we're here,' said Elizabeth, pulling a notepad and pen from her bag and signalling to a barman to come over. 'Have you two girls come up with any new ideas?'

Ronnie stiffened. She hated how cold Elizabeth was. How nonchalant. She never asked about personal stuff and stayed away from small talk. God forbid anyone would think there might be a nicer person behind that steely exterior. But Amber obviously noticed Ronnie's demeanour changing so was quick to pipe up.

'Why don't we have a drink and a general chat first. I haven't seen you in ages, Elizabeth. Not since … since …'

'Mum's funeral. You tore yourself away from Ronnie for a minute to come and sympathise with me.'

Amber reddened and Ronnie wanted to jump to her rescue but her friend had it under control. 'You must really miss her. She was a wonderful woman. I'm so glad you came tonight, Elizabeth. The three of us should get together more often. Just like we used to.'

That seemed to disarm Elizabeth because her mouth twitched and she looked unsure what to say. There was a glimmer of something in her eyes. Regret, maybe? It took her a moment to gather herself before responding. 'People grow apart. That's just life.'

Thankfully the barman arrived at the table at that moment, breaking the tension, and Ronnie was sorely tempted to forget her sobriety and order a double vodka. But she wasn't going to let her sister get to her so she stuck to the orange juice. Orders given, they settled back down to a conversation and somehow Elizabeth looked more relaxed as she slipped off her jacket and sat back into the seat. But she was still focused on the task in hand and wasn't allowing idle chit-chat to take over.

'So, other than looking online,' she said, her silver pen poised over a blank page, 'have you done anything else about finding Oliver?'

Ronnie shook her head. 'To be honest, I really don't know what else we can do. And you know me and computers – I barely know how to switch them on.'

'I assume you led the search there?' Elizabeth turned her attention to Amber. 'I seem to remember you being obsessed with social media.'

'Well, I wouldn't say I was obsessed but, yes, I have a good knowledge of it and, yes, I helped Ronnie to search.' She explained what they'd done and how their efforts had been futile. 'And what about you, Elizabeth? Did your search shed any light?'

'Not really. I tried searching the address that Frank gave us but it seems impossible to find out who lives there. There are lots of sites that do this reverse address search but none of them came up with anything. It's very frustrating.'

Ronnie nodded in agreement. 'I wish she'd just talked to us about this before … before …'

'I do too,' said Elizabeth, her voice low. 'I still feel so hurt by it. Why couldn't she have trusted us? What did she think we were going to do? Did she think we'd turn on her for keeping the secret for so long?'

'I'm sure she had her reasons,' said Amber. 'She was probably trying to protect you from any hurt.'

Elizabeth glared at her. 'And what would you know about hurt, Amber? You and your perfect little life.'

'Come on now,' said Ronnie, seeing the look of hurt in Amber's eyes. 'Let's not turn on each other. We're here to join forces and see what we can come up with. So this reverse address search, Elizabeth. Is there no way of finding out the name of the person living at the address?'

'It looked straightforward enough and I thought a name would just pop up, but nothing. You can find out details about the area, like the post office that looks after the mail and the local representative, so maybe we could go down that route.'

Ronnie sighed. 'It all seems very complicated. And even if we find out he still lives there, what then? Do we just send him a letter and say: "Hi, we're your twin daughters that you never knew about"?'

They all fell silent, imagining the scenario, until Amber spoke up again. 'What about your mum's friend. The one who fed her the information about Oliver in the early days. Didn't you say you have an address for him?'

'Yes,' said Ronnie, her mood lifting a little. 'It's a Dublin address so we could pay him a visit and see if he's still in touch with Oliver.'

'He's not.'

Amber and Ronnie both looked at Elizabeth, waiting for her to continue.

'I paid him a visit already,' she said, looking somewhat sheepish. 'I thought he was our only hope, since the online thing was producing nothing.'

'And you went without me?' Ronnie felt hurt.

'Like you wouldn't have gone without *me* if you'd thought about it, Ronnie? Let's face it. Neither of us wanted to join forces on this so we were each just doing what we could.'

She had a point and Ronnie conceded with a nod. 'Go on, then. What did he say? What was he like?'

Elizabeth spent the next ten minutes telling them about Albert Dunne and both girls listened with interest. It was nice to hear the things he'd said about their mother and lovely to know she'd been so popular. But it felt bittersweet because they were still no closer to finding their father. When Elizabeth had finished her story, they sipped their drinks in silence until Ronnie spoke up.

'You know, maybe we should write to him after all.'

'To Albert Dunne?' Elizabeth looked confused.

'No,' giggled Ronnie. 'To Oliver. Or at least to the address we have for him. We don't have to say what it's about but we can say we're looking up friends of our late mother.'

'I don't know,' said Elizabeth, looking thoughtful.

Amber sat up straighter. 'I think it's a great idea actually. If you've exhausted all other avenues and you don't want to go over there, it seems like the best solution.'

'It seems like a shot in the dark to me.' Elizabeth closed her notebook, not having written a single word, and sat back into the seat. 'Even if he's still at the address, maybe he won't answer. And do we keep watching the post every day hoping something will arrive from him? How long do we wait? How long do we keep hoping?'

'I know what it's like to wait and hope,' said Ronnie. 'You're probably right, Elizabeth. It's not worth it.'

'So why don't we just go, then?'

Ronnie and Amber stared at Elizabeth.

'Well? Ronnie?'

'You mean go to New York?' Ronnie couldn't believe what Elizabeth was suggesting. 'Us? Go together?'

'Yes, Ronnie. Do I need to spell it out? If we want to do this, we need to take control. Sending letters, waiting for information – that takes matters out of our own hands. Let's just do it. It's what Mum wanted, after all.'

'You're right,' said Ronnie, slamming her drink down a little too heavily, prompting a nearby barman to come and wipe the mess from the table. 'Let's just do it. I think it's the right way to go. And it's been years since I've been to New York.'

'This is not a holiday, Ronnie.' Elizabeth's scowl had returned. 'We'll be going over there with one purpose in mind. It won't be to go ice-skating at Rockefeller or shopping at Macy's. We're not children any more.'

Ronnie's face fell a little but she quickly recovered. 'I know, I know. But maybe we might fit in a sneaky walk through Central Park or a visit to Grand Central Station. Remember we used to love the Whispering Room there? Do you remember the day when Mum brought us—'

'Ronnie!'

'Surely there can be a bit of pleasure as well as business,' said Amber, squeezing Ronnie's hand under the table. 'New York is such a wonderful place.'

Elizabeth glared at Amber as though she'd just committed a cardinal sin. 'Just to be clear, Amber. It will be just me and Ronnie going on this trip. It's what Mum wanted.'

'Of course. I know that. And anyway, my days of jetting off at a minute's notice disappeared the day I had Daniel.'

'But would you have it any other way?' said Ronnie. 'And you know I'd always come over for a few days if you and Roger wanted to head off somewhere. Consider it my godmotherly duty!'

'You know, I might take you up on that some day. Daniel is cute as hell but the thoughts of a full night's sleep and not having to—'

'Sorry to interrupt,' said Elizabeth, slipping her arms into her jacket. 'But I have to head off. Let's look at our diaries, Ronnie, and see when we can best fit in a few days. The sooner the better.'

'That's fine by me. It shouldn't be too difficult for me to get away any time so let me know when is best for you.'

Elizabeth had stood up and Ronnie toyed with the idea of getting up to hug her. Although the conversation had been a bit frosty at times, it was the closest they'd been in years and Ronnie felt hopeful about their relationship. But the decision was made for her when Elizabeth gave a cursory wave of her hand and swept out the door as quickly as she'd entered.

'Wow!' said Amber, shaking her head. 'She's a cool customer. She has all the charm of a brick wall.'

'She's not that bad.'

Amber raised her eyebrows at Ronnie. 'Hello? Did you not hear how she spoke to you? I don't know how you kept your cool.'

Ronnie sighed. 'Years of practice. Maybe New York will sort us out – either way.'

'What do you mean?'

'I'm so sick of how we are with each other, Amber. We can't have a civil conversation these days. But to be honest, I miss her. I miss our closeness. Even when we'd gone our separate ways in our early twenties, I still felt that bond with her. But it's almost six years now since she broke that bond completely. I'm going to give our relationship one last try in New York and if she doesn't want to know after that, I'm going to shut her out of my life once and for all.'

Amber gasped. 'You can't do that, Ronnie. She's your sister. Your twin.'

'But what does that really mean? If she's not willing to act like my sister, then I'm not willing to allow her to be part of my life. You're the very one who told me that stress isn't conducive to getting pregnant. Well, my relationship with Elizabeth stresses me out. So if we can't sort things, then I'm afraid she'll be dead to me.'

'Ronnie!'

'No, I'm serious, Amber,' said Ronnie, a sob catching in her throat. 'If Mum was still here, I'd feel the need to keep Elizabeth in my life. But she's gone. I have you and I have Al. If Elizabeth isn't willing to be a proper sister to me, well then I don't have a sister at all!'

Chapter 11

Elizabeth had never felt so nervous. She checked the dining room one last time and was satisfied that everything looked perfect. She'd taken out their best china, a wedding gift from Nathan's aunt, and had even ironed a crisp white linen tablecloth to cover the mahogany table. A glance at the clock on the wall told her that Nathan would be home shortly and, if everything went to plan, the Thai takeaway she'd ordered should arrive at the same time. She'd bought two bottles of his favourite New Zealand sauvignon blanc, which were chilling in an ice bucket beside the table. She'd make sure his glass was refilled a few times before sharing her news.

She felt a tingle down below, signalling her need to pee yet again, so she hurried off to the bathroom upstairs. It always happened when she was nervous. She then checked herself out in the full-length mirror and knew Nathan would be happy with what he saw. She'd worn his favourite Louise Kennedy black dress and a pair of simple black heels. Her face was make-up-free except for a touch of powder, but she'd applied the deep red lipstick he loved and left her bobbed hair fall loose around her face. The doorbell rang, startling her, so after one final check in the mirror, she hurried downstairs.

The oven was on low so she placed the takeaway carefully on the bottom rail and prayed that Nathan would hurry up. She'd suggested they go out tonight. There was a new Italian restaurant only ten minutes' drive from their house and the reviews were fantastic. But Nathan didn't like Valentine's Day. He hated feeling obliged to go to a restaurant where everybody was packed in like sardines and they charged twice as much for sub-standard food, just because there was a harpist playing in the corner and the ladies were given a rose. Elizabeth agreed with him mostly, but a crowded place might have ensured a calm reaction to what she was about to tell him.

After meeting with Ronnie and Amber on Saturday night, Elizabeth had gone home feeling elated. It was the first time in a long time that anything had made her feel that way and she hadn't been sure whether it was the thought of finding Oliver or the fact that she'd felt that old spark of friendship that she used to have with the girls. She hadn't meant to suggest they go. But she'd been carried away with the excitement of it all and she'd just blurted it out. Her life had become mundane in the last number of years, and now the thought of the trip to New York, even if it was with her estranged sister, made her feel like she had a purpose. And she was missing her mum so much. She was hoping that the search would distract her from her grief and even give her something to look forward to. But she knew Nathan wouldn't have approved. He would have called a halt to it straight away and she knew she wouldn't have had the courage to defy him. So once she'd got her head around it, she'd contacted Ronnie the next day and they'd agreed on dates, before ringing Frank to tell him the good news. She knew Nathan wouldn't be happy, but the flights and hotel were booked now, so he could hardly stop her.

When she heard his keys in the door she took a deep breath and went out to the hallway to greet him. 'Hi, love,' she said, taking his jacket from him and kissing him lightly on the cheek. 'How was your day?'

He looked at her suspiciously. 'Fine. Why are you all dressed up? I told you I didn't want to go out tonight.'

'I know. I just thought we could celebrate Valentine's Day here ourselves.' She led the way into the kitchen. 'I have Thai food in the oven and I've set out the dining room for us.'

'You know I'm not into stupid made-up days like this, Elizabeth. Why do you insist on pushing me?'

'Relax. It's nothing fancy. We both have to eat and I just thought it would be nice to spend some quality time together.'

'Well, I had a big dinner with clients at lunchtime,' he said, kicking off his shoes and leaving them in the middle of the floor. 'But I suppose I could manage a little.'

Elizabeth breathed a sigh of relief. He was obviously in a bad mood but at least he was going to sit down and eat with her. Sometimes when he got into a mood, he'd give her the silent treatment all night, even though it would be nothing to do with her.

'Just let me hop into the shower first and I'll be back down. Actually, that food smells good. I'm probably hungrier than I thought.'

It did smell good and Elizabeth felt her stomach rumble as she began to relax. She took the food from the oven and placed the cartons in the centre of the table. She'd ordered loads – all Nathan's favourite things – and had even brought a Bailey's cheesecake home for dessert. She placed the warm plates on grey slate placemats, which had been a present from Nathan's sister. Elizabeth despised them. They were hard and uneven and she always felt it was like having her plate on the ground, but Nathan seemed to like them so she was happy to put up with them for tonight.

'This looks lovely, Elizabeth.' He kissed her on the top of the head before sitting down. 'You've gone to a lot of trouble.'

'Not really,' she said, opening the cartons and releasing the delicious aroma. 'There's not much to ordering takeaway.'

'Nonsense. It's all in the organisation. I could get used to this, you know.'

'Well, don't get too used to it. Work is getting very busy so I don't foresee many days where I'll get home before you.'

'You should delegate more, Elizabeth. Spend more time at home. You're the boss, after all.'

'Nathan, it's precisely *because* I'm the boss that I need to be there. I can't just swan off whenever I feel like it.' The words were out of her mouth before she realised it and she could have kicked herself. She wasn't making a very good argument for swanning off to New York for a week. Still, they were having a nice chat and with a few more glasses of wine in him, he'd have forgotten that comment.

The food was delicious and the conversation flowed. Nathan seemed relaxed, and all trace of his bad mood was gone. Elizabeth knew she'd have to say something so she refilled their glasses and took a big swig of hers.

'Careful, Elizabeth. I don't want to have to carry you up to bed.'

'I'm going to New York.' Her head was already swimming but she took another gulp of the wine.

Nathan stopped his fork just before it reached his mouth and Elizabeth watched as grains of egg fried rice dropped onto his plate. 'What do you mean you're going to New York?'

'What do you think I mean, Nathan? New York. In America. I'm going there.'

'Don't get smart with me,' he said, throwing his fork down onto his plate. 'I need to know details.'

Elizabeth took a deep breath. 'Well, you know how we've been looking for Oliver and you know that the last address for him is in New York? Well, Ronnie and I are going to go over there and see what we can find out.'

'No, you're not.'

'S ... sorry?'

'You're not going, Elizabeth. I've never heard anything so stupid in all my life. Going on a wild-goose chase like that.'

'It's not a wild-goose chase. We have an address, and ... and ...'

'You see? An address and nothing else. What were you thinking?'

'But it's all arranged.'

'Well, unarrange it, then.'

'Nathan, I can't. Frank has gone ahead and booked the flights and confirmed with the hotel. Everything is sorted and I've even cleared my diary in work.'

'Oh, you've cleared your diary, have you?' He pushed his plate away and sat back, cradling his glass of wine. 'I thought being the boss meant you couldn't just swan off whenever you felt like it.'

Dammit! She'd hoped he wouldn't remember. 'But this is different. I'm not going until next week so I'm not just abandoning ship at the last minute. I'll work late over the coming days and plan ahead.'

'Next week?' Nathan's tone was sharp. Menacing. 'How long for? You can't just abandon your commitments at the drop of a hat.'

'It's just for a week, Nathan. I'll be back before you know it.'

'And what about the black-tie event the weekend after next? Will you be gone for that? And Stephen's brother's wedding?'

She knew she'd be missing those two occasions when Ronnie suggested the dates and it was actually a relief. She hated going to stuff connected with Nathan's job. It was always so boring and she was forced into playing the role of a Stepford Wife, something she abhorred.

'Well, Elizabeth?' He was still waiting for an answer. 'Are the dates clashing?'

'I'll be gone for those two events, yes. But there'll be plenty more. You'll probably be better off without me there, anyway. It will give you more time to schmooze with the boss.'

Nathan stood up suddenly and began to pace the floor. 'Cancel it, please, Elizabeth.'

'Cancel?' She was momentarily confused.

'The trip. Cancel the trip.' She could see that the veins were beginning to stick out on the side of his neck and his nostrils were flaring open and shut. It was never a good sign.

'I wish you hadn't made me say it,' he continued. 'You should never have booked it all in the first place without consulting me.'

'I'm not cancelling.' Her words were quiet but her resolve was strong. She wasn't going to let him stop her.

'What did you say?' He stopped his pacing and stared at her, his face red. 'Don't provoke me, Elizabeth. You'll ring Frank and tell him to cancel the trip. Or at least your part of it. Maybe Ronnie can take that good-for-nothing, Al, with her instead.'

'Why are you so down on him, Nathan? He's a decent guy.'

'And why are you defending him? Again!'

Elizabeth had had enough. She stood up suddenly and pushed

her chair back. 'I'm not getting drawn into an argument about this, Nathan. And I'm not cancelling the trip. I'm going this day week, the twenty-first of February, and I'll be gone until Thursday of the following week. I'll be gone for eight days so you'll have to deal with it.'

She tried to walk past him to head upstairs but he grabbed her arm roughly. 'Not if I have anything to do with it, you won't!'

'Nathan! Let go. You're hurting me.'

He released his grasp immediately and his tone became softer. 'You know I'd never hurt you, Elizabeth. But I have to insist you forget about this silliness of going to New York.'

Elizabeth tried to fight back the tears as she moved towards the door. 'I'm going to lie down for a bit. I have a splitting headache.'

'Not a migraine again?' His tone changed immediately. 'Poor pet. You go on up and get some rest and I'll bring you up a cup of tea in a while.'

She nodded and headed upstairs. The only reason he'd turned all nice and sweet was because he thought he'd won. He'd made his feelings clear and he knew she'd never go against him. And usually, she wouldn't. But this was different. This wasn't about her and Nathan. It was about her and her mum. Her and Ronnie. Her and her father. She wasn't going to let Nathan bully her into throwing all that away. She closed the bedroom door behind her, praying he wouldn't come up. She felt drained and couldn't face another argument. Lying on the bed, her mind wandered to another time Nathan had put his foot down. They'd only been married a short while and things were going well. Or so she thought.

'Mum is taking me and Ronnie to London for the weekend,' she said, as they sat eating dinner in a little city centre restaurant.

'Why?' Nathan looked puzzled.

Elizabeth laughed. 'Does there have to be a reason? It's been ages since the three of us have gone away together. Ronnie and I aren't speaking at the moment and I think Mum wants to fix us.'

'But I thought you hated Ronnie?'

'I'm not her biggest fan, Nathan, but Mum has been so sick and I just want to make her happy.'

'Don't do it.'

Elizabeth stopped eating, her knife and fork in mid-air. 'Don't do what?'

'Don't go to London. They're manipulating you. Your mum is using her illness to guilt you into being friends with Ronnie again. Stand up for yourself, Elizabeth.'

'But I—'

'Come on, darling. You know I'm right. And besides, we have Leonard Finn's party on Saturday night and I'm dying to show you off to everybody. You can't let me down.'

'But I'll be letting Mum down if I cancel.'

'Elizabeth, I'm your husband. Your loyalties are to me now.' His tone had changed. It was firmer. More demanding. And Elizabeth knew she'd do as he asked.

A tingle on her face startled her out of her reverie and she realised she was crying at the memory. She really needed to hold strong this time and not let Nathan manipulate her as he'd done so many times in the past. As she looked around the pristine bedroom, she felt cold inside. Even the shadow from the orange sky couldn't bring life to the sterile white walls and crisp bedclothes. The oak wooden floor was as gloomy as Elizabeth felt and she wished, as she often did, that she had somebody to talk to.

She grabbed her phone from where it was charging on her locker and scrolled down through her recent calls. They were mostly work-related. Tears sprang to her eyes and the numbers blurred. There was a time when her call log would be full of her mother's number. She used to speak to her a few times a day and the conversation never ran dry. She missed her so much. If only she could ring her now. Talk to her. Tell her how she felt. She'd tell her she forgave her for keeping such a big secret from them. None of it would matter. Not if she had her mother back. But she knew she was only chasing shadows and she'd need to start accepting that life was different now.

She heard the telly go on downstairs and knew it would probably be a while before she'd see that cup of tea Nathan had promised. But she was glad. She really didn't want to talk to him right now. She looked at her phone again and toyed with the idea of ringing Frank. He was always available, always willing to chat, but in truth, she shouldn't be relying on him so much. Then there was Amanda, her loyal assistant. Amanda was lovely. Elizabeth had confided a lot in her lately and she was a good listener. But did she really want to take that relationship out of the workplace? She decided not, as she scrolled down through the contacts. That's when Amber's name caught her eye. They used to be such good friends, back in the day. The Three Musketeers, they used to call themselves – her, Amber and Ronnie. Until it had all fallen apart. No, Amber had made her choice and Elizabeth wouldn't be going there again. Although she hated to admit it, that only left one person, so she called the number and waited.

Chapter 12

'Right, you can come in now. But don't expect anything too fabulous – I may have put too much chilli on the potatoes and the steak sort of burnt while I was trying to unstick the roasted vegetables from the dish.'

Ronnie giggled as she entered the kitchen, as Al juggled pots and pans, beads of sweat dancing on his forehead. 'Here, let me help with that.'

'No, no, you sit down. I told you I was making you a Valentine's Day feast so that's what you're going to get.'

'But I feel bad letting you do all the work,' she said, watching as a rogue potato popped out of the tray and landed on Al's bare foot.

'Shit, shit, shit,' he said, dancing around the floor. 'Maybe I'm not cut out for this cooking lark.'

'I'll get the plates,' said Ronnie, trying not to laugh at him as he examined the burn on his foot. 'Actually, it all looks really nice, if you don't count the mess.'

Al refused to allow her to help and limped over to the counter to bring the plates to the table. 'Sorry about that. You know what a messy cook I am, though. It's impossible to keep the place clean and have four or five different pots and pans on the go at the same time.'

Ronnie felt a surge of love for Al as he placed the plate in front of her, his face like a child's, waiting to be praised. 'Thanks, love. It really does look delicious. Now come and sit down before you fall down.'

He didn't need to be asked twice and plonked down on the chair beside her. 'So, who were you talking to on the phone just then?' he said, spearing a potato with his fork.

'Elizabeth, would you believe?'

'Elizabeth! What did she want? Was she ringing to brag about the posh restaurant they're in? I bet they're in one of those Michelin star places.'

'They're not, actually,' said Ronnie, cutting slivers from her charred steak. 'They're at home. And she sounded weird.'

'Weird how?'

'It's hard to explain. She seemed vulnerable almost. It was she who rang me, but it was as though she didn't know why. When I asked her what was up, she just babbled something about checking the time of the flight. But Frank emailed the same details to us both.'

'Strange, alright. Maybe she's trying to smooth things over between you two before you head off together.'

Ronnie shook her head. 'It would take more than a phone call at this stage to smooth things over. It's been too long and too many hurtful things have been said.'

'But you'd like things to change, wouldn't you?'

'Of course I would. You know I would. But I don't want to just gloss over it and pretend the last few years didn't happen. If we ever resolve things between us, I want a proper conversation. She needs to tell me why she turned on me. Why she suddenly didn't want to be my sister. Or my friend.' She cursed the way the words caught in her throat.

Al reached out and took her hand. 'Well, she's the one who's losing out, love. And I'm sure she knows that too.'

Ronnie didn't want to waste the evening talking about her sister so she decided to change the subject. 'That was delicious, Al. You're really not a bad cook when you put your mind to it.'

'Now, are you being serious or are you having a laugh at my expense?'

'No, honestly. It was lovely. You were very good to do everything yourself.'

Al stood up to clear away the plates. 'Are you ready for dessert, then?'

'Dessert?'

'Yes, Ronnie. You know the sweet stuff that comes after a main meal?'

'Smartass.' She laughed. 'You didn't do dessert really, did you?'

'Well, I made a chocolate mousse earlier and that's chilling. I just have to make the French meringue for the top and the raspberry coulis to finish. I won't be long.'

'Seriously?' said Ronnie, feeling doubtful. Al loved to cook but he could burn a boiled egg. His only ever attempt at making dessert was a rhubarb pie with roll-out pastry. And even at that, he forgot to put the sugar into the rhubarb and it actually made Ronnie's eyes water.

'Here we go,' he said, placing a box of Marks & Spencer chocolate éclairs on the table. 'I know they're your favourites.'

'So, what happened to the chocolate mousse cake, then? Is that for later?'

'Nah. It looked too fancy-schmancy so I decided I wouldn't bother.'

'Well, thank God for that,' said Ronnie, grabbing one of the cakes and greedily taking a bite. 'You can't beat a good éclair.'

Al laughed and took one himself. 'So, what do you want to do when we clear up here? It's still early so how about a movie?'

'Have you any in mind?'

'Not really. Or we could always check and see what those ovulation sticks of yours say. If they say it's a good time to do the biz, it would be rude to ignore it!'

'Do the biz!' Ronnie pretended to look shocked. 'So that's what we're calling it now, are we? Is that some sort of hipster language? Did you learn it from the youngsters in the shop?'

'I may have overheard a couple of them talking.' His eyes twinkled and Ronnie couldn't think of anything better than lying in bed making love to him.

'Well, why don't we just head on into the bedroom and not wait until the stick tells us to. I feel like being a rebel.'

'Ronnie Cunningham! You little minx! You head on in and I'll clear up here and load the dishwasher. I won't be long.'

She felt slightly guilty leaving him to do the cleaning up after he'd spent hours cooking but she knew he didn't mind. But that wasn't all she felt guilty about. She'd done an ovulation test earlier and it had shown that she was at her peak time for love-making, so she wasn't being as rebellious as Al thought. The only reason she hadn't told him was because she didn't want to make things too clinical. She didn't want him to think she only wanted him at certain times. She hated that it had come to that but she so desperately wanted a baby and she'd try anything that was going to give them the best possible chance to conceive.

She quietly closed the bedroom door and reached under the bed for the Marks & Spencer bag she'd left there earlier. Knowing Al was cooking for her, she'd decided to give him a treat by buying some sexy underwear for herself. She knew she was overweight but Al loved her curves and always made her feel good about herself. She took the black lace knickers and bra from the bag and knew she was going to make him happy. Within minutes she was lying on top of the bedclothes, just as Al made an appearance.

'Wow!' he said, giving a low whistle. 'You look utterly amazing.'

She blushed. 'You have to say that.'

'No, I don't. And you really do.' He stripped off immediately and lay down beside her. 'You're beautiful, Ronnie. Have I told you today that I love you?'

Her heart leapt. It was their little thing. Their special phrase. And she loved hearing him say it. They made love gently at first, and then more passionately, until they were both sweat-ridden and exhausted. Al was a considerate and generous lover and Ronnie felt completely satisfied when she slipped beneath the covers afterwards.

'I feel this could be it,' she said, as she rolled onto her side so that Al could spoon her. 'I think maybe we've made a baby. Wouldn't it be perfect? A little Valentine's baby.'

Al didn't say anything so she turned around to face him. 'What's up, Al? Don't you think it would be wonderful?'

'Of course it would,' he said. 'But I just hate you getting your hopes up all the time. I know it's exciting to think about it but the disappointment every month is killing us. It's hard to see you so upset.'

Ronnie bit her lip. 'I know. But when it does happen, it will be even more special.'

He nodded and she kissed him on the lips. It was funny, she'd never really thought too much about how Al was feeling. He must get disappointed and upset each month too, but he was too busy looking after her to show it. Poor Al. She made a mental note to pay him a bit more attention instead of being too caught up in her own disappointment.

Within minutes he was snoring softly but Ronnie was wide awake. Annoyingly, she couldn't stop thinking about Elizabeth. The phone call earlier had unsettled her a little. Elizabeth had been acting out of character. It was as though she'd wanted to tell her something but then changed her mind. Ronnie wasn't used to seeing that side of Elizabeth – the vulnerable, almost childlike side. She'd sounded quiet. Sad. Although Ronnie had had some of those quiet, sad moments too since their mum had died. So maybe that's all it was. She was thinking of their mum and just needed to talk to someone who understood.

Their big trip to New York was looming and Ronnie was both excited and nervous. Part of her dreaded being cooped up with her sister for a whole week, but another part of her was glad. They'd had some good times in New York when they were younger. There'd be a lot of memories and Ronnie was sure that it would bring them closer together. At least that was what she was hoping for. Surely with them spending so much time together, Elizabeth would have to talk. To explain herself. If they finally did what they should have done years ago and sat down and properly talked about things, maybe, just maybe, they could get their relationship back on track. And then there was the reason for their trip. Oliver Angelo. Would they ever find him? And if they did, what would he say? What would *they* say? They really needed to talk more and iron out a few details.

Ronnie glanced at Al and he was in a deep sleep so she shoved back her side of the duvet gently, slipped on her robe that was on the floor beside the bed and headed to the living room. It was still only 10.30 so it wasn't too late to ring her sister. Ronnie had found Elizabeth to be unapproachable throughout the last few years but that's not how she'd been earlier. So maybe now was the perfect time to discuss their plans for New York. She wanted to know what Elizabeth was thinking. Was she excited about the prospect of finding their father? Was she scared? It would be good to have a civilised chat, for a change. She grabbed her mobile from the coffee table and called the number before she changed her mind.

'Ronnie, what can I do for you?' Her voice was sharp. Frosty.

'Hi, Elizabeth. Is this a good time? I'm sorry I had to cut our conversation short earlier but Al was just cooking for—'

'What is it, Ronnie? What do you want?'

Ronnie was taken aback. She definitely hadn't expected *that*. 'I just thought you might like to have a chat about New York. About our plans. You seemed to want to talk earlier.'

'That was earlier,' she said, spitting out the words. 'It's a bit late in the night for chit-chat, isn't it?'

'Well, it's just that we're both busy during the day and it's only a week away. How are you feeling about things? About finding our … finding Oliver? I sensed you were a bit down earlier.'

'Well, you sensed wrong. Mum wanted us to find Oliver so we're doing it. Or at least we're going to try. If we fail, it won't be for the want of trying so we won't beat ourselves up over it.'

Her tone was clipped, almost business-like. And Ronnie was beginning to lose patience. It was always the same - she'd be nice to Elizabeth and Elizabeth would freeze her out. A few months would pass with barely any contact and then Ronnie would try again, but to no avail. Each time she'd swear it was the last, but she was like a little puppy dog, always coming back for more. But Elizabeth had one final chance in New York and that was it.

'Are you still there, Ronnie? Is that it? Can I go now?'

'Yes, you can go,' said Ronnie, trying to mimic Elizabeth's frosty tone. 'And I'll see you at the airport next week.'

She ended the call before Elizabeth could say any more and felt annoyed with herself yet again for being the one making the effort. She could hear Al's snores coming from the bedroom and suddenly she just wanted to be in his arms. She rushed back into the room and dropped her robe on the floor. This was her happy place – curled up with Al. When she was with him, nothing else mattered. Not Oliver Angelo and certainly not Elizabeth. All she cared about right at that moment was the man she loved, and the possibility that they'd just created another life.

Chapter 13

'Shit, shit, shit, shit, shit,' said Elizabeth, flopping down on the bed out of breath, and kicking her overflowing suitcase. She'd spent the last hour and a half trying to fit everything into her case and, when she finally did, it was way over the weight allowance. She'd taken out a pair of shoes and a heavy sweater, but it had still weighed too much. Then she'd taken out her hairdryer. She knew they'd have one in the hotel but hers was top of the range and made her hair sleek and glossy. But even that hadn't been enough.

'Maybe it's a sign,' said Nathan, coming out of the en-suite with a towel wrapped around his waist.

Elizabeth sat up and looked at him. 'A sign of what? What do you mean?'

'A sign that maybe you're doing the wrong thing, going off thousands of miles to look for somebody you don't even know.'

Elizabeth sighed and kept quiet. She was sick of Nathan's negativity. Ever since she'd told him about the trip to New York, he'd been very offhand with her. He'd taken every opportunity to make her feel like she was doing something bad and hadn't wanted to know any details about the trip at all. She'd tried to talk to him about it – to make him see sense. But he hadn't budged. Usually Elizabeth would give in to him. But not on this occasion. She'd made her decision and had stayed strong and, despite his efforts, she hadn't changed her mind. She took a few more things out of the case and weighed it again.

'Well, thank God for that,' she said, sweat forming at the edges of her newly blow-dried hair. 'If you're finished in there, I need to hop into the shower before Frank comes.'

'It's all yours.' He turned to face her, dropping his towel to the floor, and Elizabeth could tell what was coming next. 'And this is all yours too. Or at least it could be, if you stayed home with me.'

'Nathan. Please. Don't do this.'

'Don't do what? Don't try to seduce my own wife?' His face turned dark. 'You'll be gone a whole week, Elizabeth. A man has needs.'

She hesitated for a moment before sweeping past him and into the en-suite. 'I'm sorry, Nathan, but Frank will be here in ten minutes and I need to be ready.'

She could hear him slamming the wardrobe doors as she stepped out of her robe and felt a mixture of fear and relief. She'd be gone shortly and wouldn't have to put up with him guilt-tripping her any more. But she was already worried about what things would be like between them when she returned. Nathan didn't like to have his authority challenged and that's exactly what she was doing.

She lathered the shower gel over her body, careful to avoid wetting her hair as the warm water shot from the powerful jets. She noted how skinny she'd become and was shocked to feel her ribs sticking out. She'd never been overweight but the stress of the last few months had supressed her appetite. Hopefully her week in New York would fix that. She'd always gained a few pounds during her previous visits and with any luck this time wouldn't be an exception.

Minutes later she was dressed and dragging her suitcase downstairs. She left it in the hall and went to see Nathan in the kitchen. He was sitting on a high stool at the counter, his phone in one hand, a piece of buttered toast in the other. He looked so handsome and her heart softened towards him. He was very demanding and expected her to behave in a certain way, but she was sure he loved her. And she loved him. So much.

'Nathan, I don't want us to part on an argument.'

'Hmmm?' He didn't look up from his phone.

'Nathan, please. Frank is going to be here any minute now and I don't want to go without your blessing.'

He stopped what he was doing and looked at her, his eyebrows raised.

'I *am* going,' she said, quickly. 'But I just want you to put your arms around me, tell me you love me and say you understand.'

Something in his face softened and his lip twitched. 'I do love you, Elizabeth.'

'I love you too,' she said, rushing over to him and throwing her arms around him. 'I'll ring you every day to give you an update and I'll be back before you know it.'

The doorbell rang at that moment and Nathan pushed her away. Not roughly, but assertively. 'You should get that. I assume it's for you.'

'Nathan, I—'

'Go, Elizabeth.' The steely look was back on his face. 'You wouldn't want to keep Frank waiting.'

She was about to say something but he had already turned his attention back to his phone. With a heavy heart, she headed out the hallway to the front door, making sure to force a smile onto her face.

'Here, let me get that,' said Frank, taking the suitcase from her and at the same time greeting her with a kiss. 'Jeez. Have you got bricks in there or something?'

Elizabeth followed him out to the car. 'That suitcase has been packed, unpacked and packed again until it was just perfect. Twenty-three kilograms exactly.'

Frank laughed as he hauled the case into the open boot and opened the passenger door for her. 'You're just like Belinda, you know.'

'How?' said Elizabeth, her heart leaping at the mention of her beloved mother's name.

'You're so organised. So poised. She was the very same.'

If only he knew. She might look poised on the outside but, inside, she was a mess. 'It's so good of you to take me and Ronnie to the airport, Frank. Should I ring Ronnie and tell her we'll be there in a few minutes?'

'It's no problem. I want to make sure you girls get on that flight. And don't worry about Ronnie. There's a change of plan. Al wanted to bring her out himself so I said we'd see them there.'

Of course he did, thought Elizabeth. They were on the 10.50 a.m. Aer Lingus flight direct to JFK and Frank had kindly offered to bring the two girls to the airport. Elizabeth had immediately accepted, knowing that Nathan definitely wouldn't be offering. She might have known that Al wouldn't dream of letting Ronnie go without a proper send-off. Lucky her. She felt a rush of hate for her sister.

Half an hour later, all four of them were heading towards the departure gates, Ronnie and Al hand in hand as she and Frank made small talk. She knew by his tone that he felt sorry for her. Her mother had always known when she and Nathan had fallen out and Frank was just as astute.

'Ring me as soon as you get there,' he said, as they arrived at the departure gate. 'And keep in touch. I'll be keen to know how you're both getting on.'

Elizabeth hugged him, trying not to look at Ronnie and Al, who were having a long, lingering kiss. 'Don't worry. You'll be the first to know if we find him.'

'Of course you will,' said Ronnie, finally tearing herself away from Al. She gave Frank a warm hug before turning back to her man for another kiss.

'Take care, you two,' said Al, giving Elizabeth an awkward hug. 'And the best of luck with finding Oliver. I'll keep everything crossed for you.'

Elizabeth smiled faintly before moving towards the barrier. 'Let's go, Ronnie. It's getting busy and we have to go through security and preclearance. It might take a while.'

'Right,' said Ronnie, turning to give Al one last kiss. 'I'll ring you tonight, love. Take care.'

All the lovey-dovey stuff was giving Elizabeth a headache and she was glad when it was just her and Ronnie. It felt strange to be walking through the airport with her sister. It reminded her of their past trips, but it made her sad that their mother wasn't with them this time. Before the girls had fallen out, they'd regularly travelled with their mother. And even after their big bust-up, they'd gone away a few times when Belinda had organised it. It was their thing. Elizabeth used to look forward to those trips, until she met Nathan and he put a stop to them. 'You're all grown up now, Elizabeth,' he'd say, every time she'd mention going away without him. 'From now on, any holidays you take will be with me.' She'd accepted it because she loved him and she knew he loved her. But now, in light of this trip, she was beginning to realise how much he'd held her back from her family and she was beginning to resent it.

'Are you thinking about her?' said Ronnie, bursting into Elizabeth's thoughts.

'What?'

'Mum. Are you thinking about her? It's weird to be here without her, isn't it? Especially going to New York.'

'I suppose.'

'I mean,' continued Ronnie, 'how many times did the three of us come through here together? Life can be really strange, can't it?'

They'd come to security and Elizabeth was happy she didn't have to respond to Ronnie, as they lifted their hand luggage into containers and ensured their liquids were in clear bags. She really wasn't ready for the level of chit-chat her sister seemed to want. She was still reeling from her exchange with Nathan earlier and seeing the two lovebirds together hadn't helped her mood. When they'd finally got through all the checks, they were both tired and ready for something to eat, so they grabbed a coffee and scone and found two seats at a table in the corner.

'Are you nervous?' said Ronnie, sipping her coffee and watching Elizabeth carefully.

'Why would I be nervous? I love flying. Or did you forget that?' She knew she was being unnecessarily sharp. 'I have such a hectic life that a few hours with no emails or phone calls is bliss for me.'

'I wasn't talking about the flying part.'

'Oh.'

'Come on, Elizabeth. We're going to be cooped up together on a plane for the next seven hours or so and then a whole week in New York with just each other for company. You can't keep giving me the frosty treatment.'

'This trip isn't about you and me, Ronnie. We're here for a single purpose, so let's not forget that.'

Ronnie sighed loudly. 'I'm sure you won't let me, Elizabeth. Actually, this coffee is leaving a sour taste in my mouth. I think I'll go and take a walk before we're confined to our seats. I'll see you at the gate.'

Elizabeth watched as she walked away. Ronnie was right. They needed to find a way of getting along over the next week or it would be an unbearable trip. She needed to try and put the past aside, at least until they were back to Dublin and things could be normal again.

Elizabeth glanced at Ronnie, who was engrossed in a movie, her earphones blocking out the rest of the world. She wished she could relax like her sister. She was always on edge, always overthinking things. Ronnie seemed to live this simple, carefree life whereas Elizabeth worried all the time. It wasn't fair. Ronnie laughed out loud and Elizabeth quickly looked around to see if everyone was staring at them. But nobody was. Everyone was doing their own thing and Ronnie's laughter hadn't even registered with them.

She glanced at her watch: 11.45. They'd only been on the flight for an hour and already she was fed up. It didn't look like Ronnie was going to talk to her anytime soon, and she couldn't really blame her. She'd been horrible to her back in the airport. Actually, she'd been pretty horrible to her for the last few years. But she deserved it. What she'd done didn't warrant Elizabeth's friendship. Elizabeth owed her nothing.

Still … it would be nice if they could talk about things. About their mother. About finding Oliver. It seemed crazy that they were taking this trip and hadn't discussed a plan of action. All the arrangements had been made through Frank and they'd had very little contact with each other. But that would have to change once they arrived in Manhattan.

She pressed the recline button on her seat and closed her eyes. Maybe if she could sleep for an hour or two, the silence between her and Ronnie wouldn't seem so unbearable. But another burst of Ronnie's laughter startled her and she cursed her sister for her state of oblivion. She turned her face towards the aisle and closed her eyes, but her peace was interrupted again. This time it was the cry of a baby that disturbed her. She opened her eyes to see a woman walk up and down the aisle, a baby cocooned in a sling across her chest. The baby was squealing and the mother was cooing and shushing, a worn-out look on her face. Elizabeth pulled her blanket up to her chin and closed her eyes tightly. But she couldn't stop the tears welling up. The baby's cries were too much, too hurtful. She lowered her face into the blanket and let the tears fall.

Chapter 14

When the car pulled up outside the Fitzpatrick Grand Central Hotel, a lump formed in Ronnie's throat. The familiar dark green canopy held up by two gold bars flooded her mind with memories and she could hear her mother say, *'Here we are again, girls. We're going to have a wonderful few days.'* She glanced at Elizabeth and she could tell her sister was having similar thoughts. She reached over and touched her hand.

'Come on, Elizabeth. Let's go in.'

For once Elizabeth didn't balk at the gesture but nodded wordlessly. Ronnie pulled out a twenty-dollar bill and handed it to the driver who smiled his approval. He helped them with their bags and bid them goodbye, leaving them standing looking at the building where they'd shared so many happy memories.

As they stepped inside, Ronnie noted that nothing much had changed since they were there last, from the decadent cream carpet to the Waterford Crystal chandelier, sparkling in the centre of the ceiling. An occasional table sat in the middle of the room, topped with a large orchid arrangement in a golden vase. A busful of people had just arrived so there was a flurry of activity. The uniforms suggested they were airline staff, presumably on an overnight stop-off before flying to another destination the following day. Ronnie and Elizabeth waited in line to check in and Ronnie's eyes were drawn to the wall at the left-hand side of the reception desk. It was filled with photographs of previous celebrity guests, including musicians and actors, and she smiled at the memory of two little girls – sisters, best friends – staring in awe at all the famous faces.

The front desk staff were as friendly as always as they checked them in, but she noted Elizabeth's face falling when they were handed the room key.

'Is that it?' said Elizabeth, looking at the receptionist questioningly. 'Just one room? Is that all we've got?'

'I … well, sorry. Let me just check again.' She tapped a few keys on her computer before shaking her head. 'Just one room booked,' she announced. 'For Ronnie and Elizabeth Cunningham.'

'Well, can we just book another then?' Elizabeth wasn't letting it go. 'I don't mind how small the room is once I have a double bed and coffee-making facilities.'

Ronnie rolled her eyes. Trust Elizabeth to find a problem. Would it have killed her to share for just a week? It's not as though they hadn't shared before. In fact, they'd never had separate rooms when they were away, even though that hadn't been for some time. They waited while the receptionist checked availability.

'I'm sorry,' she said, looking at Elizabeth. 'We're completely booked out for the next week.'

'You have nothing? Nothing at all?'

She shook her head. 'Nothing at all. But the room that's booked for you is a really lovely one. It's spacious and has two queen beds, so you won't be on top of each other.'

Elizabeth took the key reluctantly and Ronnie wanted to kill her for being so rude. 'Thanks for checking anyway,' said Ronnie, smiling at the girl. 'I'm sure the room is perfect.'

She beamed at Ronnie in return. 'Enjoy your stay and let us know if there's anything you need.'

'I can't believe Frank just booked us one room,' grumbled Elizabeth, as they took the lift up to their floor. 'What was he thinking?'

'Well, he did book at short notice so we were probably lucky to get a room at all.' Ronnie noticed how Elizabeth's face looked permanently angry and she wondered how her sister could live like that – in a constant state of angst. Always with something to say and very little of it good.

The receptionist hadn't been lying. The room was gorgeous. The décor was just as Ronnie remembered it and it was hard not to see their mother sitting at the desk, her laptop on the go, as they watched movies on the large screen.

'I'll take this one,' said Elizabeth, breaking into Ronnie's thoughts. 'It's closer to the bathroom and I drink a lot of water so usually get up during the night.'

Ronnie wasn't about to argue. She was happy to let Elizabeth have her way and, besides, if she'd had the choice, she'd have picked the bed beside the window anyway. The crisp white bed linen and plump pillows looked so inviting but a rumble from her stomach alerted Ronnie to the fact she was ravenous. She'd fallen asleep just before they'd served the food on the plane and Elizabeth hadn't thought to wake her.

'Why don't we just dump our stuff and go and get some food. I don't know about you but I'm exhausted, so I think once I get something to eat, I'll be turning in for the night.'

'Sounds good to me,' said Elizabeth. 'Just give me five minutes to freshen up and I'll be ready to go.'

Ronnie watched as Elizabeth disappeared into the bathroom, and felt suddenly happy. She was in New York, a place close to her heart, and she was with her sister. Maybe it was her mother's strange way of bringing them both together. She checked herself in the dressing-table mirror and decided she wouldn't bother freshening up. She'd have a shower and get straight into bed when she got back. She'd worn a pair of black culottes for the journey because they had an elasticated waist and they were comfortable and, aside from a few creases, they still looked fine. Her red-and-white-flowered blouse was loose and covered a multitude. Taking a hairbrush from her handbag, she undid the clip at the side of her hair and swept it back off her face. Maybe she imagined it but it seemed like she was glowing. In just over a week she'd know if she was pregnant, and she had a good feeling about it this time. Imagine finding her father and knowing she was going to be a mother all at once. It was too much happiness to even contemplate. But she was only too aware that it would all be tinged with sadness also. Her mother would never see her grandchild, nor would she see her girls united with their father.

'You feel her here too, don't you?'

Elizabeth's voice made Ronnie jump and she looked up to see her sister standing beside her.

'It's like she's really here,' continued Elizabeth. 'I could have sworn I actually smelt her perfume when I went into the bathroom. I know that sounds weird, though.'

Ronnie shook her head. 'No, no, it doesn't. I definitely feel she's here with us. She's left us with a mission and she's watching to make sure we don't let her down.'

It was a rare moment of camaraderie between the girls as they left the hotel room and Ronnie felt hopeful about the week ahead. She glanced at Elizabeth as they rode in the lift in silence and noticed she looked more relaxed, less angry. Was it possible that the Ice Queen might be thawing? Only time would tell.

They found a little diner just around the corner from the hotel and even picky Elizabeth had agreed to give it a go. Ronnie had feared that her sister would insist on finding somewhere more upmarket but she'd been uncharacteristically compliant. The crumbling grey paint and graffiti on the façade belied the spotlessly clean, buzzing interior, and the girls were grateful to find a table straight away. They were both about to order the steak, but Ronnie's eyes almost popped out of her head when she saw the waitress serving a plate of stacked pancakes to another table.

'I'll have the pancakes instead,' she said decisively, handing the menu back to their server.

'Ronnie, you can't have pancakes for dinner.'

'Why not? They're great jet-lag food.'

Elizabeth rolled her eyes. 'And that's a scientific fact, is it?'

'Oh, yes,' said the server, winking at Ronnie. 'People come here from all over just to cure their jet lag with Frankie's famous pancakes.'

'Good to know,' said Ronnie, laughing.

'Do you want bacon with that?' The server, a spritely middle-aged woman with a thick New York accent, smiled broadly and Ronnie was reminded why she loved this city so much.

She nodded. 'Yes, please. Extra crispy.'

'Maple syrup?'

'Of course.'

'Some sausage and hash brown on the side?'

'I might as well.'

'Jesus, Ronnie,' said Elizabeth, as the server disappeared into the kitchen. 'That's a heart attack on a plate. It's no wonder you're …'

Ronnie raised an eyebrow. 'So fat?'

'I … I wasn't going to say that.' Elizabeth reddened.

'Yes, you were, Elizabeth. And you're probably right. But I'm happy.'

Elizabeth didn't respond, so Ronnie continued. 'And what about you? You're thin and beautiful, you have a great job, a husband, you own your own house. Are *you* happy? Because I have to say, it doesn't always seem that way to me.'

'Don't be ridiculous,' said Elizabeth, a little too quickly. 'Of course I'm happy. But as I said before, we're not here to talk about us. We have a job to do and we need to focus on that.'

Ronnie sighed. 'Okay, Elizabeth. You win. No more small talk. From now on we just concentrate on finding Oliver and then we can get back to not talking to each other.'

'Well, I didn't mean that exactly.'

'I don't really care any more,' said Ronnie, her voice low. 'Let's just focus on what we have to do. By this time next week, we'll be on our way home.'

They ate their food in relative silence, Elizabeth using the excuse of needing to check emails on her phone. The pancakes, as promised, were delicious and Ronnie felt in a better mood with a full stomach.

'So let's make some plans for tomorrow,' she said, as she wiped some maple syrup from her plate with the last bite of pancake. 'Why don't we just head out directly to the address in the morning? There's no point in waiting around because if he doesn't live there any more, we'll need the rest of the week to try and track him down.'

Elizabeth took a sip of her iced tea and nodded. 'Sounds like a plan. You said you checked details of trains?'

'Yes. Mount Kisco is where we're going and it's about an hour away by train. But trains leave regularly from Grand Central so we should get one easily any time.'

'Right,' said Elizabeth, looking more relaxed. 'Let's just get up early and go. We can grab a piece of fruit to eat on the way.'

Ronnie was horrified at the thought of not eating. 'We shouldn't go too early. It will be busy at the station. Maybe some breakfast first?'

Elizabeth shrugged. 'I won't be able to eat a thing. You know what my stomach is like when I'm nervous.'

'And are you nervous?' Ronnie was a little surprised.

'Of course I'm nervous. Aren't you? Tomorrow we could possibly find ourselves face to face with our father and he doesn't even know we exist.'

'Well, when you put it like that …' said Ronnie, beginning to feel a little panicked.

Elizabeth continued. 'What if he doesn't believe us? What if he starts asking for DNA tests and everything? What if we have to go through the indignity of all that just to prove our mother wasn't lying?'

'Whoa!' Ronnie could see Elizabeth was getting worked up. 'You're getting way ahead of yourself there. We don't even know if we'll find him so there's no point in thinking about DNA tests at this stage. Let's just take it one step at a time.'

The server came to clear the plates, giving the girls a few moments to gather their thoughts. But Elizabeth was right. There was a lot to think about and really they hadn't given much consideration to what might happen. If they found Oliver, he was hardly going to open up his arms and engulf them in a hug. Thirty years he'd missed. Thirty years of his twin daughters' lives. And even if he did believe them, he'd likely be confused or sad or angry. Or worse still, he might not want to have anything to do with them. There could be a lot of pain ahead for them and they'd need to brace themselves for what was to come.

'Let's just go,' said Elizabeth, breaking into Ronnie's thoughts. 'I'm exhausted and we have a big day tomorrow.'

Ronnie nodded, before they paid the bill and left. It was like something had shifted slightly between them as they walked back towards the hotel. Elizabeth didn't seem so prickly and Ronnie felt more comfortable with her. Maybe their common goal was bringing them closer together. Or maybe they were just bound up in the fear of what might unfold tomorrow. Either way, it was nice not to be arguing, for a change. They were both ready for sleep as soon as they got back to the hotel and, although it was still early, it was well past midnight in Ireland. Their bodies hadn't adjusted yet so they gave in and fell gratefully into bed.

'What do you hope for?' Elizabeth's voice cut through the darkness and startled Ronnie.

'What do you mean?'

'Tomorrow. And the day after and the day after. What do you want to happen? Do you want us to have a father?'

'That's a funny question,' said Ronnie, not sure how to answer. 'But yes. Of course I want us to have a father. I wouldn't be looking for him otherwise.'

Elizabeth persisted. 'But if we find him, what role do you want him to play? Do you want him to be a big part of our lives, or just there in the background?'

Ronnie's hand went automatically to her stomach and she thought about the baby she so desperately wanted. A picture came to her mind of an elderly man swinging a baby in the air. A grandfather for her baby – that's what she wanted. Her mum was gone so she wanted an extension to her own tiny little family.

'Ronnie?'

'Sorry, I was drifting off there. It must be the jet lag. I don't know, to be honest. I suppose we'll have to see what he's like. What he wants from us, if anything.'

'We're doing this mostly for Mum, though, aren't we?' said Elizabeth. 'To fulfil her wishes. Would you really want a total stranger getting involved in our lives now? After all these years?'

'I haven't really thought too much beyond finding him, to be honest. Let's just see what tomorrow brings. 'Night, Elizabeth.'

'Goodnight, Ronnie. Sleep well.'

'Goodnight, Mum,' said Ronnie and Elizabeth in unison, as their mother turned off the light in the bedroom they shared.

'Goodnight, my darlings. Sleep tight. Don't let the bed-bugs bite.'

Elizabeth waited until she was sure their mother was back downstairs before tiptoeing across the room and slipping under the covers into Ronnie's bed. 'Move over, will you. You're taking up the whole bed.'

'Well, it is my bed, after all,' said Ronnie, shuffling across closer to the wall. 'Now, tell me what you said to Imelda Rogers today. She's a right bitch, that one.'

They chatted and giggled well into the night until sleep overtook them. They were co-conspirators. Partners in crime. Best friends. They had something very special – a twin bond that was the envy of everyone in school. They felt very fortunate to have each other and nothing or nobody would ever tear them apart.

Chapter 15

It was 11 a.m. when they stepped off the train in Mount Kisco station and Elizabeth's nerves were frayed. This was their father's town. The place where he lived. It felt surreal to be so close to him. That was, if he still lived there. They hopped into a taxi and gave the driver the address.

As they drove through the little village, Elizabeth was amazed at how different it was to Manhattan. It reminded her of Stars Hollow, the fictional village in *Gilmore Girls*. One of her guilty pleasures was to binge-watch episodes of *Gilmore Girls* when Nathan wasn't around, and she'd always thought that places like that just didn't exist. Yet here they were in a fantastic, sleepy town, with its quaint shopfronts and quirky houses. It said on the internet that the population was less than 10,000 and somehow she felt strangely at home.

'Here we are,' said the driver, slowing down as they drove along a leafy suburban street. 'Do you want me to drive right up to the house or just let you out here?'

'Don't drive up!' said Ronnie, panic in her voice. 'I mean, just here is fine, thanks.'

Elizabeth was glad to see that Ronnie looked nervous too. She was always so relaxed and nothing seemed to faze her. They stood on the road as the car drove away and looked up the driveway towards the house.

'Oh my God,' said Elizabeth, speaking for the first time since they'd left the train station. 'It's just one house. I assumed from Google Maps that it was a block of apartments.'

Ronnie nodded. 'That's what I thought. But you're right. It's definitely one house. God, look at the size of it.'

It was a gorgeous red-brick mansion, built on two different levels. The large front door was painted white, as were the two garage doors, and the window shutters were all black. It was set in a stunning garden that boasted a variety of trees and shrubs and Elizabeth could feel herself drooling at the thought of what the inside must look like. But there was no point in standing and staring at it all day.

'Right, are we ready to go and see who's home?' said Elizabeth, watching as Ronnie's face changed from awe to worry. 'That's what we're here for, after all.'

'You're right,' said Ronnie. 'Let's do it.'

They walked up the driveway and Elizabeth began to shake with fear. She didn't even balk when Ronnie linked their arms, and was actually quite comforted by it. The sheer height of the door was intimidating and Elizabeth felt like she was standing in front of a fairy-tale castle. There was no doorbell in sight but a large brass knocker with a lion's head sat above the handle, inviting them to announce their presence. They looked at each other before Ronnie took hold of the brass handle and banged it loudly four times.

'For God's sake, Ronnie! Once would have been enough.'

'Sorry.' She looked sheepish.

'Oh, shit,' said Elizabeth, moving back a few steps. 'Somebody's coming.'

The door opened and a woman dressed like she was ready to mount a horse stood in front of them. Forties, Elizabeth guessed. Too young to be Oliver's partner and too old to be his daughter. She felt her hopes beginning to slip away.

'Yes?' she said, rather gruffly. Not a trace of a smile.

'Sorry for bothering you,' said Ronnie, her voice remarkably strong, considering the circumstances. 'But we're looking for … for somebody.'

'Anyone in particular?' She was already impatient so Elizabeth decided to take charge.

'We're looking for Oliver Angelo. Does he live here?'

The woman shook her head immediately. 'No, sorry. You must have the wrong house.'

'We've come from Ireland,' said Elizabeth quickly, afraid the woman was going to close the door and that would be the end of it. 'He was an old friend of our mother's and this is the last address we have for him.'

Her face softened and a smile crept across her lips. 'You've come all the way from Ireland? I went there with my husband last fall and we had a blast. There was one night we went to that pub on the quays in Dublin. You know the one – where they play the Irish folk music and everybody sings. We were still there at two in the morning. You Irish certainly know how to have a good time.'

'We certainly do,' said Ronnie, smiling back at the woman. 'So, have you ever heard of Oliver Angelo at all? He would have lived here from the late eighties.'

'That's a pretty long time ago,' said the woman, looking thoughtful. 'And I can't say the name rings a bell.'

'When did you buy the house? Maybe you bought it from him? Or his family?' Elizabeth couldn't believe that they could come up against a complete dead end. There must be something to follow up on.

She shook her head. 'We just moved in a couple of years ago. Bought the house from a couple of rich kids. They were only a year married and were in the middle of a divorce. Very sad, really.'

'And before that?' said Ronnie, looking as panicked as Elizabeth felt. 'Do you know who lived here before that?'

'Sorry, I really don't think I can help you. According to the estate agent, the house has changed ownership a lot. You might have to trace this guy another way.'

There was nothing more to say. They were defeated. The first hour of looking for their father and they'd already failed. Elizabeth tried to hold back the tears as they thanked the woman and walked back down the driveway.

'What now?' she said, as they reached the tree-lined street. 'What's the point in us staying a week in New York if that's the end of our search?'

Ronnie sat down heavily on the kerb and sighed. 'It can't be the end. We'll just have to put our heads together and think of another way.'

'But that's just it.' Elizabeth took off her jacket and placed it on the kerb, before sitting down. 'There *is* no other way. We had one lead, just one tiny piece of information to help us find Oliver. We tried and we failed.'

'We can't give up,' said Ronnie, pleading with her sister. 'There has to be something else. Another way. We should give Frank a ring when we get back to the hotel and see if he can help.'

Elizabeth felt defeated. 'I'm sure if there'd been any more information, Frank would have given it to us before we left. No, Ronnie, it's the end. I know it is.' A sob caught in her throat and she suddenly found tears running down her cheeks.

'Ah, Elizabeth, don't be so upset. It'll be okay.' Ronnie reached out and took her hand and Elizabeth didn't pull away. 'We're not thinking straight now so let's give it a while and we might come up with something later.'

Elizabeth began to cry even harder. She couldn't stop herself. It was as though she'd opened the floodgates and now she couldn't close them. The tears just kept coming and coming until Ronnie began to look panicked.

'Please, Elizabeth. I hate seeing you like this.' She moved in closer and put her arm around her sister's shoulders. 'It's just a shock. We were so sure we'd find him here. I know it's upsetting, but—'

'It's not just that,' she snivelled. 'It's just, it's just …'

'What is it, then? What's got you so upset?'

Elizabeth took a tissue from her bag and blew her nose. 'Everything. Everything is wrong. Nothing ever works out for me.'

'What do you mean?' said Ronnie, watching her carefully. 'From where I stand, you have a great life – a fabulous job, a great husband, a lovely house. What's wrong about all that?'

Elizabeth hesitated for a moment but she was feeling vulnerable. It was a long time since she'd had somebody to talk to – to properly talk to. And Ronnie was there and she was being kind and really she was the only one Elizabeth had ever properly confided in. She suddenly wanted to tell her everything – from her relationship with Nathan to her unbearable sadness about other stuff in her life.

'I wouldn't know where to begin,' she said, in barely a whisper.

Ronnie's voice was gentle, encouraging. 'Take your time, Elizabeth. I'm going nowhere.'

She nodded and wiped her eyes. 'I can't believe I'm talking to you about this. And it's not easy to say it, but Nathan—'

'Are you two girls okay? Can I help you with anything?'

The voice startled them both and they looked up to see an elderly woman hovering over them.

'It's just I noticed you from my window over there.' She nodded towards the house across the road, which was mostly shadowed by trees. 'You looked a little lost. And I can see now you're upset too.'

With tears still wet on her face, Elizabeth realised there was no point in denying it. 'We've just had a bit of a disappointment, that's all. We'll be fine. But thanks.'

'You're Irish,' she said, the lines crinkling up at the sides of her eyes as she smiled. 'I guessed you weren't local. What brings you here to our little town? Are you visiting somebody?'

'We were,' said Ronnie, standing up. 'Or at least we thought we were. It turns out the person doesn't live here any more.'

The old lady shook her head and frowned. 'That's a real shame. But maybe I can help. I've lived here for a lot of years.'

Elizabeth perked up at this piece of information. 'Elizabeth Cunningham,' she said, standing up and holding out her hand. 'And this is my sister, Ronnie.'

'Nice to meet you,' the woman said, shaking their hands. 'I'm Tilly. Now, who is it you're looking for? Did I see you coming out of the Bentleys' house? They moved in about two years ago.'

Ronnie nodded. 'The one just behind us here. The lady said she didn't know the man we were looking for. He's a … an old friend of our mother's. Oliver Angelo. Did you know him?'

Tilly looked thoughtful but then shook her head. 'Name doesn't ring a bell. When did he live here, do you know?'

'Late eighties or early nineties maybe,' said Elizabeth, her hope dwindling again. 'He would have been with his girlfriend. They were probably around thirty years old when they came to live here.'

The expression on Tilly's face changed from defeat to excitement. 'Hang on. I remember something. There was a young girl who left here when she was in her teens. John and Lizzie's daughter. She came back here to live with them a few years later. Brought a guy with her.'

'That's them! That must be them.' Ronnie almost fell over with excitement.

'Skye her name was. Although I don't know what sort of a makey-up name that is. But she—'

'That's definitely her,' said Elizabeth, shocked to hear the familiar name. 'Skye was his girlfriend. So you knew them? What were they like? What was he like?'

Tilly laughed. 'I'm not sure I ever actually spoke to him but he seemed nice enough. Why don't you girls come in for a cup of coffee and I can tell you anything I know. And you can tell me why you're looking for this guy.'

Elizabeth noticed Ronnie's hesitation so she jumped in straight away. 'That would be great, Tilly. Thanks so much. Anything you could tell us would be a great help.'

Tilly beamed, and the girls followed her up her driveway.

Elizabeth felt drained but excited. She couldn't believe the range of emotions she'd gone through already that day and it looked like there'd be more to come. But she was grateful that the woman had interrupted them when she had. She was grateful that they were going to learn more about Oliver but she was also grateful that Tilly had stopped her from telling Ronnie way too much about her life. Something she would have most definitely regretted.

Stepping inside the house was like leafing through the pages of a glossy interiors magazine. The cream-tiled hallway led into a huge, beautifully decorated living room, which was linked by a gorgeous archway to the kitchen. Elizabeth had never seen anything like it. They sank back into one of the plush brown leather sofas while Tilly busied herself making coffee, and Elizabeth couldn't help wondering if the other house was like this – if Oliver had lived a privileged life over here, in stark contrast to his hippy existence in Ireland.

'This is all so weird,' whispered Ronnie, making sure Tilly couldn't hear her. 'What did Mum always tell us about not going into strangers' houses?'

Elizabeth rolled her eyes. 'I think we're safe. I don't see Tilly as the kidnapping sort.'

Ronnie giggled at that. 'You'd never know. It's always the ones you don't suspect.'

'Here we go,' said Tilly, arriving into the living room with a tray and placing it on the oak coffee table. 'Coffee and some of my pumpkin pie, freshly made this morning.'

'Thanks, Tilly.' Elizabeth sat forward, not wanting to waste a moment. 'You said you remember Skye and Oliver coming to live here. So that house was owned by Skye's parents?'

'Yes. John and Lizzie. I can't remember their surname. Actually, maybe I never knew it. I didn't know them very well.'

'But you must have talked to them,' said Ronnie. 'I mean, if you knew about their daughter leaving and then coming back.'

'I did, sometimes. Usually just a brief conversation. I'd occasionally see Lizzie in the supermarket in town and we'd chat about the children. She was a bit older than me, and Skye was her only child. I had three, but they're all grown up with families of their own now.'

'So when did they move?' said Elizabeth, anxious to know more. 'Did you keep in touch or get a forwarding address?'

Tilly shook her head. 'John died. A long time ago now. So it was just Lizzie and the two kids – Skye and her boyfriend – although they weren't kids by then. And then Lizzie's mind started to go – Alzheimer's. It's an awful thing. They had to sell up so they could afford to put her into a home.'

Ronnie shook her head. 'That's very sad. When did they leave?'

'Gosh, it's a while ago now. Must be fifteen years or more.'

Elizabeth's heart sank. 'And what about Lizzie? Did you ever visit her? Or find out how she was?'

'That's the sad part.' Tilly took her time telling the story as she sipped her coffee. 'They'd sold the house and moved Lizzie into the nursing home. But right before they were due to move to their new place, Lizzie died.'

'Oh, no,' said Ronnie. 'So did they go anyway?'

'They had no choice. They house sale had gone through and they'd already put an offer in on another place.'

Elizabeth quickly picked up on that bit of information. 'Another place? Do you have the address?'

'No,' said Tilly. 'I don't.'

'Oh.' Elizabeth's heart sank yet again. Another dead end.

'But,' continued the old lady, 'I could probably find out.'

'Really?' said Ronnie, sitting forward. 'That would be fantastic.'

'A lot of folk who lived here have moved on but I'm still in touch with a few. And the girls from my bridge club know everything about everyone. I'm sure with a bit of digging around I can get some information for you.'

Elizabeth could have kissed her. 'That's very good of you, Tilly. Can we leave our number with you, in case you find out anything?'

'Of course. Are you staying locally?'

'In the centre of Manhattan,' said Ronnie, taking out a piece of paper and writing her number on it. 'And we'll be here for the next week.'

Tilly stuffed the paper into the pocket of her slacks. 'I'm curious,' she said. 'Why would you come all the way from Ireland to look for your mother's friend? I'm sure you have a very good reason.'

Ronnie glanced at Elizabeth but neither said anything.

'Sorry,' said Tilly, beginning to stack up the cups on the tray. 'Don't mind me. I'm a seventy-five-year-old woman living alone and I'm always dying for a bit of news. It just sounds like there could be an interesting story behind all of this.'

'I suppose you could say that,' said Elizabeth, searching Ronnie's face for approval. Ronnie nodded, so she continued. 'Mum died a few months ago.'

'Oh, sweethearts. I'm so sorry to hear that. Losing a mother is a terrible, terrible thing.'

Elizabeth nodded. 'Thanks. It's been hard. But Oliver was somebody special in our mum's past. Somebody we didn't know about until after she died. And she left instructions for us to find him.'

'Now that's really something,' said Tilly, shaking her head. 'Aren't you two good girls for doing this for your mum. I bet she's looking down on you now, cheering you on.'

'That sounds like her alright,' said Ronnie, smiling. 'She'll be making sure we're doing as she asked. Actually, I've just remembered something.' She took her bag from the floor beside the sofa and rummaged around in it. 'Here's a picture of Oliver. The only one we have. You can see if you recognise him.'

Tilly looked at the picture and smiled. 'That's him alright. And he was dressed just like that when he first arrived – all new-age and hippy. But he had that knocked out of him pretty quickly.'

'What do you mean?' Elizabeth was intrigued.

'I mean he soon ditched the funky clothes for a suit and tie. I think John got him some fancy job. Not sure what it was but he seemed to take to it well. I remember Lizzie telling me that he was a natural-born businessman.'

She handed the picture back to Ronnie and stood up. The girls took it as their cue to leave so they were quick to follow suit. They thanked her as they headed outside and she promised to ring them with any news over the next day or two. They both felt drained as they stepped back out onto the street and called a taxi to bring them back to the station. As they waited, Elizabeth thought back to something Tilly had said. So their father had switched from being a carefree hippy, to a responsible businessman. Natural-born, apparently. Just like her.

'You're good at this job, aren't you?' said Belinda to Elizabeth, as they discussed the clients they'd just met. 'It's in your blood, Elizabeth. You're a natural-born businesswoman.'

For the first time since her mother's revelations, Elizabeth felt a real connection to her father. They weren't as different as she'd initially thought. A smile crept across her face and she felt happier than she'd been in a long time.

Chapter 16

'Come on, Elizabeth. Don't be such a wet blanket.'

'Seriously, Ronnie. We're not twelve any more. Why would you want to make fools of us like that?'

Ronnie linked her arm and pulled her towards the ticket desk. 'You used to love skating,' she said, determined to get her sister on the ice. 'And if I remember correctly, you were quite good at it too.'

'That was a long time ago,' said Elizabeth, frowning. 'I'll be on my bum in seconds.'

'All the more fun, then.' Ronnie wasn't taking no for an answer. They'd had lunch in Times Square and had decided to go for a walk afterwards. As soon as they'd spotted the ice rink at Rockefeller, Ronnie knew they'd have to go in. It had been their favourite place to go when they were younger. They'd beg their mother to bring them almost every day and they'd have a ball, skating around for hours, before enjoying a hot chocolate to warm themselves up.

Ten minutes later, they held on to the side rail of the rink, terrified, as hundreds of capable skaters glided past. Some were practically babies, and yet they pirouetted and leaped, speeding around with no fear whatsoever.

'We can do this,' said Ronnie, more confidently than she felt.

'Remember how we used to fly around? I'm sure we can do it again. Come on. I'll let go if you will.'

Elizabeth sighed. 'Right, let's do it.' And all of a sudden, she was gone. She pushed herself away from the rail and glided right into the middle of the rink. She looked startled at first, and then a smile filled her face. Ronnie was still holding on as she came towards her, but Elizabeth wasn't going to let her stay there. She grabbed her hand as she passed and, although Ronnie stumbled, she soon found her feet. Before long, both of them were skating proficiently around and around, and they were both loving every moment of it. They couldn't believe it when their session was up, and even considered going again.

'Maybe we should leave it for today,' said Elizabeth, exiting the rink with the rest of the crowd. 'We could always come back another day?'

Ronnie agreed. 'Yes, I think one session is enough for today. I won't be able to walk tomorrow if I do any more. Hot chocolate?'

'Of course.'

Ronnie's hands were numb as they sat with their drinks so she wrapped them around the steaming cup. She glanced at Elizabeth, who was lost in thought, but she actually looked happy for once. They were just there for a particular purpose, she'd said. Not to have fun. But there was no denying that they'd just had the best fun they'd had in a long time. It had felt good. Like old times. And she knew Elizabeth had felt it too. Maybe now would be a good time to try and break down some of the barriers between them.

'Remember earlier?' said Ronnie, breaking the silence. 'When we were sitting outside on the street. Just before Tilly came out to us.'

Elizabeth stiffened. 'What about it?'

'You were going to say something. To tell me something.'

'I don't remember,' said Elizabeth, not meeting Ronnie's eye.

'Of course you remember. You were upset. Crying.'

'Are you calling me a liar?'

Ronnie spoke in a gentle tone. 'No, I'm not saying you're a liar. But I do think you were about to tell me something and now you're not so sure.'

Elizabeth shook her head but Ronnie continued. 'It was about Nathan, wasn't it? You were going to tell me something about him.'

'Ronnie, I really don't want to talk about it. I was just emotional earlier.' She buried her chin in her puffer jacket, as though trying to silence herself.

'Is there something wrong between you two? Are you having problems?'

Elizabeth glared at her. 'You'd love that, wouldn't you? Do you hate me that much?'

'Elizabeth!' said Ronnie, shocked at her sister's response. 'Who said anything about hate? And despite what you think, I wouldn't want you and Nathan to be having problems. I want you to be happy. But I can't help thinking you're not. Something is definitely not right with you and I wish you'd talk to me.'

Ronnie knew she'd hit a nerve when Elizabeth's expression changed. The anger lines on her forehead softened and her eyes became moist again. She played idly with her now-empty cup and opened and closed her mouth a number of times, as though trying to find the right words. Ronnie waited patiently.

'Nathan is great,' she said eventually. 'He's gorgeous and generous and he looks after me really well.'

'But?'

'And I love him. I really, really love him. And I know he loves me.'

'But?' Ronnie was anxious for her to say what was really on her mind.

'It's just he can be a bit … a little bit difficult.'

'Difficult how?'

Elizabeth sighed. 'He's just a bit demanding. He makes the rules and I'm supposed to abide by them.'

Ronnie couldn't imagine Elizabeth in that role. She'd always been so bossy, even when they were little children; it was hard to imagine her allowing somebody else to boss her around. But she listened patiently as Elizabeth continued.

'It's hard to explain, really. He just has this way of making me feel inferior. He dictates what time we eat and what we're going to have. He decides when we'll go out and where we'll go. He even tells me what I should wear. And if I go against any of his wishes, I'll pay the price.'

Ronnie gasped. 'He hits you? Oh my God, Elizabeth. I'm so—'

'No, no. He doesn't hit me. He's never hurt me physically. He wouldn't do that. He just hurts me with his words sometimes. That's all.'

Ronnie didn't know what to think. 'But emotional abuse is just as awful as physical abuse. You need to do something about it. You can't stay with him if he's making you feel this way.'

Elizabeth looked panicked. 'Don't be ridiculous. Of course I'm going to stay with him. It's nothing serious. It's just how he is. And he adores me. He'd hate it if he thought I was upset.'

'But Elizabeth, you've just said that he practically rules your life. Doesn't let you make any decisions. I'm surprised you of all people would let him away with that.'

Elizabeth bowed her head and Ronnie felt bad.

'Sorry, that came out wrong. I just mean that you shouldn't tolerate that. You shouldn't let him make you feel so inferior.'

'I know you mean well, Ronnie, but I can handle Nathan. I shouldn't have said anything at all. I suppose it's just been a bit of an emotional day.'

'I'm glad you did,' said Ronnie. 'And I'll be keeping my eye on Nathan from now on. If he hurts you, he'll have me to deal with.'

'Oh God, please don't say anything. He'd go mad if he knew I was talking to you about him. He's very private.'

'I won't say a word.' Ronnie noticed the panic in Elizabeth's eyes and wondered if she'd told her the whole truth. 'But I really think you should talk to him. If he loves you as much as you say he does, he'll listen.'

Elizabeth nodded silently and pushed her chair back from the table. 'We should be getting back. I could really do with a shower after being on that grubby train and we'll need to work out what to do next.'

Ronnie stood up and buttoned up her tweed coat before they headed outside. The Manhattan air whipped at their faces as they walked back towards the hotel and Ronnie could almost feel icicles forming at the tip of her nose. Despite her thermal hat and gloves, she was freezing and couldn't wait to get back to the warmth of the hotel room. She glanced sideways at Elizabeth and felt a surge of love for the sister she thought she'd lost.

'Look at you, Elizabeth,' she said. 'You're beautiful and you're powerful and any man would be thrilled to have you. Don't ever let anybody make you feel inferior.'

Elizabeth stopped walking and turned to her sister. Her cheeks were red and Ronnie wasn't sure if it was from blushing or the wind. Either way, she looked pleased with the compliment and Ronnie was rewarded with a smile.

'It's good of you to say that, Ronnie. Especially since … since, you know …'

'Regardless of what's happened between us, I'd hate for anybody to hurt you.' A thought suddenly struck Ronnie and she laughed out loud.

'What?' said Elizabeth, as they began to walk again. 'What's so funny?'

'It's like a role reversal.'

'What do you mean?'

'Remember back in school? When I used to get teased about my weight. About my strangeness. You were always there for me.'

Elizabeth shrugged, but Ronnie continued.

'It's true. You really got me through some hard times. You told me the same thing that I just told you. You told me I was beautiful, inside and out, and not to ever believe anything different.'

'You have a great memory. I can barely remember the name of the school, never mind anything that was said there.'

'Don't be coy, Elizabeth. You know you were my saviour at that school. I never would have got through those awful years without you.'

'Well, you seem to be doing pretty well now. You're not the same insecure girl you were back then.'

Ronnie linked her arm with Elizabeth's as they turned the corner towards the hotel. 'No, I'm not. I'm happy and proud of who I am now. I feel very lucky to have such a great life.'

'And I'm very happy for you,' said Elizabeth, but her tone was sharp. She unlinked her arm from Ronnie's. 'I'm glad that everything has worked out so well for you. I'm delighted that your life is so much richer for not having me in it.'

'What are you talking about?' said Ronnie, stopping outside the door of the hotel. 'I never said that. You know I didn't.'

'Just shut up, Ronnie, with your inspirational words and philosophy about life. You think you know it all. Well, you don't.'

Ronnie was stunned. 'I … I don't know what's come over you. I never said I knew it all. I was just trying to make you remember … make *us* remember the good times. Where did it all go wrong? We used to be so close. What happened, Elizabeth? What happened to make you hate me so much?'

'Life, Ronnie. That's what happened.' Elizabeth's glare was filled with hatred, before she turned and went through the hotel door without a backward glance. Ronnie was shocked. Everything had turned sour so quickly and she couldn't get her head around it. But her bewilderment soon turned to anger. How dare Elizabeth speak to her like that. All Ronnie had done – all she'd ever done – was try to fix them. She didn't know why they were broken, but they were, and Ronnie was always trying to make things better.

Suddenly she didn't want to see Elizabeth. She didn't want to endure her silent treatment, nor did she want to argue. If her sister was expecting her to follow her through the bedroom door, she'd be left waiting. Ronnie wasn't going to go after her like a little puppy dog. She looked around uncertainly until she remembered the little coffee shop at the end of the street. It was exactly what she needed at the moment – a nice warm cup of tea and some time to herself. She hadn't even had time to digest everything that had happened that morning but now she was going to make time. She slung her bag over her shoulder and dug her hands deep into her pockets before walking away from the hotel. It was hard to believe they'd only arrived the previous day. How was she going to put up with another five days of Elizabeth, especially if she was in that mood? Maybe she should have listened to Elizabeth's advice in the first place. This wasn't supposed to be a holiday or a bonding session. They were here with one purpose, so Ronnie was going to put everything else out of her mind and focus on finding their father.

The coffee shop was quiet so Ronnie picked a nice table at the window. She liked to watch the world go by. It relaxed her and took her mind off her own troubles. But it was hard to forget the horrible exchange she'd had with Elizabeth. She'd been so vicious. Ronnie wasn't used to being on the receiving end of such nastiness. She felt suddenly lonely and longed for Al. She wished he was here beside her, comforting her, telling her nothing else mattered except the two of them. A glance at her phone told her it was 5 p.m. – 10 p.m. over in Ireland. She hadn't been able to talk to Al all day because he had back-to-back appointments and was working late but she reckoned he should be home by now. Well, there was only one way to find out.

'Hi, love.' His tone was soothing and Ronnie felt a lump in her throat.

'It's good to hear your voice, Al. Are you just in?'

'Yep,' he said. The line was so clear, it was as though he was next door. 'So, how is the Big Apple? How is the search going?'

She smiled and began to relax. 'New York is great but the search isn't going well. Oliver doesn't live at that address any more so we have to look elsewhere.'

'Oh, no.' He sounded genuinely disappointed. 'So what's next?'

'We're not sure yet. We have a few leads so we're going to follow up on them. But to be honest, it's not looking very hopeful.'

'I'm so sorry, love. I know how much you wanted to find him. How are you getting on with Elizabeth?'

'Don't get me started,' said Ronnie, taking a sip of her tea, ready to launch into the whole sorry saga.

'That bad, eh?'

'You have no idea. She's just so …' All of a sudden, she didn't want to talk about Elizabeth and how horrible she'd been. She didn't want to give that woman a moment more of her precious time.

'Go on.'

She could picture Al sitting on their little two-seater sofa, one arm behind his head, his legs stretched out in front of him.

'She's just so annoying,' she said eventually. 'And she snores.'

'Is that all?' She could hear the smile in Al's voice. 'I thought you were going to say that you two had had a massive row or something.'

'Nope. Now let's forget about Elizabeth and tell me about your day.'

She spent the next ten minutes chatting to Al about all sorts of other things, and when she eventually ended the call, she was overwhelmed with loneliness. Without her mother, and with her sister so angry, Al was her only family. He was her life and he was more than three thousand miles away. She finished her tea and checked the time. There was no way she was going back to the hotel anytime soon so she ordered another cup and took her well-worn book out of her bag. Just like her clothes, she always bought her books in second-hand shops, and she'd spotted this one just before they'd left Dublin. It was Patricia Scanlan's *City Girl* and the cover had flooded her mind with memories. She recalled as a little girl how her mother had loved Patricia Scanlan's books and how there was always one lying around the house. She used to say it was her comfort book. It was like a hug, she'd said, the sort of book that you read and re-read when you needed a little injection of happy. She opened the book and settled down for a read. And within minutes, her mother was with her. And she knew everything was going to be okay.

Chapter 17

Elizabeth checked her phone again but still nothing. She'd rung Nathan three times since she'd got back to her room and he hadn't answered. It was way too late for him to be in work so he was either gone out or gone to bed. But the latter was hardly likely, since it was still only 10.30 p.m. back home and Nathan never went to bed before midnight. She threw her phone onto the locker and lay down on the bed. Her head was pounding and she felt miserable. Damn Ronnie for bringing out the worst in her. For making her so angry that she couldn't articulate what she wanted to say.

She sat up and rooted in her handbag for some paracetamol. If she didn't fend off that headache, it could escalate very quickly. She'd often have to take to her bed, the room completely dark, in an effort to quell the pain in her head. Her mother used to say she got the headaches from spending too much time at her computer, but Elizabeth knew they were stress-related. She found what she was looking for and popped two of the pills into her mouth, washing them down with some of the bottled water she'd bought earlier. Now if only she could wash her troubles away so easily.

Her phone buzzed and she grabbed it immediately, hoping it would be Nathan. But it was just her mobile network, to tell her she'd exceeded her data limit. After just one day! The news just kept getting better and better. She switched the phone off and back on again. Surely Nathan would have tried to get in touch by now. She hadn't heard from him since she'd left the previous morning and she was beginning to worry. She desperately wanted to hear from him – to know that he wasn't angry with her any more. She needed somebody in her life to be on her side. Her phone sprang back to life but there was still nothing. She threw it roughly onto the bed, fixed the feather pillows beneath her head and closed her eyes. The jet lag was beginning to kick in and she knew she should fight it, but a little snooze might improve her mood.

Before long she began to drift off, her rhythmic heartbeat like a whispered lullaby, making her feel calm and relaxed. Even when a picture of Ronnie came unbidden into her mind, it didn't make her feel anxious. She pictured her sister as an awkward thirteen-year-old. They'd just started secondary school and Ronnie felt out of place. Her ample figure and quirky style elicited stares from the other girls, and sometimes some cruel words. But Elizabeth wasn't having it. Nobody was going to mess with her sister and she made sure those judgemental girls knew it. She was going to have her back, no matter what. Because that's what sisters did. They looked out for each other.

The ring of her phone startled her and it took her a few seconds to realise where she was. But she managed to grab it before it stopped and was relieved and delighted to hear Nathan's voice.

'Nathan! Where have you been? I've rung you loads of times.'

Silence.

'Nathan? Are you there?'

'Yes, I'm here.'

'Thank God. I thought the line had gone dead. It's so good to hear your voice. I'm going mad here with nobody to talk to. That is, except Ronnie, and you know how I feel about her.' She paused to take a breath. 'Nathan?'

'Elizabeth, it's getting late and I have to be up for a breakfast meeting in the morning. Was there something urgent?'

It was like a slap in the face. 'Well, no. I just wanted to talk to you. I miss you.'

'I miss you too.' His tone was softer. 'But while you're swanning around over there, don't forget I have a job to go to. We can't all just drop everything and head off on a holiday.'

'It's not a holiday.' She was stung by his words. 'You know that. I didn't want to come over here at all. But it's what Mum wanted.'

'I know. So you keep telling me. But you knew how I felt. And yet you still went. Don't expect me to be happy about it.'

Elizabeth sighed. 'I don't see what the problem is, Nathan. You go off on business trips all the time and I don't make a fuss about it. Why should it be different when I go?'

'The difference is I have no choice. It's my job.'

She knew there was no point in trying to make him understand. Nathan was stubborn and believed he was always right. And besides, she'd had enough with arguments already today.

'So where were you?' she said, in an attempt to defuse the situation.

'When?'

'Earlier, when I rang. I couldn't get you all evening.'

'Just at a work thing.'

'What sort of thing?'

He hesitated for a moment before answering. 'A meal for some

German clients who are in town. I didn't really want to go but Stephen insisted.'

She turned on her side and cradled the phone to her ear. 'And what about Gloria? Was she there?'

'What does that matter?'

'No need to be defensive. I was just wondering.'

'Well, yes. She was there, as a matter of fact. Just as you should have been.'

Not this again. 'Nathan, please. Can you stop trying to make me feel guilty? I'm over here now and there's nothing I can do about it. And to be honest, you were probably right. I shouldn't have come.'

'Oh?' A hint of interest in his voice.

'Yes. It's been a disaster so far. The lead we had for Oliver didn't work out, and Ronnie and I had this huge row. She's gone off somewhere and I'm here alone in our hotel room feeling miserable.'

'My poor baby,' he said, his tone suddenly changing. 'So what are you going to do?'

'I don't know.' She sighed. 'I'm too tired to think at the moment so I'll probably just sleep on it and decide in the morning.'

'I wish you were here, baby.'

Elizabeth hugged herself at the sound of his reassuring words.

'I really do,' he continued. 'After the day I had, there's nothing I'd love more than a good round of sex. Those German guys were such hard work. It's going to take me ages to wind down.'

She bit back the tears and, suddenly, she didn't want to be talking to him any more. 'I have to go, Nathan. I'll talk to you again tomorrow.'

He didn't argue so they finished the call and Elizabeth pounded her pillow in anger. Her life with Nathan was filled with such highs and lows. Sometimes he was the most charming man in the world. He looked after her and made sure she was happy. She was the envy of every woman at every event they attended because Nathan was so charismatic and handsome. But then there were moments just like the one they'd just had, that kicked her in the guts and made her feel worthless. He hadn't wanted to know anything about the search for their father. Something that was so special to her. He hadn't wanted to know anything about the trip or about how she was feeling. And just when he'd made her believe he was really pining for her, he came out with that comment about sex. With so much else going on, sex was the last thing on her mind, and his lack of sensitivity had really hurt her.

She turned onto her other side and curled her legs up towards her chin. If she could only sleep, things might look better in the morning. But it soon became clear that, despite her exhaustion, sleep wasn't going to visit her anytime soon. Maybe a bit of fresh air would do the trick, she thought to herself, sitting up at the side of the bed. A rumble from her stomach reminded her that she hadn't eaten in hours so that decided it for her. She'd go for a short walk and pick up a sandwich on the way back.

Ten minutes later, she was strolling down the street past Grand Central Station. She had wonderful memories of walking down Third Avenue because it led to Dylan's Candy Bar. She and Ronnie used to pester their mother tirelessly to take the ten minutes' walk to the famous sweet shop and they'd whoop with delight when she'd agree. The walk there was always filled with glorious anticipation and on the way back they'd stuff themselves with way too many treats. At the corner of East 60th Street, she stopped to look across at the iconic shopfront. It was just as she remembered, with its colourful stripes and paintings of candy, and she was almost tempted to go in. But coffee was more of a priority, since her headache hadn't left and she was hoping a caffeine fix would do the trick. So she turned around and headed back towards the hotel. She knew there were a few coffee shops close by so she'd grab something to go and have it back in the room.

It was difficult to walk through the hordes of people rushing in and out of Grand Central Station as she passed and she found herself looking for Ronnie's face in the crowd. It was stupid, she knew, but she was beginning to get a little worried. Earlier, she couldn't have cared less if Ronnie never came back but, now that she'd calmed down, she wanted to know that her sister was safe. If Nathan had been a bit nicer to her, maybe she wouldn't have cared about Ronnie. But at the moment, Ronnie was all she had and she should probably try a bit harder with her.

It was coming up to seven o'clock when she reached the corner of East 44th Street, where the hotel was located, and she was pleased to see the coffee shop on the corner was still open. She remembered how their delicious bacon baps used to taste all those years ago and her mouth watered in anticipation. There was no queue so she ordered her bap and coffee, and grabbed three bottles of still water from the fridge to keep her going through the night. Just a few minutes later she turned around to leave, her precious coffee warming her freezing cold hands, when she spotted Ronnie sitting at a table beside the window. What were the chances? She hesitated for a moment, unsure what to do. She could just slip out unnoticed. Go back to the hotel as planned and eat alone. Or she could swallow her pride and go and join her. Ronnie was chatting animatedly on the phone and Elizabeth felt jealous. Her sister had such a great support network. She had Al and Amber and countless good friends, all willing to listen and to be there for her when she needed them. Elizabeth, on the other hand, had nobody. The sound of Ronnie's laughter startled her and suddenly she wanted to be with her. So without further hesitation, she strode across the shop and tapped Ronnie on the shoulder.

'Anybody sitting here?' she said, making Ronnie jump.

'I have to go,' said Ronnie, talking into the phone. 'Elizabeth is here. I'll give you a buzz tomorrow if I have any news.' She threw the phone into her bag and looked at Elizabeth. 'Well, are you going to sit down or what?'

Elizabeth slipped into the seat and placed her coffee and unopened sandwich in front of her. 'Have you been here since earlier?' It was all she could think to say.

Ronnie nodded and looked at her suspiciously. 'Yes. How did you know I was here?'

'I didn't,' said Elizabeth, taking the sandwich out of its paper and placing it on a serviette. 'I came in to get something to eat and take it back to the hotel. I just spotted you as I was leaving.'

'Let me guess,' said Ronnie, her face stony. 'It made your day.'

'Don't be sarcastic, Ronnie. We're both here now so let's just try and get on.' Ronnie didn't reply so Elizabeth was forced to continue. 'I'm sorry, okay? I shouldn't have got so annoyed earlier. I can't help it. I just feel angry sometimes.'

A glimmer of a smile crept onto Ronnie's face. 'Sometimes? I'd say all of the time – or at least most of it.'

Elizabeth was about to object but how could she? Ronnie was right. She was always angry. She wasn't sure why, but it was like she didn't know how to be any other way. Everything seemed to trigger her temper these days and she didn't know how to control it.

Ronnie continued, 'But you're here now so let's call a truce. I've been telling Al and Amber about going to the house today. They're so disappointed for us. How about you? Did you speak to Nathan?'

'Yes. We chatted for ages earlier. He was gutted about it too.' She didn't meet Ronnie's eye.

'Al said he'd try and come up with some ideas for us. I know it seemed we'd reached a dead end this morning, but I'm sure something will turn up. There must be another way.'

Elizabeth took a bite of her floury bap and it was just as delicious as she remembered it. 'It feels like we've been here a week already, doesn't it? It's been the longest day ever.'

Ronnie nodded. 'It seems like ages since we were at the airport and that was only yesterday. Maybe we should just get some sleep and look at things with fresh eyes in the morning. I don't know about you, but I'm exhausted.'

'Me too. It's been an emotional day, and us arguing didn't help.'

'Agreed. Let's try and get on for the rest of the time we have here. Fighting with each other isn't going to help us find Oliver. We need to pull together on this.' Ronnie's eyes twinkled. 'There'll be plenty of time for fighting when we're back home in Ireland.'

'True,' said Elizabeth. She was beginning to relax and enjoy the banter. 'We can be nice to each other over here before normal hating resumes when we're home.'

At that moment, a buzzing sound from Ronnie's bag startled them both. She reached in and grabbed the phone, checking the display. 'It's an unknown number. I should probably leave it.'

'Answer it,' said Elizabeth. 'It could be something important.'

Ronnie did as she was told and put the phone to her ear. Elizabeth waited patiently, curious to know who her sister was talking to. She wished she could hear the other side of the conversation. Ronnie seemed excited.

'Yes. Yes. I know … That's great. You're very good …' Ronnie looked at Elizabeth and pointed to the phone. 'We're in a coffee shop beside the hotel … What? Now? … Are you sure? Okay … Okay … Okay … Yes … Yes … See you then …'

'So what was that all about?' said Elizabeth, as Ronnie ended the call. She was bursting to know what was going on.

Ronnie beamed. 'I think our day just got better.'

'Go on.'

'That was Tilly. Remember, the woman from earlier?'

'Of course I remember. What did she say?'

'She didn't say very much on the phone but she's on her way over to our hotel now to tell us more.'

'Does she have news?' Elizabeth was shocked at how quickly the woman had got back to them. 'She didn't waste any time, did she?'

Ronnie stood up. 'Come on. She said she was in Grand Central Station so she'll be at the hotel in a minute.'

Elizabeth followed, still trying to find out what the woman had said. 'Do you think she has good news? Has she found out something about Oliver?'

'I don't know what it is exactly,' said Ronnie, puffing as they hurried back towards the hotel. 'But she sounded excited and said that our search for Oliver Angelo is far from over.'

Chapter 18

They were waiting in the hotel foyer when Tilly breezed in. Ronnie was praying she'd have something concrete to tell them because they really didn't need another setback. They stood up to greet her and she smiled broadly as she approached them.

'Hello, girls,' she said, kissing them both on the cheek and hugging them as though they were her best friends in the world. 'I didn't think I'd be seeing you both again so soon.'

'Neither did we.' Elizabeth was first to sit back down and the others followed suit. 'We were delighted to get your call.'

Ronnie nodded her agreement. 'It was a lovely surprise. And you're very good to come all this way to see us.'

'It's no problem,' said Tilly, looking around the beautifully decorated lobby. 'Isn't this place gorgeous? It's such a central location.'

Ronnie nodded. 'It's great. We love it. We used to come here with our mother but we haven't been in a number of years.'

'And you're here to find her friend now. She'd be very proud of you both.'

Elizabeth shifted in her chair and it was obvious she was getting impatient. 'So, Tilly, you said you had some news on our ... on Oliver?'

'Yes,' she said, rooting in her handbag. Her brown leather Prada bag contrasted beautifully with her mustard belted trench coat and, together with her perfectly applied make-up, it was hard to believe she was a woman in her seventies. 'Here we go.'

She produced an envelope from her bag and the girls waited with bated breath as she opened it. There were two pictures. They looked old and the edges were curled and torn, but Tilly handled them as though they were the most precious things in the world. She placed them on the table in front of the girls and waited for them to say something.

Ronnie noticed Elizabeth rolling her eyes and hoped she wouldn't say anything offensive. Tilly was obviously lonely and was delighted to have people to talk to. She probably spent her days rattling around in that big house alone, not seeing anybody from one end of the day to the other. So Ronnie humoured her and took a look at one of the pictures. And then she saw him. Oliver Angelo. The ink was faded but it was definitely him. He had the same long hair and rugged features. His hippy clothes were replaced with more formal slacks and shirt and he was probably a few years older than he was in their picture, but Ronnie was in no doubt that it was their father.

'Where did you get these?' she said, picking up the other picture to have a better look. 'And who are all the other people?'

'What people?' said Elizabeth, suddenly interested. 'Here, give me a look.'

Tilly smiled, delighted to have elicited a response. 'It was a street party we had back in the nineties. The first picture is Oliver, with his arm around Skye. And that's John and Lizzie, Skye's parents, behind them.' She scanned her finger over the faded picture. 'And that's my friend Eleanor on Oliver's left and her husband beside her.'

Elizabeth looked stunned. 'I can't believe you have pictures of him. What about this one?' She held the second picture up so Tilly could explain.

Ronnie knew what her sister was thinking because she was thinking the same thing. In the picture, Oliver had a toddler in his arms – a little blond-haired boy with cheeky eyes and a devilish smile. Could it be that their father had another child? Other children? Maybe they had half-brothers and -sisters that they didn't know about. It had crossed Ronnie's mind on a couple of occasions but she'd pushed the thought away, preferring to deal with things as they happened.

'The child is Skye's cousin or nephew or something, if that's what you're wondering.' Tilly was more perceptive than they gave her credit for. 'I remember some relations coming to stay with them. There were a few kids, I think. I only remember this because Lizzie thought they'd never leave. She said she'd offered to put them up for a few nights and they ended up staying for weeks. I can't remember why they were there in the first place but—'

'But how did you get these, Tilly?' said Elizabeth, impatient as always. 'And how on earth are they going to help us find Oliver?'

'Elizabeth!' Ronnie was mortified at her sister's attitude. Tilly was only trying to help and there was no need to be rude to her.

Elizabeth at least had the grace to look sheepish. 'I'm sorry, but I just keep feeling that we're taking one step forward and two steps back.'

'But the pictures aren't all,' said Tilly, not in the slightest bit fazed by Elizabeth's rebuff. 'I have other information too. I got these from my friend Eleanor. She had a good camera, back in the day, and used to enjoy taking photographs. Anyway, after you two left this morning, I gave Eleanor a ring. We play bridge together so we meet up regularly. She used to live on my street. She was there for years and years. Until one day she decided she didn't want to clatter about in that big house alone. So she sold up and went to live in a gated community – a smaller house, where she'd feel safe and still have lots of people around her.'

'So you rang Eleanor …' Ronnie was getting impatient now.

'Yes. I told her about your search for Oliver and she remembered him well. She said she had some old pictures from her days in the street so she was going to have a look through them.'

'And she found these,' said Ronnie, running her fingers over the thinning paper.

'Yes. We aren't scheduled to play bridge until next Tuesday so we decided to meet for lunch in Manhattan. And when she gave me these, I couldn't wait to pass them on to you.'

Ronnie smiled at the woman. 'You're very good, Tilly. We really appreciate you taking the time to help us like this. But you said you had other information?'

'That's what I was trying to tell you.' Tilly was loving having their attention. 'My friend Eleanor was pretty good friends with Lizzie, Skye's mum. Eleanor is older than me, you see. I'm about ten years—'

'And?' said Elizabeth, not prepared to hear another story.

'And she gave me the address of the nursing home.'

The girls looked at her blankly.

'The nursing home that Lizzie moved into before she died. Eleanor went to visit her there a couple of times.' She waited for the girls to react but they were still trying to digest the information, so she continued.

'If you check the records with them, they'll probably have phone numbers of family members. They're bound to have one for Skye. She was an only child so she would have made all the arrangements.'

'Brilliant!' Elizabeth sat back in the chair. 'And if we manage to contact Skye, that's it. We should be able to find Oliver.'

Tilly nodded. 'I guess you will. I hope it all works out for you girls.'

'You've been such a brilliant help, Tilly,' said Ronnie, reaching out and touching the woman's bony, liver-spotted hand. 'Hasn't she, Elizabeth?'

Elizabeth nodded. 'We're very lucky to have found you this morning. So this nursing home ... you said you had an address?'

Tilly reached into her bag again and pulled out a piece of paper. 'Here you go. It's in Brooklyn so it's very close. And Eleanor remembered Lizzie's surname too. Lizzie Granger. It's all written down there so it should be all you need.'

Ronnie took the piece of paper and examined it. 'That's perfect. We can go there tomorrow and see what we can find out. We can't thank you enough for this.'

'No need to thank me,' said Tilly, beaming. 'I'm just glad I could help.'

'I'm just realising,' said Ronnie suddenly, 'we never even offered to buy you a cup of coffee. Where are our manners? Would you like to come into the bar for a coffee or a drink? Or maybe something to eat?'

Tilly shook her head. 'Not at all. You girls have a lot to talk about so I'll get out of your way.' She stood up, zipping her bag closed and securing it over her shoulder.

'Thanks again,' said Elizabeth, as they all walked towards the hotel door. 'We'd be sitting here wondering what to do next if we hadn't met you.'

Tilly turned to look at them both, a question in her eyes. 'He's your father, isn't he?'

'Wh …what?' The question took Ronnie by surprise.

'Oliver. He's your father. You don't have to tell me if you don't want to but I was thinking about it and it's a hell of a journey to make just to find an old friend of your mother's.'

Ronnie composed herself quickly. 'He was a very good friend. He was good to her, back in the day. And our mother wanted to find him before she died. So we're just doing this for her. In her mem—'

'Yes, he's our father,' said Elizabeth, her voice barely a whisper. Ronnie glared at her but she continued, 'We didn't know about him until after our mother died so we wanted to find him. To meet him.'

Tilly nodded. 'I thought so. I may not have known him well but I can definitely see the resemblance.'

'Really?' said Elizabeth. 'Ronnie or me?'

'Both of you, dear. You're both like him.'

Ronnie was taken aback. 'But me and Elizabeth are completely different. How can we both be like him?'

'You're not as different as you think,' said Tilly, looking from one to the other. 'Yes, physically you're not alike but I can see something very similar about you. You're very lucky to have each other. If you have a sister, you'll always have a friend.'

She left them with those words of wisdom as she disappeared out the door and both girls stood for a moment, lost in thought. Ronnie eventually broke the silence.

'She's lovely, isn't she?'

'And wise,' said Elizabeth, looking at Ronnie. 'Come on, let's go to bed.'

Ronnie nodded and they headed towards the lift. Sometimes they didn't need words to know what each other was thinking. It was a twin thing. A friend thing. And Ronnie all of a sudden felt grateful for that moment in time.

'Elizabeth, are you awake?' Ronnie's voice cut through the darkness of the room and hung there, awaiting a response.

Eventually Elizabeth replied sleepily. 'Just about. What's wrong?'

'Why did you say it? Why did you tell Tilly about Oliver?'

'Ronnie, can we discuss this in the morning? I'm too tired for another argument.'

'It's not an argument,' said Ronnie. 'I don't mind that you said it. But I'm just curious to know why. I thought you didn't want to tell her.'

'Because,' said Elizabeth, yawning, 'it's the truth. Oliver *is* our father. And although it initially made me uncomfortable to say it, I quite like the sound of it now. We have a father, Ronnie, an actual father. And if all goes to plan, we're going to meet him very soon.'

Chapter 19

The wind whipped across their faces as they crossed the bridge and Elizabeth was thankful for the woolly scarf that she had wrapped right up to her chin. At least the promised snow hadn't materialised and the clear skies suggested the forecasters might have been wrong. She glanced to her left at Ronnie, who also looked frozen, her hands buried deep in her coat pockets, her collar pulled right up past her ears. Elizabeth followed her gaze to the view of the Manhattan skyline and she was immediately transported back to the past. Crossing Brooklyn Bridge was one of their mother's favourite things to do in New York. She used to say that it made her feel alive. The two girls used to moan about having to walk across it when they were little, but as they got older, they grew to love it just like she did.

'Beautiful, isn't it?' said Ronnie, gesturing towards the fabulous view. 'I'll never get tired of seeing it.'

Elizabeth nodded. 'I know. I'm glad we decided to do this.'

They'd both been awake since 7 a.m., filled with excitement and anticipation about the day ahead. They'd googled the nursing home last night and found, to their delight, that it was still there. They'd thought about ringing to make their enquiries but Ronnie had suggested that they might find out more if they went in person. Elizabeth had agreed, and proposed that they walk across the bridge and then get a taxi to the address from the other side. It was still only 8.30 a.m. but there were already hordes of people crossing in each direction and cyclists constantly ringing their bells to clear their lane.

'She's beautiful, isn't she?' said Elizabeth, pulling Ronnie closer to her as a cyclist almost knocked her over.

'Who's beautiful?'

'Her.' Elizabeth nodded towards the Statue of Liberty, who was majestically holding her torch high into the New York sky. 'I don't know what it is about her, but she always makes me feel emotional.'

'You're a big softie really, aren't you?' teased Ronnie, and Elizabeth laughed.

'Don't tell anyone,' she said. 'It would ruin my reputation.'

It took them close to an hour to get to the Brooklyn side of the bridge and although they hadn't yet had breakfast, they decided to get a taxi to the home straight away. They flagged one down within minutes and gave him the address. As it turned out, they could have walked as the place was only two minutes away.

When Elizabeth thought of a nursing home, she imagined an old house surrounded by trees. There'd be wooden benches dotted here and there in the beautifully planted gardens, so the residents could go there to greet their visitors or just to relax. There'd be no sounds except the chirping of birds and whistles from crickets. This place certainly wasn't what she'd expected. Glentree Nursing Home was situated in a high-rise building right on the street. The traffic sounds were deafening and the only sign of anything green were the two half-dead planters at each side of the front door.

'God, it's awful, isn't it?' said Ronnie, echoing exactly what Elizabeth was thinking. 'Definitely not somewhere I could imagine leaving somebody I loved.'

Elizabeth nodded her head in agreement. 'Definitely not. But we don't have to worry about that. Come on. Let's go and see what we can find out.'

'Yes?' said a woman behind the front desk, as they walked through the door. 'What can I help you with?' She didn't even look up from the book she was reading. She was engrossed in it, one elbow leaning on the desk and a hand cradling her head. It was obviously a slow day.

'We're looking for somebody,' said Ronnie, stepping right up to the desk.

'Name?'

'Ronnie. Ronnie Cunningham. And this is my sister, Elizabeth.'

The woman looked up finally and glared from one to the other. 'I mean the name of the patient you're looking for.'

'Well, she's not a patient now,' said Elizabeth. 'Actually, she died quite a while ago.'

The woman, who according to her nametag was called Shania, raised her eyebrows. 'You're looking for a dead person?'

Elizabeth stifled a giggle. 'We're trying to trace somebody. And her mother was a patient here in the nineties. If you could just look up the file and give us the contact numbers you have, that would be great.'

'Nope.'

'What's that supposed to mean?' It was clear Ronnie was getting irate with the woman's nonchalant attitude.

'Do you seriously need me to explain the meaning of no?' She dismissed them with a wave of her hand and continued reading her book.

Elizabeth was aghast. If she heard a member of her staff speaking to a client like that, she'd fire them on the spot. She looked at Ronnie, who just shrugged and shook her head. But Elizabeth wasn't letting it go.

'So, is that a no you can't or no you won't?'

Shania snapped her book shut and took off her glasses as though ready for a fight. 'Listen, lady, you can't just barge in here with your fancy clothes and demand information. Our patients pay good money to be here, and it's usually to get away from family members like you.'

Words failed Elizabeth but luckily Ronnie was quick to interject. 'You can't speak to us like that. I want to see your manager.'

'My son, Denton, is gone to some meeting in Manhattan. I'll tell him you called.'

Jesus, thought Elizabeth, a mother and son operation. Well, there was no point in complaining about Shania to her son. They'd just have to think of another way. Although she wanted to strangle the rude woman, she decided to try a different approach.

'Listen, Shania,' she said, her voice softer, 'I'm sorry we got off on the wrong foot. It's just that me and my sister here are trying to trace our mother's long-lost friend and this place is the only lead we have.'

Shania didn't dismiss them this time so Ronnie joined in.

'The woman's name was Lizzie Granger and she was a patient here in the nineties.'

Both girls waited with bated breath while Shania tapped her long gel nails on the desk. 'Give me that name again,' she said, turning to her computer. 'Let me see what I can find out.'

'Thank you *so* much,' said Ronnie, beaming. 'She was only here a short time before she died but I'm sure you'll still have records.'

'Wait. Hang on a minute.' Shania stopped what she was doing. 'Are you saying she died when she was here?'

Elizabeth felt their last hope slipping away. 'I think so, but she was old and sick and she would have died wherever she was.'

The woman looked from Ronnie to Elizabeth, her face turning dark again. 'Are you two lawyers? Because the nineties were a long time ago – way before my son took over. So if you're trying to—'

'Please, Shania,' said Elizabeth, desperate for the woman to keep checking the computer. They were just a few clicks away from finding Skye's phone number. 'We're not trying to do anything except find our mother's friend.'

'Sorry, I can't help you.' She pushed her wheelie chair away from the computer and glared at the girls. 'Now, is there anything else I can help you with?'

'Please,' pleaded Ronnie. 'Can't you just check the records? We're only looking for a phone number. We have no interest in knowing anything about the woman or how she died.'

'Just what are you saying exactly?'

'We're not saying anything,' said Elizabeth, getting more and more desperate. 'You're reading way too much into this. As my sister said, all we want is a number.'

'Sorry, no.'

'Please.'

'If you can make sure the door clicks properly closed on your way out, please.' And that was that. She picked up her book again and began to read. There was no way they were getting any information from her. Nothing would convince her that they weren't trying to sue the home for some sort of negligence, and the more they pleaded, the more she was digging her heels in. There was no point in pursuing it any further so they turned and left, making sure they clicked the door shut.

'What now?' said Ronnie, leaning against the wall outside. 'We were so close to getting a number there. I can't believe she clammed up like that.'

Elizabeth was close to tears. 'That's been the story of this search, hasn't it? So near and yet so far. I'm not sure we're ever going to find Oliver. I never thought it would be so difficult.'

'I know. But we can't give up yet. Something will turn up. Maybe we'll ring Frank later and see if he has any ideas. I told him we'd keep him updated anyway.'

'Right,' said Elizabeth, wrapping her scarf back around her neck, ready to head off. 'Let's go and get some breakfast. It's too early to ring Frank so maybe we can relax for a while.'

Ronnie buttoned up her coat and shoved her hands into her pockets. 'Great idea. I'm starving.'

'Excuse me,' came a voice from behind, just as they were walking away from the building. 'Hold on a minute.'

They turned to see a young guy, maybe around sixteen or seventeen, small and weedy looking with thick black-rimmed glasses. He looked nervous as he approached them and Elizabeth automatically checked the zip was closed tightly on her bag.

'I heard you back there,' he said, looking from one to the other. 'Talking to my grandma.'

Elizabeth wasn't sure what to say but he wasn't waiting for a response.

'She's a grumpy old bird. Never has time for anyone. Lazy as hell, too.'

'What's this got to do with us?' said Ronnie, looking confused.

'Because I heard what you're looking for and maybe I can help.'

Elizabeth perked up at that. 'Is that right? Can you check out a name for us? Do you even know how to access the computer system?'

'I work here every day,' he said. 'I got into a bit of trouble so Dad brings me here to keep an eye on me. I'm good with technology so I help them with that side of things and the rest of the time I'm just a general dogsbody.'

'So you'd be willing to get us that phone number?' said Ronnie. 'And you'd be able to do it without your father or grandma knowing?'

He stuck his hands into the pockets of his chinos. 'It should be no problem. The only thing is …'

'What?' Here we go again, thought Elizabeth. One step forward and two steps back.

'Well, Dad is as mean as fuck and only pays me a pittance. If you want your information, you'll have to pay for it.'

Elizabeth balked at the teenager's foul tongue. 'Are you crazy? We're not going to pay you to get us information.'

'How much?' said Ronnie, and Elizabeth glared at her, not believing her ears.

'Five hundred.'

Ronnie laughed. 'You've got to be joking. Right, come on, Elizabeth. We're wasting our time here.'

Elizabeth felt like she was in some parallel universe as Ronnie linked her arm and marched forward. 'Ronnie, what were you thinking?' she whispered. 'Are you completely out of your mind?'

'Three hundred,' came a voice from behind.

Ronnie winked at Elizabeth before turning around. 'I'll give you fifty dollars to get me all the details from that file. Any names, numbers or addresses.'

'Nah. Can't do it for fifty.'

Ronnie rummaged in her bag and took out a crisp fifty-dollar bill. She dangled it in front of his face. 'Take it or leave it. I reckon that's a pretty good rate for two minutes' work.'

He hesitated for a moment before snapping the fifty from her hands. 'Deal. Now, give me the name of the patient.'

'But how do we know you won't just take the money and run?' said Elizabeth, unable to believe that they'd entered negotiations with this whippersnapper.

'He won't do that,' said Ronnie, keeping her eyes on the boy. 'Because if he doesn't come back to us with the information, we'll be back to tell his father or grandma what he's been up to.'

Elizabeth took a pen and paper from her bag and scribbled down Lizzie's name. She handed it to him and waited while he examined it. 'Right,' he said, pointing down the street. 'Go and wait in that coffee shop down there and I'll be back to you as soon as I can.'

And with that, he was gone. Ronnie let out a long breath and Elizabeth shook her head. 'Jesus Christ, Ronnie. Where did you learn to talk like that? I don't know whether to be shocked by what I just saw or to admire you.'

Ronnie laughed. 'Actually, I'm shaking now. I don't know where that bravado came from but fingers crossed it might just have worked.'

Elizabeth felt a wave of affection for her sister at that moment – something she hadn't experienced in a long time. So in an uncharacteristic display of friendship, she linked her arm as they walked towards the coffee shop. Maybe things were beginning to look up.

'I feel like I've just walked into an episode of *House of Cards*,' said Elizabeth, wrapping her hands around her steaming mug of coffee. 'I feel so … so corrupt.'

Ronnie threw back her head and laughed. 'How do you think I feel? I was the chief negotiator. If anyone is going to be arrested, it will be me.'

'Oh God,' said Elizabeth, giggling. 'Don't say that. And let's never speak of this again.'

'Well, that was quick,' said Ronnie, nodding in the direction of the door. Their co-conspirator had just arrived and was looking shifty as he scanned the shop. Ronnie waved to him and he came over.

'This is everything that was on the file,' he said, handing over a piece of paper. 'A name, address and a phone number. And you didn't get this from me.'

He scurried out the door, leaving the girls staring at the piece of paper. Skye Granger was the name that was written down. Not Skye Angelo – not that that meant anything. It was immediately clear, however, that the address wasn't going to help because it was the same one they had for Oliver. But the number was something new and Elizabeth felt excited to possibly be just a phone call away from their father.

'So,' said Ronnie, picking up the piece of paper. 'I suppose you'll be wanting me to memorise this and then eat it.'

Elizabeth looked at her and saw the smile on her lips. It was a long time since she'd felt so connected to Ronnie, so relaxed with her. It felt good. It felt right. Who would have thought that while searching for her father, she might just find her sister again?

Chapter 20

'This is Anne. Leave a message after the beep.'

'The little shit,' said Ronnie, throwing her phone onto the bed. 'I can't believe he gave us the wrong number.'

'No matter how many times you ring it, Ronnie, the message isn't going to change.'

Ronnie sighed. 'I know, I know. But it's just he seemed so sure. And the address is right. He couldn't have known that if he hadn't looked it up. I just don't understand why he'd give us a wrong number.'

'Maybe she gave her phone to somebody else,' said Elizabeth, looking pensive. 'Maybe she upgraded and gave or sold her old phone to somebody.'

Ronnie shook her head. 'She would have kept her own number, even with a new phone. It's the wrong number. It has to be.'

'Well, should we go back to the home and confront that guy about it? We don't have many options left.'

'I need to think,' said Ronnie, standing up and stretching her arms above her head. 'Every time we seem to reach a dead end, a new lead turns up, so there must be something else we're forgetting.'

Elizabeth sat on the bed, lost in thought, as Ronnie paced back and forth. They'd decided not to phone the number from the café earlier, for fear they'd get talking to Skye or even Oliver, and the conversation would become emotional. So they'd headed back to the hotel to make the call from the safety of their room.

'Actually, do you know what?' said Ronnie, suddenly. 'I'm sick of this. I'm sick of all of it. I really don't think we're ever going to find Oliver.'

Elizabeth looked alarmed. 'You can't say that, Ronnie. You can't give up already. We can still look. There are still things we can do.'

'Such as?'

'I can't think of anything specific right now but I'm sure if we put our heads together, we—'

'No, Elizabeth!' Ronnie knew she was being unnecessarily sharp but she'd had enough. She was fed up chasing shadows and she suddenly didn't want to think about it any more. 'Let's just forget about Oliver and Skye and anything else that's causing us stress and just go out and have some fun.'

'Fun?' said Elizabeth, as though it was the most alien word she'd ever heard.

Ronnie rolled her eyes. 'Yes, fun. Remember that word? It means having a good time, doing something exciting, not being stressed all the time.'

'Yes, I know what fun means, thank you very much. But we can't just abandon the search. Not when we've got this far.'

'That's just it,' said Ronnie, sitting back down on the bed heavily. 'We haven't come far at all. As you said yourself yesterday, it's like taking one step forward and two steps back. We're getting nowhere fast.'

'Well, I suppose it can't do any harm to take a break for the rest of the day. There's a clutch bag I really want to get in Macy's and maybe pick up a shirt or two for Nathan.'

Ronnie was relieved. She'd rung that number about ten times and each time she was getting more and more stressed. And then she remembered her quest to get pregnant and how she should avoid stress as much as possible. She wasn't big into shopping in those crazily over-priced department stores but it might be good to take their minds off things. And since the day was nice and bright, maybe they could take a stroll through Central Park. Her mood lifted at the thought, and she could feel her shoulders drop as she began to relax.

'But just one thing,' said Elizabeth, breaking into Ronnie's thoughts. 'I think we should leave a message on that phone.'

Ronnie wasn't sure. 'Why would we bother?'

'Because something tells me that maybe it's not a wrong number. It doesn't add up. That guy knows we'd come after him if he gave us the wrong information so why would he do it? Maybe this Anne has some connection with Skye.'

'I don't know, Elizabeth.'

'What have we got to lose? Humour me.'

'Okay, okay,' said Ronnie, picking up the phone again. 'If it will keep you happy. So, what should I say?'

Elizabeth thought for a moment. 'Just say you're trying to trace somebody called Skye Granger and you were given this number. Ask this woman to ring if she knows anything.'

'Okay. And then can we go and have some fun?'

Elizabeth laughed. 'Of course. But don't tell anybody that I was having fun over here. It would completely ruin my reputation.'

Ronnie watched as her sister disappeared into the bathroom and she smiled to herself. It was nice to hear Elizabeth poking fun at herself. It wasn't something she did very often but Ronnie could see her defences coming down as she started to relax. The old Elizabeth was beginning to emerge and that was the Elizabeth she loved. Their relationship was definitely improving but Ronnie wouldn't rest until she found out what had gone wrong between them in the first place. But that was a discussion for another day. For now, she was going to enjoy a day of shopping and sightseeing, and reliving happy memories from the past.

'You can't be serious,' said Ronnie, as they stood in the handbag department of Macy's. 'You'd pay that amount of money for *that*?'

Elizabeth visibly flinched. 'It's a bargain. It's only one hundred and forty dollars. It was two hundred and ten before the sale.'

'One hundred and forty dollars for that little bag. You'd barely fit your mobile phone in it. I saw one in Penneys almost the very same for five euros. It was the same coral colour and everything.'

'You have no class, Ronnie. It's a Kate Spade so it's nothing like the trash they sell in Penneys. And it's actually warm guava, not coral.'

Ronnie held up her hands by way of surrender. 'Okay, I give in. I'm never going to talk you out of it, am I?'

Elizabeth shook her head but she was smiling, and Ronnie smiled too as she watched her go to the cash desk with her precious bag. They were having a lovely afternoon. They'd put the search on hold and had managed not to talk about it either, as they'd explored some of their favourite places in the city. They'd started with a walk around Grand Central Station, spending an unnecessarily long time in the wonderful Whispering Room, one of Manhattan's hidden gems. As children, they used to run from corner to corner of the room, whispering into the wall, each trying to decipher what the other was saying. And it was like the years had fallen away earlier and they'd become children again. They'd already skated at Rockefeller but hadn't done Top of the Rock, so they wasted no time in heading up. Their mother had always said it was better than the Empire State and both girls agreed.

'So, are we done here?' said Ronnie, as she watched her sister juggle her shopping bags like a seasoned pro. 'Because it looks like rain out there and I'd love to get to Central Park while it's still dry.'

Elizabeth agreed and they were soon on their way in a taxi. It wasn't as cold as it had been earlier but the sky was looking angry, and Ronnie feared the clouds would burst very soon. Their mum used to love taking a horse-drawn carriage around Central Park so they decided they'd have to do it – for her. Ten minutes and fifty-four dollars later, they were heading through the beautiful park with a red blanket over their knees, a tired-looking white horse leading the way. Ronnie always felt uplifted by the park. It was a place where everybody seemed happy – from children playing on the immaculately kept grass, to cyclists ringing their bells to warn people of their approach. The greenness of the park contrasted beautifully with the buildings rising like spaceships in the background and Ronnie felt tears sting her eyes at the memories.

'Do you actually like being on this yoke?' said Elizabeth, making

Ronnie jump. 'I mean, do you like sitting here with a smelly blanket over us, watching that poor, miserable horse having to pull us?'

Ronnie howled with laughter. 'Oh God, I hate it. I never liked it. But it's just that Mum used to love this so much.'

'Well, thank God for that.' Elizabeth shoved the blanket from her lap and leaned forward to speak to the guide. 'Excuse me. I think we'd like to get off now, please.'

He expertly pulled the horse to a halt and the girls jumped off, delighted to be back on their feet again.

'Well, that was a waste of fifty-four dollars,' said Elizabeth, shoving some of her smaller bags into the bigger ones to make them less awkward for walking.

'Says the girl who paid almost three times that for a bag the size of a phone.'

Elizabeth pretended to take a swipe at her but it was all in good spirits and they both chatted animatedly as they walked. When they reached the Mall, Ronnie's favourite spot in the park, they became quiet as they walked along the pedestrian pathway, beneath the arch of American Elms. There was something regal about the place. It was as though it demanded their respect, and they were happy to give it.

It was after six when they walked back out through the gates of the park, exhausted but happy. It had been a fantastic day and even the promised rain hadn't materialised.

'So, what do you want to do now?' said Elizabeth, as they crawled through traffic in their second taxi of the day. 'Are you all finished with your day of fun?'

Ronnie poked her playfully. 'I didn't hear you complaining about it. And I honestly don't want to do anything else except stuff myself with an enormous burger and a mountain of chips.'

'That's so unhealthy. How about we find a sushi bar and I'll educate you on fine dining?'

'Ugh! I can't think of anything worse. Let's just go and eat in the hotel bar. The food is delicious and at least we know I can get a burger and you can get salmon or chicken or a leaf of lettuce, if that's what you fancy.'

'That suits me fine,' said Elizabeth. 'I'm too tired to think about going out anywhere else. What time is it, anyway? My phone's gone dead and I forgot to put my watch on this morning.'

Ronnie took her phone from her bag to check the time and saw there was a voice message. She'd spoken to Al earlier, so, curious to know who'd be looking for her, she dialled voicemail and held the phone to her ear. Her eyes widened as she listened to the message and had to save it and replay it to make sure she heard it right.

'What is it?' said Elizabeth, seeing the look on Ronnie's face. 'Who was that?'

The words came out as a whisper. 'It was Anne.'

'Who the hell is Anne?' Then realisation dawned on Elizabeth. 'You mean the woman you left a message for earlier?'

Ronnie nodded. 'I was having such a great day, I'd completely forgotten about her.'

'Well, come on.' Elizabeth was getting impatient. 'What did she say?'

'She said that the phone was hers but it used to belong to Skye Granger. She's her cousin. We have her, Elizabeth. We definitely have her this time. What an end to a perfect day!'

Chapter 21

Elizabeth couldn't believe it was only Saturday morning. They'd arrived on Wednesday, just three days ago, yet it felt like they'd been there for weeks. She missed home. She missed having her own space to chill out with a glass of wine in the evenings and she missed the routine of her job. She'd checked in regularly with Amanda, expecting Cunningham Recruitment to be struggling without her, but it seemed everything was running smoothly and she didn't have to worry. But the thing that surprised her most about being away was that she wasn't really thinking too much about Nathan. She had been at first. Listening to Ronnie's annoying sleep sounds on the first night had made her long for the warmth and security of Nathan's body wrapped around hers. But as the days had gone by and she'd had more time to think, she'd realised that the break from her husband was a good thing. Hopefully he'd see how insensitive he'd been about the trip and realise how much he missed her.

'Right, it's all yours,' said Ronnie, coming out of the bathroom with a big white fluffy towel wrapped around her body and another one around her hair. 'That shower is divine. I could have stayed in there all day.'

Elizabeth agreed that it was the best shower she'd ever used. The jets of water were so powerful that it felt like she was having a

body massage every time she was in there. She grabbed a fresh pair
of knickers from her suitcase and within seconds was standing in
the large cubicle. She positioned herself so that the water hit the
knots of stress at the back of her shoulders and she finally began
to relax. Reaching for the shower gel, she squeezed out a generous
amount into her hands and lathered her body liberally with the
sweet-smelling liquid. She needed to clear her head of negative
thoughts and fill herself with positivity. Today was going to be a
good day. She could sense it. She and Ronnie had plans, and she
wanted to relax, for once. Sometimes she felt like a tightly wound
spring and it made her stressed and anxious. She was going to have
to teach herself to unwind or else she'd end up having a heart attack
or breakdown one of these days.

When she eventually stepped out of the shower she felt refreshed
and in a positive mood. If everything went to plan, they could be in
touch with Oliver by the end of the day. After Anne's message the
previous night, Ronnie had rung her back but hadn't been able to
get her. It was frustrating, but at least they had the contact number
so they hoped to talk to her at some stage during the day. She
wrapped a robe around her and walked back out into the bedroom.

'I'll just be five minutes, Ronnie. I'm going to leave my hair
to …' Her heart began to race when she saw Ronnie speaking to
somebody on the phone and she crossed her fingers that it was the
call they'd been waiting for.

'Okay. I'll talk to you later.' Ronnie threw the phone down on
the bed and, to Elizabeth's shock, she began to cry.

'God, Ronnie. What's wrong?' She rushed to her sister's side and
put an arm around her. 'What's happened? Who was that? Was it
Anne?'

Ronnie sniffed and shook her head.

'What, then? Tell me.'

'That was Amber.'

'Oh, is that all?' said Elizabeth, immediately losing interest. 'I thought it was someone important. What are you crying about?'

'It's Daniel. He's sick.'

Elizabeth wasn't sure how to react. 'What's wrong with him?'

'They took him into hospital earlier,' said Ronnie, wiping her nose with the edge of the towel she had wrapped around her. 'He was vomiting and had a rash. They thought he had meningitis at first so they had to do a lumbar puncture.'

Elizabeth knew all about lumbar punctures. They were the most horrendous things ever. She'd had to have one once in her teens when she'd had suspected meningitis herself, and she'd never forget the pain. She pictured the tiny little boy having to have that awful needle into his spine and she felt like crying herself. But then she thought about Amber and how she'd betrayed her, and she found it hard to be sympathetic.

'Is he okay now?' It was the best she could manage.

Ronnie nodded. 'The test was clear but he still has a terrible bug. They're keeping him in and giving him fluids by a drip. Poor little thing. And Amber is in bits.'

She began to cry again and Elizabeth felt conflicted. She felt sorry for the child. Of course she did. But Amber didn't deserve him. She didn't deserve to have a perfect, beautiful little boy, someone who adored her, looked up to her and relied on her for everything. It just wasn't fair. Life wasn't fair.

'I'm glad you're here, Elizabeth,' said Ronnie suddenly. 'I'm glad we're here together.'

The comment took Elizabeth by surprise and she felt a lump in her throat. 'Me, too.'

'But don't you think it's time we had a proper talk?' Ronnie continued. 'About us. About what prompted that blow-up on our twenty-fifth birthday. I think we need to have that conversation if we're going to move forward.'

Elizabeth clammed up. She didn't want to go over things. She didn't want to dredge up the past. She was enjoying spending time with Ronnie again but if she allowed herself to think about things – about what Ronnie had done – she'd end up hating her all over again. She'd never be able to forgive her but she could forget. If Ronnie allowed her to.

'Elizabeth?' Ronnie was looking at her, waiting for a response. 'Are you going to finally tell me why things turned so sour between us? What happened, Izzy? Why did you stop being my friend?'

'Don't, Ronnie.' Tears welled up in Elizabeth's eyes on hearing her sister use her childhood pet name. As children, they'd hated their names. Elizabeth and Veronica. They were too stuffy, they'd thought. So they'd renamed themselves Izzy and Ronnie. Until the age of about twelve when Elizabeth began to think that Izzy wasn't a good business name so she reverted to Elizabeth.

Ronnie took her hand. 'We've been through a lot these last few years. We can get through—'

The loud shrill of Elizabeth's phone startled them both and she grabbed it quickly, thankful for the interruption.

'Hi, Nathan. It's good to hear your voice.'

'And yours too, sweetheart. I miss you.'

Elizabeth breathed a sigh of relief. 'I miss you too. But I'll be home soon. How come you're ringing so early? It's not even 5 a.m. over there.'

'An early meeting in Limerick. I just thought I'd check in on you before I head off.'

'I've so much to tell you,' she said, watching Ronnie pottering around the room. She felt smug. Ronnie wasn't the only one with an attentive partner. 'It looks like we have a lead on—'

'What are you wearing right now?'

'Wh … what?'

'Under your clothes. What have you on?'

'Nathan! I don't think this is the time.'

'Come on, Elizabeth. I'm so horny.'

She didn't know how to respond and was aware that Ronnie was probably listening to every word.

'I wouldn't have to ask you if you'd just stayed at home, Elizabeth.' His tone had completely changed. 'Even after your blatant disregard for my feelings, I'm still being nice to you and this is what I get!'

'Nathan, don't be like that. Ronnie and I are just getting ready to go out here.' She was hoping he'd take the hint that she wasn't alone. 'And guess what? We've found Skye's cousin. In fact we're waiting for her to ring back right now. So, hopefully she'll lead us to Oliver.'

'I see,' said Nathan, and Elizabeth wondered if he'd even heard what she'd said. 'I hope you're behaving yourself over there.'

'What does that mean?'

'You know. Those American men aren't shy about approaching pretty women.'

She was about to take offence with his insinuation but he didn't give her a chance. 'Right,' he said, leaving her in no doubt that the conversation was over. 'I have to fly so I'll talk to you when I can.'

He was gone before she could say goodbye and she had to fight back tears as she threw the phone on the bed.

'Everything okay?' said Ronnie, watching her carefully.

'Everything is fine.'

'It didn't sound that way. Is Nathan giving you a hard time?'

Elizabeth glared at her sister. 'Why would you think that?'

'Well, it's just that he didn't seem to want to hear what you had to say. Did he even ask you about the search?'

'God, Ronnie. You're so high and mighty. Just because Al rings you a hundred times a day doesn't mean that we should all be like that. It's actually unhealthy to be so reliant on each other.'

'He's just interested, Elizabeth. Which is more than I can say about Nathan.'

'How dare you! How dare you presume you know anything about me and Nathan! Just butt out of my business, Ronnie.'

'I'm sorry,' said Ronnie, looking sheepish. 'I didn't mean to upset you. I just worry about you.'

'Well, there's no need.' Elizabeth stomped into the bathroom and banged the door shut. She put down the toilet seat and sat down heavily. Her head was throbbing from the anger she felt but, if she was honest, it was Nathan she was angry with and not Ronnie. She'd known for a long time that things weren't right between her and Nathan but she just hadn't been able to face up to it. Now with a bit of distance, she was beginning to see how toxic the relationship was. She knew that she deserved better. But the problem was that, despite everything, she still loved him and couldn't imagine her life without him. It was all such a mess.

'Are you okay?' said Ronnie, as Elizabeth came out of the bathroom. 'If you want to talk about—'

Elizabeth was relieved once again as Ronnie's phone began to ring. There was no way she wanted to have any deep, meaningful conversations with her sister about Nathan. Especially when Ronnie had Al – the man that could do no wrong.

'This is it!' said Ronnie, as she grabbed the phone from the end of the bed and checked the display. 'It's her. It's Anne.'

'Put it on loudspeaker,' said Elizabeth, as Ronnie took a deep breath and answered. 'Hello?'

'Hi, this is Anne.' The accent was a New York one, thick and deep. The woman sounded like she smoked a hundred cigarettes a day or else she had a very bad cold. She sounded old too. But there was a friendliness to her voice, and Elizabeth prayed it was a good sign.

'Hi, Anne. Thanks for getting back to me. My name is Ronnie Cunningham and I got your number from … from somebody.'

Elizabeth rolled her eyes. Ronnie was already managing to sound shifty.

'You said you were looking for Skye Granger?'

'Yes. You might guess from the accent that I'm Irish. Myself and my sister are in New York at the moment and we're trying to find a friend of our mother's.'

'And that's Skye?' She was wary, suspicious. But she had a right to be.

'Well, not exactly,' said Ronnie, looking at Elizabeth with raised eyebrows. Elizabeth shrugged, so Ronnie continued. 'Skye's husband, Oliver, is our mother's friend. We'd just like to get in touch with him.'

'And does your mother not have his number?'

Ronnie shifted uncomfortably on the edge of the bed. 'They lost touch a while ago. You said Skye is your cousin, is that right?'

There was a pause and then a sigh. 'Yeah. Cousins.'

'Look,' said Ronnie, 'I know we're strangers and it must seem weird that we rang like this, but all we're looking for is Oliver's phone number or address. We've come all this way. We had an address for him in Mount Kisco but we just found out he doesn't live there any more.'

'Jeez,' said Anne. 'They moved out of that place years ago. A lovely house it was, too. But Aunty Lizzie got ill and they had to sell up to pay for her care.'

'And do you have the address of where they live now? Or a number for either of them?'

'Skye and Oliver split up a good few years ago so I can't help you with a number for Oliver, I'm afraid.'

Elizabeth's eyes opened wide at that nugget of information and she could tell Ronnie was surprised too. Somehow neither of them had thought that Oliver and Skye might not be together any more.

'I'm sorry to hear that,' said Ronnie. 'What about an address?'

'Can't help you there either, I'm afraid.'

The conversation was proving fruitless and Ronnie looked desperate. 'Please, Anne. Can you ask Skye? I'm sure she has an address for him, or a number.'

'They kept in touch initially for a while but both of them moved around a bit. She lost touch with him altogether when he went back to Ireland.'

'*What?*' said Elizabeth, before clamping her hand over her

mouth. She didn't want the woman to know there were two of them listening to her.

Ronnie was quick to interject. 'He went back to Ireland? Do you mean for good? Is he still there now?'

'I presume so,' said Anne. She sounded fed up with the conversation and Elizabeth feared they'd lose her before she gave them any proper information.

'But as I said,' she continued, 'Skye lost touch with him at that stage. They both went on to lead separate lives and there was no need to keep in contact.'

Ronnie paused for a moment before continuing. 'I wonder could you give us Skye's new number, please? Or even if you could ring her for us. I know you say they didn't keep in touch but maybe she has an Irish address for him. She must have some idea where he went.'

'She didn't take an address,' Anne insisted. 'I know that for sure because she felt that the break needed to be final. No hanging on. No mess. Just a clean break.'

'I'd love to talk to her, though. Maybe you could give her my number. It's just that she might have some information that would help us with our search. Anything at all.'

'I would if I could. There's nothing I'd like better.'

Ronnie looked confused. 'So, do you and Skye not talk?'

'I talk to her all the time, sweetheart. Only she doesn't talk back. Unfortunately, Skye isn't with us any more. We lost her to a stroke six months ago. Skye is dead.'

Chapter 22

'So, what are we supposed to do now?' said Elizabeth, shoving her plate aside, her poached eggs barely touched. 'Here we are in New York while our *father* ...' she spat out the word '... is back home in Ireland.'

For once Ronnie didn't feel like finishing her pancakes. 'It's bizarre, isn't it? I mean, it's like we're chasing him and he's running away. Although that's obviously not the case.'

'Did you believe her?'

'Who?' said Ronnie, pouring herself another cup of tea from the silver pot.

'Anne. Do you think what she told us is true?'

'I've no reason to doubt her, Elizabeth. She seemed genuine enough.'

Elizabeth sighed. 'Come on. Let's get out of here. I need some fresh air.'

'Good idea. Why don't we walk to Times Square? I know what would cheer us up and take our mind off things.'

'What's that?' Elizabeth already had her arms in the sleeves of her coat and was wrapping her scarf around her neck.

'M&Ms. Let's go to the M&M shop. Remember how we loved M&Ms when we were little. Remember?'

'We're not little girls any more,' said Elizabeth, a smile creeping onto her lips. 'But it couldn't hurt to give it a try.'

As they headed down East 45th Street, the sound of the city was like music to Ronnie's ears. She loved the cut and thrust of Manhattan – the yellow cabs beeping their horns, tourists snapping pictures, the different cultures, the diversity, the madness of it all. They passed the iconic Roosevelt Hotel at Madison Avenue and Ronnie smiled to herself at the memory of the two of them as teenagers, slipping into the hotel to have a nosy. They'd been in awe of its opulence and had dreamed of coming back to stay there one day. But Fitzpatrick's Grand Central had become familiar to them and, after visiting a few times, they hadn't wanted to stay anywhere else.

A car horn beeped loudly as they stepped onto the road and they jumped back in fright. 'New York drivers are crazy,' said Elizabeth, as they watched the same driver beep his way down the street.

'But don't you just love it?' said Ronnie, linking her arm into her sister's. 'And we have three more days here with nothing else to do except enjoy the craziness.'

They continued in companionable silence, until Elizabeth spoke. 'Do you miss him?'

'Who?'

'Al. Do you miss him?'

'Of course I do,' said Ronnie, shocked that Elizabeth would even have to ask. 'Especially when I hear his voice on the phone. I want to reach out and hug him.'

Elizabeth didn't respond and Ronnie looked at her questioningly. 'And what about you and Nathan?'

'Oh, yes, I really miss him.'

'Is that supposed to sound convincing?'

'Don't,' said Elizabeth defensively. 'I don't have to convince anyone.'

'Talk to me, Elizabeth.'

'What?'

Ronnie pulled them to the outside of the path where there were fewer people and more chance of walking in a straight line. 'I'm worried about you, Elizabeth. I'm worried about your relationship with Nathan. I know you said he didn't hurt you. Well, not physically. But I know you're not happy and you don't seem to be prepared to do anything about it.'

'It's not as bad as you're making out,' said Elizabeth, but her words had no conviction.

'I've watched you two together,' said Ronnie, choosing her words carefully. 'Nathan seems so ... so intense. You don't seem very relaxed around him and, after what you told me, I can understand why.'

Elizabeth shrugged but there was something in her eyes. Ronnie could tell she was getting through to her, so she continued. 'I said it before, but mental abuse is every bit as bad as physical abuse.'

'For God's sake, Ronnie! Nathan doesn't abuse me.'

'Are you sure about that?'

Elizabeth was about to object but Ronnie got in first. 'I know we haven't been close in a long time but I still care about you, Izzy. And I can't bear to think of anybody hurting you.'

Elizabeth let out a long breath. 'I know you're right. And I've been thinking about my situation a lot these last few days. I haven't decided what I'm going to do but what I do know is that things will have to change.'

'Well, that's a start,' said Ronnie, glad that her sister was finally opening up.

'You know what makes it so hard?' said Elizabeth, as they negotiated the crowds of people. 'Everyone thinks Nathan is this sweet, loving guy.'

Not Ronnie. She'd never thought that for a minute.

'And,' Elizabeth continued, 'I'm always being told how lucky I am to have him.'

'I've never told you that once,' said Ronnie. 'I think *he's* lucky to have *you*.'

Elizabeth smiled faintly. 'We've come a long way these last few days, haven't we? Could you have imagined saying that a week ago?'

'Probably not,' laughed Ronnie. 'But, seriously, I mean it. Is there anything I can do to help?'

'Thanks, but I think I need to sort this out myself. I lied earlier.'

'About what?'

Elizabeth took a deep breath. 'About missing Nathan. I don't miss him. I'm actually glad to have a bit of time away from him. He didn't want me to come here, you know.'

'Really?' But Ronnie wasn't entirely surprised. She'd never liked Nathan and had always felt she could see through his smooth exterior. Despite always appearing to be supportive of Elizabeth, Ronnie could tell he was cold. Cold and manipulative.

They reached Times Square and the bright neon signs of the M&M shop were winking at them – inviting them in.

'So, what do you think you'll do?' said Ronnie, before they walked through the door. 'Do you think you'll leave him?'

'A couple of weeks ago I would have said definitely not. But now, I'm not so sure.'

'What's changed your mind?'

Elizabeth paused before answering. 'New York.' She looked at Ronnie with tears in her eyes. 'New York and you.'

'What do you mean?'

'He's made me feel pretty worthless, Ronnie. He talks down to me and manages to convince me that nobody else would want me. That he's the only one who'd look after me. And I had nobody else, so I believed him.'

'That's awful,' said Ronnie, shaking her head. 'So, where do I come into it?'

'Isn't it obvious? I have you now. At least I hope I have.'

Ronnie put her arm around her sister and hugged her. 'Of course you have. You've always had me but you chose to turn your back.'

Elizabeth looked embarrassed. 'Well, that's all behind us now and I feel stronger than I have in years. We've always been a great team, haven't we?'

'We have, and we will be again, but there are things we need to sort out.' Ronnie still wanted to have that conversation with Elizabeth. She needed to know what happened. She wanted to move forward with her sister but she also needed closure. Maybe it was a good thing that they found out that Oliver had gone back to Ireland. Because they now had three whole days left in New York. Three days in which they didn't have to search for clues or go and knock on doors. They could spend the time talking and reconnecting with each other. But something was telling Ronnie that things wouldn't work out as perfectly as she hoped.

'Just how many have you got, Elizabeth?' said Ronnie, as her sister counted the bags of M&Ms out onto the table in the little coffee shop. 'I just got the one bag and dumped about five million sweets into it.'

'Ugh,' said Elizabeth, scrunching up her nose. 'You put them all in there together? What about the peanut ones touching off the crispy ones? Or the mint ones being beside the pretzel ones? I got separate bags for each flavour.'

'You're way too fussy, Elizabeth. I like having a lucky bag. You just never know what you're going to get.'

Elizabeth shrugged. 'You're the one who's going to be eating them, so whatever floats your boat.'

Ronnie roared laughing. 'Whatever floats my boat? That's a very un-Elizabeth-like thing to say.'

'I'm not as predictable as you think,' said Elizabeth, tapping the side of her nose. 'And speaking of being predictable, has Frank not rung yet?'

'Not yet,' said Ronnie, checking the display on her phone. 'But there's still time.'

Frank had rung them every day since they'd arrived, and always between three and four o'clock. He wanted to know everything about the search and whether or not they were getting closer to finding Oliver. He was a good man and Ronnie often thanked God for bringing him into their lives. He'd been a wonderful friend to Belinda before she died and now he was looking out for her and Elizabeth. He was like a reliable uncle – always there for them, making sure they were okay.

'Right on cue,' said Elizabeth, smiling, as Ronnie's phone buzzed on the table and Frank's name appeared on the display.

'Hi, Frank,' said Ronnie, answering on the first ring. 'How are you?'

'I'm fine, Ronnie. A few aches and pains, but that's to be expected from an old codger like me.'

Ronnie smiled. 'You're far from old, Frank Logan. My mother never hung around with old people so you definitely must be young!'

His laugh resounded down the phone. It was a comforting sound and Ronnie hugged the mobile closer to her in an effort to block out the coffee shop noises.

'So, what's the latest?'

'Well, actually, a lot has happened since our call yesterday,' said Ronnie. 'And we're still trying to digest it all.'

'Have you managed to trace him?' Frank sounded worried and Ronnie loved him for that.

'Not exactly, but we did find out he's not in New York any more.'

'And who told you that?'

'Skye's cousin, Anne.'

'Skye's cousin? How did you contact her?'

'Remember the phone number we got at the care home? Well, she answered when we rang.'

There was silence at the other end of the phone and Ronnie guessed Frank was trying to take it all in.

'Are you there, Frank?'

'Yes, sorry. So, Skye's cousin. And what did she tell you?'

'This may surprise you, considering what you told us about Oliver and Skye's relationship, but they actually split up some time ago.'

'They did?'

'Yes. I'm not sure what happened because Anne was reluctant to give us any details. I can't blame her, really. She sounded old and we're strangers.'

'You said Oliver isn't in New York any more. Did she tell you where he's gone?'

'She did,' said Ronnie, 'and you're not going to believe it.'

'Go on.'

'He's gone back to Ireland!' Ronnie waited for the shock. For the sharp intake of breath when Frank realised he'd sent them out there on a wild-goose chase. But his response took her by surprise.

'I see.'

'Did you hear what I said, Frank? Oliver is back in Ireland. We've been over here chasing him and all the time he's been back home right under our noses.' She wanted more of a reaction from him. An apology, maybe, for sending them off to New York unnecessarily. 'Why aren't you more surprised?'

'It was an old address, Ronnie. There were no guarantees. You knew that. So, did Anne give you an Irish address for him?'

'No. She clammed up about it. Said she didn't know anything about him or his whereabouts. She'd just heard through the grapevine that he was living in Ireland now.'

'And what about Skye?' he said. 'Did she say anything about her?'

'That was the most shocking part,' said Ronnie. 'Skye died six months ago. A stroke. Very unexpected, apparently.'

Another pause.

'Frank, did you hear me?'

His voice sounded choked. 'Skye? Skye is dead? She died?'

'Yes. What's wrong? Why did you …' She suddenly remembered. 'Oh, God, Frank. You knew her, didn't you? It completely slipped my mind. I'm so sorry.'

'It was a long time ago.' Barely a whisper.

'But I shouldn't have just blurted it out like that. She was probably the same age as you. And Mum. You didn't need to hear about somebody else passing away. Are you okay?'

'I'm fine, Ronnie. It's just a shock. Listen, I'd better go. I have a million things to do here. And I really am sorry that it didn't work out over there.'

'It's fine,' said Ronnie, feeling sheepish. 'Actually, Elizabeth and I are having a good time, despite everything. We're doing a lot of sightseeing and just basically hanging out together.' She knew that would cheer him up. He was always trying to push her and Elizabeth together. Just like their mother had done.

'That's great. Really, really great. And you'll be home in a few days so we can talk again then.'

'What did he say?' said Elizabeth, after Ronnie ended the call. 'Was he shocked to hear about Skye? I didn't think he knew her very well.'

Ronnie felt unsettled. 'He was acting a bit weird.'

'Weird how?'

'I don't know,' said Ronnie, sitting back and pushing away her now-cold tea. 'He just went quiet when I mentioned about Skye. He seemed upset.'

Elizabeth shrugged. 'We'll go and see him when we get home. Now, how about we go back, grab a shower and head out on the town. I want to get drunk. Forget my troubles. Because in a few days' time, I'll be back home and things are going to get very serious.'

'Right, let's get out of here,' said Ronnie, standing up. She wondered if Elizabeth was talking about Nathan when she said things were going to get serious. Hopefully, it meant that she was going to have a really serious talk with him and maybe even consider leaving him. A night on the town sounded perfect – exactly what they both needed. But Ronnie couldn't get rid of the niggling feeling that Frank was keeping something from them. She couldn't figure out what it could be, but something was telling her they weren't going to like it at all.

Chapter 23

'Remind me why we thought this would be a good idea,' said Ronnie, shouting into Elizabeth's ear. 'I'll give it another half hour and then I'm out of here.'

Elizabeth nodded in agreement. She'd given up on trying to talk because the music was so loud. When they'd gone back to the hotel the previous evening, they'd fully intended to go out. They were going to hit some clubs, have copious amounts of alcohol and forget their troubles for one night. But Nathan had rung while they were getting ready and she'd had a heated conversation with him. By the time she'd finished the call, she hadn't been in the mood for fun and had asked Ronnie if she'd mind putting off their night out. In fairness to Ronnie, she'd been great about it and had suggested some room service, a good movie and an early night. They'd had a lovely evening. They'd chatted until late and it was the closest she'd felt to her sister in a very long time.

But when they'd woken up this morning, they'd decided to resurrect their plans for fun and had come across this place on the internet. The Chilidos Club claimed to be a legendary venue in the East Village, regularly hosting musicians of all genres. Tonight was music of the nineties, and the girls hadn't been able to resist. But it had soon become apparent that the pictures on the website had been taken at very flattering angles with good lighting, because Chilidos was a tiny place in the basement of a building that allowed way too many people in. The music was good, Elizabeth had to admit. The band were decent and were playing everything from Nirvana to the Smashing Pumpkins, but the loudness was almost too much to bear.

'I'm going to the loo,' announced Ronnie, standing up and exaggerating her words so that Elizabeth could read her lips. 'And if by chance you'd like us to leave when I get back, that would be fine by me.'

Elizabeth smiled as she watched Ronnie disappear through the graffitied door of the ladies' toilets. She was glad she'd confided in her about Nathan. She'd been brilliant – understanding and supportive and not at all judgemental. Maybe it was time to let go of the past. She'd been angry with her sister for so long now that she was sick of it. Sick of the hating and the blaming. She was getting close to Ronnie again and she had a funny feeling she was going to need her in the coming weeks and months.

The sound seemed to be getting louder and Elizabeth was beginning to feel old and tired. She might have enjoyed this scene ten years ago, but it really didn't appeal to her any more. Even when the band blasted out 'Californication' by the Red Hot Chili Peppers, one of Elizabeth's favourites, it didn't make her want to stay. She'd had three vodkas but all they were doing was giving her a thumping headache. It definitely wasn't how she'd anticipated the night unfolding.

'Come on, let's get out of here,' said Ronnie, arriving back at the table and grabbing her bag from underneath. 'I'd kill for a Big Mac and chips.'

'You're such a wild thing,' said Elizabeth, giggling. But she wasn't objecting. She'd usually turn up her nose at the idea of eating in McDonald's, but anything would be better than subjecting themselves to another minute of this place.

As soon as the cold air hit their faces, the vodka began to take its effect. Elizabeth felt woozy and linked her arm into Ronnie's to steady herself. Ronnie had been sensible and had stuck to orange juice and Elizabeth wished at that moment that she'd done the same. They'd taken the subway earlier and they'd planned to walk the few kilometres back to the hotel, but the way Elizabeth was feeling, she doubted she could walk even a fraction of that. But within minutes they spotted a McDonald's and Ronnie steered them across the road and inside.

Elizabeth wasn't sure if she wanted to eat or be sick so Ronnie just ordered her a coffee and a doughnut while she herself opted for a large Big Mac meal. But as soon as Elizabeth began to pick at the doughnut and sip the coffee, she felt a lot better and it wasn't long before she was tucking into Ronnie's chips.

'God, I felt old back there,' said Ronnie, taking a sloppy bite from her burger. 'A few years ago, I'd be up on that dance floor telling them to turn the music up.'

Elizabeth laughed. 'Me, too! Well, we're going to be thirty-one in a few weeks. It's all downhill from here.'

'Don't say that, Elizabeth. All the best years are in front of us.'

'I hope so,' said Elizabeth, quietly. 'Because from where I'm looking, the future doesn't look very bright.'

'Ah, Elizabeth. It will all work out. You and Nathan just need to talk and take it from there.'

'But it's not just about me and Nathan. There's other stuff. Stuff you know nothing about ...'

Ronnie looked startled. 'What? What stuff?'

Elizabeth was tempted to confide in her. To tell her the awful truth about what happened back then. If only Ronnie hadn't been involved. If only it had been somebody else. Then Elizabeth might have felt comfortable talking to her. She wished things were different but they weren't, and she'd just have to live with it.

'Elizabeth? What is it?'

'It's just everything. Life. Nathan, Mum, Oliver ... it just feels like there's a lot going on and I don't know when I'll ever feel properly happy again.' She felt tears prick the back of her eyes and she cursed the vodka that always made her emotional. She desperately wanted to put the past to rest and move forward with Ronnie, with their relationship, but it was very difficult.

'Don't,' said Ronnie, reaching out and touching Elizabeth's hand. 'Don't let it all get on top of you. You have me now. Remember when we were young and we felt invincible because we had each other? We can be that dynamic duo again. Us against the world.'

Elizabeth was about to respond when Ronnie's phone rang, startling them both. Ronnie grabbed it from her bag and answered.

'Hi, Al. Good, good. And you? ... That's great. And is she happy with it? ... I know ... Just in McDonald's ... Yes, with Elizabeth ...'

Elizabeth tried to tune out of the conversation. It was frustrating only hearing one side. She'd love to hear what Al was saying. She really envied both of them. They seemed to have the perfect relationship, and they were equals. Not like her and Nathan. He acted as though he was the boss of her and she allowed him to. She tapped her long fingernails on the table, hoping it would hurry Ronnie on. She didn't want to have to sit and listen to her sister cooing down the phone when she herself was feeling so low.

'It's exciting, alright,' said Ronnie. 'I know … Yes … we'll have to wait at least another week though … Me too …' She lowered her voice and Elizabeth strained to hear. 'I just have a good feeling about this. I feel, I don't know, different.'

Elizabeth coughed loudly and Ronnie got the message that time. She said her goodbyes to Al, telling him she loved him and couldn't wait to see him.

'Sorry about that,' she said, looking flushed. 'We kept missing each other's calls so I just wanted to catch him this time.'

'It's okay. You two seem to have a lot to discuss.' She was fishing now, dying to know what they'd been talking about.

Ronnie looked unsure and then she smiled. 'I wasn't going to say anything but I feel we can talk about it now. Al and I are trying for a baby.'

'A *baby*?'

'Yes. We've been trying for the last year to no avail, but things might have changed.'

'Wh … what do you mean? You're not saying you're pregnant?' She thought about Ronnie refusing vodka earlier. 'You're pregnant!'

'No, no. Well, at least, I don't think so. I don't know. Maybe.'

Elizabeth felt a dark cloud descend upon her. What had she been thinking? Why had she thought she could be friends with her sister again? Ronnie didn't need her friendship. She had Al. And now she was going to have a family. A new, perfect little family. She'd have no need for her old one.

'Well, say something, Elizabeth. What do you think?'

Elizabeth bit back the tears. 'What do I think? Do you really want to know what I think?'

'Of course I do. And I might not be pregnant at all. It's too early to know for sure. But I just have a good feeling about it. Something feels different.' She ran her hand over her stomach and suddenly Elizabeth snapped.

'You and your bloody perfect life, Ronnie. Trying to make the rest of us feel inadequate.'

Ronnie looked as though she'd been slapped in the face. 'What are you talking about? Where's this coming from?'

'You're always banging on about your perfect job and your perfect home. You think you have it all sussed out. You think you have the monopoly on happy-ever-afters.' Rage filled her mind as the words came tumbling out and she just couldn't stop them. 'And let's not forget about perfect Al. He's not as perfect as you think he is.'

'Stop,' said Ronnie, looking shocked. 'Why are you saying all this? And what do you mean about Al not being perfect?'

'Work it out for yourself.'

Ronnie paused for a moment, confusion filling her face. 'Am I missing something here? I haven't a clue what you're talking about.'

'I'm going home,' said Elizabeth, standing up to leave. 'I've had enough of this.'

Ronnie grabbed her arm. 'Tell me what you mean.'

'I'm not in the mood to talk, Ronnie.' She shrugged her away roughly and headed for the door.

'You can't just say something like that and leave me hanging,' said Ronnie, following her outside. 'Stop walking, will you? Just talk to me.'

Elizabeth stopped and turned to face Ronnie. 'You make me sick. No matter what happens, you always fall on your feet. You sail through life with not a care in the world, trampling on others along the way.'

'Trampling on who?' Ronnie looked hurt. 'You know I'd never hurt anyone. Well, not intentionally, anyway. Who are you talking about? Are you talking about yourself? Is this to do with why you fell out with me? I need you to explain, because nothing is making sense to me right now.'

Elizabeth began to walk again, tears now flowing freely down her face. She wished she hadn't started the conversation but there was no going back now. She'd thought that she could draw a line under the past. That she could move on and start afresh. But there was too much hurt and she wanted Ronnie to feel it too. To feel the hurt that she felt every single day.

'Is it something to do with Al?' said Ronnie, falling into step with her. 'What were you saying about Al not being perfect?'

'Well, he's not, is he?'

'I think he is, but you seem to think something different.'

'Hmmm!'

Ronnie stopped suddenly and pulled Elizabeth to a halt too. 'What do I have to do to get you to tell me what's going on?'

Elizabeth hated her sister at that moment. She wanted to hurt her badly. She wanted to make her feel the desolation that she herself had felt back then. She wanted her to feel like her heart was broken into a million pieces.

'Elizabeth?'

Elizabeth's face was a mess of tears and snot but she didn't care. 'So you're having a baby with Al. Perfect Al.'

'I hope to, but there are no—'

'I don't want to hear any more about your plans, Ronnie. But just be aware that perfect Al wasn't so perfect on a certain day in March last year.'

'I … I don't understand.'

Elizabeth finally twisted the knife that she'd so perfectly placed inside Ronnie's heart. 'He wasn't so perfect when he took me onto your little sofa and made mad, passionate love to me!'

Chapter 24

'You're lying,' said Ronnie, stepping back as though her sister had punched her in the face. 'Why would you say a thing like that?'

'I'm sorry, Ronnie. But I just thought you should know.'

Ronnie laughed nervously. 'You're an evil bitch, Elizabeth. Making up stuff to hurt me. I really didn't think you'd stoop so low. Never in a million years would Al go near you, so you can take your false allegations and stick them up your arse.'

'You think you're so special, don't you?' said Elizabeth, her nostrils flaring. 'You think your precious Al only has eyes for you. You're such a fool. Wake up and see what's going on around you.'

'I trust Al completely. He'd never cheat on me. And especially not with you.' But Ronnie's insides were doing somersaults and the tiniest bit of doubt was sneaking into her brain. There was no way she believed Elizabeth, but something was niggling at her. She didn't know what it was but it was making her nervous.

'You really are so naïve, aren't you, Ronnie? Just because a man tells you he loves you, and he'd never leave you, doesn't mean that he'll stay faithful. Men like to have a sniff around. Check out the menu. Have a little taster here and there.'

'Do you know what?' said Ronnie, glaring at her sister with all the hatred she could muster. 'You really are a sad human being.

And to think I wanted us to be friends again.' She turned away and began walking in the direction of the hotel.

'Actually,' said Elizabeth, walking alongside her, 'you're the one who's sad. You haven't asked me when or where or anything about our little dalliance.'

Ronnie kept walking, staring straight ahead. 'Because, Elizabeth, I know for sure that your little *dalliance*, as you call it, did *not* happen.'

'It was when you were on some work thing. A jewellery fair or something over in London last March. It just happened the once but it's enough to prove that Al isn't as wonderful as you think.'

Ronnie didn't lose a step but her insides began to crumble. Elizabeth was right. She did go on a two-day trip to London last March. How would Elizabeth have remembered that unless there was something in particular to remember it by? But no, what was she thinking? How could she even contemplate doubting Al. He loved her and he couldn't stand Elizabeth. He'd never, ever do anything like that. He'd know how much it would hurt her.

'Ha!' said Elizabeth cruelly. 'I've got you thinking now, haven't I? Doubting. You know what I'm telling you is true. Deep down you know.'

They were still quite a bit away from the hotel and Ronnie was beginning to think her legs might give way. She stopped suddenly and turned to Elizabeth, tears running down her face. 'Why are you being so horrible? I don't believe one word that's coming out of your mouth but, God, it's so upsetting to hear you say those vile things.'

Elizabeth hesitated for a moment before speaking in a softer voice. 'I'm sorry, Ronnie. I shouldn't have upset you like this.'

'So you admit you're lying? How could you? You're a cruel, heartless bitch! I hate you.'

Elizabeth looked as though she'd been slapped in the face. 'Actually, I'm not lying at all. For a moment there I was sorry I'd told you, but not any more. You needed to know.'

'Do you actually think I believe you?' said Ronnie, glaring at the sister she'd thought she loved. 'The only thing I'm upset about is how you can be so nasty. How you can make up stuff to purposely hurt me. Al would never …'

Her words trailed away and Elizabeth looked at her. 'Ronnie? You're not going to faint on me now, are you?'

Ronnie's world suddenly came crashing down on her and she knew at that moment that her life would never be the same. She remembered what was niggling at her. It was something Elizabeth had said weeks ago that she thought strange at the time. She'd forgotten about it until now but it had sat there at the back of her mind, waiting to make an appearance.

'Ronnie?'

'The Virgin Mary.'

'Sorry, what?'

'The Virgin Mary. Al's tattoo on his chest. You saw it.'

Elizabeth nodded. 'Yep. That and a whole lot of others.'

'I … I don't understand. Al wouldn't do that to me.'

'He's a man, Ronnie. Put temptation in his way and he'll give in. Men are weak creatures. I'm surprised it's taken you almost thirty-one years to learn that.'

Ronnie couldn't take it in. 'Tell me what happened.'

'I called over to talk to you about Mum,' said Elizabeth, looking down at her hands. 'Al was there and he told me you were away.

He asked me in and we had a few glasses of wine. And then one thing led to another …'

'He wouldn't. I still don't believe you. I'm going to ring him.' Ronnie was sobbing as she pulled her phone from her bag and tapped Al's number. She took a few deep breaths while the phone was ringing and managed to compose herself before she spoke.

'Hi, Ronnie. I wasn't expecting to hear from you until tomorrow. I thought you'd be at that club until the early hours.'

'I need to ask you something, Al. And you need to tell me the truth.'

'Is this a truth or dare thing? I love it when you play games with me.'

'Al, this is serious.'

'Okay, okay,' he said. 'Go on.'

'Did you …' She had to pause because the words wouldn't come out. 'Did you ever have a *thing* with my sister?'

A nervous laugh followed by a clearing of his throat. And she knew in that moment.

'Al, you said you'd be honest.'

'Well, I wouldn't say we had a *thing*.'

Ronnie needed to hear him say it. 'Did she or did she not call over to our apartment last year when I was away?'

'Well, yes, but—'

'And did something happen?' She could barely breathe.

Silence.

'Al?'

'Yes. But not in the way that …'

His words were just white noise as Ronnie began to realise that everything she'd thought was real in her life was actually a lie. How could he? How could he do that to her? And with her sister, of all people. She ended the call and stood there in a daze before walking towards the road.

'Whoa,' said Elizabeth, pulling her back. 'What did he say?'

Ronnie felt her words come out in barely a whisper. 'He didn't deny it.'

'He didn't try to explain?' Elizabeth looked surprised.

'I … I don't know. I didn't listen. I didn't want to hear.' She wanted to disappear into a black hole.

'Come on, let's just get a taxi back to the hotel,' said Elizabeth. 'You look like death.'

Despite the fact that she hated her sister at that moment, Ronnie agreed. She wasn't capable of making any rational decisions because obviously her judgement was completely askew. She just needed to be in her bed where she could go over things properly. Maybe she'd wake up and it would all have been a dream. Or a nightmare. But it all seemed too real, and Ronnie wondered if she'd ever feel normal again.

The moon cast a dim light into the room as Ronnie lay staring at the ceiling. How could her idyllic life have turned so sour in the blink of an eye? Only a few hours ago, she'd felt like the luckiest girl in the world and now she couldn't imagine ever being happy again. She and Elizabeth had journeyed back to the hotel in silence, and they'd both gone straight to bed when they got back. Ronnie couldn't even look at Elizabeth. Every time she caught a glimpse of her, she imagined her and Al naked together and it made her feel sick. She just didn't understand it. Al wasn't that type of guy. Or was it naïve of her, as Elizabeth had said, to think that he couldn't be tempted?

She turned onto her side and curled her knees up to her chest. After her phone call with Al, he'd tried ringing her a number of times but she kept declining the calls. She didn't want to speak to him. She didn't want to hear his excuses. Because there was no excuse for what had happened. What could he say? '*She seduced me.*' '*She took me by surprise.*' '*I was under her spell.*' '*It meant nothing.*' No amount of words or platitudes could ever excuse what he did and she'd never, ever forgive him.

Tears stung her eyes again but this time they didn't fall. She reckoned she probably had no tears left. The sound of soft snores began to fill the room and she realised Elizabeth had fallen asleep. She must really hate her to do what she did. She must have wanted to hurt her so badly. It made Ronnie doubly sad to think that she'd lost her sister as well as her partner. The last few months had been the most challenging of her life. She lost her mum, gained a dad, lost a dad, gained a sister, lost a partner and lost sister too. Now everyone was gone and she had nobody. She was truly alone in the world and she didn't know what she was going to do.

A thought then struck her and she felt a wave of nausea rise up to her throat. What if she was pregnant? What if she was carrying Al's baby? What would she do then? Oh, the irony of it. She and Al had wished for a baby for so long. And now, when there was a chance that her wish might just be granted, it was bittersweet because she wouldn't have Al to share it with. Or would she? Could she possibly forgive him for what he'd done? But as soon as she'd thought about the question, she already knew the answer. She couldn't stay with a man who'd done that to her. Not only had he been with her sister behind her back, but he'd hidden it all from her. Al and Elizabeth had been laughing behind her back for almost a year.

She rubbed her temples in an effort to get the pictures out of her head that kept appearing unbidden. Pictures of her beloved Al curled up naked with her sister. She wondered if he enjoyed it. If Elizabeth managed to please him. Did she find all the spots that drove him crazy and made him beg for more? Did *he* beg for more? Elizabeth said it had just happened once. But how could Ronnie believe that? How could she believe anything now? It felt like her last few years with Al had been just a lie.

The sound of laughter from outside the bedroom door was a stark contrast to her mood and she suddenly felt lonely. What the hell was she going to do now? Even before Al, she'd always had boyfriends so she'd never really contemplated living a single life. She took her phone from the locker beside her and clicked onto the photo gallery. She scrolled down and found a picture of Al. It was just from the shoulders up. He was making a funny face, as he often did, and his head was cocked to the side. God, she loved that face. Used to love. A lump formed in her throat and then it suddenly became a torrent. She clasped her hands over her mouth and made a run for the bathroom. She just reached the toilet in time to throw up, and when she was done, she sat down on the floor. Leaning her head against the cold tiles, she began to cry softly. What a mess. What a bloody, bloody mess. New York may have been her favourite city up until now, but she'd always remember it as the city that broke her heart. Broke *her*. And she felt that nothing or nobody would ever be able to put her back together again.

Chapter 25

'Hi, Amanda,' said Elizabeth, as she dipped a spoon into the froth on her cappuccino. 'I just thought I'd check in with you again.'

'It's good to hear from you,' came the chirpy voice down the phone. 'Are you having a good time over there? Have you had any luck with finding your father? I've been dying to know.'

Elizabeth smiled at the sound of the friendly voice. 'Well, in relation to our father, the short answer is no. But I can fill you in on all that when I'm home. And as to having a good time, that would have to be a no as well.'

'I'm sorry, Elizabeth. I know you went off with high hopes.'

'Don't worry about me. I'm made of rubber – I'll bounce back. But tell me about how things are going in work? Has it been chaotic without me there?'

There was a short pause before Amanda spoke – just enough to make Elizabeth's insides do a flip. 'Actually, everything has been fine. Cunningham Recruitment is a well-oiled machine, thanks to you. Interviews, assessments, meetings – everything has been running like clockwork. So if you want to stay away a bit longer, I'm happy to keep things ticking over here.'

The fact that everything was running well in her company back home should have delighted Elizabeth. She should have been relieved that things hadn't fallen apart in her absence. But it left her feeling cold. They didn't need her. If she disappeared today, the company would survive without her.

'Are you there, Elizabeth?'

'Sorry, yes. I owe you a huge thank you, Amanda. You've done a brilliant job.'

'It's not just me,' she said modestly. 'It's the whole team. You've hired good people and everyone works hard.'

Elizabeth suddenly had a thought. 'Actually, as a thank you for all your hard work, I was thinking maybe I could take you for a spa weekend when I'm home. Just the two of us. It would be a chance for a proper catch-up.' She would never have called Amanda her friend. Well, not a proper one anyway. She was a colleague, an employee. But Elizabeth was beginning to realise that she was losing everybody she was ever close to and she needed a friend. She'd always got on well with Amanda so there was no reason why they couldn't develop their friendship outside of the workplace.

'Well,' said Amanda, slowly, 'I wasn't going to ask you until you got home, but now that you've mentioned it …'

'Go on.'

'It's just that Adam and I were thinking about taking a winter break. Just for a week. Or maybe ten days. I wouldn't even consider asking for holidays except for the fact that things are running so well here.'

Elizabeth bit back the tears.

'But if you think you can't cope without me …'

'Don't be silly,' said Elizabeth, trying to sound upbeat. 'Just let me know when you want to go and we can sort out your holidays. Maybe we'll take off to a spa sometime later. Around Easter, maybe.'

'Spas aren't really my thing, to be honest. But you're very good to offer. Lunch when you get back?'

'Definitely,' said Elizabeth. 'I've got to run here. Our flight is tomorrow and I have a heap of things to do. I'll see you when I'm back in the office.'

She ended the call quickly and sat back in the little wooden coffee-shop chair. The rain was pelting down outside and it didn't do much for Elizabeth's mood. It was two days now since she'd had the big showdown with Ronnie and they hadn't spoken a word since. Ronnie had spent much of her time curled up in bed in the foetal position, not answering her phone and only getting up to use the bathroom. Elizabeth wasn't sure if she'd even washed or brushed her teeth. The atmosphere was toxic in that bedroom so Elizabeth had taken to going to the little coffee shop on the corner and spending a lot of her day there.

When she'd seen how upset Ronnie was, how completely devastated, she'd been pleased at first. It was about time Ronnie felt what it was like to have your life shattered. To have your heart broken and your plans trampled on. She needed to come out of that bubble she was living in and feel real hurt. But as time had passed, she'd begun to feel a little bit guilty. She probably hadn't handled things very well. She'd been waiting for more than six years to get back at Ronnie. But revenge wasn't as sweet as she'd expected. Somehow she'd thought she could hurt Ronnie just as she'd hurt her, and then they could call it quits. An eye for an eye. In some unfathomable part of her brain, she'd imagined they could move past everything then and start a new chapter. But it had soon become clear that Ronnie was in a bad way and would never, ever forgive Elizabeth. Maybe this really was the end for them.

A cold chill ran down Elizabeth's neck and she was filled with an overwhelming sadness.

She sighed as she scrolled down through the contacts on her phone. She wished she had somebody to talk to about all this. She'd heard Ronnie on the phone to Amber and had felt insanely jealous. There was a time when Elizabeth and Amber would have been able to talk like that. Back in the day. But not now. Amber had chosen Ronnie, and Elizabeth would never be able to forgive her. As her fingers ran down through the list, she came across Frank's name. At the moment, all Elizabeth wanted him to do was listen – and he was really good at that. She tapped his number and waited for him to answer.

'Hello, Elizabeth. What's up?'

'Hi, Frank. I was just checking in with you. Just giving you an update on how things are going over here.'

'Do you have some news? I thought things had come to a standstill with the search.'

Elizabeth paused before answering. 'No, nothing more about finding Oliver. But there's been a development with me and Ronnie.'

'Oh?' He sounded hopeful.

'We had a massive row, Frank. It was awful. We haven't spoken in two days.'

He didn't respond, so Elizabeth continued.

'It was all my fault. I've done something terrible and I don't know how to—'

'Elizabeth, I'm sorry, but I can't deal with this right now. Can we just talk when you're home?'

It was so unlike Frank to fob her off. 'But I could do with your advice. It's been awful. We said some terrible things and it all got out of hand.'

'I'm sorry that happened,' he said, his tone serious, 'but isn't that the story of your lives?'

'What do you mean?'

'Come on, Elizabeth. You and Ronnie. That's how it's been with you two since I've known you. You argue, then you don't speak, then you argue again. Nothing ever changes.'

'But Frank, this is different.'

'I doubt it.'

'But—'

'Give me a ring next week. Get yourselves home, get settled back in and we'll have a chat then. And I'm sorry I'm not much help at the moment but I'm dealing with some personal stuff myself. We'll talk next week.'

And with that he was gone. Elizabeth felt numb. Frank had always been someone she could turn to but now it looked like even he was losing interest in her. Soon she'd be completely alone. Maybe Nathan had been right when he'd told her that nobody would ever love her or care for her like he did. That he was the only one she could completely rely on. Ronnie had begun to convince her over the last few days that Nathan wasn't a good person. That he didn't treat her right. But Ronnie was wrong. Nathan loved her and right now he was the only person in the world that she had on her side. She checked the time on her phone and saw it was almost six thirty. It was lunchtime at home so maybe she'd catch him on his break. She dialled his number and waited for a reply.

'Hello …' A woman's voice startled Elizabeth. There was some muffled conversation and then Nathan came on the phone. 'Hello? Elizabeth?'

'Who was that?' she said, fear coursing through her.

'That was Chanelle, my personal assistant.'

'You don't have a personal assistant.'

'I do since I got the promotion.'

She hadn't been expecting to hear that. 'You got the promotion? The one you were after? Why didn't you tell me? Nathan, that's brilliant. I'm so proud of you.'

'I'm glad you're pleased,' he said. 'But you know that it means I'll be working longer hours from now on.'

'Oh.'

He continued. 'It comes with the job. More hours, more travel. But it will be worth it financially.'

'So how are you coping without me?' She was enjoying his good mood. She didn't see that side of him too often and it was nice not to have him criticise her. She'd been right to give him another chance. Thank God she hadn't taken Ronnie's advice.

'I've been too busy to notice, really. I've missed you, of course, but I've barely been home with all this stuff going on in work.'

There were more muffled voices in the background before he spoke again. 'Listen, Elizabeth, I'm going to have to go. I'm up to my eyes here and haven't really got time to chat right now.'

'But Nathan, I haven't spoken to you in two days. I could do with a friendly ear right now.'

'Sorry, honey, no can do. Business calls, I'm afraid. Listen, I'll try and call you tomorrow or maybe the next day.'

'But I'm coming h—'

'Speak soon, then. Bye, love.'

He ended the call abruptly, leaving Elizabeth feeling cold. Her emotions were all over the place. She was delighted for him getting that promotion because she knew how hard he'd worked for it, but if it meant him never being home, she wasn't sure it was worth it. And there was just something about that woman that bothered her. The way she'd answered the phone hadn't sounded very professional. And her voice – it was vaguely familiar. But then again she'd met a lot of his colleagues at various functions so it could be just that.

The little coffee shop was buzzing with people and she was beginning to feel claustrophobic. A family had sat down at the table beside her and the children's chairs were pushed right up against hers. It was probably time to go back anyway. They had to check out of the hotel in the morning and would be heading to the airport after that for their flight home. She took a gulp of her cappuccino and almost gagged. It was stone cold and she could feel it sliding down to her stomach. She probably needed to eat something too. A picture of Ronnie curled up in bed came into her mind and guilt began to engulf her. Maybe she should try and talk to her again. After all, they'd have to sit together on a flight tomorrow so it would be very unpleasant if they couldn't pass a civil word.

The queue at the counter had thinned out so she went up and ordered two cappuccinos and two chicken rolls. It would be a bit of a peace offering. She'd try and lure Ronnie out of bed and get her to start packing. God, what if she couldn't get her up? What if Ronnie had sunk into some sort of depression and wasn't willing to move? Elizabeth was really beginning to regret her actions. She shouldn't have said all those things, knowing the hurt it would cause. She paid for her order and headed back to the hotel.

Ronnie was still in bed, curled up on her side, but her eyes were open. They were red and puffy and Elizabeth noticed she had her phone in her hand.

'I got you this,' said Elizabeth, leaving the hot drink and roll on her locker. 'I thought you needed to eat.'

Nothing.

'Don't forget we have to be out of here by eleven in the morning,' she continued. 'So we should probably get packing so that we'll be ready to go after breakfast.'

A flicker in Ronnie's eyes. That, at least, was something.

Elizabeth sat down on the end of Ronnie's bed. 'Come on, Ronnie. You can't stay there. Please get up and eat something. You're worrying me now.'

Ronnie turned and glared at her. 'Oh, I'm worrying you, am I? I'm so sorry. I'll try to do better in the future.'

'Don't be sarcastic. I'm just trying to help.' She tried to soften her voice but Ronnie was making it difficult for her. 'Don't accept my food if you don't want to, but come and pack at least. This place is a tip. It will take us ages to sort it all out.'

Ronnie pulled herself up into a sitting position and Elizabeth was shocked at how awful she looked. Her hair was like rats' tails and she had old make-up in blotches all over her face. She was still clutching her phone and Elizabeth wondered if she'd spoken to Al yet.

'Yes, I have,' said Ronnie, giving Elizabeth an evil look before turning away.

Elizabeth was confused. 'Yes you have what?'

'Spoken to Al. That's what you were wondering, wasn't it?'

The twin thing. 'Well, yes, I suppose I was. He's been ringing you so much, I knew you'd have to talk to him eventually.'

'Well, I didn't speak to him, exactly. I couldn't bear to. It was just a text. You'll be happy to know that he's moving out.'

That took Elizabeth by surprise. 'Really? Are you not going to talk about things?'

Ronnie shook her head. 'I don't want to hear his excuses and I don't want to hear yours. I just told Al that I want him gone by the time I get home and he's agreed. So he's all yours, Elizabeth. Do with him what you want.'

'No! No, Ronnie. You have it all wrong. I don't want—'

Ronnie put her hand up, her palm almost touching Elizabeth's face. 'I don't want to hear it. It happened. The damage is done. Nothing you or Al can say can undo it. I am *not* going to talk about this any more.'

A sadness overwhelmed Elizabeth as she watched Ronnie trudge into the bathroom, her feet dragging on the floor, her head and shoulders drooped. She'd broken her. She'd completely and absolutely broken her sister. Suddenly revenge didn't taste so sweet. She'd thought she'd be happy to see Ronnie like that. To know she was feeling the same hurt that Elizabeth had felt back then. But it gave her no pleasure. Saying those words to her the other night had given Elizabeth a sense of satisfaction. But then nothing felt right. As Ronnie said, you can't undo something you've done or you can't unsay hurtful words once they've tumbled from your lips. Elizabeth lay back on Ronnie's bed and closed her eyes. In her mind, she was always going to reunite with her sister at some point. She'd thought that she could decide when it would happen. But she'd gone too far. She'd put the final nail in the coffin and there was no way she and Ronnie would ever be friends again.

Chapter 26

Ronnie's heart was heavy as she sat drinking a hot chocolate in the departures hall at JFK airport. She should have been excited now. She should have been looking forward to seeing Al after a week away and filling him in on everything that had happened. But since Elizabeth had taken her life and smashed it into a million pieces, she felt nothing but trepidation and uncertainty. She was glad at least that Elizabeth had left her alone for a bit. She'd gone shopping in the duty free, leaving Ronnie to sit and contemplate her future.

After Elizabeth's revelations the other night, Ronnie had gone into shock. She'd refused to talk to Al after her initial phone call and, despite Elizabeth's efforts, she'd had no interest in talking to her either. Al had persisted with phone calls but Ronnie hadn't felt strong enough to speak to him. So eventually she'd just texted him to tell him she wanted him gone. She wasn't going to give him a chance to explain away what he'd done. What they'd done. Her so-called boyfriend and her sister. It made her sick to think about it. She'd decided that, no matter what, she wasn't going to allow him to talk her around, to win her over. She wouldn't be a doormat like her sister. Al had been unfaithful and lied to her. He'd broken the wonderful seal of trust that she'd thought they had. And she was never, ever going to forgive him.

She sat back and watched as people whizzed past, rushing for flights, trying to keep hold of children's hands, laughing, chatting, being happy. She envied all of them. It seemed she was the only one with turmoil going on in her head. Only a few days ago, she had everything. She was getting her sister back, she had a wonderful boyfriend whom she loved with all her heart and the very likely possibility of a baby on the way. Now she was back to hating her sister and she was going home to an empty apartment because she'd insisted that Al move out. He was going to stay with a friend for a bit but he'd said that it was only temporary. But Ronnie knew she couldn't take him back. Not now. Not ever. The only bit of light in her otherwise dark future was the possibility that she could be pregnant. But even that was bittersweet because she'd have nobody to share it with. However, she wouldn't stop wanting to be a mother just because Al was gone. It would be sad to do it without him, but having a baby still meant everything to her.

She strained her neck to check the screen behind her and saw that their flight was beginning to board. She wasn't looking forward to six hours on the plane beside her sister. She could barely look at her at the moment. Elizabeth had tried to talk to her over the last couple of days but Ronnie hadn't responded well. Was she supposed to just accept what Elizabeth had done and move on? It was as though Elizabeth wanted her to be mad, shout and scream, then things could go back to normal. Nothing felt normal to Ronnie at the moment and, thanks to Elizabeth, probably nothing ever would again.

Minutes later, Elizabeth arrived back at the table laden down with duty-free bags. 'Come on, we're boarding now,' she said, opening her take-on bag and stuffing some of the plastic bags into it. 'We don't want to be last in the line.'

'What does it matter?' said Ronnie, standing up slowly. 'We have our seats booked so it's not as though we'll be left standing.'

Elizabeth didn't respond but marched forward towards the gate and Ronnie followed reluctantly. Thankfully everything from there went smoothly and just half an hour later they were belted into their seats and ready for take-off. The flight wasn't full and it looked like nobody else was going to sit in their row of three so once they were up in the air, Ronnie was going to move over and leave a space between them. It was an overnight flight so at least they could try and sleep and not have to make small talk.

Two hours into the flight, Ronnie felt her head might combust. She was sick of going over and over things and trying to make sense of it all. She glanced sideways and saw that Elizabeth was asleep, her head tilted to the right, her lips parted slightly. Even in resting mode, Elizabeth looked stern. Her features were sharp and angry and even her body looked stiff and uptight. Ronnie thought about the girl she'd adored throughout their childhood. The sister she'd relied on and shared everything with. The one person she'd thought would be there for her until the end of time. Where had that girl gone? Suddenly she wanted to know. She *needed* to know. It was time to get some answers.

'Ouch,' said Elizabeth, waking with a start as Ronnie elbowed her in the side. 'What did you do that for?'

'I want to talk.'

'So you barely say a word for the last two days and you choose the moment when I'm in a deep sleep to decide you need to talk.' She sat up and wiped the drool from the side of her mouth with the sleeve of her jacket. 'What do you want to talk about?'

'What happened, Elizabeth? What happened to you?'

She looked puzzled for a moment before replying. 'Ronnie, I've told you everything about that night. It just happened, okay? What's the point in going over and over it? Al isn't the man you thought he was. You got hurt. We all get hurt. That's life.'

'Shut up about Al,' Ronnie said, holding her hand up. 'I don't want to talk about him or your sordid affair any more. I want to know what happened to you. Why have you become so bitter? So heartless. You used to be a decent human being. Or at least I thought you were.'

'Ronnie, I …' Elizabeth looked upset suddenly, which only made Ronnie more curious.

'Tell me.'

'Just life,' she said, not looking directly at Ronnie. 'We get older, life gets harder and we have to try and cope with it as best we can.'

'I'm not buying that,' said Ronnie, determined to get answers. 'Every time I've asked you about this over the last six years, you've given me some ambiguous answer. Well, I'm not accepting it any more. We were friends, Elizabeth. Good friends. We looked out for each other, had each other's backs. And then you turned on me. Why? What happened?'

Elizabeth looked at her with tears in her eyes and Ronnie was shocked to see pain in her face. Real pain and hurt and it made her nervous. She'd always known something had happened to Elizabeth back then but she was beginning to think it was something a lot more serious than she'd imagined.

'Tell me!' Ronnie's voice was getting louder but she didn't care. She wanted answers and she wasn't going to rest until she got them. She wouldn't let Elizabeth fob her off any more.

Elizabeth's voice was barely a whisper but Ronnie just caught the words. 'Ben Wilson.'

'Ben Wilson? Now there's a name I haven't heard in a while. What's he got to do with anything?' Ronnie had dated Ben Wilson for about six months after she'd come home from her Peru trip. A bit of a tearaway and not the sort of guy her mother would have wanted for her, but Ronnie had loved him. At least she thought she had. He was funny and unpredictable and Ronnie had been drawn to his rebelliousness. Ronnie looked at her sister, still waiting for an answer, and saw she was crying. It was difficult for her to muster up any sympathy for Elizabeth after what she'd done but she was curious nonetheless.

'Right, you have to tell me now. It must be six or seven years since I've heard his name mentioned.'

'Leave it, Ronnie.' Elizabeth took a tissue from her pocket and dabbed at her eyes.

'For God's sake, Elizabeth, I'm not going to leave it. I'm sick of this. Sick of you!' She could feel the anger bubbling to the surface and she'd never felt more like lashing out at anyone. 'It's our thirty-first birthdays in a few weeks so that will make it six years since your outburst. Since the day you told me you wanted nothing to do with me ever again. And you kept that promise. So I've spent years wondering what happened, why we stopped being close. And you've refused to explain. And then just as I thought we were getting things back on track, becoming close again, I find out you slept with my boyfriend. It's more drama than I can stomach. And now you're talking about Ben Wilson. What the fuck has he got to do with anything? Just fucking tell me!'

Elizabeth flinched. 'Well, there's no need for—'

'I'm warning you, Elizabeth. If you don't start talking now I'm going to start shouting. And I'll make sure the whole plane knows what a filthy slut you are.'

'That's enough,' said Elizabeth, her tears replaced with a stern look. 'Calling me names isn't going to change things. And *you* calling *me* a slut is laughable.'

Ronnie was confused but Elizabeth continued before she could say anything.

'Ben Wilson. Your first love. Your bad-boy boyfriend that you spent months fawning over.'

'What about him?'

'He was mine first.' Elizabeth choked on the words. 'We were together before you ripped him away from me and laughed about it behind my back.'

Ronnie was completely taken by surprise. 'No, he wasn't. No, you weren't.'

'Don't pretend you didn't know, Ronnie. Don't pretend you and Amber weren't having a laugh at my expense. *Poor, sad Elizabeth. She can't hold on to her men.* Don't tell me you didn't slag me off to Ben while you were lying in bed with him.'

Ronnie's head was in a spin. She didn't know what was going on. They'd all known Ben for years. He was a local guy that they'd often meet in a city centre pub on a Saturday night. Elizabeth had never been with him. Ronnie would have known if she had. Amber used to always try to get Ronnie and Ben together and eventually they'd agreed to go out. What Elizabeth said just didn't make sense.

'Lost for words now, are you?' Elizabeth opened her seatbelt and turned right around to face Ronnie. 'I hated you, Ronnie. I hated you for taking him away from me. All those years I looked after you. All the times I had your back when you were bullied in school. Then you go and take the only good thing in my life away from me.'

'I … I didn't. I honestly don't know what you're talking about.'

Elizabeth shook her head. 'We'd been seeing each other for months, me and Ben. I'm sure Amber told you that.'

'Hang on,' said Ronnie, trying to keep up. 'What's Amber got to do with it? How would she have known?'

'Oh, she knew alright. She knew damn well that Ben and I were together. Isn't that why she encouraged you to go for him? Don't try and tell me you didn't know, because I just don't believe it.'

'I didn't. I swear.' Something wasn't adding up for Ronnie. She would have known if her sister was dating Ben. 'Why didn't you say if you and Ben were together? I don't understand. You were together for months but you never said anything about it?'

Elizabeth looked uncomfortable as she twisted a hanky in her hands. 'Mum didn't like bad boys like Ben. You above all people should know that.'

Ronnie thought back to her time with Ben and remembered how much her mother hated him and his bad reputation. 'I know she didn't like Ben but why didn't you say something to me?'

Elizabeth shrugged.

Ronnie persisted. 'I was your best friend, Elizabeth. Your twin sister. I told you everything and I thought you told me everything too. How could you keep a secret like that from me for months? It doesn't make sense.'

'I relied on you too much, Ronnie. I always seemed like the confident one, the one in control. But I never did anything without your approval. I probably would have told you after a few weeks but you went off to Peru then so it was easy to keep the relationship to myself.'

'I still can't believe you managed to keep it from me. It's not as though we didn't keep in touch. I know it wasn't the same as me being at home but you still could have said something.'

'Also,' said Elizabeth, slowly, 'I was afraid that if it got out that I was seeing him, Mum would get involved and that would be the end of it. You wouldn't have been home to back me up so I would have probably given in to her disapproval.'

Ronnie nodded. 'That much makes sense. You always cared what she thought. I, on the other hand, did my own thing, regardless of her feelings.'

'I always admired you for that, Ronnie. I wished I could be more like you. So confident in your own skin. So poised and self-assured.'

Ronnie was surprised at Elizabeth's praise and was about to say so when Elizabeth put up a hand to stop her.

'But,' said Elizabeth, her eyes dark, 'that doesn't make what you did any better. I still don't believe that you didn't know about me and Ben. Amber saw us out one night. I made her promise not to tell anyone, including you, until I was ready. She said she wouldn't. But only weeks later Ben had dumped me, you were home from your travels and next I heard you and him were an item.'

Ronnie was reeling from this information. Amber knew? How could her best friend have known this and not told her? Back then, all three of them were best friends so it seemed unlikely Amber would have done anything to jeopardise that. Unless, of course, she knew exactly what she was doing. Realisation began to dawn on Ronnie and her heart began to beat like crazy. Just when she thought things couldn't get any worse, now this.

'Tell me,' she said, looking into Elizabeth's eyes. 'Are you completely positive Amber knew you were dating Ben? Are you absolutely sure?'

'Of course I am,' Elizabeth spat. 'I specifically remember the night we met her. We were queueing up for cinema tickets and having a smooch when we spotted her looking right at us. I went over to talk to her and that's when I made her promise not to say anything.'

'She never told me.' Ronnie's voice came out in a whisper. 'And you're right. She did encourage me to get together with Ben. She kept dragging me over to talk to him when we'd see him and kept telling me we'd be perfect together. I'm so sorry, Elizabeth.'

'So you really didn't know? And he never mentioned the fact that he'd been with me?'

'I swear to God, I had no idea. If I'd known, I never would have gone near him. And in all the time we were together, he never said a word about being with you. Why didn't you say something to me back then, when I started going out with him? Why didn't you tell me? I would have dumped him straight away. I would never, ever have done that to you.'

Elizabeth shook her head. 'I can't believe you really didn't know. All this time I thought you were cruel and heartless. That you didn't give a damn about me or my feelings. It almost drove me crazy.'

'Hang on,' said Ronnie, trying to work things out in her head. 'So is that it? You mistakenly thought I betrayed you, so you shut me out of your life? Six years, Elizabeth. You've barely spoken to me in six years because of a misunderstanding?'

'It was more than that.'

'Bloody hell, Elizabeth. I'm sorry that you got hurt but that's crazy. We had something really special, you and me. A really special bond. And you went and broke it because of Ben bloody Wilson?'

'Not *just* because of Ben Wilson.'

'What, then?' said Ronnie, trying to keep her anger under control. 'I'm all ears.'

Elizabeth looked at her sister and tears were pouring down her face. 'Because of Ben Wilson. And the fact that I was pregnant with his child.'

Chapter 27

'What did you say?' Ronnie's face turned ashen. 'Pregnant? You. Pregnant?'

'Yes, Ronnie, I was pregnant. So now you know why it was such a big deal for me when Ben left me to be with you.'

'I can't get my head around this,' said Ronnie, rubbing her temples. 'Did Ben know? What did he say?'

'I never told him.' Elizabeth could barely get the words out. 'He was with you by the time I found out I was pregnant.'

Ronnie shook her head and looked at Elizabeth nervously. 'And the baby? What happened?'

Elizabeth opened her mouth but the words wouldn't come out.

'Elizabeth?' Ronnie reached over and took her hand. 'Tell me.'

'I had an abortion.' She began to sob, as big, fat tears fell in torrents down her face. She couldn't control them, nor could she control her shoulders that heaved up and down with the grief. All the hurt and guilt of the last seven years began to spill out and she feared it would never stop. Ronnie still had her hand and Elizabeth could see that she was crying too. They sat there for what seemed like ages, both lost in thought, united in grief. Eventually Ronnie spoke, her voice shaky and uncertain.

'I can't believe you were pregnant and had an abortion, and I didn't know. What were we? Twenty-four?' She squeezed Elizabeth's hand before releasing it to open her own seatbelt. She moved back into the middle seat to be closer to her. 'Tell me about it.'

Elizabeth suddenly wanted to tell her sister everything. She'd kept it all to herself for so long that it had grown inside her, making her angry and aloof. But she was sick of feeling that way. She wanted to share the burden. To tell Ronnie about that awful, awful time in her life. So she blew her nose, took a deep breath and began.

'Ben and I had been seeing each other for about four months. I really thought I loved him. He was so different to other boys I'd dated. I suppose I was attracted to the bad boy in him. And I thought he loved me too. Until one day he announced that it had been fun but he needed to move on. Or in his words, *"We should spread our wings, man. Meet new people. Have new experiences."* I was gutted.'

'And did you know at that stage that you were pregnant?'

Elizabeth shook her head. 'It was a few weeks later when I realised what was going on. I didn't know how to feel. On one hand, I saw it as an opportunity to get him back. I'd tell him we were going to have a baby and he'd come running back to me. And I quite liked the idea of having a baby, actually. It wasn't something I'd thought of before but I was mature, I'd cemented myself firmly in the family business and had enough money to be able to support a child. I was terrified but also a little bit excited.'

'Oh, Elizabeth. Why didn't you tell us? Why didn't you talk to us? Even if Ben didn't want to be involved, you would have had me. And Mum.' Ronnie's expression changed suddenly and Elizabeth knew exactly what she was thinking.

'Before you ask, Mum knew nothing about it. I told nobody. It took me a few days to get my head around it myself and by then you and Ben were together.'

'Elizabeth, I—'

Elizabeth put her hand up to stop Ronnie saying any more. 'I know, I know. You didn't know about me and Ben. But at that time – in my hormonal state – you were all plotting against me. I couldn't see beyond that.'

Ronnie sighed. 'So what happened then?'

'I made my decision quickly. You know what I'm like. If something has to be done, I don't procrastinate. A week later I was over in London having the abortion, and I was back home the next day with nobody the wiser about what I'd done.'

'Hang on,' said Ronnie, looking thoughtful. 'The trip to London to see a client. I remember. You came back and ended up in hospital. You said it was a gastric bug and we should stay away.'

Elizabeth nodded. 'We had a few clients over there so I organised a meeting with one of them so nobody would question where I was going. I got an infection when I came back. It was bad. I honestly thought I was going to die.'

'That's awful,' said Ronnie. 'I still can't believe you went through all of that and I never knew. So much for twintuition.'

Elizabeth wanted to keep going with the story. To make Ronnie understand the reason for her coldness and indifference for the last number of years. She suddenly wanted to make everything okay between them and the only way she could do it was by being honest. 'As soon as I came out of the hospital, I built a wall around myself and I was determined I'd never let anybody get close to me again. I couldn't look at you, Ronnie. Every time I saw you and knew that you were with Ben, it was like a knife to my heart. And then I'd remember the baby, and what could have been.'

'Do you ever think ...' Ronnie trailed off, not finishing the sentence.

'Do I ever think what?'

'Do you ever think about what might have happened? I mean, if you had the baby. How your life would be different.'

Elizabeth felt tears sting her eyes again and her head began thumping like crazy. She'd had enough. She didn't want to talk about it any more. Her heart began beating right up into her throat and her breathing became shallow. 'I can't, Ronnie. I can't ...'

'It's okay, it's okay,' said Ronnie, rubbing her arm. 'Just breathe. Come on. Breathe with me ... one ... two ... three ...'

Elizabeth listened to Ronnie's calm voice and her breathing quickly returned to normal. But she was absolutely exhausted. She told Ronnie that she needed to shut her eyes for a while. To clear her head of the memories that were threatening to strangle her. So she turned and laid her head against the window blind and made herself as comfortable as possible in the tiny space. She'd suffered from panic attacks when she was in her teens. They were usually exam-related and they never lasted more than a minute or two. Ronnie had always been the one to help her back then. She'd found out the correct way of handling a panic attack and had always been able to talk Elizabeth through them. It was nice that she still remembered.

Elizabeth closed her eyes tight. She wanted sleep to come but there was too much going on in her head. Despite her exhaustion, she felt a weight had been lifted off. There had been so many times in the past she'd wanted to confront Ronnie about Ben and about what had happened. But for a long time, she'd been way too hurt. Too emotional. And then when she met Nathan, he hadn't exactly encouraged her relationship with Ronnie. He knew nothing about why they'd fallen out but he seemed to think that all her attention should be on him and that her family should take a back seat.

But maybe there was still time to get their relationship back on track. They were talking again, so that had to be a good thing. And surely all those moments of closeness they'd had in New York had to account for something.

She shifted in her seat and glanced at Ronnie. She had her eyes closed but it was clear she wasn't asleep. Her eyelids were twitching and Elizabeth could tell that she also had a million things going on in her head. As she looked at her sister, she wondered how she could ever have hated her. How she could have turned her back on her. This was the sister she loved more than anything in the world. She'd have died for her when they were younger. How could she have allowed things to get so out of control?

Ronnie opened her eyes at that moment and saw Elizabeth watching her. 'Are you okay now?' she said gently. 'Feeling better?'

Elizabeth nodded. 'What you asked earlier. About if I ever thought what life would be like if I'd had the baby.'

'Elizabeth, you don't have to—'

'It's okay. I want to talk about it. And the short answer is yes. I wonder every day what my life would be like if I'd made a different decision. If I'd gone ahead and had the baby.'

'And?'

Elizabeth thought for a moment. 'My life would be very different but I think it would be good different. I'd have a six-year-old now. Imagine me, with a child.'

They both paused to imagine, before Elizabeth continued. 'But that's not all. If I'd gone ahead and had the child, we would have been having this conversation a lot sooner. We would have saved on years of misunderstandings. Years of guilt and blame and hatred.'

The captain's voice came through the intercom at that moment, announcing that he'd soon be telling them to put their seatbelts on for landing. They were just half an hour from home. It had been an exhausting and emotionally draining flight but, if the two of them could finally make peace and put their differences aside, it would have been worth it. Elizabeth put her belt on and turned back to face her sister.

'I forgive you, Ronnie.'

'Forgive me?'

'Yes. For what happened back then. I realise now that you didn't know. That it was Amber I should have been mad at and not you. I hope maybe we can put it all behind us and start to build up our relationship again.'

Ronnie looked at her in confusion. 'Are you crazy, Elizabeth?'

'Wh … what?'

'How can you forgive me when I didn't do anything wrong? Yes, I went out with Ben, but I knew nothing about you and him.'

'I know,' said Elizabeth, eager to explain herself. 'I know that now so I suppose what I'm saying is that I don't hold any grudges any more.'

'Listen,' said Ronnie, her eyes staring at Elizabeth. Cold. Unflinching. 'I'm desperately sorry for you and what you went through. I can't even imagine how painful that must have been. And I'm sorry that I didn't suspect anything at the time or at least have enough cop on to know there was something serious going on with you. I hate that we've spent so many years apart. So much time when we could have supported each other and been there for each other.'

'I feel exactly the same,' said Elizabeth. 'So much wasted time. That's why I think we should move forward now. Forget about the past.'

'You misunderstand me, Elizabeth. You may forgive me, but I don't forgive you.'

There was silence for a moment before realisation dawned on Elizabeth. 'If you're talking about the Al thing, I only told you because—'

'I don't want to hear it,' said Ronnie. 'Nothing you say will make it right.'

'But just let me explain.'

'It's too late, Elizabeth. The moment you told me you slept with my boyfriend. The man I adore – adored. The man who was going to be the father of my baby. Or babies, if we were lucky. The moment you told me that, you took my life away from me. So once we part at Dublin airport, I never, ever want to see you again for as long as I live.'

Chapter 28

There was no Al waiting at the arrivals hall to kiss Ronnie and tell her he'd missed her. No Al to pull her suitcase for her and allow her to lean her exhausted body against him. As she sat alone in a taxi, she realised that her life was going to be very different from now on. She'd literally gone from having a full and wonderful life to having nothing. Nobody. She wondered for a brief moment if she'd been too rash in telling Al to move out, but she'd had no choice. How could she even look at him knowing he'd been with Elizabeth? That must have been how Elizabeth had felt back then – hurt, betrayed, alone. But the difference was that Elizabeth had done what she did intentionally. She'd set out to hurt Ronnie, and had succeeded.

The early morning sky was a mixture of darkness and light as the taxi pulled up outside Ronnie's apartment block. It was an eerie time of the day, when the morning workers and late-night revellers met, and nobody was properly awake. She paid the taximan and he sped off, his engine breaking the tranquillity of the street. She stood looking up at her building. *Their* building, hers and Al's. And she already dreaded the emptiness. She rooted in her handbag for her keys and, once she'd found them, she took her case and headed towards the front door. She was just going to have to get used to the way things were.

As soon as Ronnie stepped into the apartment, a chill ran down her spine. It felt cold and unfamiliar. It was neat and tidy and nothing was out of place. But without Al, it would never be the same again. She dropped her suitcase and locked the door. All she wanted to do was sleep. Maybe she'd wake up and all this nastiness would be a dream. But it would be too much to hope for. With a heavy heart, she went into the kitchen and filled the kettle with water. That's when she spotted his note on the fridge.

Let me know when you're ready to talk. I haven't done anything wrong. Al x

She took the note and read it over and over. He hadn't done anything wrong? What was he thinking? In what world was it okay to sleep with your girlfriend's sister? The tone of the note was almost angry. As though he felt she'd been too harsh on him. It beggared belief.

The kettle clicked, startling her, and she took a mug from the cupboard. Her stomach rumbled, reminding her she hadn't eaten since the airport the previous day, and she suddenly had a longing for toast. Real Irish bread, lightly toasted and slathered in butter. Proper comfort food. Her mother had always said that everything always looked better when you had a strong cup of tea and a heap of toast and butter in front of you. She wished now that she'd asked the taximan to stop at a shop. She popped a teabag into the mug and poured the boiling water on top. She was happy to drink it black but opened the fridge just to see if there was any milk left from when Al was there. To her surprise, not only was there milk, but the fridge was packed full of fresh food. There was ham and cheese, tomatoes and coleslaw. There was cooked chicken and even a few of her favourite cream cakes. But the thing that stood out was the lasagne. The one she loved from her favourite Italian deli. Al must have gone out to stock up for her. To make sure she was looked after.

Tears sprang to her eyes at the thought of her boyfriend. She wished that his sleeping with Elizabeth didn't matter. She wished she could put it aside and move on. Accept Al's apology and warn him never to do anything like that again. But she couldn't. It was too hurtful and she could never look at him in the same way again. But it didn't stop her loving him. She still loved him so much it hurt. That's why it was so hard. If she could only hate him, things would be a whole lot easier. She found a fresh sliced pan in the bread bin so at least she could have her toast. She popped a couple of pieces in the toaster and checked her phone.

Amber had texted while they were in the air. She said that Daniel was fighting fit again and they couldn't wait to see her. She said to ring her as soon as she got back, no matter how early. She'd taken to getting up at six to have a half hour on her own before Daniel woke up. The calm before the storm, she called it – those blissful minutes when all was quiet and nobody looking for anything from her. Well, Amber's peace was about to be shattered because Ronnie wasn't a bit happy with her and she was going to let her know. She took her toast from the toaster and spread the slices generously with butter. After taking a large bite, she took the tea and toast into the living room and placed them on the coffee table. If she'd learned anything from the revelations of the last few days, it was not to let things fester. Deal with them and move on. If only Elizabeth had done that seven years ago. She dialled Amber's number.

'Ronnie! I was hoping you'd call. Are you just in? How was your flight? I'm dying to hear all your news.'

'Did you know about Elizabeth and Ben?' Ronnie wasn't interested in chit-chat at that moment.

'What?' Amber sounded rattled.

'I didn't ring for a catch-up, Amber. I just need to know. Did you know that Elizabeth was with Ben before I was? That they got together while I was away in Peru? She seems to think you did.'

'That was a long time ago, Ronnie. What's brought this on? And what does it matter now anyway?'

'It matters because it's the reason why Elizabeth turned her back on me. But I think you already know that.'

Amber's silence said it all.

'How could you?' said Ronnie, rage causing her voice to rise. 'How could you have known that and kept it from me? And not only that, but you encouraged me to go out with Ben. And you lied about it for all these years.'

'I'm sorry, Ronnie, I really am. I didn't intend for Elizabeth to react the way she did. I thought she'd throw a bit of a tantrum about it. That it would cause a bit of tension. But I never thought she'd start a feud that would last for so long.'

Ronnie couldn't believe what she was hearing. 'But you had the power to stop it at any stage. You could have told me why Elizabeth was so cool with me. You knew. All those years and you knew what it was all about, when I was clueless.'

'I don't know what else to say except I'm really sorry,' she said, her voice wobbling. 'Please don't be annoyed with me.'

'Well, of course I'm annoyed with you,' said Ronnie, crumbling the edges of her toast with her fingers. 'How else am I supposed to feel? Just tell me why you did it. Why did you push me towards Ben when you knew all the time he'd been with Elizabeth?'

'I was jealous,' said Amber. 'I wanted to split you up.'

Ronnie was confused. 'Me and Ben?'

'Of course not. You and Elizabeth. I wanted to drive some distance between you. You two were so tight and, even though I was your friend, I could never get close to either of you because you built a wall around yourselves.'

'No, we didn't.'

'You did, Ronnie. The three of us were best friends but really it was you and her – I was just on the outskirts.'

Ronnie bit back the tears. 'So it's really true. You purposely caused the rift between me and Elizabeth. All the times I cried to you about it. The times when I asked your advice on how to get through to her. This is unbelievable.'

'Please, Ronnie. You have to believe me that I never meant it to go that far. I didn't think Elizabeth would become so distant. And I told myself that things were changing for you two. Elizabeth was busy with her job and you weren't seeing as much of each other anyway. I convinced myself that even without my meddling, you two would have become distant.'

'How convenient,' spat Ronnie. 'I hope that made you feel better.'

'You have to admit I tried over the years to get you two talking again. I encouraged you to persevere. I asked you both on nights out to get you together. I was trying to make up for what I did.'

It was true. Amber had encouraged Ronnie to keep trying with Elizabeth, even when she wanted to give up. She'd always told her to persevere – to keep trying to break down the barriers. But that still didn't make up for what she'd done. 'Why didn't you just tell me, Amber? Just admit what you'd done and at least I could have tried to make things right.'

'I should have,' said Amber, her sniffles indicating she was crying. 'But I was scared of losing you. And as time passed, and it didn't look like you and Elizabeth would be making up any time soon, I didn't think telling you would do anyone any good.'

Ronnie sighed. She was exhausted and couldn't muster up the energy to argue for a minute longer. She hated what Amber had done but a little part of her understood it. And she couldn't lose another person in her life. Not when she'd already lost her boyfriend and sister in one fell swoop. She took a gulp of her tea and considered how much of the latest news she wanted to share. If she hadn't found out about Amber's betrayal, she would have been telling her all the gossip at this stage. Looking for her opinion, her advice.

'Ronnie, are you still there? I really am so sorry. Please don't turn your back on me. I need you in my life.'

'I need you too,' said Ronnie, her voice barely a whisper. 'I really need a friend right now.'

Amber was quick to jump in. 'Well, I'm here for you, whatever you need. Tell me what I can do. Did you and Elizabeth sort things out? I assume you did if you found out about her and Ben.'

'Oh, we sorted things out alright. We sorted a *lot* of things out. But not all for the better.'

'What do you mean?'

Ronnie paused for a moment. She was angry at Amber, but she badly needed to talk to somebody. To offload. The revelations of the last few days were weighing heavily on her and she wanted to share the burden.

'Come on, Ronnie. Tell me.'

'Well ...' she began, sitting back on the sofa and folding her two legs behind her bum. 'Elizabeth got pregnant by Ben, had an abortion and apparently it was all my fault.'

Amber gasped but Ronnie didn't give her time to comment.

'Oh, yes, and to top it all off, she put the final nail in the coffin by sleeping with Al.' Ronnie's voice caught in her throat as she said the words. 'So now not only have I lost a sister, but I've lost the great love of my life and I honestly don't know how I'm going to live without him.'

Ronnie stretched her arm out over the empty space beside her. She'd been in bed for the last two hours but sleep evaded her. Bloody jet lag. She was due in work the following day and no doubt she'd be exhausted by then. But how could she sleep with so much going on in her head? She took Al's pillow and hugged it to her. It still smelled of him and it brought tears to her eyes. But it was strangely comforting and, before long, she began to drift off.

Ronnie didn't know what was happening. The ground beneath her began to crack and suddenly there was a split. When she looked up, Al was on the other side. The crack was getting bigger and bigger and she realised there was no way she could reach him.

'Al,' she screamed, watching as he seemed to get further and further away. Then suddenly Amber was there. And so was Elizabeth. But they were all on the other side.

'Come and get me,' said Ronnie, beginning to panic. 'I can't stay here on my own.'

'Don't worry,' shouted Elizabeth. 'We'll look after the babies. They'll be safe with us.'

It was then she saw that they were all holding babies, Elizabeth, Amber and Al. Each had a baby in their arms and they were cradling them close.

'Nooooo!' screamed Ronnie, running to the edge of the crack in the earth. 'Bring my babies back.'

Suddenly they all turned their backs on her and began to walk away.

'Nooooo!' She couldn't believe what she was seeing. Surely they weren't going to leave her there? 'Come back. My babies need me.'

'Nooooo!' screamed Ronnie, sitting up in the bed. She was saturated with sweat and it took her a moment to realise she'd been dreaming. Thank God for that. But a feeling of uncertainty coursed through her and she felt unsettled. And then she remembered. Her hand went to her stomach and she thought about what she'd so desperately hoped for. What *they'd* so desperately hoped for. Her period was due in a few days but she had no signs – no cramps, no headaches. No warning that her dreams were about to be dashed. She had to ask herself if it was still her dream. Did she want to have a baby now that Al was gone? Did she really want to walk in her mother's footsteps and bring a baby up alone? But the answer was clear. Regardless of her situation, the one thing that would bring joy to her life was a baby, and she hoped and prayed that this would be the month.

Chapter 29

Elizabeth had come to a realisation about Nathan. She'd been too harsh on him. She'd been unhappy with how he was treating her but her standards were way too high. She really was lucky to have a man like him for a husband and she should be more grateful. He was the only one she could rely on. Even though they may fight or have niggly arguments about things, Nathan would always be there for her. Not like everybody else in her life.

She should never have told Ronnie about her doubts. Her sister had immediately jumped in and had advised her to leave. And, stupidly, Elizabeth had listened to her. She'd allowed herself to believe that the relationship was toxic and she should get out of it as soon as she could. But it was clear Ronnie had her own agenda and didn't have Elizabeth's best interests at heart.

The last few days had been traumatic, culminating in the flight from hell. It had been torturous, sitting on that plane, regurgitating those awful memories and trying to make Ronnie understand how she'd felt back then. Finally, everything was out in the open. She'd bared her soul and had told Ronnie everything. And it had looked like they were getting somewhere. It had been like old times. Until Ronnie had slapped her in the face with her rejection. Well, she didn't need her sister. She'd managed fine for the last six years without her, so she could continue doing the same. All she wanted now was to crawl into bed beside her husband, curl herself around his warm, sleep-filled body and allow him to look after her. Just like he always did.

She paid the taximan and took keys from her bag. The house smelled of takeaway and bleach, and she smiled at the familiarity. Compared to most other men, Nathan was a godsend in the house. He liked everything neat and tidy and cleaned more than she did. So it was a surprise to see the dirty glasses and empty takeaway containers on the kitchen counter. But she didn't care. She was home and that was all that mattered.

Torn between rushing up the stairs to her husband and feeding her growling stomach, she opted for the latter. She reckoned if her stomach was full, she could settle down for a more comfortable few hours' sleep. Her thoughts briefly flitted to Ronnie and she wondered how her sister felt going home to an empty flat. Ronnie had told Al to leave, and despite all that had happened, Elizabeth couldn't help feeling guilty about that. Still, once a day or two had passed, she was going to put it right. There'd been too many lies. Too much deceit. She and Ronnie may never get their relationship back on track but Elizabeth owed her an explanation.

She was sitting on a stool at the counter a few minutes later, tucking into her cheese and crackers, when she heard the floorboards creak upstairs. She hoped Nathan wasn't getting up for work yet because she really wanted to spend some time with him in bed. Shoving the plate away, she rushed out of the kitchen and was heading up the stairs when Nathan emerged from the bedroom looking dishevelled, his robe loosely tied around him.

'Get yourself back in there,' she said playfully. 'We have a lot of catching up to do.'

'Why are you home?' he said, looking confused. 'I thought you weren't due back until tomorrow.'

'Shows how much you listen to me.' She went and wrapped her arms around him, breathing in his smell. 'Come on. Let's go to bed for a while.'

He shut the door firmly behind him and ushered her back towards the stairs. 'I need coffee,' he said. 'You can tell me all your news downstairs.'

'Well, let me just get out of these clothes first,' she said, reaching for the door handle.'

'No!'

Elizabeth looked at her husband and fear coursed through her. 'Nathan?'

'I'm sorry. It's just the room is a mess. I haven't got around to cleaning it and I know you—'

'Let me in, Nathan.' She knew. Before she even pushed the door open, she knew what she was going to find.

'Elizabeth, wait!'

She pushed past him with a strength she didn't know she had and almost fell through the bedroom door. The woman was hunched over beside the bed with her back to the door, one leg in her trousers, her bum cheeks bursting out of her thong. She almost fell over trying to get the other leg in and it would have been laughable if it wasn't so shocking.

'Elizabeth,' said Nathan, trying to pull her back. 'Come downstairs. It's not what it looks like.'

Elizabeth laughed hysterically. 'Why do they always say that? Of course it's what it looks like. How could you? How could you do it to me?'

'Don't jump to conclusions. I know what it looks like but Gloria was just—'

'Gloria?' Elizabeth's eyes darted across to the woman, who was now fully dressed and looking as though she might faint. 'You're sleeping with Gloria?'

Nathan's mouth opened and closed but no words came out.

'I … I'd better go,' said Gloria, picking up her shoes and trying to get past where Elizabeth was standing.

But Elizabeth wasn't letting her away that easily and blocked her path. 'So, how long has this been going on? How long have you two been sneaking around behind my back? Behind Stephen's back.'

'Oh God, please don't say anything to Stephen,' said Gloria, her face panic-stricken. 'It was just once. It will never happen again.' She looked pleadingly at Nathan to back her up and Elizabeth waited to hear how he was going to get out of this one.

'Gloria, you should go. I want to speak to my wife alone.'

'But tell her, Nathan. Stephen can't know. You promised it would be okay.'

'Go,' said Nathan, his face ashen. 'This is between me and Elizabeth.'

Elizabeth glared at the other woman before standing aside to allow her to scurry downstairs. And then it was just the two of them. Her and Nathan standing in the bedroom that had been Elizabeth's sanctuary for the last few years. But as she looked around, she felt cold. Her breathing became laboured and she knew she had to get out of there. So without a word, she turned and ran downstairs and into the living room, where she threw herself onto the sofa and sobbed.

Nathan was right behind her. 'Come on, Elizabeth. Don't cry.' He kneeled down on the floor beside her. 'There's no need to be upset.'

She turned to him, enraged. 'Are you serious? I've just come home to see my husband in my bed with another woman, and there's no need to be upset?'

'I know it seems bad. It *is* bad. But there was nothing to it. It was just a stupid mistake.'

'So, I should just shrug my shoulders and say it doesn't matter?' She couldn't believe what she was hearing.

He moved her legs and sat on the sofa beside her. 'Look, I know I messed up. But you can't hold one indiscretion against me.'

'God, Nathan. Do you not think I'm entitled to be upset?' She sat up and wiped her tears in her sleeve. 'You're lucky I'm still here speaking to you at all after you've behaved like a … like a man-whore.'

'I'll let that one go for now,' he said. 'Only because you've had a shock.'

'So, how long has it been going on?' she said. 'How long have you been sleeping with that woman behind my back? Come on, then. I want to know it all.'

'There's nothing much to tell, Elizabeth. As Gloria said, it was just the once. And it won't be happening again.'

Elizabeth couldn't believe how matter-of-fact he was about the whole situation. But she wasn't going to let him get out of it that easily. 'And what do you think Stephen would say if he found out about this dalliance? I reckon you'd be saying goodbye to that promotion.'

His face turned dark and his eyes became steely. 'Don't threaten me, Elizabeth. Or you'll be sorry.'

'I … I'm not threatening you. I'm just saying.'

'Well, you need to think before you say stuff like that. Stephen is never going to know about this. Do you understand me?'

She nodded, and he continued.

'I know this situation isn't ideal, but you can't expect me to take all the blame.'

'I can't?' He was messing with her head.

'You went off and left me. I asked you not to but you didn't listen. You didn't even consider that I might have needed you. I thought our relationship was important to you.'

'It was,' she said. 'It is.'

'I was upset,' he continued. 'I thought you didn't love me. I thought that you didn't care what I thought.'

'But that's crazy, Nathan. You know I love you. Going to New York was something I had to do. And it was only for a week. Why did you have to go and sleep with her? Gloria, of all people!'

His shoulders sagged and he looked remorseful. 'It was a moment of weakness. She called into the office yesterday to collect some papers. Stephen was away on business and you weren't here. We got talking. I felt lonely and so did she. I shouldn't have let it happen. But I'm only human. We all make mistakes.'

Elizabeth wasn't sure how to feel. She was gutted – and disgusted. How could she ever sleep in her own bed again knowing Nathan and Gloria had been there together? How could she ever trust him again? But on the other hand, he was right. She'd left him without any consideration for his feelings. She'd gone thousands of miles away when he hadn't wanted her to and left him feeling sad and vulnerable. Maybe she had to take some of the blame. She looked at his handsome face, his eyes wide, begging for her to understand.

'Come on, Elizabeth. You know I'm right. We've both made mistakes. Let's just try and sort things out.'

She let out a long sigh and looked at him. 'Okay. Let's try and put this behind us. I'm not saying I can forgive you straight away but if you're telling me it was a once-off – that you love me and want to be with me – then I'll try and accept that.'

'Good girl,' he said, reaching over and pulling her into his arms. 'Because I know you, Elizabeth. And you need me. We need each other.'

She nodded and accepted his hug. What else was she going to do? He was right – she needed him. She had nobody else. And as he said, he was only human. It wasn't as though she hadn't made mistakes herself. Maybe this was punishment for some of hers.

'Come on,' he said, standing up and pulling her up with him. 'Let's go to bed.'

A picture of him and Gloria making mad, passionate love in her bed sprung to her mind and she shook her head. 'You go on up. I'm going to potter around here for a bit and not let the jet lag take a hold of me. I'll sleep better tonight if I don't sleep now.'

'Are you sure that's all it is?' He watched her carefully.

'Of course,' she said, trying to inject some levity into her tone. 'You go and sleep for a while and I'll see you when you get up.'

She watched him disappear through the living room door before flopping back down onto the sofa. If only she didn't love him so much. If only she didn't need him. He'd told her on many occasions that nobody would ever love her like he did. That nobody would ever look after her and care for her like he did. And he was probably right. She needed to try and forget about this morning and move on. But somewhere in the back of her brain was her sister's voice: *'He's manipulating you, Elizabeth. Don't put up with it. He'll brainwash you until you have no opinions of your own. Leave him now before it's too late.'*

The cemetery was quiet except for a handful of people doing a guided tour. Elizabeth always thought it strange that such a thing would have any appeal, but apparently the Glasnevin Cemetery tour was one of the highlights of things to do in Dublin. Her walk to the grave was a short one, thanks to her mother buying a plot some years ago close to the gate. The girls had thought it morbid at the time, that she was thinking about her death, but they were thankful now that it was an accessible grave in a lovely spot, and they always made sure it was topped up with fresh flowers.

She was surprised to see that the grave was looking so neat and tidy, considering the girls hadn't been around for over a week. The flowers and potted plants were wonderfully colourful and she placed her own yellow rose arrangement down amongst them. Closing her eyes, she tried to visualise her mum. She saw her sitting at her desk, her no-nonsense, short, grey, spiky hair meticulous, her face poised in concentration. But then a smile, as Elizabeth entered the room. She always made time. No matter how busy she was. She'd never turn her daughters away or push them aside. She'd been the one staple in Elizabeth's life and, since she'd left them, her world had fallen apart.

'What am I going to do, Mum?' she whispered, as she sat on her hunkers, her fingers running over the engraving on the headstone.

'Everything is such a mess. I wish you were here to tell me how to make things right.'

A breeze rose suddenly in the air and whipped across her face. It was like a kiss from her mum. It startled her but she felt calm. She knew then that her mum was with her, looking after her and guiding her in the right direction. She had to believe that, just as she had to believe everything was going to be okay. She wouldn't let herself fall further and further into an abyss. She closed her eyes and felt the breeze again. And she knew what she had to do.

Chapter 30

'You girls will be the death of me,' said Frank, scratching his grey beard. 'I thought this trip would have brought you closer together, not ripped you completely apart. What on earth happened?'

Ronnie sipped her cappuccino, unsure how much she wanted to say. Frank had rung the previous evening to ask her to lunch and she'd jumped at the chance of a friendly ear. It was two days since she'd arrived home and she hadn't spoken to a single soul. Amber had rung a few times but she hadn't taken any of her calls. She needed time – time to get her head straight, time to heal. She longed to hear Al's voice, but he hadn't made any attempt to contact her since she got back. She wanted to talk to Frank about it all, but something about how he looked made her reluctant to burden him. He seemed vulnerable, sad. And Ronnie didn't want to add to his troubles.

'So, tell me,' he continued. 'When we last spoke, I got the impression you two were getting on well and now you're telling me you're not speaking at all?'

'It's a long story, Frank. And I really don't want to get into it all now. Suffice it to say, you won't be getting us in a room together anytime soon.'

He shook his head. 'I'm really sorry to hear that. I had hoped to talk to you both about a few things. I was going to pencil in something for next week.'

'What few things?' asked Ronnie, alarmed. 'Can't you just tell me now?'

'I'd rather not,' he said, not meeting her eye. And then he looked at her and smiled. 'I'm under instructions, you see.'

Ronnie smiled too. 'Mum!'

'Of course. And you know she'd strike me down if I didn't follow her wishes.'

'Is it about Oliver? Have you got more information? I still can't believe we went all the way to New York, and he's been back here in Ireland all the time.'

'Well, if I can get you two in a room together for ten minutes, we can have a proper chat about things.'

Ronnie was about to object but he got in first. 'You don't even have to talk to each other. I'll do all the talking.'

'Okay,' sighed Ronnie. 'Now can we talk about something else, please?'

He sighed. 'Okay. But I still think you should—'

'Frank!'

'Okay, okay. Not another word. For now. Except one more thing.'

Ronnie rolled her eyes.

'It's just that I haven't been able to reach Elizabeth,' he said. 'I've rung her a few times and the call just goes to voicemail. I've also tried her in work and her secretary just says she's not available. I know you don't want to talk about her, but is there anything in particular I should know? Is there any reason she's avoiding me?'

Ronnie shook her head. 'I'd say she's just busy catching up on work stuff. You know what she's like. I'm sure she'll be in touch over the weekend.'

'I'll try her again later,' he said. 'I wouldn't want her to think I'm taking sides or anything.'

'I'm sure she wouldn't,' said Ronnie. Although she knew that it was exactly the sort of thing Elizabeth would think. But she didn't want to waste another moment talking about her sister so she swiftly changed the subject. 'How are you, anyway, Frank? You said you were dealing with some personal stuff while we were away. Is there anything I can do?'

'No, it's fine. But thanks.' He looked down at his cup and Ronnie could see a real sadness in his face.

'Is it Mum?' she said. 'I know you loved her and I'm sure you miss her just as much as we do.'

He nodded. 'It's that, amongst other things. Sometimes I forget she's gone. First thing in the morning when I wake up, she springs to my mind and I have to remember all over again that she's not here any more.'

Ronnie reached over and rubbed his hand awkwardly. 'I know how that feels. I do it all the time. And I know we're no replacement, but you have us now, me and Elizabeth. We can be your family, if you let us.'

'Thanks,' he said, his voice choked, and Ronnie could see he had tears in his eyes. He really had loved Belinda so much.

'It must have been a bit of a shock for you to hear about Skye too,' said Ronnie. 'I forgot that you knew her when I blurted it out. I could have kicked myself. Did you know her well?'

'Fairly well. And yes, it was a shock. It's made me feel old. It's strange when people your own age are beginning to die off. It makes you wonder when it's going to be your turn.'

'Don't say that, Frank. You're young and healthy. You've got plenty of years left in you.'

'Let's hope so,' he said. 'Because I have a lot of plans for the coming years and I'd be very annoyed if I popped my clogs before I had a chance to fulfil them.'

He had a twinkle in his eye and Ronnie laughed. 'On that note,' she said, 'I'm going to head off. I have a few things to do around town before I go home. I'll give you a ring next week.'

They both stood up and Frank hugged her. 'Say hello to Al for me,' he said. 'I bet he's glad to have you home.'

Ronnie didn't dare speak because she immediately felt choked up. She just nodded before walking outside into the cold March air. It was a typical Saturday afternoon in town with shoppers dashing about, keen to find the next bargain, and buskers vying for their attention. Usually the atmosphere on Grafton Street would lift her spirits, but not today. She couldn't stop thinking about Al. She was missing him like crazy. She kept going over and over things in her head but nothing was making sense. It was so out of character for Al to have slept with her sister. He just wasn't like that. It went against everything he believed in. And he'd also said in his note that he'd done nothing wrong. Maybe she should give him a chance to tell his side of the story. It couldn't hurt just to hear him out.

But there was something else niggling at her as she walked towards her bus stop on Dawson Street – something that made her walk past her own stop and on to the next. Minutes later she was on a bus, but she wasn't heading home. Being a twin was a strange thing. She'd sworn she'd never speak to Elizabeth again. She hated her and what she'd done. But she had a feeling that something was wrong. That Elizabeth was in some sort of trouble. And despite everything, she couldn't turn her back on her. As the bus sped along towards Castleknock, Ronnie wondered how her life had become so complicated.

'Ronnie!' Nathan stood at the door, a look of confusion on his face. 'What do you want?'

She was taken aback by his tone. 'To see Elizabeth. Is she here?'

'Does it look like it?' He pointed to the driveway, where his car sat alone.

'I didn't even notice,' she said. 'What time will she be back? Would you mind if I waited? Because there isn't another bus until—'

'I see you two are as close as ever,' he said, a sneer creeping across his face.

'I … I don't understand.' Ronnie was beginning to feel uncomfortable and she wondered how Elizabeth could love somebody like Nathan.

'Elizabeth doesn't live here any more so I can't help you.' He began to close the door but Ronnie stopped it with her hand.

'What do you mean she doesn't live here?'

'Can't you work it out? She's gone, Ronnie. She made a decision that she didn't want to be married any more so the stupid bitch left me.'

She was torn between surprise and satisfaction. From what Elizabeth had told her about Nathan and how he behaved, Ronnie was glad she'd left him. She knew herself how difficult it was to walk away from a relationship but her sister had done the right thing.

'So, can I go back in now?' Nathan said sarcastically. 'Or would you like more of the details?'

'Just tell me where she is,' said Ronnie, looking at him in disgust.

He shrugged. 'I couldn't tell you.'

'Couldn't or wouldn't?'

'You think you're such a smartass, Ronnie, don't you? I don't know where my wife is. Funnily enough, leaving a forwarding address wasn't top of her priority list.'

A cold chill ran down Ronnie's spine. 'If you've done anything to hurt her …'

'Oh, for God's sake! This isn't an episode of *Criminal Minds*. We argued, she left, end of story. I don't know where she is and, right now, I don't care.'

Suddenly Ronnie felt protective of her sister and was filled with hatred for the man standing in front of her. 'Okay, I'm going.' She leaned in so that her face was almost touching his. 'But if you ever call my sister a bitch again, I won't smash your face in, but I know somebody who'll do it for me.'

He paled, and Ronnie took great satisfaction in seeing his expression change. 'Get out of here,' he said, but his voice was shaky.

'Gladly,' she said, turning to walk away, but not before giving him a death stare.

She heard the front door slam closed as she walked down the driveway and she thought she was going to faint. She hated confrontations and that one had been particularly scary. She wasn't sure where she'd got the strength from but she just knew she had to stand up to that horrible man. How had Elizabeth put up with him for the last few years? He'd really had everyone fooled with his 'nice-guy' act. But she'd seen through him now and she was relieved her sister had too.

Still shaking as she arrived at the bus stop, she leaned against the wall to try and calm herself. But as she began to re-play the day's events in her head, her anxiety became worse. Frank had said that he couldn't get in touch with Elizabeth, that he'd rung her a number of times and it had just gone to voicemail. What if Nathan had done something to her? What if he'd hurt her? Maybe she should call the police and let them talk to him. Or maybe she was letting her imagination run wild. She took her phone out of her pocket and dialled a number. And waited.

Chapter 31

'Come in,' said Elizabeth, opening her hotel room door to allow Ronnie in. 'I was surprised to hear from you.'

Ronnie stepped inside and hugged her sister. 'I'm so glad you're okay. I was worried.'

Elizabeth was confused by the uncharacteristic gesture of affection. 'Why were you worried?'

'I spoke to Nathan.'

'I see.' There were four leather chairs surrounding a small round table and Elizabeth sat down on one, indicating for Ronnie to do the same. 'Did you go around to the house?'

'Yes,' said Ronnie, sitting down and watching Elizabeth carefully. 'I wanted to speak to you.'

'And what did he say? Did he tell you what happened?'

Ronnie shook her head. 'He just said you left him. He didn't elaborate and, to be honest, I wasn't sticking around to find out any more. I found him really intimidating.'

Elizabeth began to pluck some imaginary fluff from her trousers. It was just two days since they'd last seen each other. Since they'd said their goodbyes at the airport and Ronnie had told her that she never wanted to see her again. So why was she here? Why did she care?

'I know I said I didn't want to see you again,' said Ronnie, reading her mind. 'But I never wanted to see you in danger. And I couldn't help thinking that while you were with Nathan you weren't safe.'

'Well, you were right,' said Elizabeth, her voice barely a whisper. 'If I'd stayed with Nathan, I would have been in danger.'

Ronnie looked at her. 'I knew it. What did he do? Did he hurt you? You shouldn't be afraid of going to the police. I can help you.'

'Relax, Ronnie. I was in danger of being an idiot, that's all.'

'So he didn't hurt you?' said Ronnie, confusion written all over her face. 'He didn't hit you or abuse you?'

'Physically, no. But emotionally, completely.'

'Go on,' said Ronnie, sitting back in the chair. 'Tell me what happened.'

'I will, but not yet.'

'Why?'

'Before we say any more,' said Elizabeth, standing up, 'I need to talk to you about Al and me.'

Ronnie shook her head. 'Absolutely not. I really don't want to discuss Al with you at all.'

'But I need to explain. To tell you what happened.'

Ronnie stood up and headed for the door. 'I knew this was a mistake. I'm glad you're okay and that you've left that horrible man, but I'm not here to compare notes about my boyfriend.'

'Ronnie, please …'

'No, Elizabeth,' she said, her hand on the doorknob. 'I don't want to hear the details and I don't want to discuss Al with you now or ever.'

'I didn't sleep with him!'

Ronnie turned and looked at her. 'What?'

'I said I didn't sleep with him.'

'But you did. You said. And Al admitted it.'

Elizabeth shook her head. 'Please, Ronnie. Come back in and sit down. I'll tell you everything.'

'But I didn't come here for—'

'Just sit down and listen. I've picked up the phone loads of times over the last two days to talk to you about this. But then I'd chicken out, knowing how annoyed you were. You need to know this so just sit down and listen.'

Ronnie reluctantly did what she was told and waited for Elizabeth to continue.

'The night that it happened, I—'

'So it *did* happen?' said Ronnie, shaking her head.

'God, you're so impatient. Just hear me out. On the night in question, I went over to your flat.'

'Why did you go over there?' said Ronnie. 'How did you know he was alone?'

'I didn't. That's just the point. I went over to see you. To talk to you about Mum. She was upset about us – about the tension between us. And she really shouldn't have had to deal with that as well as coping with the cancer. She never said it was affecting her but I knew. I wanted to talk to you about us trying harder. At least in front of her.'

'And you found Al there alone. How convenient.'

'I know how it looks, Ronnie. But I didn't go over there with an ulterior motive. I swear I didn't know you were away.'

'But?'

'But then Al was so nice. He asked me in and he listened. He was everything Nathan wasn't and I got drawn in to the situation.'

'Seriously, Elizabeth? So it was *Al* who seduced *you*? He sucked you in and you just couldn't resist.'

Ronnie wasn't making it easy and Elizabeth couldn't blame her. 'No, that's not what I meant. I meant that I felt drawn to Al because of how he was with me. Kind and sympathetic, a good listener. And then I thought about you taking Ben away from me and how I'd felt back then. And all those awful memories of the abortion and the guilt and the absolute sadness came flooding back to me.'

She glanced over at Ronnie, who had her head in her hands, her elbows resting on the table. She looked broken and Elizabeth wanted to cry. She'd made such a mess of everything. But there were going to be no more tears. She'd walked out on Nathan and that had been one of the hardest things she'd ever done. And now she was going to fix things between her and Ronnie. She was going to make her sister listen and understand. And if she had to spend the next year or more trying to make it up to her, well, that's what she'd do.

'So I made a move on him,' she continued, mortified at the memory. 'I don't know what came over me but we were sitting side by side on the sofa and I reached over suddenly to kiss him. He jumped in fright; I had a glass of red wine in my hand and it spilled all down the front of his T-shirt.'

'The grey silk one,' said Ronnie, her voice barely a whisper. 'I noticed the stain when I was ironing and he said he'd spilled wine.'

Elizabeth nodded. 'It was a full glass of wine and completely saturated him so he whipped the top off straight away.'

'And that's how you saw the tattoo.' Ronnie was beginning to put it all together and Elizabeth was relieved.

'Yes. Well, it's not exactly subtle, is it? I caught a glance of it, then Al disappeared and returned seconds later with a different top on.'

'And then?'

'And then everything was awkward,' said Elizabeth, not daring to look at Ronnie. 'Awkward and horrible. I was mortified. I kept apologising to him and he kept assuring me it was okay. But it wasn't okay. I felt like an idiot and I just wanted to get out of there.'

Ronnie was beginning to look more interested. 'And did you? Did you leave then?'

'I was out of there like a bat out of hell,' said Elizabeth, cringing at the memory. 'Poor Al. He was trying to make me feel better about the whole thing but it was just making me feel worse. I asked him not to tell you about it and he said there was nothing to tell. Oh God, it was so humiliating. I'm so sorry, Ronnie, I really am.'

'But what about Nathan, Elizabeth? What were you thinking? And I still can't get my head around the fact you lied about it.'

'Looking back on it now, I suppose I was craving what Nathan wasn't giving me. I just wanted to be loved. To be wanted.' She looked at Ronnie with tears in her eyes. 'And I knew it was going to hurt you so that was an added bonus.'

Ronnie shook her head and her words were barely a whisper. 'So you didn't have sex with Al?'

'I've just told you everything that happened. Every single detail. I swear, Ronnie. That's all that happened.'

But Ronnie still didn't look happy. 'Then why,' she said, shaking her head, 'did Al not tell me that? Why did he let me believe what you said? It doesn't make sense.'

'I don't know,' said Elizabeth. 'Did you give him a chance to explain?'

'Well, no, I suppose I didn't. But he could have tried harder to make me listen. I've been home two days now and he hasn't tried to get in touch.'

'God, Ronnie, you're such an idiot!'

'Excuse me?' Ronnie glared at her.

'Al adores you. Do you realise that? Do you know how much he idolises you? Before I … before the incident, all he could talk about was you. He asked me if I could try harder with you because he wanted you to be happy. He loves you, you big idiot. And I'd give anything to be loved like that.'

Ronnie began to cry and Elizabeth was quick to rush to her side and put her arms around her. 'I'm so sorry for all the hurt I've caused, Ronnie. I want to make up for it now. I want to be your sister again – if you'll let me. Can you find it in your heart to forgive me?'

'We've both been idiots,' said Ronnie, hugging Elizabeth back. 'And you've been hurt too – badly. I … I can't imagine the pain you went through with the baby and everything.'

Elizabeth bit back the tears. 'That's all in the past now. Let's try and move forward. That is, if you want to?'

'I do,' said Ronnie. 'That's all I've ever wanted. I've missed you so much.'

'I think this calls for a celebration.' Elizabeth jumped up and grabbed the room service menu. 'How about we order lunch and have a proper chat. How does that sound?'

Ronnie wiped her eyes. 'It sounds perfect to me. I had a big lunch earlier but I'm starving again.'

Elizabeth watched as her sister scanned the menu and her heart lifted a little. She was thrilled. She hadn't expected that their chat would go quite so well. Having her sister back meant so much to her. But it was bittersweet, because she'd also just lost the man she thought she'd be spending the rest of her life with.

'So, what do you think about finding Oliver now?' said Ronnie, wiping up her remaining maple syrup with the last piece of pancake. 'Have you thought any more about looking for him over here?'

Elizabeth shook her head. 'To be honest, I haven't had a chance to think about it at all. I've had other things on my mind.'

'Of course. I haven't even asked you what happened with you and Nathan. What made you leave in the end?'

'Well,' said Elizabeth, remembering the scene, 'after you and I argued on the plane, I decided to give him another chance. To talk to him and try and make him see how he'd been treating me. I loved him, Ronnie. I still do.'

'So, what happened? Did he not respond well?'

'My plans for a calm and adult conversation went out the window when I came home to find him in bed with his boss's wife!'

Ronnie gasped. 'No! Are you serious?'

'Deadly serious,' said Elizabeth. 'She scurried off with her tail between her legs and he tried to justify it by telling me I shouldn't have gone to New York.'

'Bastard!'

'Yep! And I almost allowed him to talk me around. He kept telling me how much he loved me and how he'd missed me. He said that it was just a once-off and it would never happen again.'

'And what did you say?'

'I accepted what he said. I didn't want it to be over between us. I just wanted to forget I ever walked in on them and move on.'

Ronnie looked puzzled. 'Then how did you end up here? What made you walk out in the end?'

'Mum.'

'What do you mean?'

Elizabeth smiled at the memory. 'I went to see her at the cemetery, to talk to her. And I felt her, Ronnie, I really felt her presence. I know it sounds daft but she was right there with me, assuring me, comforting me. I knew right there at her graveside that I needed to leave Nathan. It was as though she'd whispered to me, told me what I needed to do. So I just went home, packed a case and left.'

'I'm so proud of you,' said Ronnie, reaching across and squeezing her hand. 'And I know Mum is looking down too, feeling proud. It must have been a difficult thing for you to do.'

'It was. But it was the right thing. It's going to take me some time to get over him but I will. I have you now to help me through it. At least I hope I do?' She looked at Ronnie for confirmation.

Ronnie began to laugh suddenly. 'I can just picture her,' she giggled.

'Who?' said Elizabeth, confused by the change in conversation.

'Mum. I can just picture her shaking her head and saying, *"Well, it's about time those two idiots got their act together!"'*

Elizabeth laughed at that. 'Poor Mum. She tried so hard to get us back together again. And she left poor Frank with the job after she died.'

'Well, we should put him out of his misery as soon as possible,' said Ronnie. 'And I think we really need to keep an eye on him. I met him earlier today and he's not himself. He was really good to Mum so I think we owe it to her to make sure he's okay.'

Elizabeth nodded. 'I feel bad now that I've been ignoring his calls. I'll give him a ring later and tell him the good news.'

'And in answer to your earlier question,' said Ronnie, her eyes twinkling, 'yes, you have me to help you through things. You'll always have me, Izzy. You and me against the world. Just like it always used to be.'

Elizabeth pushed Ronnie over in the bed so she could squeeze in beside her. Even though they were teenagers now, they still loved to sleep in the same bed sometimes.

'Another nightmare?' said Ronnie, moving over to make room for her sister. 'What was it this time?'

Elizabeth snuggled down into the duvet. 'I can't really remember. It just felt like somebody was chasing me. I woke up feeling terrified.'

'Poor you,' said Ronnie. 'Well, you're safe now. There's no need to be afraid.'

'Thanks, sis.'

'No problem, Izzy. You'll always have me. It's you and me against the world.'

Chapter 32

The rain was pelting down on Ronnie but she didn't care. She was just steps away from home and hopefully minutes away from being reunited with Al. She'd rung him before she left Elizabeth's hotel to ask him to meet her back at the flat and he'd immediately agreed. She knew she had a lot of grovelling to do but she was willing to do anything to get things back on track with him again. But he hadn't been completely blameless either. He should have told her about the incident with Elizabeth. Maybe he'd thought he was doing the right thing but keeping secrets like that was never good.

Elizabeth had insisted on driving her home but Ronnie had asked to be dropped at the nearby shops, claiming she needed to pick up a few things. It was only partially true but she wasn't ready to talk to Elizabeth about it yet. She'd been sure right from the moment she and Al had made love on Valentine's night that something was different. She'd felt different. And she'd remained positive that this month was going to be the one. The paper bag holding the precious pregnancy test rustled in her handbag as she rooted for her keys and she felt overwhelmed with excitement.

She'd been half tempted to go into the public toilets in the shopping centre to do the test but it wouldn't be a very romantic way of finding out she was pregnant for the first time. So she was hoping that the conversation with Al would go well and then they could do the test together. It would be wonderful to see the result with Al by her side so they'd have that moment to cherish forever.

As soon as she entered the lift that would take her to her third-floor apartment, she knew he was home. The distinctive, warm, masculine scent of his Jean Paul Gaultier aftershave hung in the air, indicating he'd just got there before her. She breathed in the smell and it filled her with longing. As she stepped inside the flat, she prayed that they could sort everything out – that Al still loved her. Because he was everything to her and she knew now that she couldn't live without him.

The TV was blaring and he obviously didn't hear her come in. Her heart felt like it would overflow with love as she watched his long limbs stretch over the end of the sofa, his head thrown back in laughter at whatever he was watching. How could she ever have doubted him? He'd never shown her anything but dedication and love. How could she ever have thought he'd been unfaithful?

'Hi, love,' she said, kicking off her shoes and going to sit beside him. 'Thanks for coming over.'

'Well, of course I was going to come over,' he said, sitting up to make space for her on the sofa. 'I told you to let me know whenever you were ready to talk.'

'I'm so sorry, Al. I should never have doubted you. I can't believe I was so quick to believe what Elizabeth said.'

'So she's told you, then? She's told you what really happened?'

Ronnie nodded. 'Just today. She was so convincing, Al. Honestly, she completely sucked me into her lies. She knew about the tattoo on your chest and everything, so what was I supposed to think?'

'Ronnie, you were supposed to think that I would never, ever do anything like that to you. You were supposed to know that I would never hurt you. Your problem is that you just didn't think at all. You were just ready to believe whatever came out of her mouth.'

Ronnie was taken aback. She'd imagined falling into Al's arms. She'd thought that he'd dismiss what had happened as a glitch and they could move forward with their lives, with their plans. But he seemed really angry and she wasn't sure how to handle it.

'How many times did I sit and listen to you moaning about Elizabeth?' he continued. 'About how she'd changed and how you felt so distant from her. It's me who's been there for you over the last few years when you've cried about your relationship with her and it's me who's picked up the pieces when you felt heartbroken.'

'I know, Al. But she just—'

'I'm sure she was convincing in whatever she told you. I'm sure she made the whole thing sound believable. But you just took her word and didn't even give me the chance to reply? What's that all about, Ronnie? Where did the trust go?'

Ronnie was in tears. 'It's not gone anywhere. I trust you completely. She just messed with my head. And we were so far away. I made a mistake. Please don't be angry with me.'

Al stood up and began to pace back and forth. 'It feels like such a betrayal, Ronnie. Have you any idea what I've been through these last few days? Knowing you thought so little of me? So many times I wanted to pick up the phone and explain. But I was too hurt.'

'I was stupid,' said Ronnie, tears flowing freely down her face. 'There was just so much going on. I was trying to get my relationship with Elizabeth back on track, trying to find my father and thinking of my mother at the same time. Everything just got so intense.'

'I can understand that,' he said, a little more gently. 'I know how weird you felt about going away with Elizabeth and what a big deal it was to look for your father. But I'm the one person who's stood beside you. Comforted you, supported you. When others turned their backs on you, I was always there.'

'You've always been my rock, Al.' She was trying valiantly to stop the tears but they just kept coming. 'All I can say is I'm sorry. But why did you let me continue to think you two had slept together? Why did you let me believe her lies?'

'Are you serious, Ronnie? Do you remember the conversation we had when you rang to ask me about it? You specifically asked if Elizabeth had called to the apartment and if something had happened. I'd barely got a word out of my mouth and you hung up. I tried ringing you about a hundred times straight after and you didn't answer any of my calls.'

Hearing him tell it like that, she felt ridiculous. Why had she just not let him explain?

'So then,' he continued, 'I got stubborn. I was mad as hell at you. Our relationship has been the most wonderful thing that's ever happened to me. And I thought it was the same for you.'

'It was,' she pleaded. 'It is. Can we just try to get past this, please? I just want things back the way they were. I love you, Al. You mean everything to me.'

He had his back to her and was leaning his two hands against the mantelpiece. Terror overcame her then. What if he didn't want her back? What if he felt the trust was gone and he couldn't live with that?

'Al, please say something.' She stood up and went to him, tentatively putting a hand on his shoulder. 'Al? Please don't tell me it's over.'

He swung around suddenly. 'Over? What on earth are you talking about? Of course it's not over.'

'But I thought … you were saying …' She was at a loss for words.

'I'm mad at you, Ronnie. But I love you to bits. Just because we've had a big argument, it doesn't mean we're over. Did you honestly think I'd break up with you because of this? Because of a misunderstanding?'

'I … I don't know.' Her head was in a spin.

'I think we need to argue more often – just to get you used to how it works.' A smile crept over his face. 'You're such an idiot. But you're my idiot and I'm never, ever letting you go.'

She threw her arms around him and buried her head in his chest. 'I love you so much, Al. I'm so sorry for everything.'

He gently tilted her chin up to him and kissed her long and softly on the lips. 'You know what's brilliant about having arguments like this?'

'Well, I'm not sure there's anything brilliant about it at all. But go on.'

'The making up.' He kissed her again before taking her hand and leading her towards the bedroom.

She didn't need persuasion. She couldn't think of anything nicer than lying in Al's arms, knowing that he loved her and wanted to be with her for the rest of his life. Everything was falling into place.

She had her sister back, Al had come home and hopefully she'd soon become a mother. All she needed now was to find her father, the missing piece of the puzzle, and her life would be complete.

'So, tell me again,' said Ronnie, resting her head on Al's chest. 'Why did you think it was such a good idea not to tell me about Elizabeth trying to seduce you?'

'Well, for starters, she didn't really try to seduce me. She just had an awkward moment. She spilled her wine and that was the end of it.'

'But if she hadn't spilled her wine, what would have happened?'

Al moved Ronnie's head back onto the pillow and turned on his side so he could look at her. 'Nothing would have happened. She would have realised what she was doing and would have been mortified.'

'But let's say she hadn't stopped. What would you have done?'

'Are you seriously asking me that?' said Al. 'I would have politely moved away and told her that she was making a mistake. That I loved *you* and wasn't interested in anybody else.'

'That's what I wanted to hear,' said Ronnie, snuggling down into the arch of his arm. 'But you still haven't said – why didn't you just tell me about it in the first place?'

Al sighed. 'I didn't think it was something you needed to know. You and Elizabeth were in such a bad place, it would have just made things so much worse. And besides, you had enough stresses going on with your mum being so sick, and trying to get pregnant.'

'Oh God, I almost forgot!' Ronnie jumped up from the bed and began to search for her underwear.

'What?' said Al, producing her pants from beneath the covers. 'Where are you going?'

'Just give me a minute.' She took her dressing gown from the back of the door and slipped it on before heading out to the living room. She found her handbag where she'd left it on the floor, and reached in to find the pharmacy bag. But just as she bent over, dizziness overcame her and she had to lean against the coffee table for support. After a moment of fuzziness, she made it to the kitchen, where she poured herself a glass of water. And then she felt the all-too-familiar feeling in her stomach. It was like somebody pulling her from the inside out.

'Nooooo!' she said, in a low whisper. 'Please don't let this be happening.'

She rushed into the bathroom to check and, sure enough, the bleeding had started. And not just a bit of spotting. It flowed like a torrent of rage out of her and she sat on the toilet and cried.

'Are you okay in there?' came Al's voice from outside the door. 'Are you crying?'

'I'm fine,' she managed. 'Just give me a minute.'

She sorted herself out and looked in the mirror. She was a mess. Her mascara was streaked down her cheeks and her eyes were puffy and red. It was a reflection of how she felt inside. All messed up and desperately sad. She spotted the pharmacy bag on the floor, where she'd discarded it in her rush, and kicked it against the wall. It wasn't fair. It just wasn't bloody fair.

A tapping at the door startled her and the sound of Al's voice was gentle and kind. 'Is it what I think it is, Ronnie? Come on out, love. It will be okay.'

She opened the door and fell into his arms, sobbing. 'When will it be okay, Al? When will I manage to get pregnant? What's wrong with me?'

'Come on,' he said, leading her into the living room and down onto the sofa. 'It's been a very upsetting month so maybe when everything settles down …'.

She just nodded and snuggled into him. The fact was, she was losing faith in ever getting pregnant. It was her thirty-first birthday in three weeks and she'd really hoped to have something more to celebrate than being a year older. She'd had it all planned in her head. She was going to keep it just between herself and Al until her birthday and then announce it on the day. It would have been the most special birthday ever. And now it would just be the saddest.

Al was rubbing her hair and she began to drift off. She hadn't slept properly since they'd got back from New York and the exhaustion was finally catching up with her. But thoughts were swirling around in her head, not allowing her mind to properly relax. Because so many things had happened in the last few days, Ronnie hadn't given a lot of thought to what her sister had gone through when she'd fallen pregnant. How confused she must have been. How upset to know that the father of her baby didn't want to be with her. Her head must have been a complete mess, to take the step of going to England for an abortion. And she'd had nobody – nobody to talk to, to advise her, to support her. Ronnie would have had a little niece or nephew if she'd gone through with the pregnancy. He or she would be six years old now. It was too painful to even contemplate.

'Are you still awake?' said Al, breaking into her thoughts.

Ronnie sat up and rubbed her eyes. 'Unfortunately, yes.'

'Come on.'

'What? Where?'

He took her hand and pulled her up from the sofa. 'We need to get out and not allow ourselves to wallow.'

'No, Al, I don't feel like—'

'I'm not taking no for an answer,' he said, kissing her lightly on the top of her head. 'Now go and get ready because we're going to do something fun.'

'What have you in mind?' she said, as he pushed her towards the bathroom. 'Because I'm really not in a fun sort of mood.'

'You just concentrate on getting ready and I'll tell you the plan when we're on the way. Let's just say it's something to show you how committed I am to you. I love you, Ronnie. And I want to be with you for the rest of my life.'

She didn't ask again but headed into the bathroom to shower. A wave of excitement overcame her and she wondered what Al had planned. Neither of them was a traditionalist and had never really been interested in the whole marriage thing. But maybe that was about to change. Her heart felt a little less heavy as she turned the shower on full power. Before she stepped in, she spotted the pharmacy bag on the floor, where she'd kicked it earlier. But she didn't cry. She picked it up and placed it in the cabinet under the sink. Next month would be the one. She was sure of it.

Chapter 33

Elizabeth looked out the window at the hordes of people dashing about, some with heads down trying to avoid the snow that was falling thick and fast, others looking to the sky and embracing the experience. It was typical March weather. Yesterday had been hot and humid and she'd worn nothing over her short-sleeved dress all day. But today the temperatures were below zero and even with the heat on full blast in her office, she couldn't warm up. But she was glad to be back at work – back on familiar territory. A place where she knew what she was doing. Somewhere she felt in control.

'Elizabeth,' said Amanda, tapping on her door as she walked in. 'It's Nathan again. What should I tell him this time?'

Elizabeth sighed. It was a week since she'd come home and found her husband in bed with another woman. And she felt every bit as disgusted as she had that first day. He'd rung her constantly on her mobile and she'd ignored every single call. But now he was ringing her workplace, insisting Amanda put him through to her. This was the fourth call already that day and Elizabeth was running out of patience, as well as excuses.

'Sorry about this, Amanda. You can just put him through this time.' She'd given Amanda a brief outline of what had happened and, in fairness to the young assistant, she'd been very supportive.

Amanda disappeared back out to her desk and, within seconds, she'd put the call through to Elizabeth's phone. Elizabeth allowed it to ring several times before she picked up.

'Hi, Nathan. Hold on a moment, please.'

She tapped the red button, buying her some time, aware that he hated the sound of 'Opus Number 1' playing in his ear. She kept meaning to change the monotonous on-hold music but she just hadn't got around to it yet. Her inner child whooped at the thought of Nathan being irritated with the sound and she didn't hurry to put him out of his misery. But she knew she'd have to talk to him sometime. She couldn't keep avoiding his calls. And besides, that house was half hers and it didn't seem right that she'd left him with everything, while she was living out of a hotel room. She sighed and picked up the phone.

'What do you want, Nathan?'

'Elizabeth, please don't be like that. I've been trying to get you all week.'

'I know.'

'Look,' he said, and she could hear the angst in his voice, 'I know you've had a little shock. But just come home and we can talk about it.'

'Are you serious? A little shock? Is that what you call me walking in on you and your … your fancy-woman having sex in our bed?' She couldn't believe how he was making it seem so insignificant.

'Don't exaggerate, Elizabeth. You didn't walk in on us.'

'I'm not having this conversation with you,' she said, her blood boiling. 'Not until you're ready to own what you did. Whether or whether not I actually saw you doing the deed is neither here nor there.'

'Okay, okay. I'm sorry. I know I messed up. But I love you, sweetheart. And I'm completely lost without you. Please come home.'

She didn't trust herself to say anything.

'Come on, love,' he continued. 'I'll spend the rest of my life making it up to you. Gloria is nothing to me. It was a lapse in judgement. It shouldn't have happened and it will never, ever happen again.'

Her resolve was beginning to falter. Maybe she was being too stubborn. Cutting her nose off to spite her face, as her mother would say. Everyone can make mistakes and God knows she'd made enough of them. She sat back in her chair and chewed on a pen. Nathan obviously sensed her indecision and tried again to win her over.

'Maybe we could go away. Just the two of us. We work so hard and don't see enough of each other. We could go to the Bahamas or the Seychelles. Somewhere with white sandy beaches and blue skies. Just imagine, Elizabeth. No interruptions, no distractions. Just time for us. What do you say?'

'I … I don't know.'

'Well, just hop into your car and come over here and we'll talk about it. I want to see your face. It's not the same talking to you on the phone.'

She knew she had to remain strong but it was difficult. 'I'm not ready to come home yet, Nathan.'

'That's okay. We can take it one step at a time. Just come over for now and I'll order us something to eat so we can talk. That's all I'm asking for, a chance to put things right. You can go back and sleep in the hotel if you still want to.'

She glanced at the time display on her screen and saw it was almost six o'clock. She hadn't been in a rush to leave because the thought of going back to an empty hotel room was depressing. Going home, on the other hand, sounded appealing, even if she and Nathan weren't in a good place.

'I'll think about it,' she said, swivelling from side to side in her chair. 'I do need to pick up some more clothes so perhaps I could do that at the same time.'

'Of course,' he said, and she could hear the animation in his voice. 'I'll order from that Thai place you like and if it arrives before you, I'll just stick it in the oven.'

She sighed. 'Okay. But I'm not staying for long.'

'Great. I'll see you shortly.'

She ended the call and threw her phone on the desk. What an idiot she was. Nathan only had to say jump and she asked how high. That's why she'd avoided his calls all week. She knew how he could manipulate her. And once they were face to face, he'd do everything in his power to convince her to come home. She glanced out the window and saw that the snow had stopped. Thanks to the heavy downpour, it had actually stuck and the street below was like a winter wonderland.

'Is there anything I can do for you before I go?' said Amanda, appearing at the door. 'Traffic is going to be chaotic with that snow so I want to get going as soon as possible.'

Elizabeth shook her head. 'You go. I'll see you tomorrow.'

'What about you?'

'I'll be right behind you,' said Elizabeth, finally making a decision and switching off her computer. 'It's about time I got out of here myself.'

With a heavy heart, she took the lift to the basement car park, wondering how things had become so messed up. It was as though Nathan had thrown her a line, and he was slowly reeling her in. She'd started the week with a strong resolve but after seven nights in a stuffy hotel room, listening to music booming from the nightclub below, she was beginning to falter. She sat into her car and started the ignition. She didn't want to be alone any longer. She was yearning for some human contact, something to make her feel alive. She took a deep breath and headed out into the evening traffic.

The snow was casting an eerie light as she sat in the car looking up at the house. She took a few moments before going in. She'd had enough confrontation recently to last a lifetime but she needed to do this. She began to shiver. Since switching off the engine, the car had become freezing cold, and she knew it was time. She took a deep breath before getting out and walking towards the front door.

'Come in,' said Amber, opening the door wide. 'I was surprised to get your call.'

Elizabeth hovered on the doorstep. 'A bad surprise?'

'Not at all. It's just … well … I wasn't expecting to hear from you. That's all.'

'I surprise myself sometimes,' said Elizabeth, stepping inside and wiping her feet on the doormat. 'I just thought it was time.'

Amber led the way into the little kitchen and Elizabeth's eyes opened wide when she saw how beautiful it was. The pale green wooden units contrasted beautifully with the cream shelves and, although it was somewhat cluttered, it had a wonderful homely feel to it. Elizabeth thought of her own sterile kitchen that cost a fortune and was barely used, and again was reminded of how sad her life really was.

'Are you okay?' said Amber, watching as Elizabeth looked around her.

'Sorry, I was just thinking about how lovely your house is.'

Amber laughed. 'You don't have to be nice. I know you're used to grander things than this.'

Elizabeth turned to her. 'I hate that you think of me that way, Amber. But I probably deserve it. Your house is gorgeous. Lived in. Mine is big and cold and has no character.'

Amber looked unsure of what to say but indicated for Elizabeth to sit down at the cream wooden table. She busied herself filling the kettle, and an awkward silence hung in the air. When Elizabeth had left work, she'd planned on going home to see Nathan. To talk to him. To try and sort things out. But as she'd sat in traffic heading out of the city, she'd thought about what would happen. He'd play on her vulnerability. He'd be nice to her and convince her he'd made a stupid mistake. He'd woo her and make her feel special. And she'd let him. She'd go back to him and nothing would have changed. Realisation had dawned on her that his sleeping with Gloria wasn't the problem in their relationship – that was just a symptom of something that was already broken. The problem was Nathan himself and how he behaved towards her. How he made her feel. Small and insignificant. Vulnerable and needy. And she didn't want to feel that way any more.

'I take it you're still a coffee lover?' said Amber, placing two mugs on the table and taking a carton of milk from the fridge. 'Sorry, we're probably a bit more slapdash than you're used to but we weren't expecting guests.'

'Stop, Amber.'

'What?'

'Stop making me out to be stuck-up. I'm not the person you think I am.'

Amber folded her arms and leaned against the counter. 'Are you not?'

Elizabeth shook her head, wondering if her coming here had been a good idea.

'It's just,' continued Amber, 'that you've done a pretty good job of making out you're better than us these last few years.'

She wasn't wrong, but Elizabeth wasn't about to take all the blame. 'You're probably right, Amber, but I don't think I'm the only one who's behaved badly.'

Amber shifted uncomfortably. 'I know, and I'm sorry for that. I really am.'

'Has Ronnie told you what happened back then?' said Elizabeth, watching Amber's reaction.

'Yes.'

'Everything?'

'If you mean about the pregnancy, then yes.' Amber looked at her with tears in her eyes. 'I wish you'd told us. If I'd known about—'

Elizabeth held up a hand to stop her. 'I know, I know. You never would have encouraged Ronnie to date Ben and none of this would ever have happened.'

'I can't tell you how sorry I am,' said Amber, sitting down on a chair beside Elizabeth and reaching over to take her hand. 'You must have gone through hell.'

'Without a doubt, it was the lowest point in my life. Not the pregnancy – because although I got a shock, I quite liked the idea.

But the aftermath.' She felt choked up at the memories but she wanted to share them with Amber, just as she had with Ronnie. She wanted to be surrounded by people again – people who cared for her. So she needed to begin building some bridges.

'Right,' said Amber, standing up. 'This calls for some seriously chocolatey biscuits. I think I have a few Penguin bars stashed up here.'

A few minutes later they were sipping their coffees and Elizabeth was continuing with her story. 'You know what I'm like when I make a decision,' she said. 'I trust that it's the right one and don't second guess myself. It was no different for the abortion. I decided it was the only thing to do so I organised everything pretty quickly and it was done before I had time to reconsider.'

Amber looked crestfallen. 'And afterwards?'

'I was a mess. Mentally and physically wiped out from the whole thing.'

'It sounds awful. And did you not tell anybody? You went through all that alone?'

Elizabeth nodded. 'I isolated myself from everybody. But you already know that. It was easier that way. And don't forget, I already thought you and Ronnie were laughing at me, thinking it was funny to have taken Ben away from me.'

'I can't tell you how much I regret that, Elizabeth. I didn't think you and Ben were serious. I thought it would just be something that would cause a bit of an argument between you and Ronnie. I was jealous – jealous of your friendship, your bond. I'm really, really sorry.'

'We can all take our share of the blame for what happened back then,' said Elizabeth. 'And if I'm honest, I probably was a lot more into Ben than he was into me. If it hadn't been Ronnie, he would have left me for somebody else.'

'But then you and Ronnie wouldn't have fallen out.'

Elizabeth shrugged. 'Maybe. I think I was just looking for a punchbag at the time. After I had the abortion, there were complications.'

'What sort of complications?' Amber looked worried.

'Well, let's just say that getting pregnant again may not be as easy as it was the first time.'

Amber gasped. 'Oh God, Elizabeth. That's awful.'

At that moment, the kitchen door burst open and Amber's husband, Roger, appeared, with Daniel in his arms. 'Here you go, Mummy. One nice, clean little boy, all dressed and ready for bed.'

'Mummmmmyyyyy,' said Daniel, jumping down from Roger's arms and running to Amber. 'Who's that lady?'

Amber picked him up and sat him on her lap. 'This is my friend, Elizabeth. She's Ronnie's sister.'

Daniel giggled. 'No, she isn't. Vonnie is fat and she's skinny.'

'Daniel!' said Roger, still standing at the kitchen door.

Elizabeth smiled. 'He's fine. Good to see you again, Roger.'

Roger nodded. 'Likewise. Now, if you two girls are going to be gossiping for the next while, I think I'll head off to the gym for a bit.'

'Off you go,' said Amber, tickling Daniel under the arms. 'This little man will be heading for bed as soon as he has his supper.'

'Can I watch the Simsims?' said Daniel, when Roger had left the room. 'And can I have a toastie, pleeeeeeease?'

'Okay, since you asked so nicely,' said Amber, lifting him down off her lap. 'You go and switch the telly on and I'll bring your sandwich in.'

'He's adorable,' said Elizabeth, watching as Daniel raced off in his little Thomas the Tank Engine pyjamas. 'You're so lucky.'

'I know. He means everything to me. I can't imagine my life without him.' Amber's hand shot to her mouth. 'I'm sorry, Elizabeth. That was insensitive of me.'

'It's fine. You don't have to tiptoe around me. It was a long time ago and all I want to do now is move forward.'

'So, is that what brought you here tonight? Moving forward?'

Elizabeth nodded. 'Yes. I've done a lot of thinking lately and I want to put the past behind me.'

'That's great, Elizabeth. Maybe you, me and Ronnie can team up again. Just like old times.'

'Maybe,' said Elizabeth. And then her face turned dark. 'But make no mistake. If you ever come between me and my sister again, I'll make sure you regret it.'

Chapter 34

'I absolutely love it,' said Ronnie, holding out her hand to admire her ring finger. 'It's just so perfect.'

Al took her hand and kissed it. 'Isn't it? And at least there's no chance of you losing it.'

Ronnie laughed and popped the last of her chicken into her mouth. 'I can't believe you've been planning this for so long and I never knew. You're such a romantic.'

'Stop, will you. You're ruining my tough-boy image by even saying that.'

'You're anything but tough, Al. You're the nicest, kindest, sweetest man I've ever known. Have I told you today how much I love you?'

'I love you too,' he said, reaching across the table to kiss her. 'Now, I'd better go and get ready. I want to be out of here before your guests arrive.'

'Are you sure you won't stay and join us? The others wouldn't mind, and you could help with ideas.'

'I think I'll give that one a miss.' He stood up and stretched, his T-shirt rising up, exposing his toned midriff. 'You can fill me in on everything later.'

'Okay,' said Ronnie, standing up to clear away the plates. 'You head on up for your shower and I'll sort this lot out.'

Amber and Elizabeth were due to arrive in half an hour and Ronnie couldn't help feeling excited. The last time they'd met, just before New York, things had been a lot different. Now they'd all managed to work through their problems and Ronnie was going to do all she could to bring the three of them back together again. As she loaded the plates and glasses into the dishwasher and wiped down the table, she smiled at the sound of Al's singing coming from the bedroom. He could barely hold a note but knew the words to every Queen song and the flat would often be filled with his crooning.

She took a bottle of white wine from the drinks cupboard and stuck it in the fridge. Elizabeth was driving so Ronnie knew she wouldn't touch a drop but Amber would probably have a few since Elizabeth was picking her up along the way. It was hard to imagine the two girls arriving together. Ronnie had been shocked and delighted when she'd heard of their reconciliation. Amber had rung her straight afterwards to update her and she'd spoken to Elizabeth the following day. So when Ronnie had suggested they all get together tonight, nobody had objected.

'Right, love, I'm off.' Al appeared in the kitchen, a vision of gorgeousness in just a pair of faded jeans and plain black T-shirt. He didn't need fancy clothes to make him look beautiful. He could wear anything and still be the most handsome man in the room.

'Have a good night,' said Ronnie, crossing the room to kiss him. 'I'll see you when you get in.'

'I hope your night goes well too,' he said, heading for the front door. 'And remember – no dredging up the past and no arguments. It's all about moving forward.'

'Yes, Daddy,' she giggled, before closing the door behind him.

Back in the kitchen, she busied herself filling bowls with her favourite Marks & Spencer snacks that she'd picked up earlier. Cheese puffs were her favourite but, as she poured them into the bowl, her stomach lurched. She'd just finished a long and painful period and she was still feeling a bit queasy. She reckoned it was a combination of travelling and stress that had brought her period on with such ferocity and, for about the umpteenth time that month, she cursed the fact that she was a woman. It just wasn't fair.

She brought the snacks into the living room and placed them on the coffee table. It was just five to eight so she'd have time to slap on a bit of make-up. She'd just got out of the shower before dinner and hadn't bothered doing her face. But a glance in the bathroom mirror had told her that she needed to do something to cover the black bags beneath her eyes. As she applied a thin line on the edges of her eyelid, she could see the sadness in her face. Her life was filled with good things but there was still one thing stopping her from being entirely happy. She and Al had talked about the baby situation at length over the last few days, and they'd decided that, if nothing happened soon, they were going to go and see a doctor about it. She tried to remain positive and think as she always did, that this would be the month.

The doorbell rang just as she finished applying her lip gloss, and she went to greet her guests. 'Come in, come in,' she said, kissing the two girls and taking their coats. 'You're right on time.'

There was a sense of awkwardness as the three girls sat around the coffee table and Ronnie wished they were all having a few drinks to relax them. But it was going to take a while. They were hardly going to go back to how things had been in their earlier years, when they were giggling teenagers and the best of friends. A lot of things had happened and it was going to take them all a while to get over them.

'Right,' said Amber, breaking the silence. 'I want to propose a toast.'

Ronnie nodded and picked up her glass. 'Good idea.'

'To us,' she said, holding her glass in the air. 'To forgiveness and acceptance and a bright future for all of us.'

'I'll drink to that,' said Ronnie, clinking her glass with Amber's. 'Elizabeth?'

Elizabeth looked uncertain for a moment and then held up her glass. 'To friendship.'

'To friendship,' they said in unison, and suddenly the ice was broken. The conversation began to flow and soon it was like it used to be. Ronnie was delighted. She couldn't have wished for more. It was a long time since she'd seen Elizabeth looking so relaxed and it was good to see Amber having fun. Amber had told Ronnie about Elizabeth's warning to her but, if there was tension between them, it certainly wasn't evident.

About an hour had passed before Amber brought up the reason they were there. 'So, are we going to put our heads together and come up with some ideas about finding your father? It won't be long before my brain is mush with all this wine so maybe we should talk about it now.'

Ronnie laughed. 'I'm sipping this soda water pretending it's wine, but it's not working.'

'Are you going to stay off alcohol while you're trying to …' Amber trailed off and looked from Ronnie to Elizabeth.

'It's okay,' said Ronnie. 'Elizabeth knows we're trying for a baby. And the answer is yes. I'm going to do everything I can to give myself the best possible chance. But let's not talk about that tonight. You're right, we should try and come up with some ideas about finding Oliver, now that we know he's in Ireland.'

'What about Frank?' said Amber. 'Has he got any more information that might help? What's he saying about it all?'

Elizabeth shook her head. 'He's not saying a lot, actually. I've talked to him a couple of times and he seems very down. He said he hasn't been feeling well and I didn't want to push him for information.'

Ronnie agreed. She'd spoken to Frank too and he didn't seem himself. The death of a loved one hits everyone in different ways at different times and it seemed that Frank was going through a hard time. Hearing about Skye's death seemed to have affected him, and Ronnie reckoned it brought all the memories of Belinda flooding back. He'd told her that he wanted them to come into his office again to talk about things but he was probably just trying to help. He'd been so good to them both that now it was time for them to look after him. They could go ahead with the search without his input and hopefully they'd have some news for him eventually.

'What about the old man you went to see?' said Ronnie, looking at Elizabeth. 'Albert Dunne, was it? I know you said he'd lost touch with Oliver, but maybe if we jogged his memory, he'd remember something. Maybe Oliver had a brother or sister – anything that we could follow up on.'

Amber nodded. 'That's a good idea. You said he was happy to talk to you, didn't you, Elizabeth?'

'Yes, he was a lovely man. Very willing to chat, but I honestly doubt he has any more information. But I suppose it couldn't hurt to try.'

'Maybe if we both go,' said Ronnie to Elizabeth. 'I could say I wanted to meet him since he was a friend of our mother's.'

Elizabeth nodded. 'But I had one more idea. I'm not sure if it will help but I had this done.' She reached into her handbag and pulled out a sheet of paper that was carefully folded. She opened it up and placed it on the table for the girls to see.

'What is it?' said Amber, turning her head to the side to try and decipher the picture.

'The tattoo!' said Ronnie, clapping her hands together. 'You had it blown up.'

'Yes, it was all I could think of doing. I brought it to a photo shop and asked them to get me the clearest picture possible of it. At least we can see exactly what it is now.'

They all took turns to look closely at the picture. It was, as they'd already suspected, the international peace sign – a circle with a line running down the middle, intersected by an upside-down V. The sign itself was in black but there was a feather attached to the bottom of it, and it was filled with a myriad of colours. There seemed to be a chain attached to the top of the circle on either side, which was why they'd originally thought it was a necklace. It was obviously cleverly designed to look that way.

'It's beautiful, isn't it?' said Amber, examining the picture. 'And really distinctive too.'

Elizabeth took the picture from her. 'That's exactly what I was thinking. It's so distinctive that maybe we have a chance of tracing him that way.'

Ronnie was intrigued. 'What do you mean?'

'Isn't it obvious?' said Elizabeth, stabbing a finger at the picture. 'Maybe we can trace Oliver through a tattoo shop. He probably got the tattoo in Dublin so we can check what shops were open in the eighties. I don't imagine there'd be too many.'

Amber slammed her drink down on the table. 'Oops, sorry! I'm getting a bit too excited. But that's a brilliant idea. If they keep original designs on file, they might just have contact details of the people who got them.'

'Exactly!' Elizabeth was smiling, and Ronnie's heart soared.

'I can ask Al,' she said. 'He'd be able to check what tattoo parlours were around back then and he could probably get in touch with them for us. You're a genius, Elizabeth. I never would have thought of that.'

Elizabeth beamed. 'So, I'll leave this with you and you can have a word with Al about it.'

'Of course,' said Ronnie, holding out her hand to take the picture.

'What's that?' said Amber, suddenly, pointing to Ronnie's hand. 'On your finger.'

Ronnie smiled. She'd been waiting for one of them to notice it. 'Do you like it?' she said, holding her hand out for the girls to examine it.

Amber gasped. 'It's stunning. Wow!'

'Beautiful,' said Elizabeth. 'But what does this mean?'

'We're not getting married, if that's what you're asking. It's not really our thing. But it's a symbol of our commitment, our love. He has a matching one. He designed it, and surprised me earlier in the week.'

'Oh my God,' said Amber, shaking her head. 'He's the perfect man. Can you ask him to have a word with Roger? His idea of romance is clearing up Daniel's toys before I get home from work!'

They all laughed at that and Ronnie felt happy. The tattoos were a great idea. Al had drawn a design based on an antique ring and he'd surprised Ronnie with a visit to his shop. He had one of his best tattoo artists ink the rings onto their wedding fingers and Ronnie had almost burst with happiness. It was such a thoughtful gesture, combining her love of antique jewellery with his love of tattoos. They didn't need a piece of paper to tell them they were committed to each other. This way they could wear their memories forever. Her thoughts turned then to her father. She wondered what was behind his choice of tattoo. Was he alone when he got it? Was he with Skye or maybe he was with their mother. She hoped that he could tell her the story himself someday. As she glanced at her own tattoo, she suddenly felt a bond with Oliver. Although she didn't know him, he'd become one of the most important people in her life.

Chapter 35

Elizabeth was finally feeling strong enough to face Nathan. She was home almost two weeks and had managed to avoid him for most of that time. If she'd agreed to see him before now, there was no doubt in her mind that she would have caved in to his charms. But numerous chats with both Ronnie and Amber over the last week, and a lot of soul-searching, told her that Nathan just wasn't good for her. It was a toxic relationship and she needed to put an end to it, no matter how heartbreaking that might be. So she'd packed up all her stuff and was on the way back to the house. He'd had it easy these last couple of weeks. He'd been able to stay there whereas she'd been stuck in a hotel room. But not any more. She was moving home. She hoped he'd do the decent thing and move out, but if not, she was going to leave him in no doubt that they were no longer a couple.

It was just before eight o'clock when she parked her car in the driveway, and she was glad to see Nathan's car there. She'd decided against warning him she was coming. She didn't want to make a big deal of it – she just wanted to be back where she belonged. After all, they'd only bought that particular house because it was close to where her mother lived, close to where she'd grown up. Nathan didn't care where he lived, whereas Elizabeth had a very close affinity with the area and didn't want to be anywhere else.

The cloudy sky cast an eerie light into the car as she checked her lipstick in the mirror, and she suddenly felt nervous. What if she walked in on him and Gloria again? Or even worse, what if he had somebody different there? Maybe he'd had a string of women these last few years and she'd been oblivious to it all. But there was no point in speculation. She needed to confront him and that's what she was going to do.

As soon as the door opened, she relaxed. She'd wondered briefly if he'd have changed the locks, so she was thankful he hadn't stooped so low. A clattering from the kitchen told her he was up, so she took a deep breath and headed in.

'Hello, Nathan.'

'Elizabeth! I didn't hear you come in. You frightened the life out of me.' He was dressed in a pair of boxers and a white T-shirt and, even with his dishevelled hair, he looked handsome.

'Sorry about that. It would have felt weird to ring the doorbell in my own house.'

'Of course you shouldn't have rung the bell. Come here.' He went to hug her but she signalled for him to stop.

'I'm not here to make up, Nathan. We have a few things to sort out.'

'That's what I've been trying to tell you,' he said, running his hand through his silver hair. 'I was angry with you for leaving but I understand why you did it. And you staying away isn't going to solve anything. We need to work things out here together.'

'Well, I'm back now.' She sat up on a high stool at the kitchen counter. 'But it's only because this is my home. It's where I want to be.'

'I'm happy you're back, love.' He sat down beside her. 'And I know you're not ready to forgive me yet, but in time you will. I know it. I'll work on making you trust me again.'

She shook her head. 'I said I wasn't here to make up.'

'I heard you. But in time—'

'No!' She didn't want there to be any uncertainty. 'You and me are over. There's not going to be any making up or building trust. I want you out, Nathan. I want you to pack your bags and leave this house. When things settle down we can sell up.'

'What are you saying, Elizabeth? You want to separate? Don't be so ridiculous. We're married. You can't go off in a huff because you don't like something I did.'

She couldn't believe what she was hearing. 'God, Nathan, you're unbelievable. This is not some childish spat where one person is sulking because the other got the bigger slice of cake. We're talking about you sleeping with Gloria. Your betrayal. Your infidelity. Adultery. Need I go on?'

'You're upset,' he said, cocking his head to the side as if trying to console a puppy. 'And I understand. Really, I do.'

'Are you mad?' said Elizabeth, standing up and glaring at him. 'I'm not looking for your understanding and of course I'm upset. What I want is you out of here so that we can start proceedings for a legal separation.'

He looked hurt. 'Don't say that. We can work it out. I keep telling you it meant nothing. Gloria means nothing to me. It was all just a stupid mistake.'

She realised then that she'd have to take a different tack with him because he seemed to think she was just having some sort of tantrum and it would all settle down. 'It's not just you sleeping with Gloria. There's a lot more to it than that.'

'Is there? Because unless I'm completely wrong at reading the situation, you were in love with me before you left for New York. You can't just suddenly decide that ...' His eyes narrowed and slowly he began to nod his head. 'Of course. It's only dawning on me now.'

'What is?' She was finding it difficult to keep up with his thought process.

'You've found somebody else, haven't you? That's why you're so determined to get me out. You were just using my little slip-up as an excuse.'

'Don't be ridiculous.'

'It's all making sense now,' he said, standing up and pacing back and forth. 'You were so keen to get away to New York and wouldn't listen to reason. And then you came back with a plan to leave me and I handed everything to you on a plate.'

'Nathan, you're just being stupid now.'

He glared at her and there was steel in his eyes. 'Don't call me stupid, Elizabeth. Although maybe I *was* stupid to fall right into your trap.'

'I don't have anybody else,' she said, leaning against the counter and folding her arms. 'So don't try and deflect from what you've done. I know that's what you're doing so there's no point in denying it.'

'Well, if you have nobody else waiting in the wings for you, then what is it? You said there's a lot more to it. So go on, I'm dying to hear.'

She let out a long sigh. She hadn't been planning on explaining things to him. She'd thought that he'd get it. Did he honestly not think he'd treated her badly? Could he not see how dominant he was over her? How much he'd suffocated her?

'It's the way you make me feel,' she said finally. 'I don't want to feel that way any more.'

'And how do I make you feel, Elizabeth? Because I thought I always made you feel special. And loved.'

He was right, in a way. She'd always felt special when she was on his arm. Every head in a room would turn when he'd walk in and she'd always felt extremely lucky to be his wife. He was obviously sensing a chink in her armour, so he continued.

'Well? Can you honestly say I haven't made you feel loved?'

He did love her. She was pretty sure of that. Whenever they'd go out to an event, he'd always have an arm draped lovingly over her shoulder to let the world know she was his. It had always made her feel very loved and cherished. Her resolve was beginning to wane.

'Elizabeth, love,' he said, walking towards her and taking her hands in his. 'All this nonsense needs to stop. We love each other, you and me. We have a very special bond that can't be broken. I made a stupid mistake and I've paid the price for it. I've had to spend three weeks without you now and I can't bear it. I can't bear to be apart from you any longer. I love you, sweetheart. Please say you love me too.'

She had to bite back the tears as she looked into his pleading eyes – the eyes that she'd loved from the moment she saw them. Maybe she'd been too rash. Was she crazy to throw away a marriage without a proper discussion? Without getting some help or counselling?

'Elizabeth?'

'I do love you, Nathan. But that's not the issue. I can't go on like this. *We* can't go on. I'm scared of you. I'm scared I'll do something that you don't like or say something that displeases you. I live in fear of your disapproval and that's no way for a wife to feel. We're not equals. I'm like your understudy – always in your shadow and scared to take the limelight.'

He looked genuinely shocked. 'Am I really that bad? I can't believe you've been feeling like that and never told me. I'm so sorry, sweetheart. I really, really am. I'll do better. I'll make sure you don't ever feel that way again.'

'I … I don't know.'

'Come on. Remember the day we got married? When we danced to Bryan Adams' 'Everything I Do'? I meant every word of that song when I sang it to you. Remember? You made me promise that I meant those words and that we'd always fight to stay together, no matter what happened.'

She nodded. 'But it was a fairy-tale. This is reality.'

'It's as real as it gets,' he said, squeezing her hands. 'And I'm fighting for you now. For us. We can take it as slowly as you like. Just move back in and we'll take it day by day.'

'Well, I suppose it's silly paying for a hotel room when we have a big house like this. But if I agree – and I'm saying *if* – I won't be sleeping in the same bed as you. It will be purely an arrangement of convenience.'

'But you'll be willing to see how things go? To consider giving us another chance?'

'Maybe.' She just couldn't help herself.

'That's all I needed to know,' said Nathan, pulling her to him and hugging her tight. 'Now let's get your stuff in out of the car and back where it belongs. I need to talk to you then about Stephen.'

She wriggled out of his embrace and looked at him. 'What about Stephen?'

'We need a plan. To figure out what we're going to say to him. He heard Gloria on the phone to me and put two and two together. We need to deflect attention from it.'

'Wh … what do you mean?'

'Well, I was thinking that maybe we could arrange for him to come over here and you could flirt with him. Seduce him. You know how he always gives you the eye. Then if I walked in on the two of you, it would be perfect.'

'Perfect?' She didn't like the sound of this.

'Yes. At the moment he only *suspects* there's something going on between Gloria and me, but if he found out for sure, I'd definitely lose my job.'

'I'm not following.'

'Come on, Elizabeth. Catch up. If we can turn things around that *he's* the one doing the cheating, then there's no way he'll come for me.'

She felt like she'd been slapped in the face. 'So you actually want me to sleep with your boss so that you won't lose your job?'

'Well, you don't have to go that far but, basically, yes. It's important. I can't lose this job or we'll lose everything.'

Elizabeth suddenly saw her husband with new eyes. Instead of the ruggedly handsome man who had made her swoon in the past, she now saw somebody with an ugly soul. Somebody who would do whatever was needed to get what he wanted. He didn't care who he hurt along the way or who he trod on. He was selfish and single-minded and she couldn't believe he'd almost managed to reel her back in.

'Actually,' she said, moving away from him and taking her handbag from the stool where she'd left it, 'you don't have to move out at all. You can stay here and I'll leave again.'

'What do you mean? I thought you were—'

'Well, you thought wrong, Nathan. I will never, ever let you manipulate me again. I'm going upstairs to collect some more of my stuff and then I'll be going.' Her heart pounded like crazy as she took the stairs two at a time and began to pull stuff out of the wardrobe. There was a large suitcase under the bed so she stuffed as much as she could fit into it before zipping it closed and turning to leave. Nathan was at the bedroom door watching her.

'I'm warning you, Elizabeth. You'll regret it if you leave now.'

'The only thing I regret,' she said, pushing past him, 'is ever setting eyes on you.'

She hurried downstairs, dragging the case behind her. There was a pile of post for her on the hall table so she grabbed it and stuck it under her arm. She could barely breathe as she tried to juggle her bags to open the door, and it was only when she got to the car that she released a long, slow exhale. She quickly glanced back towards the house but he hadn't come after her. He'd never do that. He wouldn't want neighbours to know there was something going on. He'd hate for them to think he was anything less than perfect. She hauled the bags into the boot of the car, threw the letters on the seat beside her and sped off down the road. Once she'd got to a safe distance, she knew she'd have to stop the car for fear she'd crash, given her heightened state of anxiety. She pulled in to a petrol station and parked beside a wall. Closing her eyes, she began to breathe, slow and steady, just like Ronnie would tell her. She imagined Ronnie's voice: *'Breathe, one, two three ...'* and soon her breathing steadied and she began to feel normal again.

Tears sprang to her eyes when she realised the enormity of her situation. She'd checked out of the hotel, thinking she'd be going home, so now she had nowhere to go. Everything was such a mess. She reached down to get a tissue from her handbag, and that's when she saw it. It was in the pile of post she'd taken from the house. It looked more daunting than the other letters, if that was possible. More urgent. So she opened it immediately.

Nothing could have prepared her for the words in that letter. She read them again and again until they blurred in front of her eyes. She must be a really bad person. Because karma seemed to have set its sights on her and it wasn't going to rest until it had finished her off completely.

Chapter 36

Ronnie stood up and leaned her face against the cold tiled wall of the bathroom. That was the third time she'd been sick since she woke up and it wasn't even ten o'clock. She cursed the curry she'd had with Al the previous night. Since they'd been having a nice relaxing Sunday, they'd decided to give cooking a miss and try out the new Indian takeaway that everyone was raving about. Well, she certainly wouldn't be going there again. She'd been due in work but she'd had to ring in sick, and she hated doing that. She'd only ever missed four days since she'd started there ten years before, and two of those were for her mother's funeral.

Back in bed, she lay wide awake, thinking about her sister. Elizabeth had been very withdrawn these last few days and Ronnie was worried about her. They'd had a lovely evening with Amber just over a week ago, but something must have happened since then because Elizabeth was acting strangely. She'd rung Ronnie last Wednesday, asking if she'd mind her staying at their mum's house for a while until she got herself sorted. Ronnie hadn't minded one bit and had actually wondered why she hadn't done that in the first place rather than staying in a hotel. They had decided to put the house on the market, since each of them had their own home and hadn't planned on moving, but things had changed now for Elizabeth. But it wasn't just that – it was how she was acting. Ronnie had rung her for a chat a few times and she'd fobbed her off. She'd also tried to get her talking about the search for Oliver but she hadn't seemed interested. She hadn't been cold or aloof, as she'd been in the past. She'd seemed down – depressed, almost. And Ronnie's heart went out to her.

A rumble from her stomach caused Ronnie to sit up, wondering if she was going to be sick again, but she realised she was actually starving. Hopefully, she'd seen the last of the vomiting and would be able for something to eat soon. Her mobile was on her locker so she took it up and dialled Elizabeth's number.

'Elizabeth Cunningham.' She sounded just like their mother, and Ronnie's heart leapt when she heard it.

'Hi, Elizabeth. It's Ronnie.'

'Sorry, Ronnie, I was expecting a business call. Are you okay?'

'What makes you ask that?'

'I don't know. You just sound a bit rough.'

Ronnie smiled at her perception. 'A bit of food poisoning, actually. I'm a lot better now, thankfully. But more importantly, how are you? I'm worried about you.'

There was silence, and Ronnie's heart skipped a beat.

'Elizabeth? Is there something you're not telling me? What's happened?'

'I'm fine. It's just this whole thing with Nathan. It's getting me down. I know I've done the right thing in leaving him. But it's hard, you know?'

Ronnie knew. She'd felt that way for the short time she'd been apart from Al. She hadn't been able to cope without him. But then again, Al was ten times the man Nathan was.

'So, what do you think will happen? Are you two finished completely? Or do you think there's a chance you'll reconcile?'

'No,' she said, determination in her voice. 'Me and Nathan are finished. I've had a few wobbles, but I'm never going back to him. I'm pretty sure of that.'

'Oh, Elizabeth, I'm so sorry. I know I encouraged you to leave him but I know it can't be easy for you. What can I do? Just tell me what you need. I want to be able to help you.'

'You're very good, Ronnie, but there's nothing you can do. Letting me stay in Mum's house is enough.'

'You don't need my permission to stay there. It's your house too.'

'I know, but I didn't want you to think I was assuming it was okay. And I know we're going to put it on the market shortly, but I just need time to get myself sorted.'

'Of course. Take as much time as you need.'

'Thanks.' It was barely a whisper.

'So, anyway,' said Ronnie, in an attempt to lighten the mood. 'I was thinking that maybe we could pay Albert Dunne a visit together. You know, the man you called on before we went to New York. Mum's friend.'

'I don't know, Ronnie.'

'Come on. You want to continue to look for Oliver, don't you?'

'Of course I do. It's just I have a lot on at the moment.'

Ronnie was determined to get her thinking about something other than Nathan. 'I understand that, but it might take your mind off things. Al has been doing a bit of searching in relation to Oliver's tattoo. He's contacted some tattoo shops that were around back then to see if he can trace the design. He's not having much luck, though.'

'I suppose it was a long shot,' said Elizabeth. 'It feels as though we're never going to find him.'

'Come with me to Albert Dunne's house. I think we should tell him the whole story this time. What have we got to lose? It might jog his memory.'

'Why don't you go on your own, rather than me turning up again? He might feel a bit intimidated by both of us landing on his doorstep.'

Ronnie thought for a moment. 'Actually, you're probably right. I'm off work today so I might head on over there later.'

'Good idea. Let me know how you get on.'

Ronnie's stomach rumbled again and this time she was certain it was hunger. 'I have to go, Elizabeth. I'll give you a buzz later and fill you in. Or maybe I could pop over?'

'I'm planning to go to bed early and catch up on some reading, so just ring me and we can chat.'

Ronnie said her goodbyes and replaced the phone on her locker. She swung her legs out of the bed and stood up, fully expecting to be weak and wobbly, but she felt surprisingly well. She'd get herself some tea and toast and if that successfully stayed down, she'd shower and call a taxi to bring her to Albert Dunne's house. She knew she spent way too much on taxis but she really couldn't face buses today. A bubble of excitement formed in her stomach. It was good to have something to focus on – to take her mind off not getting pregnant. Looking for her father these last weeks had saved her from dwelling on the negative, and whatever the outcome, she'd be always grateful for that.

'Mr Dunne? I'm Ronnie Cunningham. Belinda Cunningham's daughter.'

A beam of a smile split the old man's face and he held open the door wide. 'Well, isn't this a lovely surprise? I had a visit from your sister too a few weeks ago.'

'Yes, Elizabeth said she came to see you. I hope you don't mind me coming too?'

'Not at all, not at all, once you stop with the Mr Dunne and call me Albert. Come in. I'll stick the kettle on.'

Ronnie followed him through the narrow hallway into the little kitchen, where he indicated for her to sit down. 'I know you told Elizabeth anything you remembered about Oliver Angelo, but I just thought I'd come and tell you why we're so keen to find him. And maybe you might remember something else. Anything at all that might help us.'

'Now that sounds intriguing,' he said, placing two mugs on the table. 'Elizabeth said she was trying to trace him to find out more about your mum's early years. But I could tell there was more to it than that.'

Ronnie nodded. 'He's our father.' She let the words hang in the air.

'I knew it,' he said, clapping his hands together. 'As soon as your sister had left, I was thinking about it and I said to myself: *I bet he's their father.* I always knew your mother and Oliver had a connection and I was always surprised they didn't get together. Tea or coffee?'

'Tea, please,' said Ronnie, surprised but delighted that she hadn't shocked the old man with her revelation. 'So, do you think they would have got together if Oliver hadn't had a girlfriend already?'

He brought the freshly made pot of tea to the table and sat down. 'I'm sure of it. It was a funny situation. Oliver and Skye had been together since they were teenagers. They were like the same person and it was a very easy-going relationship. They were almost like brother and sister.'

'And it wasn't like that with Mum and him?'

He shook his head. 'There was a spark there. I saw it right from the start. Whenever we'd all meet up, I saw it in Oliver's eyes. When he'd talk to your mum, something would light up inside him.'

Ronnie was thrilled with this nugget of information. 'And did he ever say anything about her? Did you never speak to him about what you saw?'

'I did, actually,' said Albert. 'We had a chat about it once. He admitted he had feelings for Belinda but he also loved Skye. It was as though ...' He trailed off, and Ronnie was dying to know more.

'Go on,' she said, willing him to continue.

'It was as though he thought he wasn't good enough for Belinda. She was a businesswoman – a rich girl who was used to the finer things.' He coughed awkwardly. 'I'm sorry, love. I don't want you to think I'm speaking ill of her. Belinda was a lovely woman. She never acted as though she was better than us but I think it got into Oliver's head.'

Ronnie nodded. 'I understand what you're saying. So he never pursued her, then? He just kept it as a friendship?'

'Yes,' said Albert, pouring the tea into the mugs. 'It was probably the easiest option for him to stay with Skye. She was a lovely girl too. They had the same passions and worked well together.'

Ronnie thought for a moment about telling him about Skye but decided against it. There was no need to bring him more bad news. And what purpose would it serve anyway? She was there to get information about Oliver and nothing more.

'You must miss her,' he continued, stirring spoon after spoon of sugar into his tea.

That caught Ronnie by surprise. 'Who?'

'Your mum. I can't believe she's gone. It's very sad.'

'Yes,' said Ronnie, 'I miss her a lot. She was a fantastic woman and a great mother. Elizabeth and I are lost without her.'

They both sat in silence for a moment until Ronnie realised she needed to progress things. It was great finding out about the past, about the relationship between Oliver and Belinda. But that wasn't going to help her find him. She needed to try to get Albert to think back – to find something that might help her.

'We went to New York, you know,' she said, sipping her tea. 'Me and Elizabeth. We went over and found the address you gave us.'

'Did you really?' Albert looked impressed. 'All the way over there? My God, you really are on a mission.'

Ronnie smiled. 'We really want to find him and we were sure that was the way. But as it turns out, he came back to Ireland some years ago.'

'No!' said Albert, shaking his head. 'I'm so sorry I gave you that address. It's my fault you went over there.'

'Not at all, Albert. It was a good trip. It gave me and Elizabeth time to catch up and to relive some of our childhood memories. It's all good.'

'So, are you no closer to finding him, then?'

Ronnie shook her head. 'We don't have much to go on. I was hoping you might remember something else.'

He looked thoughtful and then his eyes lit up. 'It's not much, but I do remember one small thing.'

Ronnie sat forward. 'Go on.'

'Oliver and Skye went off one day to get matching tattoos. Oliver wanted to get his right on the front of his chest and I thought he was mad. But he went ahead and got it all the same.'

Ronnie's heart fell. 'The international peace sign?'

'That's the one. You already knew?'

'I knew about Oliver's tattoo. We saw it in a picture. Right in the centre of his chest. The peace sign with a colourful feather coming from the end of it.'

Albert shook his head. 'There was no feather, as far as I recall. It was just the peace sign. I remember because Sky's one was on her shoulder.'

'Maybe he added the feather at a later stage,' said Ronnie. 'You don't happen to remember the shop where they had it done, do you?'

'Not specifically. But it was somewhere over close to St Stephen's Green. I know that because we all met up in the park afterwards and Oliver was white in the face. He said he hadn't realised it would be so painful.'

Ronnie smiled at that. It wasn't a lot of information but it was something. Maybe it would help Al to identify the shop and they could take it from there. Her stomach rumbled and all of a sudden she felt queasy again. She probably shouldn't have had that toast so soon after being sick. She needed to get out of there so she pushed her chair back and stood up.

'Thanks so much for your help, Albert. It's been lovely talking to you.'

'And you too,' said the old man, following her out to the front door. 'It's nice to remember old times. You and your sister are welcome here anytime.'

She was just about to reply when he spoke again. 'Actually, I'm only thinking of it now but I assume you know that Oliver isn't his real name?'

'What?'

'Oliver Angelo. Did you not know? It's just a name he called himself. Same with Skye. Your father was born with a much more ordinary name but it didn't suit his hippie lifestyle. They never changed officially but we only ever knew them as Skye and Oliver.'

Chapter 37

'There's somebody here to see you,' said Amanda, appearing at Elizabeth's office door just as she was packing up to leave.

Elizabeth rolled her eyes and quickly scanned her diary. 'I've nothing down for this afternoon and I'm in a hurry. Who is it?'

'She says her name is Amber Webb and she's a friend of yours.' Amanda walked towards Elizabeth and lowered her voice. 'I'm assuming it's *the* Amber? She's exactly as you described her.'

Elizabeth was taken aback. 'Yes, that's her. I don't know what she's doing here, though. You can send her in. But I have to be out of here in ten minutes at the most so can you please come and interrupt us if she's still here.'

'Will do,' said Amanda, disappearing back out the door.

Elizabeth shut down her computer and checked herself in her little compact mirror. She dabbed a bit of powder under her eyes, in an attempt to hide the grey folds of skin that she'd gained from lack of sleep, and applied a touch of lip gloss. Amber was the last person she'd expected to see and she was curious as to why she was here.

'Hi, Elizabeth,' said Amber, walking in and looking around her. 'Wow! This place is amazing. What a gorgeous office!'

Elizabeth smiled weakly. 'It was Mum's. It's pretty special alright. So, what brings you here?'

Amber sat down on a chair at the front of the desk. 'I'm worried about you, Elizabeth. And so is Ronnie. We know you're going through a tough time with all the Nathan stuff but we don't want you to start alienating yourself from us again.'

'I've just been busy,' said Elizabeth, not meeting Amber's eye. 'I'm trying to catch up on work that wasn't done while I was away.'

'But you've been avoiding our calls and not telling us what's been going on. Look at me, Elizabeth.'

She really didn't want to get into an emotional confrontation but she did as Amber asked and looked across at her.

'I'm here for you,' said Amber, reaching over and taking her hand. 'I know you'll probably never fully forgive me for what I did, but I want to make it up to you. I want to be your friend, just like I was when we were teenagers. I want you to share your troubles with me and let me help you.'

It was all too much for Elizabeth. It had been a long time since anybody had cared for her that way – since anybody had taken the time to want to help her. A lot of it was her own fault because she'd alienated herself from everybody, but seeing Amber sitting in front of her now brought memories of their childhood back to her and she couldn't keep the tears in.

'Oh, Elizabeth,' said Amber, rushing to her side. 'What's wrong? What's happened?'

Elizabeth took a moment to gather herself. 'I just feel that karma is coming to get me. Every time I think things are beginning to go right for me, something bad happens.'

'Is it Nathan? Is he giving you a hard time?' Amber pulled a chair over so she could sit beside Elizabeth. 'I'm sure it's not easy going through a separation. But please, Elizabeth, let me and Ronnie help you. We don't want you to shut us out.'

Elizabeth shook her head. 'It's not Nathan. Well, it's that too, but there's something else.'

Amber looked worried. 'What is it? Come on, you can tell me. I want to help.'

Elizabeth thought for a moment and then realised she didn't want to cope with everything on her own any more. She needed a friend. So she reached for her handbag and pulled out the envelope. Slipping the folded letter out from inside, she handed it to Amber and waited for her response.

Amber read it carefully as Elizabeth watched, and when she looked up she had tears in her eyes. 'When did you get this?'

'Last week. I took it with the rest of my post from the house when I walked out on Nathan for good.'

'And have you done anything about it?'

Elizabeth nodded. 'It took me a while but I finally made the call today. That's where I'm going now, actually.'

'Right, I'm coming with you.' Amber stood up and handed the letter back to Elizabeth. 'And I'm not taking no for an answer.'

For just a split second, Elizabeth was going to object, and then she nodded. 'Thank you. I could do with the company.'

She put the letter back into her bag and stood up to leave. Irregular cells, the letter said. Just like that. Two words that could change the course of her life and they'd typed them as though they were typing a shopping list. She hadn't thought much about the cervical smear test she'd had before going to New York so the letter had come as a massive shock. But she was going to deal with it. Whatever the outcome, she wouldn't be coping alone.

'Are you nervous?' said Amber, as they sat in the doctor's surgery. 'It's not nice but it will be over in a few seconds.'

Elizabeth nodded. 'I'm not nervous about the test at all. It's the outcome I'm scared stiff about.'

'It's going to be fine.' Amber found her hand and squeezed it. 'You're going to be okay.'

'Am I? It's funny how people say that. As if they know what the outcome is going to be.'

'I'm sorry. I suppose I'm just trying to keep your spirits up.'

Elizabeth looked at her then. 'No, *I'm* sorry. I haven't exactly been nice to you lately. I shouldn't have threatened you like that after we talked things through. I shouldn't have said what I did about you coming between me and Ronnie.'

Amber shook her head. 'I deserved it. I did a terrible thing and I feel very lucky that you and Ronnie are prepared to forgive me.'

'It's in the past,' said Elizabeth.

The doctor came out to call a name and she felt her heart pounding. But it wasn't her turn and she breathed a sigh of relief.

'So you and Nathan,' said Amber, slowly. 'I don't want to pry, but you said you got the letter when you left him for the final time. Does that mean you went back and left again?'

Elizabeth nodded. 'I went back to sort some stuff out. And he was lovely at first. He almost won me over again. Because that's what he does best. He could charm the birds off the trees.'

'I only met him a couple of times but that's the impression I got from him too – charming and charismatic. I thought he was especially attentive to you at your mum's funeral. I remember thinking how lucky you were to have him.'

'Huh! If you'd seen him when we got home, you wouldn't have thought that.'

'Why? What did he do?'

Elizabeth cringed at the memory. 'It wasn't what he did. He told me to pull myself together. That I was a big girl and didn't need to be crying all the time.'

Amber gasped. 'Are you serious? The bastard.'

'Yep. Isn't it funny to think I put up with that for so long? What was I thinking?'

'You were in love, Elizabeth. And thanks to me, you didn't have a sister or a best friend to turn to. I really am so sorry for all you've been through.'

'Love really blinds us, doesn't it?' Elizabeth thought about how naïve she'd been, how unwilling to acknowledge Nathan's faults. 'But now that I've allowed myself to step out of the situation and look in, I don't like what I see one bit.'

'So, is that it, then? Are you two finished for good?'

'Definitely,' said Elizabeth. 'I'm not saying it's going to be easy but I know it's the right thing to do. It's weird. I still love him. And I still miss him. But I feel strangely free. It was a suffocating relationship.'

'Well, I'm here for you, whenever you need me. And I know Ronnie is too.'

They sat in silence, lost in thought, until Elizabeth's eyes were drawn to a woman who'd just come in with a double buggy. Two little identical girls, around one year old, sat side by side. One was asleep, her head leaned to one side, her tiny rosebud mouth open slightly and blowing bubbles with every breath. The other was sucking her thumb, taking everything in. She caught Elizabeth's eye and turned her head away shyly. A lump formed in Elizabeth's throat as a picture of her and Ronnie as children came into her mind. Life was wonderful back then – simple and straightforward. Until adulthood had come and slapped them all in the face.

'Are you going to tell Ronnie?' Elizabeth jumped as Amber's voice broke into her thoughts.

'Not yet.'

'But why? I really think you should tell her.'

The woman with the buggy sat down and the sleeping child began to cry as she woke up. Her sister reached over and put her hand on her face to comfort her. Elizabeth smiled at the scene.

'Because,' she said, nodding her head towards the babies, 'I want to protect her. I don't want her to worry unless she has to. If it's bad news, of course she'll have to know. And if it's good, well, then I'll have spared her unnecessary heartache.'

'Good for you,' said Amber.

Elizabeth lowered her voice. 'You know Mum's cancer was found through a cervical smear test?'

Amber nodded. 'I know. But that doesn't mean it will be the same for you.'

'Here's hoping,' said Elizabeth, crossing fingers on both hands.

'Elizabeth Cunningham.' The doctor's voice filled the little surgery and Elizabeth took a deep breath.

'Good luck,' said Amber, squeezing her hand briefly before she stood up.

'Thanks.' She followed the doctor into the little room and closed her eyes for a moment. *'Stay with me, Mum. You were such a trooper through all your illness. Send me some of your strength and if you have any influence up there, please let the outcome of this be a good one.'*

Chapter 38

'I don't think you should look for your father any more,' said Al, as he and Ronnie walked hand in hand down Grafton Street. 'At least, not for the moment.'

Ronnie stopped walking and looked at him. 'What? Why would you say that? I thought you were in favour of me finding him.' She felt hurt.

He pulled her closer to him and began walking again. 'I *do* want you to find him, but I think the search is taking its toll on you.'

'I know a lot has happened over the last few weeks,' she said. 'But I feel we're getting so close. He's here, Al, here in Ireland. Probably in Dublin. We can't give up now.'

'I don't want you to give up, Ronnie. But maybe just take a step back for a while. Let things settle down. Maybe if you're not thinking about it so much, something will turn up.'

Ronnie felt unsettled by Al's words. She'd thought he was fully supportive of the search but now he was saying the opposite. All of a sudden, the skies darkened and rain began to pelt down – big, icy raindrops whipped across their faces, prompting them to run for the nearest shelter. Luckily, they were close to a coffee shop so they stepped inside and grabbed a table, before more people decided to shelter from the rain. Minutes later, they were sipping frothy cappuccinos and Ronnie wanted to know more about what Al had said.

'So tell me,' she said, cupping her hands around the steamy drink. 'Why do you want me to stop looking now? When we're getting so close. We've only just found out that Oliver Angelo isn't his real name and Albert has promised he'll do a bit of digging for us. And then there's the tattoo. If you can find out—'

'Ronnie, stop.'

She looked at him in confusion. 'What?'

Al sighed. 'I've done everything I can to find out about that tattoo, but it's hopeless. The peace sign is a generic one. Every tattoo parlour does them. And the feather is very common too. Even if we did know where he got it done, I don't think it would help. We don't know the date or even the year. And there would be thousands of people who would have got similar tattoos.'

Ronnie's heart fell, but she quickly recovered. 'But we can't give up just because one lead doesn't prove fruitful. Frank said he wants to see Elizabeth and me so I think he might have some more information.'

'Listen, love,' he said, reaching across and taking her hand. 'I know you want to find your father and I'm completely behind you. But look at how it's been affecting you these last few weeks. You've been exhausted and sick and, dare I say it, a lot more grumpy than usual.'

'That was just the food poisoning,' she reasoned. 'I didn't get much sleep with that and I've been trying to catch up.'

'Look, Ronnie. I know how much you want a baby. How much we both want it. And look at what's happened this month. We've lost an opportunity because you were sick.'

Ronnie thought he was being very unfair. She'd done an ovulation test the previous week and it showed she was at her most fertile. But then she'd got sick that same day and their plans for a night of passion were forgotten.

'I know it wasn't your fault,' he continued. 'But I think you're under an enormous amount of stress and it's definitely not helping you.'

'You're probably right.' She relented. 'I haven't felt my best since we came back from New York, if I'm honest.'

'That's exactly what I mean,' he said, looking relieved. 'You've had so much to cope with lately. Elizabeth and Amber and the search for Oliver and the thing with you and me …'

She nodded. 'Thank God it's all worked out, though. Especially you and me. I couldn't bear it if I lost you.'

'Well, you're not going to,' he said. 'I'm here for keeps. That's why I want to make sure you're okay and don't end up having some sort of breakdown. Why don't you just let things settle for a while? Enjoy your newfound relationship with Elizabeth. Relax for a bit, and when you feel stronger you can start looking for Oliver again.'

She couldn't argue with that. It felt like they were going around and around in circles looking for Oliver and it was beginning to drive her mad. Al could be right about the stress. Maybe that's what was making her feel so ill. She hoped she hadn't developed an ulcer or something because she really didn't need that on top of everything else. And he was right about the baby thing. Having a baby was their priority but she'd lost sight of that these last couple of weeks. She'd been either too tired or too sick for love-making, and in another week or so, she'd be devastated when her period would arrive.

'You know I only want the best for you,' said Al, breaking into her thoughts. 'For us.'

Ronnie looked at his concerned face and she knew he was telling the truth. 'I know you do,' she said, scooping the froth from the sides of her cup with a spoon. 'I want a baby more than anything, so if the stress of the search is affecting that, then I need to take a step back.'

Al nodded. 'It won't be forever. I just want you to relax for a while. Take some time out for you. Do something fun to take your mind off everything.'

'I'll tell you what I would like to do,' she said, watching Al carefully. 'It's not exactly fun but I think it's time.'

'What's that?'

'I want to get checked out. To find out why I'm not getting pregnant. We said we'd give it a year and it's been more than that. I don't want to wait any longer.'

'I don't know, Ronnie. That's a whole other lot of stress.'

'It is,' she agreed. 'But wouldn't it be better to know? What if there was something wrong with me that could be easily fixed? We could be trying to get pregnant forever and it may never happen. But with a bit of intervention, it could all get sorted out.'

He looked unsure still, so she wanted to get him onside.

'Why don't I just go to my GP, for starters? Have a word with her. See what she suggests. Surely that can't hurt. And if she wants to refer me to a specialist, we can talk about it again.'

'I suppose that's fair enough,' he said, looking relieved. 'Let's just take it step by step. I just can't bear the thought of a load of tests – people messing around with our bits.' He nodded towards his nether region and Ronnie began to giggle.

'You're such a typical man,' she said. 'I won't let anyone mess with your precious bits unless they really have to.'

'Well, that's a relief,' he said, pretending to wipe his brow. 'So, why don't we make a start right now.'

She looked at him questioningly and he laughed.

'I mean, why don't you ring your doctor now and see if you can get an appointment for today. It's still early and if she can squeeze you in, at least it would get the ball rolling.'

'Brilliant idea,' she said, delighted. 'I'll do that now.'

She loved how Al always put a positive spin on things. It was her birthday in five days and she'd desperately wanted to be pregnant by then. And since that wasn't going to happen, at least she'd have taken a step towards finding out why. She wanted her birthday to be happy this year. Despite not being pregnant, there were a lot of other good things in her life. She and Al were stronger than ever and her relationship with Elizabeth was improving all the time. She realised how lucky she was and she was never going to take that for granted. She pulled her phone out of her bag and dialled the number for her doctor.

Ronnie curled her legs up beneath her on the little leather sofa and sipped her tea. They'd just come home from town and Al was gone to the gym, leaving her alone with her thoughts. The day seemed endless and it was still just after three. They'd both been in work for the morning and had finished at lunchtime. They'd met for a bite to eat and then walked down Grafton Street towards the bus stop. That's when the rain had started and they'd ended up in that coffee shop, where a lot of important decisions had been made.

She'd rung her doctor and luckily got a cancellation for later. She was seeing her at half four and was looking forward to chatting about the pregnancy situation. Or lack of it.

She flicked through the channels on the telly but nothing took her interest. She wasn't really a telly sort of girl. She much preferred to read a book or listen to music, but today she couldn't seem to settle down to anything. Her thoughts turned to Al and what he had said about finding her father. Much as she wanted to find him, Al was probably right. It had caused her a lot of stress recently, and everybody knew that stress while trying to get pregnant wasn't ideal. She felt a bit guilty abandoning the search, especially when Elizabeth was so keen. But she'd understand. It was important for Ronnie to do the right thing for herself at the moment.

She hadn't spoken to Frank since the previous week so maybe she'd give him a buzz. He'd been very good to both her and Elizabeth and he deserved to know what she was thinking. And anyway, she wanted to invite him to their birthday drinks on Tuesday. She and Elizabeth had decided they didn't want to have a big celebration. It would be their first birthday without their mother so they were going to mark it by having a small family get-together in the house they grew up in. A few drinks and nibbles and a chance to relax and have a chat. She muted the telly and took her mobile from the pocket of her skirt. He answered on the first ring.

'Hi, Ronnie. You wouldn't believe it but I was just about to give you a ring.'

'Were you? For anything in particular?'

'Not really. I haven't spoken to you in a while and I was hoping to see yourself and Elizabeth over the next few days.'

She smiled at that. It was good to have somebody like Frank

looking out for them. He was like their favourite uncle – somebody who was always there if they needed him. Somebody they could rely on no matter what.

'Ronnie?'

'Sorry, Frank. Yes, that would be lovely. That was one of the reasons I was ringing you. Myself and Elizabeth would like you to come over to Mum's house on Tuesday evening. Around seven, if you can make it. We're just having a low-key celebration and we'd love you to be there.'

'Ah! Your thirty-first birthdays. You're getting old.'

Ronnie laughed, but was amazed he remembered. And not only that, he even knew how old they were. 'I feel old,' she said, smiling. 'It's been a long year.'

'Very long,' said Frank, and she could hear the sadness in his voice. 'So, what else did you want to talk to me about? You said there was something else?'

Ronnie didn't want to disappoint him so she chose her words carefully. 'It's about the search for Oliver. It's been very stressful, Frank. And I might need to take a step back for a little while.'

There was a pause before he replied. 'I can understand that. But wait until I see you and Elizabeth on Tuesday. I have some more information for you.'

She felt a bolt of excitement and then remembered what she and Al had spoken about. 'It's just that Al and I are trying to have a baby. We have been for a while but nothing is happening. And the stress of everything isn't helping. I know you're trying to do right by our mother and you're only trying to help, but I need to start looking after myself better. And that means not chasing after something that I might never find.'

'A baby!' His voice was just a whisper. 'A little child of your own.'

Something in his voice brought a tear to Ronnie's eye. 'Yes, Frank. If all goes to plan. So you'll understand why I can't dedicate any more time to the search at the moment.'

'Of course. Don't think about it for one more minute.'

'Thanks, Frank. I knew you'd understand.' A wave of nausea overtook her and she sat up quickly, clasping her hand over her mouth. As Al had said, her illness was stress-related, so she was right to try and eliminate any worries or pressures from her life.

'I have to go, Frank,' she said, standing up and walking towards the bathroom as she spoke. 'I'll see you Tuesday.'

'See you then,' he said. 'And, Ronnie?'

'Yes?'

'Your mum would be very happy. Having a grandchild would have made her the happiest woman in the world. And I know she's with you now, looking after you. So, have faith. It will happen.'

She thanked him and threw the phone down before running to the bathroom. Sitting on the floor, she retched painfully into the toilet bowl, at the same time crying at the beautiful words that Frank had just spoken.

Chapter 39

Elizabeth sang to herself as she placed the trays of food in the oven. Today was already proving to be one of the best birthdays she'd ever had. The day had started with the arrival of a massive bouquet of flowers from Amanda. Elizabeth had become very close to her assistant of late and she was happy now to call her a friend. Amanda had insisted she take the day off for her birthday, saying that she'd look after everything in her absence, and Elizabeth had agreed. But the best bit of the day had been the phone call from her doctor. The smear test she'd had was clear. No sign of any irregular cells, so no cancer. The repeat test was clear. She'd cried with relief and immediately rang Amber to share the news. She hadn't told Ronnie about it so there was no need to now.

She filled some bowls with snacks and laid them out on the coffee table in the living room. Her guests would be arriving in an hour and she couldn't wait to celebrate. She'd woken up that morning fearing Nathan would either call to the house or ring persistently, knowing it was her birthday, but it was already almost six and she hadn't heard a word. And she was surprisingly okay with that. The less she heard from him, the easier it was to put him out of her mind and get on with her life.

She glanced around the room and was satisfied that everything was ready, so she poured herself a large glass of white wine and sat down on the sofa. Six months ago, she never would have believed she'd be in this situation – waiting for her sister to arrive so that they could celebrate their birthdays together. She was still reeling over her split with Nathan but everything else in her life was coming together and she was beginning to feel really happy. Cunningham Recruitment was going from strength to strength and she was even thinking of expanding over the next couple of years. The company was very important to her, as her mother had grown it from nothing, and she was going to do all she could to make sure it became one of the biggest names in recruitment in Ireland.

Before long, the doorbell rang, startling her, and she stood up to greet the first of her guests. A gust of wind blew suddenly when she opened the front door, and Amber almost fell into the hall.

'Jesus!' she said, pulling leaves from her hair. 'It's crazy weather out there. I almost got blown down the street.'

Elizabeth laughed at the sight of her friend. She was barely more than five feet tall and her long blonde hair was almost covering her elf-like face. 'Are you on your own? I thought you were bringing Roger and Daniel?'

'It's just me,' she said, taking off her coat and placing it on the coatstand. 'Daniel had a bit of a temperature so I decided to leave him at home with Roger. Actually, I'm quite glad to get out on my own. Does that make me sound awful?'

'Not at all,' said Elizabeth, leading the way into the living room and pouring her friend a glass of red. 'I'm just glad you're here.'

Amber took the drink gladly and sat down on an armchair. 'Happy birthday, by the way. You'll have to wait until Ronnie is here for your presents.'

'Ah, you shouldn't have,' said Elizabeth, beaming. It had been a long time since she'd had a present from Amber, and her heart soared.

'Of course I should have. Although I can't beat the present you got already today. You must have been so relieved to hear the test was all clear.'

'Oh God, you have no idea. Isn't it brilliant? I had myself half dead and buried.'

'Don't say that,' scolded Amber, her face turning dark. 'I'm not ready to give you up just yet.'

'Sorry. But I was just so delighted. I've been worried sick.'

Amber nodded sombrely. 'I can imagine. So, what time are the others coming?'

Just then the doorbell rang and Elizabeth smiled. 'Right about now, I'd say.'

It was Ronnie, Al and Frank. There were kisses and hugs all around, before they joined Amber in the living room for another round of kisses. Elizabeth went to check on the food in the oven while Ronnie poured the drinks, and before long they were all sitting around, tucking into onion bhajis and samosas, chicken satay on a stick and spring rolls. All courtesy of Marks & Spencer, as Elizabeth's cooking skills left a lot to be desired.

As they all chatted animatedly, Elizabeth glanced across at Ronnie and noted how fabulous she looked. Her skin was glowing and she had a twinkle in her eye. Deciding not to pursue the search for Oliver was a good decision for her. She needed to rid herself of the stress, and although Elizabeth was keen to keep searching, she understood Ronnie's motivation. Having a baby meant a lot to them, and Elizabeth wanted it for them too. She couldn't wait to be an aunty. Maybe someday she'd be lucky enough to find love and to have a child of her own, but for now she'd settle for a niece or nephew who she could spoil rotten.

'I'd like to propose a toast,' said Amber, raising her glass. 'To my two best friends in the world. I'm so happy you're both in my life and here's to many more years of friendship. Happy birthday. To Elizabeth and Ronnie.'

They all clinked glasses and Elizabeth noted that Frank looked a bit pale. He hadn't said much since he'd arrived and she could see beads of sweat on his forehead. He wasn't wearing a tie but she'd seen him open the top button of his shirt a few minutes before, and he was now pulling at his collar. She hoped he wasn't ill but something told her there was something going on with him. As she watched him, he suddenly took a pen from his pocket and tapped it on his glass. Everybody stopped talking and looked over at him.

'I just want to say something,' he said, loosening his collar further. 'Elizabeth and Ronnie, you know how much you mean to me. And how much your mother meant to me.' His eyes filled with tears and his breathing became heavy.

'Are you okay, Frank?' said Elizabeth. 'Hold on, I'll get you some water.' She returned a moment later with a glass of water, which Frank took gratefully.

'Just give me a moment,' he said, sipping the water. 'Me and my damn emotions getting the better of me.'

They waited in silence, all eyes on Frank, until Ronnie suddenly spoke up. 'Actually, while you're recovering, Frank, I want to say something myself.'

All eyes turned to Ronnie then, and suddenly Elizabeth knew. 'As you all know,' said Ronnie, her eyes darting towards Al, 'these last few months have been very topsy-turvy and we've all had our fair share of upset. But I want today to be a new start for us all. So Al and I want to share …'

A glass suddenly smashed on the floor, startling them, and they all jumped to their feet when they saw Frank slowly slipping down in his chair.

'Frank!' said Ronnie, rushing to his side. 'Frank, what's wrong?'

'Call an ambulance,' said Al, pushing the chair away and laying him down on the floor.

'Can't … breathe …' rasped Frank, as he pulled at his collar and rolled his head from side to side. 'Help …'

Elizabeth was crying. 'It's okay, Frank. Help is on the way. Just try and stay calm. Breathe with me … one … two … three …' But it was clear to Elizabeth that this was a whole lot more serious than her panic attacks.

They could do nothing but make him comfortable until the ambulance arrived minutes later. Thankfully they'd been returning from a call-out and had been just down the street when the 999 call had come in. Frank was still conscious, but barely, as the two paramedics rushed into the room and began working on him. Everyone stood back to give them space. They worked swiftly and within minutes had him on a stretcher with monitors attached to him. They'd opened his shirt to attach some wires to his chest and just as they were about to wheel him out to the ambulance, Elizabeth saw it. She gasped out loud and Ronnie looked at her quizzically. And then she saw it too. Right there in the centre of his chest. The international peace sign, with a colourful feather attached.

Chapter 40

Ronnie and Elizabeth sat in a little family room at the hospital, waiting for news on Frank. They'd barely spoken a word since they'd arrived there, both lost in thought. They were in shock. Nothing could have prepared them for what they'd seen back at the house, and now they didn't even know if Frank was going to make it.

'Had you any idea?' said Elizabeth, breaking the silence. 'I mean, did you ever suspect?'

Ronnie shook her head. 'Never. God, I can't get my head around it. What does it mean?'

'Well, I think it's pretty clear what it means, Ronnie. Frank is our father.'

'But why would he have sent us off like that? We went all the way to New York for, apparently, absolutely no reason. I just don't get it.'

'Well, let's hope he gets the chance to explain,' said Elizabeth, in a whispered voice. 'Regardless of anything, I couldn't bear to lose him.'

'Me neither,' said Ronnie, and they fell silent again.

'Okay, are you Frank Logan's family?' A doctor appeared at the door of the room and both girls jumped up from their seats.

'Yes ... well, no ... well, yes, I suppose we are.' Ronnie's head was in a spin and thankfully Elizabeth took over.

'We're his daughters. Is he okay?'

Ronnie's heart leapt at Elizabeth's words.

'Yes,' said the young doctor, her hands buried deeply in her white coat. 'He's absolutely fine. He just needs some rest and he'll be as right as rain.'

'Was it a heart attack?' said Ronnie, tears of relief welling up in her eyes.

The doctor shook her head. 'No. It seems to have been a panic or anxiety attack. The symptoms can be the same and it seems that your father had a pretty serious one.'

Their father. Frank Logan, their dad. Ronnie couldn't get her head around it. 'Thank you,' she said, holding out her hand to shake the doctor's. 'Can we go in and see him now?'

'Of course. Not for too long, though. He needs to sleep. We'll keep him overnight for observation but he should be okay to go home tomorrow. As soon as we have a bed ready, we'll be taking him up to the ward.'

The doctor disappeared and Ronnie clutched Elizabeth's hand. 'Is this really happening, Izzy? Have we found our father? Could it really be Frank? I can't take it in.'

'It looks like it,' said Elizabeth, squeezing her hand in return. 'Let's just go in and talk to him. See what he has to say.'

The colour had come back to his cheeks and he was breathing normally, much to the girls' relief. His eyes were closed so they quietly pulled up two chairs to sit and wait. The steady beeps from the machines in the room were making Ronnie sleepy and she feared she'd doze off. But suddenly Frank's eyes opened, and he smiled and nodded his head when he saw the girls.

'I'm sorry,' he whispered. 'I didn't mean to give you such a fright.'

'Don't you dare be sorry,' said Elizabeth, taking his hand. 'I, of all people, know what those panic attacks are like. They're all-consuming and you feel as though you can't breathe.'

He nodded. 'I've had a few before but that was a bad one. I thought it was a heart attack.'

'So did we,' said Ronnie, smiling at him. 'Thank God it wasn't.'

'This ticker is in full working order, according to the doctors,' he said, patting his chest. Then a serious look came over his face and he looked at the girls. 'I need to tell you something. It's going to come as a big shock and I hope you can forgive me for keeping it from you for so long.'

Ronnie glanced at Elizabeth and she nodded. 'We know,' said Ronnie. 'We saw the tattoo.'

It took him a moment to process what she'd said and then his hand went to his chest. 'You saw it? Oh God, I hate that you found out like that. I'm so sorry.'

'So it's true?' said Elizabeth, her eyes open wide. 'You're our father?'

He nodded. 'Yes, I am. Is that okay?'

'It's more than okay,' said Ronnie, her cheeks wet with tears. 'I couldn't imagine a better father. You've been like a dad to us for years anyway. This is the best news ever.'

Frank rolled his head back to the centre of the pillow and looked to the ceiling. His breaths began to quicken and Ronnie stood up, ready to call a doctor. But to her surprise, he began to cry. Big fat tears poured down his face and he sobbed like a baby. Both girls took his hands in theirs and sat in silence until his sobs subsided. Elizabeth handed him a clump of tissues from a box beside the bed and he wiped his face and let out a huge sigh.

'I've wanted to tell you for so long,' he said. 'It was killing me that you didn't know, but I had to wait until the time was right.'

'I don't understand,' said Elizabeth. 'Why did you have to wait? And why didn't Mum tell us? All this searching for Oliver, going over to New York, visiting old friends of Mum's ... what was that all about?'

Frank smiled then and his whole face lit up. 'Your mum was a very clever lady. Going to New York was never about finding Oliver.'

'What do you mean?' Ronnie was intrigued.

'It was about getting you two back together. Do you think for a moment that a woman like Belinda Cunningham leaves room for error when she makes plans? She had everything arranged, right down to the finest details. I was under instructions to send you off on this search and to make sure you did it together. And only when you two had finally got your act together was I to tell you the truth.'

Ronnie shook her head. 'And what if we hadn't become friends again? Would you never have told us?'

'Belinda knew that wouldn't have happened. Knowing you as she did, she was certain that you just needed to work matters out. She told me that things might get worse for you before they got better and it seems she was right. Again.'

'So you really are Oliver Angelo,' said Elizabeth, sitting back in her chair. 'I have to say, you're not what I expected.'

Frank laughed. 'Did you expect a sixty-one-year-old hippie? My hippie days are long gone, I'm afraid. My alternative living was ironed out of me in New York when we went to live with Skye's family.'

'Of course,' said Ronnie, realisation dawning on her. 'You and Shirley. You were Oliver and Skye. Shirley was Skye.'

'Yes,' said Frank, looking down at his hands. 'Now you know why I got such a shock when I heard of her passing. Despite the fact we split up in the end, I loved her, you know. We spent a lot of years together and I'm very sad that she's gone.'

'I'm so sorry,' said Elizabeth, squeezing his hand. 'You've had some terrible losses these last few months.'

'Yes, but look at what I've gained.' Frank looked at them both. 'I hope you'll accept me as your father. Having you two as daughters is the best possible thing that could happen to me. I love you both so much. I've had a few years to take it all in but I know that both of you will need some time.'

'Exactly when did you know?' said Ronnie, a million questions forming in her mind. 'Did you really not know about us for all those years you were away?'

'Not a clue,' he said. 'After Skye and I split up and I came home for my father's funeral, I met up with your mum. She knew I was in a bad way – depressed and drinking too much. So she told me. She gave me something to live for. And that's when I decided to move home to Ireland for good.'

'Did you ever think about Mum?' said Elizabeth. 'During the years when you were living in New York. Did you ever think about what life would have been like if you'd chosen her instead of Skye?'

He nodded. 'All the time. That's why I got the feather.'

'The feather?'

'Yes.' He pulled back his shirt to expose his tattoo. 'Skye and I went and got matching tattoos – the international peace sign. But later when I was in America, I missed your mother so much. My own mother used to always say, *"Feathers appear when angels are near"* and your mum was like an angel in my head. I thought about her often and, when I was going through a bad patch, I used to close my eyes and imagine your mum giving me advice.'

'So you got the feather,' said Ronnie, tears welling up again. 'The feather was to remind you of Mum.'

'Yes,' said Frank. 'I got a colourful one because rainbows are a sign of happiness and that's how I felt when I thought of your mother.'

Elizabeth let out a long breath. 'You must have really loved her. All those years away and she was always on your mind.'

'She was the great love of my life, if I'm honest. Skye was wonderful and I did love her – but it was a different love. Your mum has always been the one.'

Silence filled the room as they all tried to take in the events of the night. Until Frank finally looked at Ronnie. 'What were you going to tell us?'

'What do you mean?'

'Back at the house. You were about to make an announcement, until I stole your thunder by having my anxiety attack.'

Ronnie smiled, and her heart thumped with excitement. 'I think I can forgive you,' she said. 'But what I wanted to tell you all is …' she couldn't believe she was going to say the words '… Al and I are going to have a baby. I'm pregnant.'

'I knew it,' said Elizabeth, reaching over to hug her sister. 'I guessed it straight away. I'm so happy for you. For both of you. How far gone are you?'

'Seven and a half weeks. Apparently, my period was a false one, or something like that. The doctor did a pregnancy test on Thursday and it was positive, so on account of the bleeding, she sent me to have a scan.'

'And everything was okay?'

'It's early days,' said Ronnie. 'But we heard a heartbeat, so that's a good start.'

Elizabeth clapped her hands together. 'The news just keeps getting better and better.'

Ronnie looked at Frank, who'd been very quiet. 'And what about you, Grandad? Are you happy?'

He nodded, and his tears said it all.

Acknowledgements

As I'm writing this, I'm looking out the window at a snow-covered garden and I'm counting my blessings. Being a writer is a dream come true for me – doing something I love, and being able to call it a job, is an honour and a privilege. But one of the best parts is the twenty-second commute to the back of the house while wearing my pyjamas, big fluffy unicorn slippers and no make-up. I don't even have to do the school run any more, as the children are older, so it's literally bed to office with a slight detour for a cup of tea on the way. Who wouldn't love my job?

As with all my books, writing *In Search of Us* has been a pleasure. But the process wasn't without its challenges. I began, as I always do, with a seed of an idea, and then began to develop my characters. As each character sprang to life for me, I began to get more and more excited. Their stories began to form in my mind and I could see it all unfolding. And then I began to write what would be a compelling, exciting and interesting story. I tend to fly by the seat of my pants as I write – I keep going without planning too much or looking back because I want to be all floaty and creative and let it all 'flow out of me'! And then, when I reach a certain stage, I begin to read it back. Just, you know, to make sure it's as brilliant as

I thought it was. So I began to read through what I'd written of *In Search of Us*, expecting to be wowed by my talent, and that's when I realised it was rubbish! I knew I'd have to perform some miracle editing or else my words would be destined for the bin. And that's where my wonderful family come in.

My husband, Paddy, is my rock and my biggest cheerleader. When I get disheartened and feel like I can't finish a book or think that my writing is worse than terrible, he's always there to encourage me and talk me through my meltdowns. He'll happily read what I've written and offer calm and helpful advice. He makes me believe in myself and, even more importantly, he does the ironing. Thanks, Paddy, for everything.

Although my children are growing up and are fast heading for adulthood, I feel very lucky to have them all still at home with me. My eldest, Eoin, has just turned twenty-one and I still can't get my head around it. Last I checked, I was only in my mid-twenties – where does the time go? But all of them in their own way contribute to my writing day. Whether it's bringing a cup of tea to me in my office when a deadline is approaching or giving their feedback on titles or covers, it's wonderful to get their input and to know they're as proud of me as I am of them. Eoin, Roisin, Enya and Conor, I love you very much and I appreciate your support and love more than you'll ever know.

When I looked back on the acknowledgements for my last book, *Falling Softly*, I felt an overwhelming sadness. I thanked, as I always do, my mother-in-law, Mary, for being so encouraging and lovely and for always reading my books with such enthusiasm. Sadly, we lost her last year, but I still wanted to remember her here and acknowledge what a huge part of my life she was. *Falling Softly* was on her locker when she died and I feel honoured that perhaps she was enjoying some of my words in her final days.

Huge thanks to my own parents, Paddy and Aileen Chaney, who have always encouraged me to follow my heart and do what makes me happy. They're such a great support to me in my writing and in every other aspect of my life, and I don't know what I'd do without them. Thanks to my one and only sibling, Gerry Chaney, and to his lovely wife, Denyse, for all their support. As a self-professed technophobe, I know I only have to lift the phone to Gerry and he'll talk me calmly through whatever technical nightmare I find myself in and Denyse's advice is invaluable when it comes to the first draft of my books. She's always the first to read it, even before my editor, and her keen eye always spots what needs to be fixed.

Writing can be a very lonely thing, especially when a deadline is looming, and I'm locked away in my cave for weeks without seeing another soul. Well maybe I exaggerate, but you get the gist. I'm very lucky to have a wide network of friends who understand when I'm not in touch and are always ready to take me for a coffee or a drink when I finally emerge. A special thanks to Lorraine Hamm, a wonderful friend who I can count on for anything, and thanks to Denise Deegan and Angie Pierce for the coffees, calls and encouragement. To Niamh Greene and Michelle Jackson – you two girls bring so much happiness into my life. I live for our indulgent nights away when we plot and plan and solve the problems of the world. A particular mention has to go to a special group of ladies – Carmel, Lorna, Grace, Leigh, Kathleen, Eimer, Clodagh, Amanda, Sheena, Aileen, Teresa, Judith, Elaine, Nuala, Amanda, Nicola, Veronica and Mary. They are my neighbours and have become my good friends. I feel blessed to live amongst them. Thank you all for the fun and the laughs and for always being there. I've recently taken up golf and I've found it to be a wonderful outlet away from my desk. I want to sincerely thank the wonderful ladies of Hermitage Golf Club for their warm welcome and eternal patience.

And now to the professionals who take this book from its raw state and make it into the finished product. First of all, thank you to my lovely agent, Tracy Brennan, from the Trace Literary Agency. This year is already shaping up to be a very exciting one, thanks to Tracy, and I look forward to many years of excitement ahead. To the team at Hachette Ireland – thank you for all you do for me and my books. I couldn't wish to work with better. Thanks to Ciara Doorley, my editor. Ciara is a wizard of words and always manages to put that extra sparkle into my books. Thanks to Joanna Smyth, who is always there to answer queries and is forever patient. Thanks to Ruth Shern, who gets stuck with me for a day travelling around the book shops in Dublin and patiently waits while I yap (and sometimes shop!) when I'm supposed to be signing. And to the rest of the team – Breda, Jim, Bernard and Siobhan. Thanks to Aonghus Meaney for his meticulous copy-editing and Emma Dunne for her proofreading. They manage to spot the things that I can't see, despite me reading and rereading a hundred times.

Thanks to Vanessa O'Loughlin from writing.ie and inkwellwriters.ie. As well as being a talented author, Vanessa gives so much time to Irish writers – whether it's helping with their manuscripts or pointing them in the right direction. Vanessa has been there for me since I began writing and I'm very grateful for her friendship and guidance. It can be a scary thing when a book first goes out into the world and, sometimes, we dread the reviews. But they're very important and I want to say a special thank you to all the book bloggers both here in Ireland and abroad, for taking the time to read and review my books. Most of them don't get paid for what they do, so I'm very grateful to each and every one of them. Thank you to the booksellers, who work so hard to promote and sell my books. It still makes me emotional to see my books on the shelves.

Last, but not least, I want to say a huge thank you to you, my wonderful readers. You are the most important part of this process because, without you, what would be the point? I'm humbled and grateful that you choose my book to read and, furthermore, that you parted with your hard-earned money to buy it. It's such an honour to have my characters enter your lives and I hope with all my heart that you enjoy *In Search of Us*. If you'd like to get in touch, please feel free – you'll find me on my website mariaduffy.ie or on twitter @mduffywriter. I'm also on Facebook. You know me – I love a good chat – and I especially love to hear from readers.

I wish you all health and happiness.

Maria x

January 2018

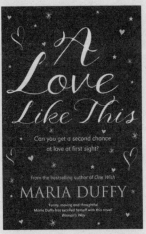

A LOVE LIKE THIS

'Do you believe in destiny?'

'Yes, definitely.'

William and Donna, born on the same day in Dublin, have almost met many times – on their tenth birthday, when Donna spotted Will carrying a colourful bunch of balloons; the day Will, a law student, visited the bakery where Donna worked; and an introduction by mutual friends that never came to pass. Over the years, they have kept just missing each other.

Then, on a sunny day at a café in Auckland, they finally meet. And, in that moment, thousands of miles away from home, they're exactly where they're supposed to be.

But a terrible disaster strikes, and they are separated – left with the memory of the brief time they had together, and dreams of what might have been.

Perhaps all is not lost however, and fate will bring them together once more …

Also available as an ebook

ONE WISH

Becky is used to her young daughter asking tricky questions, but lately Lilly has become fascinated by one in particular – why she doesn't have a father. And Becky realises that it's not a subject she can ignore for much longer.

What Becky remembers about Lilly's dad would fit on a Post-it: his name is Dennis, he's a successful property developer – and he doesn't know he has a daughter. And when she finally locates him, he's not at all what she expected.

Dennis might not be everyone's idea of the perfect dad. But as Becky gets to know him, she begins to wonder if she was wrong not to let him into Lilly's life before now. And she can't help but think about her own family, the people she left far behind.

Is it ever too late to change your mind, and welcome someone from your past into your present?

Also available as an ebook

THE LETTER

Ellie Duggan is getting married in seven weeks. But just before she sets off for a fun-filled New York hen party weekend, she finds a letter addressed to her sister Caroline.

Dated only weeks before Caroline died in a tragic accident, it contains some startling information which forces Ellie to face some truths about herself, Caroline's death – and even her forthcoming marriage.

Ellie has spent the three years since Caroline's death running from the truth. But as the weekend in New York comes to a close, she makes a drastic decision. As Ellie finally lays old ghosts to rest, she realises that the truth can set you free. But will she be willing to take the risk?

Also available as an ebook

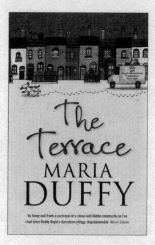

THE TERRACE

St Enda's Terrace, nestled in the heart of Dublin city, is like any other closeknit community – there's the newly-weds planning on having a baby; the single mother raising her children on her own; the upwardly mobile couple who bought in the height of the boom, and the long-timers to whom everyone goes for advice.

But behind every closed door, there are secrets. And when the street syndicate wins the national lottery, but the ticket is nowhere to be found, these neighbours are about to discover just how much has been kept hidden . . .

As friendships and relationships are put to the test in the search for the missing ticket, the residents of St Enda's learn that, while good times might come and go, good friends are forever.

Also available as an ebook

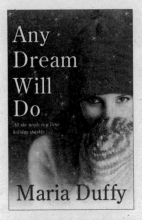

ANY DREAM WILL DO

It seemed harmless at the time – a few white lies here and there to make her life seem more exciting. And as far as thirty-something Jenny Breslin was concerned, it wasn't as though her online friends would ever find out the truth, right?

But then one night Jenny sends out a drunken message inviting her cyber-buddies to stay at her house in Dublin for a few days. And, as the acceptances start flooding in, Jenny starts to panic . . .

Where is she going to find the gorgeous boyfriends she's boasted about? How is she going to convince her online friends that her job at the bank is as glamorous and exciting as she's led them to believe?

And how is she going to get around the fact that her profile picture is years out of date, and taken in a flattering light?

When Jenny comes face-to-face with her three online friends, it turns out she's not the only one who's been stretching the truth. As true identities are exposed, friendships are put to the test. But as Jenny navigates the weekend, she learns that real friendship means accepting people as they are.

Also available as an ebook

FALLING SOFTLY

Holly couldn't be happier.

Christmas, her favourite time of year, is only seven weeks away and her boyfriend has just popped the question. So what if their life together could use a bit more excitement, or if her future mother-in-law is already interfering in their wedding plans – this is the future that Holly wants. Isn't it?

Josh's future is all laid out too.

He and girlfriend Stephanie are moving into their brand new home and, with a baby on the way, they're about to enter an exciting chapter of their lives together. But something isn't quite right, and Josh can't put his finger on what.

As the festive season approaches, will Holly and Josh manage to push their doubts aside? Or will they find themselves wishing they were spending Christmas with someone else?

Also available as an ebook